THE NEWCASTLE FORGOTTEN FANTASY LIBRARY
VOLUME XIX

THE ROOTS OF THE MOUNTAINS

# THE ROOTS OF THE MOUNTAINS WHEREIN IS TOLD SOMEWHAT OF THE LIVES OF THE MEN OF BURG/DALE THEIR FRIENDS THEIR NEIGHBOURS THEIR FOEMEN AND THEIR FELLOWS IN ARMS BY WILLIAM MORRIS

WHILES CARRIED O'ER THE IRON ROAD,
WE HURRY BY SOME FAIR ABODE;
THE GARDEN BRIGHT AMIDST THE HAY,
THE YELLOW WAIN UPON THE WAY,
THE DINING MEN, THE WIND THAT SWEEPS
LIGHT LOCKS FROM OFF THE SUN-SWEET HEAPS—
THE GABLE GREY, THE HOARY ROOF,
HERE NOW—AND NOW SO FAR ALOOF.
HOW SORELY THEN WE LONG TO STAY
AND MIDST ITS SWEETNESS WEAR THE DAY,
AND 'NEATH ITS CHANGING SHADOWS SIT,
AND FEEL OURSELVES A PART OF IT.
SUCH REST, SUCH STAY, I STROVE TO WIN
WITH THESE SAME LEAVES THAT LIE HEREIN.

NEWCASTLE PUBLISHING CO., INC.
NORTH HOLLYWOOD, CALIFORNIA

1979

## BIBLIOGRAPHICAL NOTE

This Newcastle edition is an unabridged reprinting of the 1896 edition published by Longmans, Green, London. It contains a new introduction by Richard Mathews. *The Roots of the Mountains* was first published in 1889 by Longmans, Green, London. Of that edition, 250 copies were printed on large paper.

## PUBLISHER'S NOTE

We apologize for the omission of the new introduction scheduled for this edition, but it did not reach us in time to make the printing deadline.

A NEWCASTLE BOOK
FIRST PRINTING APRIL 1979
PRINTED IN THE UNITED STATES OF AMERICA

# CONTENTS.

# THE ROOTS OF THE MOUNTAINS

## CHAPTER I. OF BURGSTEAD AND ITS FOLK AND ITS NEIGHBOURS.

ONCE upon a time amidst the mountains and hills and falling streams of a fair land there was a town or thorp in a certain valley. This was well-nigh encompassed by a wall of sheer cliffs; toward the East and the great mountains they drew together till they went near to meet, and left but a narrow path on either side of a stony stream that came rattling down into the Dale: toward the river at that end the hills lowered somewhat, though they still ended in sheer rocks; but up from it, and more especially on the north side, they swelled into great shoulders of land, then dipped a little, and rose again into the sides of huge fells clad with pine-woods, and cleft here and there by deep ghylls: thence again they rose higher and steeper, and ever higher till they drew dark and naked out of the woods to meet the snow-fields and ice-rivers of the high mountains. But that was far away from the pass by the little river into the valley; and the said river was no drain from the snow-fields white and thick with the grinding of the ice, but clear and bright were its waters that came from wells amidst the bare rocky heaths.

The upper end of the valley, where it first began to open out from the pass, was rugged and broken by rocks and ridges of water-borne stones, but presently it smoothed itself into mere grassy swellings and knolls, and at last into a fair and fertile plain swelling up into a green wave, as it were, against the rock-wall which encompassed it on all sides save where the river came gushing out of the strait pass at the east end, and where at the west end it poured itself out of the Dale toward the lowlands and the plain of the great river.

Now the valley was some ten miles of our measure from that place of the rocks and the stone-ridges, to where the faces of the hills drew somewhat anigh to the river again at the west, and then fell aback along the edge of the great plain ; like as when ye fare a-sailing past two nesses of a river-mouth, and the main-sea lieth open before you.

Besides the river afore-mentioned, which men called the Weltering Water, there were other waters in the Dale. Near the eastern pass, entangled in the rocky ground was a deep tarn full of cold springs and about two acres in measure, and therefrom ran a stream which fell into the Weltering Water amidst the grassy knolls. Black seemed the waters of that tarn which on one side washed the rocks-wall of the Dale ; ugly and aweful it seemed to men, and none knew what lay beneath its waters save black mis-shapen trouts that few cared to bring to net or angle : and it was called the Death-Tarn.

Other waters yet there were : here and there from the hills on both sides, but especially from the south side, came trickles of water that ran in pretty brooks down to the river ; and some of these sprang bubbling up amidst the foot-mounds of the sheer-rocks ; some had cleft a rugged and strait way through them, and came tumbling down into the Dale at diverse heights from their faces. But on the north side about halfway down the Dale, one stream somewhat bigger than the others, and dealing with softer ground, had cleft for itself a wider way ; and the folk had laboured this way wider yet, till they had made them a road running north along the west side of the stream. Sooth to say, except for the strait pass along the river at the eastern end, and the wider pass at the western, they had no other way (save one of which a word anon) out of the Dale but such as mountain goats and bold cragsmen might take ; and even of these but few.

This midway stream was called the Wildlake, and the way along it Wildlake's Way, because it came to them out of the wood, which on that north side stretched away from nigh to the lip of the valley-wall up to the pine woods and the high fells on the east and north, and down to the plain country on the west and south.

2

Now when the Weltering Water came out of the rocky tangle near the pass, it was turned aside by the ground till it swung right up to the feet of the Southern crags; then it turned and slowly bent round again northward, and at last fairly doubled back on itself before it turned again to run westward ; so that when, after its second double, it had come to flowing softly west-ward under the northern crags, it had cast two thirds of a girdle round about a space of land a little below the grassy knolls and tofts aforesaid; and there in that fair space between the folds of the Weltering Water stood the Thorp whereof the tale hath told.

The men thereof had widened and deepened the Weltering Water about them, and had bridged it over to the plain meads ; and athwart the throat of the space left clear by the water they had built them a strong wall though not very high, with a gate amidst and a tower on either side thereof. Moreover, on the face of the cliff which was but a stone's throw from the gate they had made them stairs and ladders to go up by ; and on a knoll nigh the brow had built a watch-tower of stone strong and great, lest war should come into the land from over the hills. That tower was ancient, and therefrom the Thorp had its name and the whole valley also; and it was called Burgstead in Burgdale.

So long as the Weltering Water ran straight along by the northern cliffs after it had left Burgstead, betwixt the water and the cliffs was a wide flat way fashioned by man's hand. Thus was the water again a good defence to the Thorp, for it ran slow and deep there, and there was no other ground betwixt it and the cliffs save that road, which was easy to bar across so that no foe-men might pass without battle, and this road was called the Port-way. For a long mile the river ran under the northern cliffs, and then turned into the midst of the Dale, and went its way west-ward a broad stream winding in gentle laps and folds here and there down to the out-gate of the Dale. But the Portway held on still underneath the rock-wall, till the sheer-rocks grew some-what broken, and were cumbered with certain screes, and at last

3

the wayfarer came upon the break in them, and the ghyll through which ran the Wildlake with Wildlake's Way beside it, but the Portway still went on all down the Dale and away to the Plain-country.

That road in the ghyll, which was neither wide nor smooth, the wayfarer into the wood must follow, till it lifted itself out of the ghyll, and left the Wildlake coming rattling down by many steps from the east; and now the way went straight north through the woodland, ever mounting higher, (because the whole set of the land was toward the high fells,) but not in any cleft or ghyll. The wood itself thereabout was thick, a blended growth of diverse kinds of trees, but most of oak and ash ; light and air enough came through their boughs to suffer the holly and bramble and eglantine and other small wood to grow together into thickets, which no man could pass without hewing a way. But before it is told whereto Wildlake's Way led, it must be said that on the east side of the ghyll, where it first began just over the Portway, the hill's brow was clear of wood for a certain space, and there, overlooking all the Dale, was the Mote-stead of the Dalesmen, marked out by a great ring of stones, amidst of which was the mound for the Judges and the Altar of the Gods before it. And this was the holy place of the men of the Dale and of other folk whereof the tale shall now tell.

For when Wildlake's Way had gone some three miles from the Mote-stead, the trees began to thin, and presently afterwards was a clearing and the dwellings of men, built of timber as may well be thought. These houses were neither rich nor great, nor was the folk a mighty folk, because they were but a few, albeit body by body they were stout carles enough. They had not affinity with the Dalesmen, and did not wed with them, yet it is to be deemed that they were somewhat akin to them. To be short, though they were freemen, yet as regards the Dalesmen were they well-nigh their servants ; for they were but poor in goods, and had to lean upon them somewhat. No tillage they

had among those high trees ; and of beasts nought save some
flocks of goats and a few asses. Hunters they were, and char-
coal-burners, and therein the deftest of men, and they could shoot
well in the bow withal : so they trucked their charcoal and their
smoked venison and their peltries with the Dalesmen for wheat
and wine and weapons and weed; and the Dalesmen gave them
main good pennyworths, as men who had abundance wherewith
to uphold their kinsmen, though they were but far-away kin.
Stout hands had these Woodlanders and true hearts as any; but
they were few-spoken and to those that needed them not somewhat surly of speech and grim of visage: brown-skinned they
were, but light-haired ; well-eyed, with but little red in their
cheeks : their women were not very fair, for they toiled like the
men, or more.   They were thought to be wiser than most men
in foreseeing things to come.   They were much given to spells,
and songs of wizardry, and were very mindful of the old story-
lays, wherein they were far more wordy than in their daily speech.
Much skill had they in runes, and were exceeding deft in scoring them on treen bowls, and on staves, and door-posts and roof-
beams and standing-beds and such like things.  Many a day when
the snow was drifting over their roofs, and hanging heavy on the
tree-boughs, and the wind was roaring through the trees aloft and
rattling about the close thicket, when the boughs were clattering
in the wind, and crashing down beneath the weight of the gathering
freezing snow, when all beasts and men lay close in their lairs,
would they sit long hours about the house-fire with the knife or the
gouge in hand, with the timber twixt their knees and the whetstone
beside them, hearkening to some tale of old times and the days
when their banner was abroad in the world; and they the while
wheedling into growth out of the tough wood knots and blossoms
and leaves and the images of beasts and warriors and women.
They were called nought save the Woodland-Carles in that
day, though time had been when they had borne a nobler name :
and their abode was called Carlstead.  Shortly, for all they had

and all they had not, for all they were and all they were not,
they were well-beloved by their friends and feared by their foes.
Now when Wildlake's Way was gotten to Carlstead, there
was an end of it toward the north; though beyond it in a right
line the wood was thinner, because of the hewing of the Carles.
But the road itself turned west at once and went on through the
wood, till some four miles further it first thinned and then ceased
altogether, the ground going down-hill all the way: for this was
the lower flank of the first great upheaval toward the high mountains. But presently, after the wood was ended, the land broke
into swelling downs and winding dales of no great height or depth,
with a few scattered trees about the hill-sides, mostly thorns or
scrubby oaks, gnarled and bent and kept down by the western
wind: here and there also were yew-trees, and whiles the hill-
sides would be grown over with box-wood, but none very great;
and often juniper grew abundantly. This then was the country
of the Shepherds, who were friends both of the Dalesmen and the
Woodlanders. They dwelt not in any fenced town or thorp, but
their homesteads were scattered about as was handy for water and
shelter. Nevertheless they had their own stronghold; for amidmost of their country, on the highest of a certain down above a
bottom where a willowy stream winded, was a great earthwork:
the walls thereof were high and clean and overlapping at the entering in, and amidst of it was a deep well of water, so that it was
a very defensible place: and thereto would they drive their flocks
and herds when war was in the land, for nought but a very great
host might win it; and this stronghold they called Greenbury.
These Shepherd-Folk were strong and tall like the Woodlanders,
for they were partly of the same blood, but burnt they were both
ruddy and brown: they were of more words than the Woodlanders,
but yet not many-worded. They knew well all those old story-lays,
(and this partly by the minstrelsy of the Woodlanders,) but they
had scant skill in wizardry, and would send for the Woodlanders,
both men and women, to do whatso they needed therein. They

6

were very hale and long-lived, whereas they dwelt in clear bright air, and they mostly went light-clad even in the winter, so strong and merry were they. They wedded with the Woodlanders and the Dalesmen both; at least certain houses of them did so. They grew no corn; nought but a few pot-herbs, but had their meal of the Dalesmen; and in the summer they drave some of their milch-kine into the Dale for the abundance of grass there; whereas their own hills and bents and winding valleys were not plenteously watered, except here and there as in the bottom under Green-bury. No swine they had, and but few horses, but of sheep very many, and of the best both for their flesh and their wool. Yet were they nought so deft craftsmen at the loom as were the Dales-men, and their women were not very eager at the weaving, though they loathed not the spindle and rock. Shortly, they were merry folk well-beloved of the Dalesmen, quick to wrath, though it abode not long with them; not very curious in their houses and halls, which were but little, and were decked mostly with the handiwork of the Woodland-Carles their guests; who when they were abiding with them, would oft stand long hours nose to beam, scoring and nicking and hammering, answering no word spoken to them but with aye or no, desiring nought save the endurance of the daylight. Moreover, this shepherd-folk heeded not gay raiment overmuch, but commonly went clad in white woollen or sheep-brown weed.

But beyond this shepherd-folk were more downs and more, scantily peopled, and that after a while by folk with whom they had no kinship or affinity, and who were at whiles their foes. Yet was there no enduring enmity between them; and ever after war and battle came peace; and all blood-wites were duly paid and no long feud followed: nor were the Dalesmen and the Woodlanders always in these wars, though at whiles they were. Thus then it fared with these people.

But now that we have told of the folks with whom the Dales-men had kinship, affinity, and friendship, tell we of their chief abode, Burgstead to wit, and of its fashion. As hath been told, it lay upon the land made nigh into an isle by the folds of the Weltering Water towards the uppermost end of the Dale; and it was warded by the deep water, and by the wall aforesaid with its towers. Now the Dale at its widest, to wit where Wildlake fell into it, was but nine furlongs over, but at Burgstead it was far narrower; so that betwixt the wall and the wandering stream there was but a space of fifty acres, and therein lay Burgstead in a space of the shape of a sword-pommel: and the houses of the kinships lay about it, amidst of gardens and orchards, but little ordered into streets and lanes, save that a way went clean through everything from the tower-warded gate to the bridge over the Water, which was warded by two other towers on its hither side.

As to the houses, they were some bigger, some smaller, as the house-mates needed. Some were old, but not very old, save two only, and some quite new, but of these there were not many: they were all built fairly of stone and lime, with much fair and curious carved work of knots and beasts and men round about the doors; or whiles a wale of such-like work all along the house-front. For as deft as were the Woodlanders with knife and gouge on the oaken beams, even so deft were the Dalesmen with mallet and chisel on the face of the hewn stone; and this was a great pastime about the Thorp. Within these houses had but a hall and solar, with shut-beds out from the hall on one side or two, with whatso of kitchen and buttery and out-bower men deemed handy. Many men dwelt in each house, either kinsfolk, or such as were joined to the kindred.

Near to the gate of Burgstead in that street aforesaid and facing east was the biggest house of the Thorp; it was one of the two abovesaid which were older than any other. Its door-posts and the lintel of the door were carved with knots and twining stems fairer than other houses of that stead; and on the wall beside the door carved over many stones was an image

8

wrought in the likeness of a man with a wide face, which was
terrible to behold, although it smiled: he bore a bent bow in his
hand with an arrow fitted to its string, and about the head of him
was a ring of rays like the beams of the sun, and at his feet was
a dragon, which had crept, as it were, from amidst of the blossomed knots of the door-post wherewith the tail of him was yet
entwined.   And this head with the ring of rays about it was
wrought into the adornment of that house, both within and without, in many other places, but on never another house of the Dale;
and it was called the House of the Face.  Thereof hath the tale
much to tell hereafter, but as now it goeth on to tell of the ways
of life of the Dalesmen.

In Burgstead was no Mote-hall or Town-house or Church,
such as we wot of in these days; and their market-place was
wheresoever any might choose to pitch a booth: but for the most
part this was done in the wide street betwixt the gate and the
bridge.   As to a meeting-place, were there any small matters
between man and man, these would the Alderman or one of the
Wardens deal with, sitting in Court with the neighbours on the
wide space just outside the Gate: but if it were to do with greater
matters, such as great manslayings and blood-wites, or the making
of war or ending of it, or the choosing of the Alderman and the
Wardens, such matters must be put off to the Folk-mote, which
could but be held in the place aforesaid where was the Doom-ring
and the Altar of the Gods; and at that Folk-mote both the Shepherd-Folk and the Woodland-Carles foregathered with the Dalesmen, and duly said their say.   There also they held their great
feasts and made offerings to the Gods for the Fruitfulness of the
Year, the Ingathering of the Increase, and in Memory of their
Forefathers.  Natheless at Yule-tide also they feasted from house
to house to be glad with the rest of Midwinter, and many a cup
they drank at those feasts to the memory of the fathers, and the
days when the world was wider to them, and their banners fared
far afield.

But besides these dwellings of men in the field between the wall and the water, there were homesteads up and down the Dale whereso men found it easy and pleasant to dwell : their halls were built of much the same fashion as those within the Thorp; but many had a high garth-wall cast about them, so that they might make a stout defence in their own houses if war came into the Dale.

As to their work afield; in many places the Dale was fair with growth of trees, and especially were there long groves of sweet chestnut standing on the grass, of the fruit whereof the folk had much gain. Also on the south side nigh to the western end was a wood or two of yew-trees very great and old, whence they gat them bow-staves, for the Dalesmen also shot well in the bow. Much wheat and rye they raised in the Dale, and especially at the nether end thereof. Apples and pears and cherries and plums they had in plenty; of which trees, some grew about the borders of the acres, some in the gardens of the Thorp and the homesteads. On the slopes that had grown from the breaking down here and there of the Northern cliffs, and which faced the South and the Sun's burning, were rows of goodly vines, whereof the folk made them enough and to spare of strong wine both white and red.

As to their beasts; swine they had a many, but not many sheep, since herein they trusted to their trucking with their friends the Shepherds ; they had horses, and yet but a few, for they were stout in going afoot; and, had they a journey to make with women big with babes, or with children or outworn elders, they would yoke their oxen to their wains, and go fair and softly whither they would. But the said oxen and all their neat were exceeding big and fair, far other than the little beasts of the Shepherd-Folk ; they were either dun of colour, or white with black horns (and those very great) and black tail-tufts and ear-tips. Asses they had, and mules for the paths of the mountains to the east ; geese and hens enough, and dogs not a few, great hounds stronger than wolves, sharp-nosed, long-jawed, dun of colour, shag-haired.

As to their wares; they were very deft weavers of wool and flax, and made a shift to dye the thrums in fair colours; since both woad and madder came to them good cheap by means of the merchants of the plain country, and of greening weeds was abundance at hand. Good smiths they were in all the metals: they washed somewhat of gold out of the sands of the Weltering Water, and copper and tin they fetched from the rocks of the eastern mountains; but of silver they saw little, and iron they must buy of the merchants of the plain, who came to them twice in the year, to wit in the spring and the late autumn just before the snows. Their wares they bought with wool spun and in the fleece, and fine cloth, and skins of wine and young neat both steers and heifers, and wrought copper bowls, and gold and copper by weight, for they had no stamped money. And they guested these merchants well, for they loved them, because of the tales they told them of the Plain and its cities, and the manslayings therein, and the fall of Kings and Dukes, and the uprising of Captains.

Thus then lived this folk in much plenty and ease of life, though not delicately nor desiring things out of measure. They wrought with their hands and wearied themselves; and they rested from their toil and feasted and were merry: to-morrow was not a burden to them, nor yesterday a thing which they would fain forget: life shamed them not, nor did death make them afraid.

As for the Dale wherein they dwelt, it was indeed most fair and lovely, and they deemed it the Blessing of the Earth, and they trod its flowery grass beside its rippled streams amidst its green tree-boughs proudly and joyfully with goodly bodies and merry hearts.

## CHAPTER II.  OF FACE-OF-GOD AND HIS KINDRED.

A man
cometh from
out of the
wood.

TELLS the tale, that on an evening of late autumn when the weather was fair, calm, and sunny, there came a man out of the wood hard by the Mote-stead aforesaid, who sat him down at the roots of the Speech-mound, casting down before him a roe-buck which he had just slain in the wood. He was a young man of three and twenty summers; he was so clad that he had on him a sheep-brown kirtle and leggings of like stuff bound about with white leather thongs; he bore a short-sword in his girdle and a little axe withal; the sword with fair wrought gilded hilts and a dew-shoe of like fashion to its sheath. He had his quiver at his back and bare in his hand his bow unstrung. He was tall and strong, very fair of fashion both of limbs and face, white-skinned, but for the sun's tanning, and ruddy-cheeked: his beard was little and fine, his hair yellow and curling, cut some-what close, but for its length so plenteous, and so thick, that none could fail to note it. He had no hat nor hood upon his head, nought but a fillet of golden beads.

As he sat down he glanced at the dale below him with a well-pleased look, and then cast his eyes down to the grass at his feet, as though to hold a little longer all unchanged the image of the fair place he had just seen. The sun was low in the heavens, and his slant beams fell yellow all up the dale, gilding the chestnut groves grown dusk and grey with autumn, and the black masses of the elm-boughs, and gleaming back here and there from the pools of the Weltering Water. Down in the midmost meadows the long-horned dun kine were moving slowly as they fed along the edges of the stream, and a dog was bounding about with exceeding swiftness here and there among them. At a sharply curved bight of the river the man could see a little vermilion flame flickering about, and above it a thin blue veil of smoke hanging in the air, and clinging to the boughs of the willows anear; about it were a dozen menfolk clear to see, some sitting, some standing,

12

some walking to and fro, but all in company together: four of
these were brown-clad and short-skirted like himself, and from
above the hand of one came a flash of light as the sun smote upon
the steel of his spear.   The others were long-skirted and clad
gayer, and amongst them were red and blue and green and white
garments, and they were clear to be seen for women.  Just as the
young man looked up again, those of them who were sitting down
rose up, and those that were strolling drew nigh, and they joined
hands together, and fell to dancing on the grass, and the dog and
another one with him came up to the dancers and raced about and
betwixt them; and so clear to see were they all and so little, being far away, that they looked like dainty well-wrought puppets.

The young man sat smiling at it for a little, and then rose up
and shouldered his venison, and went down into Wildlake's Way,
and presently was fairly in the Dale and striding along the Portway beside the northern cliffs, whose greyness was gilded yet by
the last rays of the sun, though in a minute or two it would go
under the western rim.   He went fast and cheerily, murmuring
to himself snatches of old songs; none overtook him on the road,
but he overtook divers folk going alone or in company toward
Burgstead; swains and old men, mothers and maidens coming
from the field and the acre, or going from house to house; and
one or two he met but not many.  All these greeted him kindly,
and he them again; but he stayed not to speak with any, but went
as one in haste.

It was dusk by then he passed under the gate of Burgstead;
he went straight thence to the door of the House of the Face, and
entered as one who is at home, and need go no further, nor abide
a bidding.

The hall he came into straight out of the open air was long and
somewhat narrow and not right high; it was well-nigh dark now
within, but since he knew where to look, he could see by the
flicker that leapt up now and then from the smouldering brands
of the hearth amidmost the hall under the luffer, that there were

but three men therein, and belike they were even they whom he
looked to find there, and for their part they looked for his coming,
and knew his step.

He set down his venison on the floor, and cried out in a cheery
voice: 'Ho, Kettel! Are all men gone without doors to sleep so
near the winter-tide, that the Hall is as dark as a cave? Hither
to me! Or art thou also sleeping?'

A voice came from the further side of the hearth: 'Yea, lord,
asleep I am, and have been, and dreaming; and in my dream I
dealt with the flesh-pots and the cake-board, and thou shalt see
my dream come true presently to thy gain.'

Quoth another voice: 'Kettel hath had out that share of his
dream already belike, if the saw sayeth sooth about cooks. All
ye have been away, so belike he hath done as Rafe's dog when
Rafe ran away from the slain buck.'

He laughed therewith, and Kettel with him, and a third voice
joined the laughter. The young man also laughed and said:
'Here I bring the venison which my kinsman desired; but as
ye see I have brought it over-late: but take it, Kettel. When
cometh my father from the stithy?'

Quoth Kettel: 'My lord hath been hard at it shaping the
Yule-tide sword, and doth not lightly leave such work, as ye
wot, but he will be here presently, for he has sent to bid us dight
for supper straightway.'

Said the young man: 'Where are there lords in the dale,
Kettel, or hast thou made some thyself, that thou must be always throwing them in my teeth?'

'Son of the Alderman,' said Kettel, 'ye call me Kettel, which
is no name of mine, so why should I not call thee lord, which is no
dignity of thine, since it goes well over my tongue from old use
and wont? But here comes my mate of the kettle, and the
women and lads. Sit down by the hearth away from their hurry,
and I will fetch thee the hand-water.'

The young man sat down, and Kettel took up the venison

and went his ways toward the door at the lower end of the hall; but ere he reached it it opened, and a noisy crowd entered of men, women, boys, and dogs, some bearing great wax candles, some bowls and cups and dishes and trenchers, and some the boards for the meal.

The young man sat quiet smiling and winking his eyes at the sudden flood of light let into the dark place; he took in without looking at this or the other thing the aspect of his Fathers' House, so long familiar to him; yet to-night he had a pleasure in it above his wont, and in all the stir of the household; for the thought of the wood wherein he had wandered all day yet hung heavy upon him. Came one of the girls and cast fresh brands on the smouldering fire and stirred it into a blaze, and the wax candles were set up on the daïs, so that between them and the new-quickened fire every corner of the hall was bright. As aforesaid it was long and narrow, over-arched with stone and not right high, the windows high up under the springing of the roof-arch and all on the side toward the street; over against them were the arches of the shut-beds of the house-mates. The walls were bare that evening, but folk were wont to hang up hallings of woven pictures thereon when feasts and high-days were toward; and all along the walls were the tenter-hooks for that purpose, and divers weapons and tools were hanging from them here and there. About the daïs behind the thwart-table were now stuck for adornment leavy boughs of oak now just beginning to turn with the first frosts. High up on the gable wall above the tenter-hooks for the hangings were carven fair imagery and knots and twining stems; for there in the hewn stone was set forth that same image with the rayed head that was on the outside wall, and he was smiting the dragon and slaying him; but here inside the house all this was stained in fair and lively colours, and the sun-like rays round the head of the image were of beaten gold. At the lower end of the hall were two doors going into the butteries, and kitchen, and other

15

out-bowers ; and above these doors was a loft upborne by stone pillars, which loft was the sleeping chamber of the goodman of the house ; but the outward door was halfway between the said loft and the hearth of the hall.

So the young man took the shoes from his feet and then sat watching the women and lads arraying the boards, till Kettel came again to him with an old woman bearing the ewer and basin, who washed his feet and poured the water over his hands, and gave him the towel with fair-broidered ends to dry them withal.

Scarce had he made an end of this ere through the outer door came in three men and a young woman with them ; the fore-most of these was a man younger by some two years than the first-comer, but so like him that none might misdoubt that he was his brother ; the next was an old man with a long white beard, but hale and upright ; and lastly came a man of middle-age, who led the young woman by the hand. He was taller than the first of the young men, though the other who entered with him out-went him in height ; a stark carle he was, broad across the shoulders, thin in the flank, long-armed and big-handed ; very noble and well-fashioned of countenance, with a straight nose and grey eyes underneath a broad brow : his hair grown some-what scanty was done about with a fillet of golden beads like the young men his sons. For indeed this was their father, and the master of the House.

His name was Iron-face, for he was the deftest of weapon-smiths, and he was the Alderman of the Dalesmen, and well-beloved of them ; his kindred was deemed the noblest of the Dale, and long had they dwelt in the House of the Face. But of his sons the youngest, the new-comer, was named Hall-face, and his brother the elder Face-of-god ; which name was of old use amongst the kindred, and many great men and stout warriors had borne it aforetime : and this young man, in great love had he been gotten, and in much hope had he been reared, and therefore had he been named after the best of the kindred. But

16

his mother, who was hight the Jewel, and had been a very fair woman, was dead now, and Iron-face lacked a wife.

Face-of-god was well-beloved of his kindred and of all the Folk of the Dale, and he had gotten a to-name, and was called Gold-mane because of the abundance and fairness of his hair.

As for the young woman that was led in by Iron-face, she was the betrothed of Face-of-god, and her name was the Bride. She looked with such eyes of love on him when she saw him in the hall, as though she had never seen him before but once, nor loved him but since yesterday; though in truth they had grown up together and had seen each other most days of the year for many years. She was of the kindred with whom the chiefs and great men of the Face mostly wedded, which was indeed far away kindred of them. She was a fair woman and strong : not easily daunted amidst perils : she was hardy and handy and light-foot : she could swim as well as any, and could shoot well in the bow, and wield sword and spear : yet was she kind and compassionate, and of great courtesy, and the very dogs and kine trusted in her and loved her. Her hair was dark red of hue, long and fine and plenteous, her eyes great and brown, her brow broad and very fair, her lips fine and red : her cheek not ruddy, yet nowise sallow, but clear and bright : tall she was and of excellent fashion, but well-knit and well-measured rather than slender and wavering as the willow-bough. Her voice was sweet and soft, her words few, but exceeding dear to the listener. In short, she was a woman born to be the ransom of her Folk.

Now as to the names which the menfolk of the Face bore, and they an ancient kindred, a kindred of chieftains, it has been said that in times past their image of the God of the Earth had over his treen face a mask of beaten gold fashioned to the shape of the image ; and that when the Alderman of the Folk died, he to wit who served the God and bore on his arm the gold-ring between the people and the altar, this visor or face of God was laid over the face of him who had been in a manner his priest, and therewith he was borne to mound; and the new Alderman and priest had it in charge to fashion a new visor for the God; and whereas for long this great kindred had been chieftains of the people, they had been, and were all so named, that the word Face was ever a part of their names.

## CHAPTER III. THEY TALK OF DIVERS MATTERS IN THE HALL.

NOW Face-of-god, who is also called Gold-mane, rose up to meet the new-comers, and each of them greeted him kindly, and the Bride kissed him on the cheek, and he her in like wise; and he looked kindly on her, and took her hand, and went on up the hall to the daïs, following his father and the old man; as for him, he was of the kindred of the House, and was foster-father of Iron-face and of his sons both; and his name was Stone-face: a stark warrior had he been when he was young, and even now he could do a man's work in the battlefield, and his understanding was as good as that of a man in his prime. So went these and four others up on to the daïs and sat down before the thwart-table looking down the hall, for the meat was now on the board; and of the others there were some fifty men and women who were deemed to be of the kindred and sat at the endlong tables.

So then the Alderman stood up and made the sign of the Hammer over the meat, the token of his craft and of his God. Then they fell to with good hearts, for there was enough and to spare of meat and drink. There was bread and flesh (though not Gold-mane's venison), and leeks and roasted chestnuts of the grove, and red-cheeked apples of the garth, and honey enough of that year's gathering, and medlars sharp and mellow: moreover, good wine of the western bents went up and down the hall in great gilded copper bowls and in mazers girt and lipped with gold.

But when they were full of meat, and had drunken somewhat, they fell to speech, and Iron-face spake aloud to his son, who had but been speaking softly to the Bride as one playmate to the other: but the Alderman said: 'Scarce are the wood-deer grown, kinsman, when I must needs eat sheep's flesh on a Thursday, though my son has lain abroad in the woods all night to hunt for me.'

And therewith he smiled in the young man's face; but Gold-mane reddened and said: 'So is it, kinsman, I can hit what I can see; but not what is hidden.'

Iron-face laughed and said: 'Hast thou been to the Woodland-Carles? are their women fairer than our cousins?'

Face-of-god took up the Bride's hand in his and kissed it and laid it to his cheek; and then turned to his father and said: 'Nay, father, I saw not the Wood-carles, nor went to their abode; and on no day do I lust after their women. Moreover, I brought home a roebuck of the fattest; but I was over-late for Kettel, and the flesh was ready for the board by then I came.'

'Well, son,' quoth Iron-face, for he was merry, 'a roebuck is but a little deer for such big men as are thou and I. But I rede thee take the Bride along with thee the next time; and she shall seek whilest thou sleepest, and hit when thou missest.'

Then Face-of-god smiled, but he frowned somewhat also, and he said: 'Well were that, indeed! But if ye must needs drag a true tale out of me: that roebuck I shot at the very edge of the wood nigh to the Mote-stead as I was coming home: harts had I seen in the wood and its lawns, and boars, and bucks, and loosed not at them: for indeed when I awoke in the morning in that wood-lawn ye wot of, I wandered up and down with my bow unbent. So it was that I fared as if I were seeking something, I know not what, that should fill up something lacking to me, I know not what. Thus I felt in myself even so long as I was underneath the black boughs, and there was none beside me and before me, and none to turn aback to: but when I came out again into the

The offer of
Iron-face to
his son.

sunshine, and I saw the fair dale, and the happy abode lying
before me, and folk abroad in the meads merry in the eventide;
then was I full fain of it, and loathed the wood as an empty thing
that had nought to give me; and lo you! all that I had been
longing for in the wood, was it not in this House and ready to
my hand?—and that is good meseemeth.'

Therewith he drank of the cup which the Bride put into his
hand after she had kissed the rim, but when he had set it down
again he spake once more:

'And yet now I am sitting honoured and well-beloved in the
House of my Fathers, with the holy hearth sparkling and gleaming down there before me; and she that shall bear my children
sitting soft and kind by my side, and the bold lads I shall one
day lead in battle drinking out of my very cup: now it seems to
me that amidst all this, the dark cold wood, wherein abide but
the beasts and the Foes of the Gods, is bidding me to it and drawing me thither. Narrow is the Dale and the World is wide; I
would it were dawn and daylight, that I might be afoot again.'

And he half rose up from his place. But his father bent his
brow on him and said: 'Kinsman, thou hast a long tongue for
a half-trained whelp: nor see I whitherward thy mind is wandering, but if it be on the road of a lad's desire to go further and
fare worse. Hearken then, I will offer thee somewhat! Soon
shall the West-country merchants be here with their winter truck.
How sayest thou? hast thou a mind to fare back with them, and
look on the Plain and its Cities, and take and give with the
strangers? To whom indeed thou shalt be nothing save a purse
with a few lumps of gold in it, or maybe a spear in the stranger's
band on the stricken field, or a bow on the wall of an alien city.
This is a craft which thou mayst well learn, since thou shalt be
a chieftain; a craft good to learn, however grievous it be in the
learning. And I myself have been there; for in my youth I desired sore to look on the world beyond the mountains; so I went,
and I filled my belly with the fruit of my own desires, and a bitter

20

meat was that ; but now that it has passed through me, and I Face-of-god will not go to the Plain. yet alive, belike I am more of a grown man for having endured its gripe.  Even so may it well be with thee, son ; so go if thou wilt ; and thou shalt go with my blessing, and with gold and wares and wain and spearmen.'

'Nay,' said Face-of-god, 'I thank thee, for it is well offered; but I will not go, for I have no lust for the Plain and its Cities; I love the Dale well, and all that is round about it ; therein will I live and die.'

Therewith he fell a-musing ; and the Bride looked at him anxiously, but spake not.  Sooth to say her heart was sinking, as though she foreboded some new thing, which should thrust itself into their merry life.

But the old man Stone-face took up the word and said :

' Son Gold-mane, it behoveth me to speak, since belike I know the wild-wood better than most, and have done for these threescore and ten years ; to my cost.  Now I perceive that thou longest for the wood and the innermost of it ; and wot ye what? This longing will at whiles entangle the sons of our chieftains, though this Alderman that now is hath been free therefrom, which is well for him.  For, time was this longing came over me, and I went whither it led me : overlong it were to tell of all that befell me because of it, and how my heart bled thereby.  So sorry were the tidings that came of it, that now meseemeth my heart should be of stone and not my face, had it not been for the love wherewith I have loved the sons of the kindred.  Therefore, son, it were not ill if ye went west away with the merchants this winter, and learned the dealings of the cities, and brought us back tales thereof.'

But Gold-mane cried out somewhat angrily, ' I tell thee, fosterfather, that I have no mind for the cities and their men and their fools and their whores and their runagates.  But as for the wood and its wonders, I have done with it, save for hunting there along with others of the Folk.  So let thy mind be at ease ; and for

21

the rest, I will do what the Alderman commandeth, and whatso
my father craveth of me.'

'And that is well, son,' said Stone-face, 'if what ye say
come to pass, as sore I misdoubt me it will not. But well it
were, well it were! For such things are in the wood, yea and
before ye come to its innermost, as may well try the stoutest
heart. Therein are Kobbolds, and Wights that love not men,
things unto whom the grief of men is as the sound of the fiddle-
bow unto us. And there abide the ghosts of those that may not
rest; and there wander the dwarfs and the mountain-dwellers,
the dealers in marvels, the givers of gifts that destroy Houses;
the forgers of the curse that clingeth and the murder that flitteth
to and fro. There moreover are the lairs of Wights in the
shapes of women, that draw a young man's heart out of his body,
and fill up the empty place with desire never to be satisfied, that
they may mock him therewith and waste his manhood and
destroy him. Nor say I much of the strong-thieves that dwell
there, since thou art a valiant sword; or of them who have been
made Wolves of the Holy Places; or of the Murder-Carles, the
remnants and off-scourings of wicked and wretched Folks—men
who think as much of the life of a man as of the life of a fly.
Yet happiest is the man whom they shall tear in pieces, than
he who shall live burdened by the curse of the Foes of the Gods.'

The house-master looked on his son as the old carle spake,
and a cloud gathered on his face a while; and when Stone-face
had made an end he spake:

'This is long and evil talk for the end of a merry day, O
fosterer! Wilt thou not drink a draught, O Redesman, and
then stand up and set thy fiddle-bow a-dancing, and cause it
draw some fair words after it? For my cousin's face hath grown
sadder than a young maid's should be, and my son's eyes gleam
with thoughts that are far away from us and abroad in the wild-
wood seeking marvels.'

Then arose a man of middle-age from the top of the endlong

22

bench on the east side of the hall: a man tall, thin and scant-
haired, with a nose like an eagle's neb: he reached out his hand
for the bowl, and when they had given to him he handled it, and
raised it aloft and cried:

'Here I drink a double health to Face-of-god and the Bride,
and the love that lieth between them, and the love betwixt them
twain and us.'

He drank therewith, and the wine went up and down the
hall, and all men drank, both carles and queens, with shouting
and great joy. Then Redesman put down the cup (for it had
come into his hands again), and reached his hand to the wall
behind him, and took down his fiddle hanging there in its case,
and drew it out and fell to tuning it, while the hall grew silent
to hearken: then he handled the bow and laid it on the strings
till they wailed and chuckled sweetly, and when the song was well
awake and stirring briskly, then he lifted up his voice and sang:

### The Minstrel saith:

'O why on this morning, ye maids, are ye tripping
    Aloof from the meadows yet fresh with the dew,
Where under the west wind the river is lipping
    The fragrance of mint, the white blooms and the blue?

For rough is the Portway where panting ye wander;
    On your feet and your gown-hems the dust lieth dun;
Come trip through the grass and the meadow-sweet yonder,
    And forget neath the willows the sword of the sun.

### The Maidens answer:

Though fair are the moon-daisies down by the river,
    And soft is the grass and the white clover sweet;
Though twixt us and the rock-wall the hot glare doth quiver,
    And the dust of the wheel-way is dun on our feet;

Yet here on the way shall we walk on this morning
    Though the sun burneth here, and sweet, cool is the mead;

23

For here when in old days the Burg gave its warning,
Stood stark under weapons the doughty of deed.

Here came on the aliens their proud words a-crying,
And here on our threshold they stumbled and fell ;
Here silent at even the steel-clad were lying,
And here were our mothers the story to tell.

Here then on the morn of the eve of the wedding
We pray to the Mighty that we too may bear
Such war-walls for warding of orchard and steading,
That the new days be merry as old days were dear.'

Therewith he made an end, and shouts and glad cries arose
all about the hall ; and an old man arose and cried : ' A cup to the
memory of the Mighty of the Day of the Warding of the Ways.'
For you must know this song told of a custom of the Folk, held
in memory of a time of bygone battle, wherein they had overthrown a great host of aliens on the Portway betwixt the river
and the cliffs, two furlongs from the gate of Burgstead. So
now two weeks before Midsummer those maidens who were
presently to be wedded went early in the morning to that place
clad in very fair raiment, swords girt to their sides and spears in
their hands, and abode there on the highway from morn till even
as though they were a guard to it. And they made merry there,
singing songs and telling tales of times past : and at the sun-
setting their grooms came to fetch them away to the Feast of the
Eve of the Wedding.

While the song was a-singing Face-of-god took the Bride's
hand in his and caressed it, and was soft and blithe with her ;
and she reddened and trembled for pleasure, and called to mind
wedding feasts that had been, and fair brides that she had seen
thereat, and she forgot her fears and her heart was at peace again.

And Iron-face looked well-pleased on the two from time to
time, and smiled, but forbore words to them.

But up and down the hall men talked with one another about

24

things long ago betid : for their hearts were high and they desired deeds ; but in that fair Dale so happy were the years from day to day that there was but little to tell of. So deepened the night and waned, and Gold-mane and the Bride still talked sweetly together, and at whiles kindly to the others ; and by seeming he had clean forgotten the wood and its wonders.

Then at last the Alderman called for the cup of good-night, and men drank thereof and went their ways to bed.


CHAPTER IV.   FACE-OF-GOD FARETH TO THE WOOD AGAIN.

WHEN it was the earliest morning and dawn was but just beginning, Face-of-god awoke and rose up from his bed, and came forth into the hall naked in his shirt, and stood by the hearth, wherein the piled-up embers were yet red, and looked about and could see nothing stirring in the dimness : then he fetched water and washed the night-tide off him, and clad himself in haste, and was even as he was yesterday, save that he left his bow and quiver in their place and took instead a short casting-spear; moreover he took a leathern scrip and went therewith to the buttery, and set therein bread and flesh and a little gilded beaker ; and all this he did with but little noise ; for he would not be questioned, lest he should have to answer himself as well as others.

Thus he went quietly out of doors, for the door was but latched, since no bolts or bars or locks were used in Burgstead, and through the town-gate, which stood open, save when rumours of war were about.   He turned his face straight towards Wildlake's Way, walking briskly, but at whiles looking back over his shoulder toward the East to note what way was made by the dawning, and how the sky lightened above the mountain passes.

By then he was come to the place where the Maiden Ward
was held in the summer the dawn was so far forward that all
things had their due colours, and were clear to see in the shadow-
less day. It was a bright morning, with an easterly air stirring
that drave away the haze and dried the meadows, which had
otherwise been rimy; for it was cold. Gold-mane lingered on
the place a little, and his eyes fell on the road, as dusty yet as in
Redesman's song; for the autumn had been very dry, and the
strip of green that edged the outside of the way was worn and
dusty also. On the edge of it, half in the dusty road, half on
the worn grass, was a long twine of briony red-berried and black-
leaved; and right in the midst of the road were two twigs of
great-leaved sturdy pollard oak, as though they had been thrown
aside there yesterday by women or children a-sporting; and the
deep white dust yet held the marks of feet, some bare, some shod,
crossing each other here and there. Face-of-god smiled as he
passed on, as a man with a happy thought; for his mind showed
him a picture of the Bride as she would be leading the Maiden
Ward next summer, and singing first among the singers, and he
saw her as clearly as he had often seen her verily, and before him
was the fashion of her hands and all her body, and the little
mark on her right wrist, and the place where her arm whitened,
because the sleeve guarded it against the sun, which had long
been pleasant unto him, and the little hollow in her chin, and
the lock of red-brown hair waving in the wind above her brow,
and shining in the sun as brightly as the Alderman's cunningest
work of golden wire. Soft and sweet seemed that picture, till
he almost seemed to hear her sweet voice calling to him, and desire of her so took hold of the youth, that it stirred him up to go
swiftlier as he strode on, the day brightening behind him.

Now was it nigh sunrise, and he began to meet folk on the
way, though not many; since for most their way lay afield, and
not towards the Burg. The first was a Woodlander, tall and
gaunt, striding beside his ass, whose panniers were laden with

26

charcoal.  The carle's daughter, a little maiden of seven winters, Face-of-god maketh neighbours. was riding on the ass's back betwixt the panniers, and prattling to herself in the cold morning; for she was pleased with the clear light in the east, and the smooth wide turf of the meadows, as one who had not often been far from the shadow of the heavy trees of the wood, and their dark wall round about the clearing where they dwelt.  Face-of-god gave the twain the sele of the day in merry fashion as he passed them by, and the sober dark-faced man nodded to him but spake no word, and the child stayed her prattle to watch him as he went by.

Then came the sound of the rattle of wheels, and, as he doubled an angle of the rock-wall, he came upon a wain drawn by four dun kine, wherein lay a young woman all muffled up against the cold with furs and cloths; beside the yoke-beasts went her man, a well-knit trim-faced Dalesman clad bravely in holiday raiment, girt with a goodly sword, bearing a bright steel helm on his head, in his hand a long spear with a gay red and white shaft done about with copper bands.  He looked merry and proud of his wain-load, and the woman was smiling kindly on him from out of her scarlet and fur; but now she turned a weary happy face on Gold-mane, for they knew him, as did all men of the Dale.

So he stopped when they met, for the goodman had already stayed his slow beasts, and the goodwife had risen a little on her cushions to greet him, yet slowly and but a little, for she was great with child, and not far from her time.  That knew Gold-mane well, and what was toward, and why the goodman wore his fine clothes, and why the wain was decked with oak-boughs and the yoke-beasts with their best gilded bells and copper-adorned harness.  For it was a custom with many of the kindreds that the goodwife should fare to her father's house to lie in with her first babe, and the day of her coming home was made a great feast in the house.  So then Face-of-god cried out: 'Hail to thee, O Warcliff!  Shrewd is the wind this morning, and thou dost well to heed it carefully, this thine orchard, this thy garden, this thy

Face-of-god
cannot tell of
his road.

fair apple-tree! To a good hall thou wendest, and the Wine of Increase shall be sweet there this even.'

Then smiled Warcliff all across his face, and the goodwife hung her head and reddened. Said the goodman: 'Wilt thou not be with us, son of the Alderman, as surely thy father shall be?'

'Nay,' said Face-of-god, 'though I were fain of it: my own matters carry me away.'

'What matters?' said Warcliff; 'perchance thou art for the cities this autumn?'

Face-of-god answered somewhat stiffly: 'Nay, I am not;' and then more kindly, and smiling, 'All roads lead not down to the Plain, friend.'

'What road then farest thou away from us?' said the goodwife.

'The way of my will,' he answered.

'And what way is that?' said she; 'take heed, lest I get a longing to know. For then must thou needs tell me, or deal with the carle there beside thee.'

'Nay, goodwife,' said Face-of-god, 'let not that longing take thee; for on that matter I am even as wise as thou. Now good speed to thee and to the new-comer!'

Therewith he went close up to the wain, and reached out his hand to her, and she gave him hers and he kissed it, and so went his ways smiling kindly on them. Then the carle cried to his kine, and they bent down their heads to the yoke; and presently, as he walked on, he heard the rumble of the wain mingling with the tinkling of their bells, which in a little while became measured and musical, and sounded above the creaking of the axles and the rattle of the gear and the roll of the great wheels over the road: and so it grew thinner and thinner till it all died away behind him.

He was now come to where the river turned away from the sheer rock-wall, which was not so high there as in most other places, as there had been in old time long screes from the cliff, which had now grown together, with the waxing of herbs and the

28

washing down of the earth on to them, and made a steady slope More neigh-
or low hill going down riverward.  Over this the road lifted itself bours come on
above the level of the meadows, keeping a little way from the to the road;
cliffs, while on the other side its bank was somewhat broken and women to wit.
steep here and there.  As Face-of-god came up to one of these
broken places, the sun rose over the eastern pass, and the meadows
grew golden with its long beams.  He lingered, and looked back
under his hand, and as he did so heard the voices and laughter
of women coming up from the slope below him, and presently a
young woman came struggling up the broken bank with hand
and knee, and cast herself down on the roadside turf laughing
and panting.  She was a long-limbed light-made woman, dark-
faced and black-haired : amidst her laughter she looked up and
saw Gold-mane, who had stopped at once when he saw her; she
held out her hands to him, and said lightly, though her face
flushed withal :

'Come hither, thou, and help the others to climb the bank ;
for they are beaten in the race, and now must they do after my
will ; that was the forfeit.'

He went up to her, and took her hands and kissed them, as
was the custom of the Dale, and said :

'Hail to thee, Long-coat! who be they, and whither away this
morning early ? '

She looked hard at him, and fondly belike, as she answered
slowly : 'They be the two maidens of my father's house, whom
thou knowest ; and our errand, all three of us, is to Burgstead,
to the Feast of the Wine of Increase which shall be drunk this
even.'

As she spake came another woman half up the bank, to whom
went Face-of-god, and, taking her hands, drew her up while she
laughed merrily in his face: he saluted her as he had Long-
coat, and then with a laugh turned about to wait for the third ;
who came indeed, but after a little while, for she had abided,
hearing their voices.  Her also Gold-mane drew up, and kissed

29

her hands, and she lay on the grass by Long-coat, but the second maiden stood up beside the young man. She was white-skinned and golden-haired, a very fair damsel, whereas the last-comer was but comely, as were well-nigh all the women of the Dale.

Said Face-of-god, looking on the three : ' How comes it, maidens, that ye are but in your kirtles this sharp autumn morning ? or where have ye left your gowns or your cloaks?'

For indeed they were clad but in close-fitting blue kirtles of fine wool, embroidered about the hems with gold and coloured threads.

The last-comer laughed and said : ' What ails thee, Goldmane, to be so careful of us, as if thou wert our mother or our nurse ? Yet if thou must needs know, there hang our gowns on the thorn-bush down yonder; for we have been running a match and a forfeit ; to wit, that she who was last on the highway should go down again and bring them up all three ; and now that is my day's work: but since thou art here, Alderman's son, thou shalt go down instead of me and fetch them up.'

But he laughed merrily and outright, and said : ' That will I not, for there be but twenty-four hours in the day, and what between eating and drinking and talking to fair maidens, I have enough to do in every one of them. Wasteful are ye women, and simple is your forfeit. Now will I, who am the Alderman's son, give forth a doom, and will ordain that one of you fetch up the gowns yourselves, and that Long-coat be the one; for she is the fleetest-footed and ablest thereto. Will ye take my doom? for later on I shall not be wiser.'

' Yea,' said the fair woman, ' not because thou art the Alderman's son, but because thou art the fairest man of the Dale, and mayst bid us poor souls what thou wilt.'

Face-of-god reddened at her words, and the speaker and the last-comer laughed; but Long-coat held her peace: she cast one very sober look on him, and then ran lightly down the bent; he drew near the edge of it, and watched her going; for her light-foot slimness was fair to look on: and he noted that when she was nigh the thorn-bush whereon hung the bright-broidered gowns, and deemed belike that she was not seen, she kissed both her hands where he had kissed them erst.

Thereat he drew aback and turned away shyly, scarce looking at the other twain, who smiled on him with somewhat jeering looks ; but he bade them farewell and departed speedily; and if they spoke, it was but softly, for he heard their voices no more.

He went on under the sunlight which was now gilding the out-standing stones of the cliffs, and still his mind was set upon the Bride; and his meeting with the mother of the yet unborn baby, and with the three women with their freshness and fairness, did some-how turn his thought the more upon her, since she was the woman who was to be his amongst all women, for she was far fairer than any one of them; and through all manner of life and through all kinds of deeds would he be with her, and know more of her fair-ness and kindness than any other could: and him-seemed he could see pictures of her and of him amidst all these deeds and ways.

Now he went very swiftly; for he was eager, though he knew not for what, and he thought but little of the things on which his eyes fell. He met none else on the road till he was come to Wild-lake's Way, though he saw folk enough down in the meadows ; he was soon amidst the first of the trees, and without making any stay set his face east and somewhat north, that is, toward the slopes that led to the great mountains. He said to himself aloud, as he wended the wood : 'Strange ! yestereven I thought much of the wood, and I set my mind on not going thither, and this morning I thought nothing of it, and here am I amidst its trees, and wending towards its innermost.'

His way was easy at first, because the wood for a little space was all of beech, so that there was no undergrowth, and he went lightly betwixt the tall grey and smooth boles ; albeit his heart was nought so gay as it was in the dale amidst the sunshine. After a while the beech-wood grew thinner, and at last gave out

A path before
him that
seemeth like a
slot of men.

altogether, and he came into a space of rough broken ground with
nought but a few scrubby oaks and thorn-bushes growing thereon
here and there.  The sun was high in the heavens now, and
shone brightly down on the waste, though there were a few white
clouds high up above him.  The rabbits scuttled out of the grass
before him; here and there he turned aside from a stone on which
lay coiled an adder sunning itself; now and again both hart and
hind bounded away from before him, or a sounder of wild swine
ran grunting away toward closer covert.  But nought did he see
but the common sights and sounds of the woodland; nor did he
look for aught else, for he knew this part of the woodland indif-
ferent well.

He held on over this treeless waste for an hour or more, when
the ground began to be less rugged, and he came upon trees again,
but thinly scattered, oak and ash and hornbeam not right great,
with thickets of holly and blackthorn between them.  The set
of the ground was still steadily up to the east and north-east, and
he followed it as one who wendeth an assured way.  At last before
him seemed to rise a wall of trees and thicket; but when he drew
near to it, lo! an opening in a certain place, and a little path as
if men were wont to thread the tangle of the wood thereby;
though hitherto he had noted no slot of men, nor any sign of
them, since he had plunged into the deep of the beech-wood.  He
took the path as one who needs must, and went his ways as it
led.  In sooth it was well-nigh blind, but he was a deft woodsman, and by means of it skirted many a close thicket that had
otherwise stayed him.  So on he went, and though the boughs
were close enough overhead, and the sun came through but in
flecks, he judged that it was growing towards noon, and he wotted
well that he was growing aweary.  For he had been long afoot,
and the more part of the time on a rough way, or breasting a
slope which was at whiles steep enough.

At last the track led him skirting about an exceeding close
thicket into a small clearing, through which ran a little wood-

land rill amidst rushes and dead leaves: there was a low mound The token of near the eastern side of this wood-lawn, as though there had a dwelling of once been a dwelling of man there, but no other sign or slot of men. man was there.

So Face-of-god made stay in that place, casting himself down beside the rill to rest him and eat and drink somewhat. Whatever thoughts had been with him through the wood (and they had been many) concerning his House and his name, and his father, and the journey he might make to the cities of the Westland, and what was to befall him when he was wedded, and what war or trouble should be on his hands—all this was now mingled together and confused by this rest amidst his weariness. He laid down his scrip, and drew his meat from it and ate what he would, and dipping his gilded beaker into the brook, drank water smacking of the damp musty savour of the woodland ; and then his head sank back on a little mound in the short turf, and he fell asleep at once. A long dream he had in short space ; and therein were blent his thoughts of the morning with the deeds of yesterday; and other matters long forgotten in his waking hours came back to his slumber in unordered confusion : all which made up for him pictures clear, but of little meaning, save that, as oft befalls in dreams, whatever he was a-doing he felt himself belated.

When he awoke, smiling at something strange in his gone-by dream, he looked up to the heavens, thinking to see signs of the even at hand, for he seemed to have been dreaming so long. The sky was thinly overcast by now, but by his wonted woodcraft he knew the whereabouts of the sun, and that it was scant an hour after noon. He sat there till he was wholly awake, and then drank once more of the woodland water ; and he said to himself, but out loud, for he was fain of the sound of a man's voice, though it were but his own:

'What is mine errand hither? Whither wend I? What shall I have done to-morrow that I have hitherto left undone?

Or what manner of man shall I be then other than I am
now ?'

Yet though he said the words he failed to think the thought, or
it left him in a moment of time, and he thought but of the Bride
and her kindness. Yet that abode with him but a moment, and
again he saw himself and those two women on the highway edge,
and Long-coat lingering on the slope below, kissing his kisses on
her hands ; and he was sorry that she desired him overmuch, for
she was a fair woman and a friendly. But all that also flowed
from him at once, and he had no thought in him but that he also
desired something that he lacked : and this was a burden to him,
and he rose up frowning, and said to himself, ' Am I become a
mere sport of dreams, whether I sleep or wake ? I will go back-
ward—or forward, but will think no more.'

Then he ordered his gear again, and took the path onward
and upward toward the Great Mountains ; and the track was
even fainter than before for a while, so that he had to seek his
way diligently.


CHAPTER V.   FACE-OF-GOD FALLS IN WITH MENFOLK
ON THE MOUNTAIN.

NOW he plodded on steadily, and for a long time the forest
changed but little, and of wild things he saw only a few
of those that love the closest covert. The ground still
went up and up, though at whiles were hollows, and steeper
bents out of them again, and the half-blind path or slot still led
past the close thickets and fallen trees, and he made way without let or hindrance. At last once more the wood began to thin,
and the trees themselves to be smaller and gnarled and ill-
grown: therewithal the day was waning, and the sky was quite
clear again as the afternoon grew into a fair autumn evening.

Now the trees failed altogether, and the slope grown steeper

34

was covered with heather and ling; and looking up, he saw before him quite near by seeming in the clear even (though indeed they were yet far away) the snowy peaks flushed with the sinking sun against the frosty dark-grey eastern sky; and below them the dark rock-mountains, and below these again, and nigh to him indeed, the fells covered with pine-woods and looking like a wall to the heaths he trod.

He stayed a little while and turned his head to look at the way whereby he had come; but that way a swell of the oak-forest hid everything but the wood itself, making a wall behind him as the pine-wood made a wall before. There came across him then a sharp memory of the boding words which Stone-face had spoken last night, and he felt as if he were now indeed within the trap. But presently he laughed and said: 'I am a fool: this comes of being alone in the dark wood and the dismal waste, after the merry faces of the Dale had swept away my foolish musings of yesterday and the day before. Lo! here I stand, a man of the Face, sword and axe by my side; if death come, it can but come once; and if I fear not death, what shall make me afraid? The Gods hate me not, and will not hurt me; and they are not ugly, but beauteous.'

Therewith he strode on again, and soon came to a place where the ground sank into a shallow valley and the ling gave place to grass for a while, and there were tall old pines scattered about, and betwixt them grey rocks; this he passed through, climbing a steep bent out of it, and the pines were all about him now, though growing wide apart, till at last he came to where they thickened into a wood, not very close, wherethrough he went merrily, singing to himself and swinging his spear. He was soon through this wood, and came on to a wide well-grassed wood-lawn, hedged by the wood aforesaid on three sides, but sloping up slowly toward the black wall of the thicker pine-wood on the fourth side, and about half a furlong overthwart and endlong. The sun had set while he was in the last wood, but it was

still broad daylight on the wood-lawn, and as he stood there he
was ware of a house under the pine-wood on the other side, built
long and low, much like the houses of the Woodland-Carles, but
rougher fashioned and of unhewn trees.  He gazed on it, and said
aloud to himself as his wont was :

'Marvellous! here is a dwelling of man, scarce a day's journey
from Burgstead; yet have I never heard tell of it : may happen
some of the Woodland-Carles have built it, and are on some errand
of hunting peltries up in the mountains, or maybe are seeking
copper and tin among the rocks.  Well, at least let us go see what
manner of men dwell there, and if they are minded for a guest to-
night; for fain were I of a bed beneath a roof, and of a board with
strong meat and drink on it.'

Therewith he set forward, not heeding much that the wood he
had passed through was hard on his left hand; but he had gone
but twenty paces when he saw a red thing at the edge of the wood,
and then a glitter, and a spear came whistling forth, and smote
his own spear so hard close to the steel that it flew out of his hand ;
then came a great shout, and a man clad in a scarlet kirtle ran
forth on him.  Face-of-god had his axe in his hand in a twinkling,
and ran at once to meet his foe ; but the man had the hill on his
side as he rushed on with a short-sword in his hand.  Axe and
sword clashed together for a moment of time, and then both the
men rolled over on the grass together, and Face-of-god as he fell
deemed that he heard the shrill cry of a woman.  Now Face-of-
god found that he was the nethermost, for if he was strong, yet
was his foe stronger; the axe had flown out of his hand also, while
the strange man still kept a hold of his short-sword; and presently,
though he still struggled all he could, he saw the man draw back
his hand to smite with the said sword ; and at that nick of time the
foeman's knee was on his breast, his left hand was doubled back
behind him, and his right wrist was gripped hard in the stranger's
left hand.  Even therewith his ears, sharpened by the coming death,
heard the sound of footsteps and fluttering raiment drawing near ;

36

something dark came between him and the sky; there was the A fair woman. sound of a great stroke, and the big man loosened his grip and fell off him to one side.

Face-of-god leapt up and ran to his axe and got hold of it; but turning round found himself face to face with a tall woman holding in her hand a stout staff like the limb of a tree. She was calm and smiling, though forsooth it was she who had stricken the stroke and stayed the sword from his throat. His hand and axe dropped down to his side when he saw what it was that faced him, and that the woman was young and fair; so he spake to her and said:

'What aileth, maiden? is this man thy foe? doth he oppress thee? shall I slay him?'

She laughed and said: 'Thou art open-handed in thy proffers: he might have asked the like concerning thee but a minute ago.'

'Yea, yea,' said Gold-mane, laughing also, 'but he asked it not of thee.'

'That is sooth,' she said, 'but since thou hast asked me, I will tell thee that if thou slay him it will be my harm as well as his; and in my country a man that taketh a gift is not wont to break the giver's head with it straightway. The man is my brother, O stranger, and presently, if thou wilt, thou mayst be eating at the same board with him. Or if thou wilt, thou mayst go thy ways unhurt into the wood. But I had liefer of the twain that thou wert in our house to-night; for thou hast a wrong against us.'

Her voice was sweet and clear, and she spake the last words kindly, and drew somewhat nigher to Gold-mane. Therewithal the smitten man sat up, and put his hand to his head, and quoth he:

'Angry is my sister! good it is to wear the helm abroad when she shaketh the nut-trees.'

'Nay,' said she, 'it is thy luck that thou wert bare-headed, else had I been forced to smite thee on the face. Thou churl, since when hath it been our wont to thrust knives into a guest, who is come of great kin, a man of gentle heart and fair face? Come hither and handsel him self-doom for thy fool's onset!'

37

The man rose to his feet and said : 'Well, sister, least said, soonest mended. A clout on the head is worse than a woman's chiding; but since ye have given me one, ye may forbear the other.'

Therewith he drew near to them. He was a very big-made man, most stalwarth, with dark red hair and a thin pointed beard; his nose was straight and fine, his eyes grey and well-opened, but somewhat fierce withal. Yet was he in nowise evil-looking; he seemed some thirty summers old. He was clad in a short scarlet kirtle, a goodly garment, with a hood of like web pulled off his head on to his shoulders : he bore a great gold ring on his left arm, and a collar of gold came down on to his breast from under his hood.

As for the woman, she was clad in a long white linen smock, and over it a short gown of dark blue woollen, and she had skin shoes on her feet.

Now the man came up to Face-of-god, and took his hand and said : 'I deemed thee a foe, and I may not have over-many foes alive : but it seems that thou art to be a friend, and that is well and better; so herewith I handsel thee self-doom in the matter of the onslaught.'

Then Face-of-god laughed and said: 'The doom is soon given forth ; against the tumble on the grass I set the clout on the head ; there is nought left over to pay to any man's son.'

Said the scarlet-clad man : 'Belike by thine eyes thou art a true man, and wilt not bewray me. Now is there no foeman here, but rather maybe a friend both now and in time to come.' Therewith he cast his arms about Face-of-god and kissed him. But Face-of-god turned about to the woman and said: 'Is the peace wholly made ?'

She shook her head and said soberly : 'Nay, thou art too fair for a woman to kiss.'

He flushed red, as his wont was when a woman praised him ; yet was his heart full of pleasure and well-liking. But she laid her hand on his shoulder and said: 'Now is it for thee to choose

38

betwixt the wild-wood and the hall, and whether thou wilt be a
guest or a wayfarer this night.'

As she touched him there took hold of him a sweetness of pleasure he had never felt erst, and he answered: 'I will be thy guest and not thy stranger.'

'Come then,' she said, and took his hand in hers, so that he scarce felt the earth under his feet, as they went all three together toward the house in the gathering dusk, while eastward where the peaks of the great mountains dipped was a light that told of the rising of the moon.

## CHAPTER VI. OF FACE-OF-GOD AND THOSE MOUNTAIN-DWELLERS.

A YARD or two from the threshold Gold-mane hung back a moment, entangled in some such misgiving as a man is wont to feel when he is just about to do some new deed, but is not yet deep in the story; his new friends noted that, for they smiled each in their own way, and the woman drew her hand away from his. Face-of-god held out his still as though to take hers again, and therewithal he changed countenance and said as though he had stayed but to ask that question:

'Tell me thy name, tall man; and thou, fair woman, tell me thine; for how can we talk together else?'

The man laughed outright and said: 'The young chieftain thinks that this house also should be his! Nay, young man, I know what is in thy thought, be not ashamed that thou art wary; and be assured! We shall hurt thee no more than thou hast been hurt. Now as to my name; the name that was born with me is gone: the name that was given me hath been taken from me: now I belike must give myself a name, and that shall be Wild-wearer; but it may be that thou thyself shalt one day give me another, and call me Guest.'

39

His sister gazed at him solemnly as he spoke, and Face-of-god
beholding her the while, deemed that her beauty grew and grew
till she seemed as aweful as a Goddess; and into his mind it
came that this over-strong man and over-lovely woman were
nought mortal, and they withal dealing with him as father and
mother deal with a wayward child : then for a moment his heart
failed him, and he longed for the peace of Burgdale, and even the
lonely wood. But therewith she turned to him and let her hand
come into his again, and looked kindly on him and said : ' And
as for me, call me the Friend; the name is good and will serve
for many things.'

He looked down from her face and his eyes lighted on her hand,
and when he noted even amid the evening dusk how fair and
lovely it was fashioned, and yet as though it were deft in the
crafts that the daughters of menfolk use, his fear departed, and
the pleasure of his longing filled his heart, and he drew her hand
to him to kiss it; but she held it back. Then he said: ' It is the
custom of the Dale to all women.'

So she let him kiss her hand, heeding the kiss nothing, and
said soberly :

' Then art thou of Burgdale, and if it were lawful to guess,
I would say that thy name is Face-of-god, of the House of
the Face.'

' Even so it is,' said he, ' but in the Dale those that love me
do mostly call me Gold-mane.'

' It is well named,' she said, ' and seldom wilt thou be called
otherwise, for thou wilt be well-beloved. But come in now, Gold-
mane, for night is at hand, and here have we meat and lodging
such as an hungry and weary man may take; though we be
broken people, dwellers in the waste.'

Therewith she led him gently over the threshold into the hall,
and it seemed to him as if she were the fairest and the noblest of
all the Queens of ancient story.

When he was in the house he looked and saw that, rough as

40

it was without it lacked not fairness within. The floor was of hard-trodden earth strewn with pine-twigs, and with here and there brown bearskins laid on it: there was a standing table near the upper end athwart the hall, and a daïs beyond that, but no endlong table. Gold-mane looked to the shut-beds, and saw that they were large and fair, though there were but a few of them; and at the lower end was a loft for a sleeping chamber dight very fairly with broidered cloths. The hangings on the walls, though they left some places bare which were hung with fresh boughs, were fairer than any he had ever seen, so that he deemed that they must come from far countries and the City of Cities: therein were images wrought of warriors and fair women of old time and their dealings with the Gods and the Giants, and Wondrous wights; and he deemed that this was the story of some great kindred, and that their token and the sign of their banner must needs be the Wood-wolf, for everywhere was it wrought in these pictured webs. Perforce he looked long and earnestly at these fair things, for the hall was not dark yet, because the brands on the hearth were flaming their last, and when Wild-wearer beheld him so gazing, he stood up and looked too for a moment, and then smote his right hand on the hilt of his sword, and turned away and strode up and down the hall as one in angry thought.

But the woman, even the Friend, bestirred herself for the service of the guest, and brought water for his hands and feet, and when she had washed him, bore him the wine of Welcome and drank to him and bade him drink; and he all the while was shamefaced; for it was to him as if one of the Ladies of the Heavenly Burg were doing him service. Then she went away by a door at the lower end of the hall, and Wild-wearer came and sat down by Gold-mane, and fell a-talking with him about the ways of the Dalesmen, and their garths, and the pastures and growths thereof; and what temper the carles themselves were of; which were good men, which were ill, which was loved and which scorned; no otherwise than if he had been the goodman of some neighbouring

G

dale; and Gold-mane told him whatso he knew, for he saw no
harm therein.

After a while the outer door opened, and there came in a woman
of some five-and-twenty winters, trimly and strongly built; short-
skirted she was and clad as a hunter, with a bow in her hand and
a quiver at her back: she unslung a pouch, which she emptied at
Wild-wearer's feet of a leash of hares and two brace of mountain grouse; of Face-of-god she took but little heed.

Said Wild-wearer: 'This is good for to-morrow, not for to-
day; the meat is well-nigh on the board.'

Then Gold-mane smiled, for he called to mind his home-coming
of yesterday. But the woman said:

'The fault is not mine; she told me of the coming guest but
three hours agone.'

'Ay?' said Wild-wearer, 'she looked for a guest then?'

'Yea, certes,' said the woman, 'else why went I forth this
afternoon, as wearied as I was with yesterday?'

'Well, well,' said Wild-wearer, 'get to thy due work or go
play; I meddle not with meat! and for thee all jests are as
bitter earnest.'

'And with thee, chief,' she said, 'it is no otherwise; surely I
am made on thy model.'

'Thy tongue is longer, friend,' said he; 'now tarry if thou
wilt, and if the supper's service craveth thee not.'

She turned away with one keen look at Face-of-god, and departed through the door at the lower end of the hall.

By this time the hall was dusk, for there were no candles there,
and the hearth-fire was but smouldering. Wild-wearer sat silent
and musing now, and Face-of-god spake not, for he was deep in
wild and happy dreams. At last the lower door opened and the fair
woman came into the hall with a torch in either hand, after whom
came the huntress, now clad in a dark blue kirtle, and an old
woman yet straight and hale; and these twain bore in the victuals and the table-gear. Then the three fell to dighting the

board, and when it was all ready, and Gold-mane and Wild-wearer were set down to it, and with them the fair woman and the huntress, the old woman threw good store of fresh brands on the hearth, so that the light shone into every corner ; and even therewith the outer door opened, and four more men entered, whereof one was old, but big and stalwarth, the other three young : they were all clad roughly in sheep-brown weed, but had helms upon their heads and spears in their hands and great swords girt to their sides ; and they seemed doughty men and ready for battle. One of the young men cast down by the door the carcass of a big-horned mountain sheep, and then they all trooped off to the out-bower by the lower door, and came back presently fairly clad and without their weapons. Wild-wearer nodded to them kindly, and they sat at table paying no more heed to Face-of-god than to cast him a nod for salutation.

Then said the old woman to them : ' Well, lads, have ye been doing or sleeping ?'

' Sleeping, mother,' said one of the young men, ' as was but due after last night was, and to-morrow shall be.'

Said the huntress : ' Hold thy peace, Wood-wise, and let thy tongue help thy teeth to deal with thy meat ; for this is not the talking hour.'

' Nay, Bow-may,' said another of the swains, ' since here is a new man, now is the time to talk to him.'

Said the huntress : ' 'Tis thine hands that talk best, Wood-wont ; it is not they that shall bring thee to shame.'

Spake the third : ' What have we to do with shame here, far away from dooms and doomers, and elders, and wardens, and guarded castles ? If the new man listeth to speak, let him speak ; or to fight, then let him ; it shall ever be man to man.'

Then spake the old woman : ' Son Wood-wicked, hold thy peace, and forget the steel that ever eggeth thee on to draw.'

Therewith she set the last matters on the board, while the three swains sat and eyed Gold-mane somewhat fiercely, now that

43

words had stirred them, and he had sat there saying nothing, as
one who was better than they, and contemned them; but now
spake Wild-wearer:

'Whoso hungreth let him eat! Whoso would slumber, let
him to bed. But he who would bicker, it must needs be with
me. Here is a man of the Dale, who hath sought the wood in
peace, and hath found us. His hand is ready and his heart is
guileless: if ye fear him, run away to the wood, and come back
when he is gone; but none shall mock him while I sit by: now,
lads, be merry and blithe with the guest.'

Then the young men greeted Gold-mane, and the old man
said: 'Art thou of Burgstead? then wilt thou be of the House
of the Face, and thy name will be Face-of-god; for that man
is called the fairest of the Dale, and there shall be none fairer
than thou.'

Face-of-god laughed and said: 'There be but few mirrors in
Burgdale, and I have no mind to journey west to the cities to see
what manner of man I be: that were ill husbandry. But now I have
heard the names of the three swains, tell me thy name, father!'

Spake the huntress: 'This is my father's brother, and his name
is Wood-father; or ye shall call him so: and I am called Bow-
may because I shoot well in the bow: and this old carline is my
eme's wife, and now belike my mother, if I need one. But thou,
fair-faced Dalesman, little dost thou need a mirror in the Dale so
long as women abide there; for their faces shall be instead of
mirrors to tell thee whether thou be fair and lovely.'

Thereat they all laughed and fell to their victual, which was
abundant, of wood-venison and mountain-fowl, but of bread was
no great plenty; wine lacked not, and that of the best; and
Gold-mane noted that the cups and the apparel of the horns and
mazers were not of gold nor gilded copper, but of silver; and he
marvelled thereat, for in the Dale silver was rare.

So they ate and drank, and Gold-mane looked ever on the
Friend, and spake much with her, and he deemed her friendly

44

indeed, and she seemed most pleased when he spoke best, and led him on to do so. Wild-wearer was but of few words, and those somewhat harsh; yet was he as a man striving to be courteous and blithe; but of the others Bow-may was the greatest speaker.

Wild-wearer called healths to the Sun, and the Moon, and the Hosts of Heaven; to the Gods of the Earth; to the Woodwights; and to the Guest. Other healths also he called, the meaning of which was dark to Gold-mane; to wit, the Jaws of the Wolf; the Silver Arm; the Red Hand; the Golden Bushel; and the Ragged Sword. But when he asked the Friend concerning these names what they might signify, she shook her head and answered not.

At last Wild-wearer cried out: 'Now, lads, the night weareth and the guest is weary: therefore whoso of you hath in him any minstrelsy, now let him make it, for later on it shall be over-late.'

Then arose Wood-wont and went to his shut-bed and groped therein, and took from out of it a fiddle in its case; and he opened the case and drew from it a very goodly fiddle, and he stood on the floor amidst of the hall and Bow-may his cousin with him; and he laid his bow on the fiddle and woke up song in it, and when it was well awake she fell a-singing, and he to answering her song, and at the last all they of the house sang together; and this is the meaning of the words which they sang:

*She singeth.*
Now is the rain upon the day,
    And every water's wide;
Why busk ye then to wear the way,
    And whither will ye ride?

*He singeth.*
Our kine are on the eyot still,
    The eddies lap them round;

45

All dykes the wind-worn waters fill,
And waneth grass and ground.

*She singeth.*

O ride ye to the river's brim
In war-weed fair to see?
Or winter waters will ye swim
In hauberks to the knee?

*He singeth.*

Wild is the day, and dim with rain,
Our sheep are warded ill;
The wood-wolves gather for the plain,
Their ravening maws to fill.

*She singeth.*

Nay, what is this, and what have ye,
A hunter's band, to bear
The Banner of our Battle-glee
The skulking wolves to scare?

*He singeth.*

O women, when we wend our ways
To deal with death and dread,
The Banner of our Fathers' Days
Must flap the wind o'erhead.

*She singeth.*

Ah, for the maidens that ye leave!
Who now shall save the hay?
What grooms shall kiss our lips at eve,
When June hath mastered May?

*He singeth.*

The wheat is won, the seed is sown,
Here toileth many a maid,

46

And ere the hay knee-deep hath grown
Your grooms the grass shall wade.

     *They sing all together.*
Then fair befall the mountain-side
Whereon the play shall be!
And fair befall the summer-tide
That whoso lives shall see.

Face-of-god thought the song goodly, but to the others it was well known. Then said Wood-father :

'O foster-son, thy foster-brother hath sung well for a wood abider; but we are deeming that his singing shall be but as a starling to a throstle matched against thy new-come guest. Therefore, Dalesman, sing us a song of the Dale, and if ye will, let it be of gardens and pleasant houses of stone, and fair damsels therein, and swains with them who toil not overmuch for a scant livelihood, as do they of the waste, whose heads may not be seen in the Holy Places.'

Said Gold-mane : 'Father, it is ill to set the words of a lonely man afar from his kin against the song that cometh from the heart of a noble house ; yet may I not gainsay thee, but will sing to thee what I may call to mind, and it is called the Song of the Ford.'

Therewith he sang in a sweet and clear voice : and this is the meaning of his words :

In hay-tide, through the day new-born,
    Across the meads we come ;
Our hauberks brush the blossomed corn
    A furlong short of home.

Ere yet the gables we behold
    Forth flasheth the red sun,
And smites our fallow helms and cold
    Though all the fight be done.

In this last mead of mowing-grass
  Sweet doth the clover smell,
Crushed neath our feet red with the pass
  Where hell was blent with hell.

And now the willowy stream is nigh,
  Down wend we to the ford;
No shafts across its fishes fly,
  Nor flasheth there a sword.

But lo! what gleameth on the bank
  Across the water wan,
As when our blood the mouse-ear drank
  And red the river ran?

Nay, hasten to the ripple clear,
  Look at the grass beyond!
Lo ye the dainty band and dear
  Of maidens fair and fond!

Lo how they needs must take the stream!
  The water hides their feet;
On fair kind arms the gold doth gleam,
  And midst the ford we meet.

Up through the garden two and two,
  And on the flowers we drip;
Their wet feet kiss the morning dew
  As lip lies close to lip.

Here now we sing; here now we stay:
  By these grey walls we tell
The love that lived from out the fray,
  The love that fought and fell.

When he was done they all said that he had sung well, and

that the song was sweet. Yet did Wild-wearer smile somewhat; and Bow-may said outright: 'Soft is the song, and hath been made by lads and minstrels rather than by warriors.'

'Nay, kinswoman,' said Wood-father, 'thou art hard to please; the guest is kind, and hath given us that I asked for, and I give him all thanks therefor.'

Face-of-god smiled, but he heeded little what they said, for as he sang he had noted that the Friend looked kindly on him; and he thought he saw that once or twice she put out her hand as if to touch him, but drew it back again each time. She spake after a little and said:

'Here now hath been a stream of song running betwixt the Mountain and the Dale even as doth a river; and this is good to come between our dreams of what hath been and what shall be.' Then she turned to Gold-mane, and said to him scarce loud enough for all to hear:

'Herewith I bid thee good-night, O Dalesman; and this other word I have to thee: heed not what befalleth in the night, but sleep thy best, for nought shall be to thy scathe. And when thou wakest in the morning, if we are yet here, it is well; but if we are not, then abide us no long while, but break thy fast on the victual thou wilt find upon the board, and so depart and go thy ways home. And yet thou mayst look to it to see us again before thou diest.'

Therewith she held out her hand to him, and he took it and kissed it; and she went to her chamber-aloft at the lower end of the hall. And when she was gone, once more he had a deeming of her that she was of the kindred of the Gods. At her departure him-seemed that the hall grew dull and small and smoky, and the night seemed long to him and doubtful the coming of the day.

## CHAPTER VII. FACE-OF-GOD TALKETH WITH THE FRIEND ON THE MOUNTAIN.

SO now went all men to bed; and Face-of-god's shut-bed was over against the outer door and toward the lower end of the hall, and on the panel about it hung the weapons and shields of men. Fair was that chamber and roomy, and the man was weary despite his eagerness, so that he went to sleep as soon as his head touched the pillow; but within a while (he deemed about two hours after midnight) he was awaked by the clattering of the weapons against the panel, and the sound of men's hands taking them down; and when he was fully awake, he heard withal men going up and down the house as if on errands : but he called to mind what the Friend had said to him, and he did not so much as turn himself toward the hall; for he said : 'Belike these men are outlaws and Wolves of the Holy Places, yet by seeming they are good fellows and nought churlish, nor have I to do with taking up the feud against them. I will abide the morning. Yet meseemeth that she drew me hither : for what cause ?'

Therewith he fell asleep again, and dreamed no more. But when he awoke the sun was shining broad upon the hall-floor, and he sat up and listened, but could hear no sound save the moaning of the wind in the pine-boughs and the chatter of the starlings about the gables of the house ; and the place seemed so exceeding lonely to him that he was in a manner feared by that loneliness.

Then he arose and clad himself, and went forth into the hall and gazed about him, and at first he deemed indeed that there was no one therein. But at last he looked and beheld the upper gable, and there underneath a most goodly hanging was the glorious shape of a woman sitting on a bench covered over with a cloth of gold and silver ; and he looked and looked to see if the woman might stir, and if she were alive, and she turned her head toward him, and lo it was the Friend; and his heart rose to his mouth for wonder and fear and desire. For now he doubted whether the other folk were aught save shows and shadows, and she the Goddess who had fashioned them out of nothing for his bewilderment, pre- sently to return to nothing.

Yet whatever he might fear or doubt, he went up the hall towards her till he was quite nigh to her, and there he stood silent, wondering at her beauty and desiring her kindness.

Grey-eyed she was like her brother; but her hair the colour of red wheat: her lips full and red, her chin round, her nose fine and straight. Her hands and all her body fashioned exceeding sweetly and delicately; yet not as if she were an image of which the like might be found if the craftsman were but deft enough to make a perfect thing, but in such a way that there was none like to her for those that had eyes to behold her as she was; and none could ever be made like to her, even by such a master-craftsman as could fashion a body without a blemish.

She was clad in a white smock, whose hems were broidered with gold wire and precious gems of the Mountains, and over that a gown woven of gold and silver: scarce hath the world such another. On her head was a fillet of gold and gems, and there were wondrous gold rings on her arms: her feet lay bare on the dark grey wolf-skin that was stretched before her.

She smiled kindly upon his solemn and troubled face, and her voice sounded strangely familiar to him coming from all that loveliness, as she said: 'Hail, Face-of-god! here am I left alone, although I deemed last night that I should be gone with the others. Therefore am I fain to show myself to thee in fairer array than yesternight; for though we dwell in the wild-wood, afar from the solace of folk, yet are we not of thralls' blood. But come now, I bid thee break thy fast and talk with me a little while; and then shalt thou depart in peace.'

Spake Face-of-god, and his voice trembled as he spake: 'What art thou? Last night I deemed at whiles once and again that thou wert of the Gods; and now that I behold thee thus, and it is broad daylight, and of those others is no more to be seen than if they had never lived, I cannot but deem that it is even so, and that thou comest from the City that shall never perish. Now if thou be a goddess, I have nought to pray thee, save to slay me speedily if thou hast a mind for my death.  But if thou art a woman——'

She broke in : 'Gold-mane, stay thy prayer and hold thy peace for this time, lest thou repent when repentance availeth not.  And this I say because I am none of the Gods nor akin to them, save far off through the generations, as art thou also, and all men of goodly kindred.  Now I bid thee eat thy meat, since 'tis ill talking betwixt a full man and a fasting ; and I have dight it myself with mine own hands ; for Bow-may and the Wood-mother went away with the rest three hours before dawn.  Come sit and eat as thou hast a hardy heart ; as forsooth thou shouldest do if I were a very goddess.  Take heed, friend, lest I take thee for some damsel of the lower Dale arrayed in Earl's garments.'

She laughed therewith, and leaned toward him and put forth her hand to him, and he took it and caressed it ; and the exceeding beauty of her body and of the raiment which was as it were a part of her and her loveliness, made her laughter and her friendly words strange to him, as if one did not belong to the other ; as in a dream it might be.  Nevertheless he did as she bade him, and sat at the board and ate, while she leaned forward on the arm of her chair and spake to him in friendly wise.  And he wondered as she spake that she knew so much of him and his : and he kept saying to himself : 'She drew me hither ; wherefore did she so ?'

But she said : 'Gold-mane, how fareth thy father the Alderman ? is he as good a wright as ever ?'

He told her : Yea, that ever was his hammer on the iron, the copper, and the gold, and that no wright in the Dale was as deft as he.

Said she : 'Would he not have had thee seek to the Cities, to see the ways of the outer world ?'

'Yea,' said he.

52

She said : 'Thou wert wise to naysay that offer; thou shalt have enough to do in the Dale and round about it in twelve months' time.'

'Art thou foresighted?' said he.

'Folk have called me so,' she said, 'but I wot not. But thy brother Hall-face, how fareth he?'

'Well;' said he, 'to my deeming he is the Sword of our House, and the Warrior of the Dale, if the days were ready for him.'

'And Stone-face, that stark ancient,' she said, 'doth he still love the Folk of the Dale, and hate all other folks?'

'Nay,' he said, 'I know not that, but I know that he loveth us, and above all me and my father.'

Again she spake : 'How fareth the Bride, the fair maid to whom thou art affianced?'

As she spake, it was to him as if his heart was stricken cold; but he put a force upon himself, and neither reddened nor whitened, nor changed countenance in any way; so he answered : 'She was well the eve of yesterday.' Then he remembered what she was, and her beauty and valour, and he constrained himself to say : 'Each day she groweth fairer; there is no man's son and no daughter of woman that does not love her; yea, the very beasts of field and fold love her.'

The Friend looked at him steadily and spake no word, but a red flush mounted to her cheeks and brow and changed her face; and he marvelled thereat; for still he misdoubted that she was a Goddess. But it passed away in a moment, and she smiled and said :

'Guest, thou seemest to wonder that I know concerning thee and the Dale and thy kindred. But now shalt thou wot that I have been in the Dale once and again, and my brother oftener still; and that I have seen thee before yesterday.'

'That is marvellous,' quoth he, 'for sure am I that I have not seen thee.'

53

'Yet thou hast seen me,' she said; 'yet not altogether as I am now;' and therewith she smiled on him friendly.

'How is this?' said he; 'art thou a skin-changer?'

'Yea, in a fashion,' she said. 'Hearken! dost thou perchance remember a day of last summer when there was a market holden in Burgstead; and there stood in the way over against the House of the Face a tall old carle who was trucking deer-skins for diverse gear; and with him was a queen, tall and dark-skinned, somewhat well-liking, her hair bound up in a white coif so that none of it could be seen; by the token that she had a large stone of mountain blue set in silver stuck in the said coif?'

As she spoke she set her hand to her bosom and drew something from it, and held forth her hand to Gold-mane, and lo amidst the palm the great blue stone set in silver.

'Wondrous as a dream is this,' said Face-of-god, 'for these twain I remember well, and what followed.'

She said: 'I will tell thee that. There came a man of the Shepherd-Folk, drunk or foolish, or both, who began to chaffer with the big carle; but ever on the queen were his eyes set, and presently he put forth his hand to her to clip her, whereon the big carle hove up his fist and smote him, so that he fell to earth noseling. Then ran the folk together to hale off the stranger and help the shepherd, and it was like that the stranger should be mishandled. Then there thrust through the press a young man with yellow hair and grey eyes, who cried out, "Fellows, let be! The stranger had the right of it; this is no matter to make a quarrel or a court case of. Let the market go on! This man and maid are true folk." So when the folk heard the young man and his bidding, they forebore and let the carle and the queen be, and the shepherd went his ways little hurt. Now then, who was this young man?'

Quoth Gold-mane: 'It was even I, and meseemeth it was no great deed to do.'

'Yea,' she said, 'and the big carle was my brother, and the tall queen, it was myself.'

54

'How then,' said he, 'for she was as dark-skinned as a dwarf, and thou so bright and fair?'

She said: 'Well, if the woods are good for nothing else, yet are they good for the growing of herbs, and I know the craft of simpling; and with one of these herbs had I stained my skin and my brother's also. And it showed the darker beneath the white coif.'

'Yea,' said he, 'but why must ye needs fare in feigned shapes? Ye would have been welcome guests in the Dale howsoever ye had come.'

'I may not tell thee hereof as now,' said she.

Said Gold-mane: 'Yet thou mayst belike tell me wherefore it was that thy brother desired to slay me yesterday, if he knew me, who I was.'

'Gold-mane,' she said, 'thou art not slain, so little story need be made of that: for the rest, belike he knew thee not at that moment. So it falls with us, that we look to see foes rather than friends in the wild-woods. Many uncouth things are therein. Moreover, I must tell thee of my brother that whiles he is as the stalled bull late let loose, and nothing is good to him save battle and onset; and then is he blind and knows not friend from foe.'

Said Face-of-god: 'Thou hast asked of me and mine; wilt thou not tell me of thee and thine?'

'Nay,' she said, 'not as now; thou must betake thee to the way. Whither wert thou wending when thou happenedst upon us?'

He said: 'I know not; I was seeking something, but I knew not what—meseemeth that now I have found it.'

'Art thou for the great mountains seeking gems?' she said. 'Yet go not thither to-day: for who knoweth what thou shalt meet there that shall be thy foe?'

He said: 'Nay, nay; I have nought to do but to abide here as long as I may, looking upon thee and hearkening to thy voice.'

Her eyes were upon his, but yet she did not seem to see him, and for a while she answered not; and still he wondered that mere words should come from so fair a thing; for whether she moved foot, or hand, or knee, or turned this way or that, each time she stirred it was a caress to his very heart.

He spake again: 'May I not abide here a while? What scathe may be in that?'

'It is not so,' she said; 'thou must depart, and that straightway: lo, there lieth thy spear which the Wood-mother hath brought in from the waste. Take thy gear to thee and wend thy ways. Have patience! I will lead thee to the place where we first met and there give thee farewell.'

Therewith she arose and he also perforce, and when they came to the doorway she stepped across the threshold and then turned back and gave him her hand and so led him forth, the sun flashing back from her golden raiment. Together they went over the short grey grass of that hill-side till they came to the place where he had arisen from that wrestle with her brother. There she stayed him and said:

'This is the place; here must we part.'

But his heart failed him and he faltered in his speech as he said:

'When shall I see thee again? Wilt thou slay me if I seek to thee hither once more?'

'Hearken,' she said, 'autumn is now a-dying into winter: let winter and its snows go past: nor seek to me hither; for me thou should'st not find, but thy death thou mightest well fall in with; and I would not that thou shouldest die. When winter is gone, and spring is on the land, if thou hast not forgotten us thou shalt meet us again. Yet shalt thou go further than this Woodland Hall. In Shadowy Vale shalt thou seek to me then, and there will I talk with thee.'

'And where,' said he, 'is Shadowy Vale? for thereof have I never heard tell.'

She said: 'The token when it cometh to thee shall show thee thereof and the way thither. Art thou a babbler, Gold-mane?'

He said: 'I have won no prize for babbling hitherto.'

She said: 'If thou listest to babble concerning what hath be-

56

fallen thee on the Mountain, so do, and repent it once only, that The woman goeth into the house. is, thy life long.'

'Why should I say any word thereof?' said he. 'Dost thou not know the sweetness of such a tale untold?'

He spake as one who is somewhat wrathful, and she answered humbly and kindly:

'Well is that. Bide thou the token that shall lead thee to Shadowy Vale. Farewell now.'

She drew her hand from his, and turned and went her ways swiftly to the house: he could not choose but gaze on her as she went glittering-bright and fair in that grey place of the mountains, till the dark doorway swallowed up her beauty. Then he turned away and took the path through the pine-woods, muttering to himself as he went:

'What thing have I done now that hitherto I had not done? What manner of man am I to-day other than the man I was yesterday?'


## CHAPTER VIII. FACE-OF-GOD COMETH HOME AGAIN TO BURGSTEAD.

FACE-OF-GOD went back through the wood by the way he had come, paying little heed to the things about him.

For whatever he thought of strayed not one whit from the image of the Fair Woman of the Mountain-side.

He went through the wood swiftlier than yesterday, and made no stay for noon or aught else, nor did he linger on the road when he was come into the Dale, either to speak to any or to note what they did. So he came to the House of the Face about dusk, and found no man within the hall either carle or queen. So he cried out on the folk, and there came in a damsel of the house, whom he greeted kindly and she him again. He bade her bring the washing-water, and she did so and washed his feet and his hands. She was a fair maid enough, as were most in the Dale, but he heeded her little ; and when she was done he kissed not her cheek for her pains, as his wont was, but let her go her ways unthanked. But he went to his shut-bed and opened his chest, and drew fair raiment from it, and did off his wood-gear, and did on him a goodly scarlet kirtle fairly broidered, and a collar with gems of price therein, and other braveries. And when he was so attired he came out into the hall, and there was old Stone-face standing by the hearth, which was blazing brightly with fresh brands, so that things were clear to see.

Stone-face noted Gold-mane's gay raiment, for he was not wont to wear such attire, save on the feasts and high days when he behoved to. So the old man smiled and said :

'Welcome back from the Wood! But what is it? Hast thou been wedded there, or who hath made thee Earl and King?'

Said Face-of-god : 'Foster-father, sooth it is that I have been to the wood, but there have I seen nought of manfolk worse than myself. Now as to my raiment, needs must I keep it from the moth. And I am weary withal, and this kirtle is light and easy to me. Moreover, I look to see the Bride here again, and I would pleasure her with the sight of gay raiment upon me.'

'Nay,' said Stone-face, 'hast thou not seen some woman in the wood arrayed like the image of a God? and hath she not bidden thee thus to worship her to-night? For I know that such wights be in the wood, and that such is their wont.'

Said Gold-mane : 'I worship nought save the Gods and the Fathers. Nor saw I in the wood any such as thou sayest.'

Therewith Stone-face shook his head; but after a while he said : 'Art thou for the wood to-morrow?'

'Nay,' said Gold-mane angrily, knitting his brows.

'The morrow of to-morrow,' said Stone-face, 'is the day when we look to see the Westland merchants : after all, wilt thou not go hence with them when they wend their ways back before the first snows fall?'

58

'Nay,' said he, 'I have no mind to it, fosterer; cease egging me on hereto.' They will have him go to the Cities.

Then Stone-face shook his head again, and looked on him long, and muttered: 'To the wood wilt thou go to-morrow or next day; or some day when doomed is thine undoing.'

Therewith entered the service and torches, and presently after came the Alderman with Hall-face; and Iron-face greeted his son and said to him: 'Thou hast not hit the time to do on thy gay raiment, for the Bride will not be here to-night; she bideth still at the Feast at the Apple-tree House: or wilt thou be there, son?'

'Nay,' said Face-of-god, 'I am over-weary. And as for my raiment, it is well; it is for thine honour and the honour of the name.'

So to table they went, and Iron-face asked his son of his ways again, and whether he was quite fixed in his mind not to go down to the Plain and the Cities: 'For,' said he, 'the morrow of to-morrow shall the merchants be here, and this were great news for them if the son of the Alderman should be their faring-fellow back.'

But Face-of-god answered without any haste or heat: 'Nay, father, it may not be: fear not, thou shalt see that I have a good will to work and live in the Dale.'

And in good sooth, though he was a young man and loved mirth and the ways of his own will, he was a stalwarth workman, and few could mow a match with him in the hay-month and win it; or fell trees as certainly and swiftly, or drive as straight and clean a furrow through the stiff land of the lower Dale; and in other matters also was he deft and sturdy.

CHAPTER IX. THOSE BRETHREN FARE TO THE YEW-WOOD WITH THE BRIDE.

NEXT morning Face-of-god dight himself for work, and took his axe; for his brother Hall-face had bidden him go down with him to the Yew-wood and cut timber there,

On the road
to the Yew-
wood.

since he of all men knew where to go straight to the sticks that would quarter best for bow-staves; whereas the Alderman had the right of hewing in that wood. So they went forth, those brethren, from the House of the Face, but when they were gotten to the gate, who should be there but the Bride awaiting them, and she with an ass duly saddled for bearing the yew-sticks. Because Hall-face had told her that he and belike Gold-mane were going to hew in the wood, and she thought it good to be of the company, as oft had befallen erst. When they met she greeted Face-of-god and kissed him as her wont was; and he looked upon her and saw how fair she was, and how kind and friendly were her eyes that beheld him, and how her whole face was eager for him as their lips parted. Then his heart failed him, when he knew that he no longer desired her as she did him, and he said within himself: 'Would that she had been of our nighest kindred! Would that I had had a sister and that this were she!'

So the three went along the highway down the Dale, and Hall-face and the Bride talked merrily together and laughed, for she was happy, since she knew that Gold-mane had been to the wood and was back safe and much as he had been before. So indeed it seemed of him; for though at first he was moody and of few words, yet presently he cursed himself for a mar-sport, and so fell into the talk, and enforced himself to be merry; and soon he was so indeed; for he thought: 'She drew me thither: she hath a deed for me to do. I shall do the deed and have my reward. Soon will the spring-tide be here, and I shall be a young man yet when it comes.'

So came they to the place where he had met the three maidens yesterday; there they also turned from the highway; and as they went down the bent, Gold-mane could not but turn his eyes on the beauty of the Bride and the lovely ways of her body: but presently he remembered all that had betid, and turned away again as one who is noting what it behoves him not to note. And he said to himself: 'Where art thou, Gold-mane? Whose art thou?

60

Yea, even if that had been but a dream that I have dreamed, yet would that this fair woman were my sister!'

So came they to the Yew-wood, and the brethren fell to work, and the Bride with them, for she was deft with the axe and strong withal. But at midday they rested on the green slope without the Yew-wood; and they ate bread and flesh and onions and apples, and drank red wine of the Dale. And while they were resting after their meat, the Bride sang to them, and her song was a lay of time past; and here ye have somewhat of it:

'Tis over the hill and over the dale
  Men ride from the city fast and far,
If they may have a soothfast tale,
  True tidings of the host of war.

And first they hap on men-at-arms,
  All clad in steel from head to foot:
Now tell true tale of the new-come harms,
  And the gathered hosts of the mountain-root.

Fair sirs, from murder-carles we flee,
  Whose fashion is as the mountain-trolls';
No man can tell how many they be,
  And the voice of their host as the thunder rolls.

They were weary men at the ending of day,
  But they spurred nor stayed for longer word.
Now ye, O merchants, whither away?
  What do ye there with the helm and the sword?

O we must fight for life and gear,
  For our beasts are spent and our wains are stayed,
And the host of the Mountain-men draws near,
  That maketh all the world afraid.

61

They left the chapmen on the hill,
    And through the eve and through the night
They rode to have true tidings still,
    And were there on the way when the dawn was bright.

O damsels fair, what do ye then
    To loiter thus upon the way,
And have no fear of the Mountain-men,
    The host of the carles that strip and slay?

O riders weary with the road,
    Come eat and drink on the grass hereby!
And lay you down in a fair abode
    Till the midday sun is broad and high;

Then unto you shall we come aback,
    And lead you forth to the Mountain-men,
To note their plenty and their lack,
    And have true tidings there and then.

'Tis over the hill and over the dale
    They ride from the mountain fast and far;
And now have they learned a soothfast tale,
    True tidings of the host of war.

It was summer-tide and the Month of Hay,
    And men and maids must fare afield;
But we saw the place were the bow-staves lay,
    And the hall was hung with spear and shield.

When the moon was high we drank in the hall,
    And they drank to the guests and were kind and blithe,
And they said: Come back when the chestnuts fall,
    And the wine-carts wend across the hythe.

Come oft and o'er again, they said;
    Wander your ways; but we abide

For all the world in the little stead;
For wise are we, though the world be wide.

Yea, come in arms if ye will, they said;
And despite your host shall we abide
For life or death in the little stead;
For wise are we, though the world be wide.

So she made an end and looked at the fairness of the dale spreading wide before her, and a robin came nigh from out of a thornbush and sung his song also, the sweet herald of coming winter; and the lapwings wheeled about, black and white, above the meadow by the river, sending forth their wheedling pipe as they hung above the soft turf.

She felt the brothers near her, and knew their friendliness from of old, and she was happy; nor had she looked closer at Goldmane would she have noted any change in him belike; for the meat and the good wine, and the fair sunny time, and the Bride's sweet voice, and the ancient song softened his heart while it fed the desire therein.

So in a while they arose from their rest and did what was left them of their work, and so went back to Burgstead through the fair afternoon; by seeming all three in all content. But yet Goldmane, as from time to time he looked upon the Bride, kept saying to himself: 'O if she had been but my sister! sweet had the kinship been!'

CHAPTER X.   NEW TIDINGS IN THE DALE.

IT was three days thereafter that Gold-mane, leading an ass, went along the highway to fetch home certain fleeces which were needed for the house from a stead a little west of Wildlake; but he had gone scant half a mile ere he fell in with a throng of folk going to Burgstead. They were of the Shepherds ; they had weapons with them, and some were clad in coats of fence. They went along making a great noise, for they were all talking each to each at the same time, and seemed very hot and eager about some matter. When they saw Gold-mane anigh, they stopped, and the throng opened as if to let him into their midmost ; so he mingled with them, and they stood in a ring about him and an old man more ill-favoured than it was the wont of the Dalesmen to be.

For he was long, stooping, gaunt and spindle-shanked, his hands big and crippled with gout : his cheeks were red after an old man's fashion, covered with a crimson network like a pippin ; his lips thin and not well hiding his few teeth ; his nose long like a snipe's neb. In short, a shame and a laughing-stock to the Folk, and a man whom the kindreds had in small esteem, and that for good reasons.

Face-of-god knew him at once for a notable close-fist and starve-all fool of the Shepherds ; and his name was now become Penny-thumb the Lean, whatever it might once have been.

So Face-of-god greeted all men, and they him again ; and he said : ' What aileth you, neighbours ? Your weapons are bare, but I see not that they be bloody. What is it, goodman Penny-thumb ?'

Penny-thumb did but groan for all answer ; but a stout carle who stood by with a broad grin on his face answered and said :

' Face-of-god, evil tidings be abroad ; the strong-thieves of the wood are astir ; and some deem that the wood-wights be helping them.'

' Yea, and what is the deed they have done ?' said Gold-mane.

Said the carle : ' Thou knowest Penny-thumb's abode ?'

' Yea surely,' said Face-of-god ; ' fair are the water-meadows about it ; great gain of cheese can be gotten thence.'

' Hast thou been within the house ?' said the carle.

' Nay,' said Gold-mane.

64

Then spake Penny-thumb : 'Within is scant gear : we gather
for others to scatter ; we make meat for others' mouths.'

The carle laughed : 'Sooth is that,' said he, 'that there is little gear therein now ; for the strong-thieves have voided both hall and bower and byre.'

'And when was that ?' said Face-of-god.

'The night before last night,' said the carle, 'the door was smitten on, and when none answered it was broken down.'

'Yea,' quoth Penny-thumb, 'a host entered, and they in arms.'

'No host was within,' said the carle, 'nought but Penny-thumb and his sister and his sister's son, and three carles that work for him ; and one of them, Rusty to wit, was the worst man of the hill-country. These then the host whereof the goodman telleth bound, but without doing them any scathe ; and they ransacked the house, and took away much gear ; yet left some.'

'Thou liest,' said Penny-thumb ; 'they took little and left none.'

Thereat all men laughed, for this seemed to them good game, and another man said : 'Well, neighbour Penny-thumb, if it was so little, thou hast done unneighbourly in giving us such a heap of trouble about it.'

And they laughed again, but the first carle said : 'True it is, goodman, that thou wert exceeding eager to raise the hue and cry after that little when we happed upon thee and thy housemates bound in your chairs yesterday morning. Well, Alderman's son, short is the tale to tell : we could not fail to follow the gear, and the slot led us into the wood, and ill is the going there for us shepherds, who are used to the bare downs, save Rusty, who was a good woodsman and lifted the slot for us ; so he outwent us all, and ran out of sight of us, so presently we came upon him dead-slain, with the manslayer's spear in his breast. What then could we do but turn back again, for now was the wood blind now Rusty was dead, and we knew not whither to follow the fray ; and the man himself was but little loss : so back we turned, and told goodman Penny-thumb of all this, for we had left him

65                                                                K

alone in his hall lamenting his gear; so we bided to-day's morn,
and have come out now, with our neighbour and the spear, and
the dead corpse of Rusty. Stand aside, neighbours, and let the
Alderman's son see it.'

They did so, and there was the corpse of a thin-faced tall
wiry man, somewhat foxy of aspect, lying on a hand-bier covered
with black cloth.

'Yea, Face-of-god,' said the carle, 'he is not good to see now
he is dead, yet alive was he worser: but, look you, though the man
was no good man, yet was he of our people, and the feud is with us;
so we would see the Alderman, and do him to wit of the tidings,
that he may call the neighbours together to seek a blood-wite for
Rusty and atonement for the ransacking. Or what sayest thou?'

'Have ye the spear that ye found in Rusty?' quoth Gold-mane.

'Yea verily,' said the carle. 'Hither with it, neighbours; give
it to the Alderman's son.'

So the spear came into his hand, and he looked at it and said:
'This is no spear of the smiths' work of the Dale, as my father
will tell you. We take but little keep of the forging of spear-
heads here, so that they be well-tempered and made so as to ride
well on the shaft; but this head, daintily is it wrought, the blood-
trench as clean and trim as though it were an Earl's sword. See
you withal this inlaying of runes on the steel? It is done with
no tin or copper, but with very silver; and these bands about the
shaft be of silver also. It is a fair weapon, and the owner hath
a loss of it greater than his gain in the slaying of Rusty; and he
will have left it in the wound so that he might be known hereafter, and that he might be said not to have murdered Rusty but
to have slain him. Or how think ye?'

They all said that this seemed like to be; but that if the man
who had slain Rusty were one of the ransackers they might have
a blood-wite of him, if they could find him. Gold-mane said that
so it was, and therewithal he gave the shepherds good-speed and
went on his way.

66

But they came to Burgstead and found the Alderman, and in due time was a Court held, and a finding uttered, and outlawry given forth for the manslaying and the ransacking against certain men unknown. As for the spear, it was laid up in the House of the Face.

But Face-of-god pondered these matters in his mind, for such ransackings there had been none of in late years; and he said to himself that his friends of the Mountain must have other folk, of which the Dalesmen knew nought, whose gear they could lift, or how could they live in that place. And he marvelled that they should risk drawing the Dalesmen's wrath upon them; whereas they of the Dale were strong men not easily daunted, albeit peaceable enough if not stirred to wrath. For in good sooth he had no doubt concerning that spear, whose it was and whence it came: for that very weapon had been leaning against the panel of his shut-bed the night he slept on the Mountain, and all the other spears that he saw there were more or less of the same fashion, and adorned with silver.

Albeit all that he knew, and all that he thought of, he kept in his own heart and said nothing of it.

So wore the autumn into early winter; and the Westland merchants came in due time, and departed without Face-of-god, though his father made him that offer one last time. He went to and fro about his work in the Dale, and seemed to most men's eyes nought changed from what he had been. But the Bride noted that he saw her less often than his wont was, and abode with her a lesser space when he met her; and she could not think what this might mean; nor had she heart to ask him thereof, though she was sorry and grieved, but rather withdrew her company from him somewhat; and when she perceived that he noted it not, and made no question of it, then was she the sorrier.

But the first winter-snow came on with a great storm of wind from the north-east, so that no man stirred abroad who was not compelled thereto, and those who went abroad risked life and limb

67

thereby. Next morning all was calm again, and the snow was deep, but it did not endure long, for the wind shifted to the south-west and the thaw came, and three days after, when folk could fare easily again up and down the Dale, came tidings to Burgstead and the Alderman from the Lower Dale, how a house called Greentofts had been ransacked there, and none knew by whom. Now the goodman of Greentofts was little loved of the neighbours: he was grasping and overbearing, and had often cowed others out of their due : he was very cross-grained, both at home and abroad : his wife had fled from his hand, neither did his sons find it good to abide with him : therewithal he was wealthy of goods, a strong man and a deft man-at-arms. When his sons and his wife departed from him, and none other of the Dalesmen cared to abide with him, he went down into the Plain, and got thence men to be with him for hire, men who were not well seen to in their own land. These to the number of twelve abode with him, and did his bidding whenso it pleased them. Two more had he had who had been slain by good men of the Dale for their masterful ways ; and no blood-wite had been paid for them, because of their ill-doings, though they had not been made outlaws. This man of Greentofts was called Harts-bane after his father, who was a great hunter.

Now the full tidings of the ransacking were these : The storm began two hours before sunset, and an hour thereafter, when it was quite dark, for without none could see because the wind was at its height and the drift of the snow was hard and full, the hall-door flew open ; and at first men thought it had been the wind, until they saw in the dimness (for all lights but the fire on the hearth had been quenched) certain things tumbling in which at first they deemed were wolves ; but when they took swords and staves against them, lo they were met by swords and axes, and they saw that the seeming wolves were men with wolf-skins drawn over them. So the new-comers cowed them that they threw down their weapons, and were bound in their places ; but when they

68

were bound, and had had time to note who the ransackers were, they saw that there were but six of them all told, who had cowed and bound Harts-bane and his twelve masterful men; and this they deemed a great shaming to them, as might well be.

So then the stead was ransacked, and those wolves took away what they would, and went their ways through the fierce storm, and none could tell whether they had lived or died in it; but at least neither the men nor their prey were seen again; nor did they leave any slot, for next morning the snow lay deep over everything.

No doubt had Gold-mane but that these ransackers were his friends of the Mountain; but he held his peace, abiding till the winter should be over.


## CHAPTER XI. MEN MAKE OATH AT BURGSTEAD ON THE HOLY BOAR.

A WEEK after the ransacking at Greentofts the snow and the winter came on in earnest, and all the Dale lay in snow, and men went on skids when they fared up and down the Dale or on the Mountain.

All was now tidingless till Yule over, and in Burgstead was there feasting and joyance enough; and especially at the House of the Face was high-tide holden, and the Alderman and his sons and Stone-face and all the kindred and all their men sat in glorious attire within the hall; and many others were there of the best of the kindreds of Burgstead who had been bidden.

Face-of-god sat between his father and Stone-face; and he looked up and down the tables and the hall and saw not the Bride, and his heart misgave him because she was not there, and he wondered what had befallen and if she were sick of sorrow.

But Iron-face beheld him how he gazed about, and he laughed; for he was exceeding merry that night and fared as a young man.

High-tide in
the Hall of
the Face.

Then he said to his son: 'Whom seekest thou, son? is there someone lacking?'

Face-of-god reddened as one who lies unused to it, and said:
'Yea, kinsman, so it is that I was seeking the Bride my
kinswoman.'

'Nay,' said Iron-face, 'call her not kinswoman: therein is ill-
luck, lest it seem that thou art to wed one too nigh thine own
blood. Call her the Bride only: to thee and to me the name is
good. Well, son, desirest thou sorely to see her?'

'Yea, yea, surely,' said Face-of-god; but his eyes went all
about the hall still, as though his mind strayed from the place and
that home of his.

Said Iron-face: 'Have patience, son, thou shalt see her anon,
and that in such guise as shall please thee.'

Therewithal came the maidens with the ewers of wine, and
they filled all horns and beakers, and then stood by the endlong
tables on either side laughing and talking with the carles and the
older women; and the hall was a fair sight to see, for the many
candles burned bright and the fire on the hearth flared up, and
those maids were clad in fair raiment, and there was none of them
but was comely, and some were fair, and some very fair: the walls
also were hung with goodly pictured cloths, and the image of the
God of the Face looked down smiling terribly from the gable-end
above the high-seat.

Thus as they sat they heard the sound of a horn winded close
outside the hall door, and the door was smitten on. Then rose
Iron-face smiling merrily, and cried out:

'Enter ye, whether ye be friends or foes: for if ye be foemen,
yet shall ye keep the holy peace of Yule, unless ye be the foes
of all kindreds and nations, and then shall we slay you.'

Thereat some who knew what was toward laughed; but Gold-
mane, who had been away from Burgstead some days past,
marvelled and knit his brows, and let his right hand fall on his
sword-hilt. For this folk, who were of merry ways, were wont

70

to deal diversely with the Yule-tide customs in the manner of shows ; and he knew not that this was one of them.

Now was the outer door thrown open, and there entered seven men, whereof two were all-armed in bright war-gear, and two bore slug-horns, and two bore up somewhat on a dish covered over with a piece of rich cloth, and the seventh stood before them all wrapped up in a dark fur mantle.

Thus they stood a moment ; and when he saw their number, back to Gold-mane's heart came the thought of those folk on the Mountain : for indeed he was somewhat out of himself for doubt and longing, else would he have deemed that all this was but a Yule-tide play.

Now the men with the slug-horns set them to their mouths and blew a long blast ; while the first of the new-comers set hand to the clasps of the fur cloak and let it fall to the ground, and lo ! a woman exceeding beauteous, clad in glistering raiment of gold and fine web ; her hair wreathed with bay, and in her hand a naked sword with goodly-wrought golden hilt and polished blue-gleaming blade.

Face-of-god started up in his seat, and stared like a man new-wakened from a strange dream : because for one moment he deemed verily that it was the Woman of the Mountain arrayed as he had last seen her, and he cried aloud ' The Friend, the Friend !'

His father brake out into loud laughter thereat, and clapped his son on the shoulder and said : ' Yea, yea, lad, thou mayst well say the Friend ; for this is thine old playmate whom thou hast been looking round the hall for, arrayed this eve in such fashion as is meet for her goodliness and her worthiness. Yea, this is the Friend indeed !'

Then waxed Face-of-god as red as blood for shame, and he sat him down in his place again : for now he wotted what was to-ward, and saw that this fair woman was the Bride.

But Stone-face from the other side looked keenly on him.

71

Then blew the horns again, and the Bride stepped daintily up
the hall, and the sweet odour of her raiment went from her about
the fire-warmed dwelling, and her beauty moved all hearts with
love. So stood she at the high-table ; and those two who bore
the burden set it down thereon and drew off the covering, and lo!
there was the Holy Boar of Yule on which men were wont to
make oath of deeds that they would do in the coming year, according to the custom of their forefathers. Then the Bride laid
the goodly sword beside the dish, and then went round the table
and sat down betwixt Face-of-god and Stone-face, and turned
kindly to Gold-mane, and was glad ; for now was his fair face
as its wont was to be. He in turn smiled upon her, for she was
fair and kind and his fellow for many a day.

Now the men-at-arms stood each side the Boar, and out from
them on each side stood the two hornsmen : then these blew up
again, whereon the Alderman stood up and cried :

' Ye sons of the brave who have any deed that ye may be desirous of doing, come up, come lay your hand on the sword, and
the point of the sword to the Holy Beast, and swear the oath that
lieth on your hearts.'

Therewith he sat down, and there strode a man up the hall,
strong-built and sturdy, but short of stature ; black-haired, red-
bearded, and ruddy-faced : and he stood on the daïs, and took up
the sword and laid its point on the Boar, and said :

' I am Bristler, son of Brightling, a man of the Shepherds.
Here by the Holy Boar I swear to follow up the ransackers of
Penny-thumb and the slayers of Rusty. And I take this feud upon
me, although they be no good men, because I am of the kin and
it falleth to me, since others forbear ; and when the Court was hallowed hereon I was away out of the Dale and the Downs. So
help me the Warrior, and the God of the Earth.'

Then the Alderman nodded his head to him kindly, and
reached him out a cup of wine, and as he drank there went up a
rumour of praise from the hall ; and men said that his oath was

72

manly and that he was like to keep it; for he was a good man-at-arms and a stout heart.

Then came up three men of the Shepherds and two of the Dale and swore to help Bristler in his feud, and men thought it well sworn.

After that came a braggart, a man very gay of his raiment, and swore with many words that if he lived the year through he would be a captain over the men of the Plain, and would come back again with many gifts for his friends in the Dale. This men deemed foolishly sworn, for they knew the man; so they jeered at him and laughed as he went back to his place ashamed.

Then swore three others oaths not hard to be kept, and men laughed and were merry.

At last uprose the Alderman, and said: 'Kinsmen, and good fellows, good days and peaceable are in the Dale as now; and of such days little is the story, and little it availeth to swear a deed of derring-do: yet three things I swear by this Beast; and first to gainsay no man's asking if I may perform it; and next to set right above law and mercy above custom; and lastly, if the days change and war cometh to us or we go to meet it, I will be no backwarder in the onset than three fathoms behind the foremost. So help me the Warrior, and the God of the Face and the Holy Earth!'

Therewith he sat down, and all men shouted for joy of him, and said that it was most like that he would keep his oath.

Last of all uprose Face-of-god and took up the sword and looked at it; and so bright was the blade that he saw in it the image of the golden braveries which the Bride bore, and even some broken image of her face. Then he handled the hilt and laid the point on the Boar, and cried:

'Hereby I swear to wed the fairest woman of the Earth before the year is worn to an end; and that whether the Dalesmen gainsay me or the men beyond the Dale. So help me the Warrior, and the God of the Face and the Holy Earth!'

73                                                            L

Therewith he sat down; and once more men shouted for the love of him and of the Bride, and they said he had sworn well and like a chieftain.

But the Bride noted him that neither were his eyes nor his voice like to their wont as he swore, for she knew him well; and thereat was she ill at ease, for now whatever was new in him was to her a threat of evil to come.

Stone-face also noted him, and he knew the young man better than all others save the Bride, and he saw withal that she was ill-pleased, and he said to himself: 'I will speak to my fosterling to-morrow if I may find him alone.'

So came the swearing to an end, and they fell to on their meat and feasted on the Boar of Atonement after they had duly given the Gods their due share, and the wine went about the hall and men were merry till they drank the parting cup and fared to rest in the shut-beds, and whereso else they might in the Hall and the House, for there were many men there.

## CHAPTER XII.   STONE-FACE TELLETH CONCERNING THE WOOD-WIGHTS.

EARLY on the morrow Gold-mane arose and clad himself and went out-a-doors and over the trodden snow on to the bridge over the Weltering Water, and there betook himself into one of the coins of safety built over the up-stream piles; there he leaned against the wall and turned his face to the Thorp, and fell to pondering on his case. And first he thought about his oath, and how that he had sworn to wed the Mountain Woman, although his kindred and her kindred should gainsay him, yea and herself also. Great seemed that oath to him, yet at that moment he wished he had made it greater, and made all the kindred, yea and the Bride herself, sure of the meaning of the words of it: and he deemed himself a dastard that he had not done so. Then he

74

looked round him and beheld the winter, and he fell into mere
longing that the spring were come and the token from the Mountain.
Things seemed too hard for him to deal with, and he between a
mighty folk and two wayward women; and he went nigh to wish
that he had taken his father's offer and gone down to the Cities;
and even had he met his bane: well were that! And, as young
folk will, he set to work making a picture of his deeds there, had
he been there. He showed himself the stricken fight in the plain,
and the press, and the struggle, and the breaking of the serried
band, and himself amidst the ring of foemen doing most valiantly,
and falling there at last, his shield o'er-heavy with the weight of
foemen's spears for a man to uphold it. Then the victory of his
folk and the lamentation and praise over the slain man of the
Mountain Dales, and the burial of the valiant warrior, the praising
weeping folk meeting him at the City-gate, laid stark and cold in
his arms on the gold-hung garlanded bier.

There ended his dream, and he laughed aloud and said: ' I
am a fool! All this were good and sweet if I should see it myself; and forsooth that is how I am thinking of it, as if I still
alive should see myself dead and famous! '

Then he turned a little and looked at the houses of the Thorp
lying dark about the snowy ways under the starlit heavens of the
winter morning: dark they were indeed and grey, save where
here and there the half-burned Yule-fire reddened the windows
of a hall, or where, as in one place, the candle of some early waker
shone white in a chamber window. There was scarce a man
astir, he deemed, and no sound reached him save the crowing of
the cocks muffled by their houses, and a faint sound of beasts in
the byres.

Thus he stood a while, his thoughts wandering now, till presently he heard footsteps coming his way down the street and
turned toward them, and lo it was the old man Stone-face. He
had seen Gold-mane go out, and had risen and followed him that
he might talk with him apart. Gold-mane greeted him kindly,

75

though, sooth to say, he was but half content to see him; since he
doubted, what was verily the case, that his foster-father would
give him many words, counselling him to refrain from going to
the wood, and this was loathsome to him; but he spake and said:

'Meseems, father, that the eastern sky is brightening toward
dawn.'

'Yea,' quoth Stone-face.

'It will be light in an hour,' said Face-of-god.

'Even so,' said Stone-face.

'And a fair day for the morrow of Yule,' said the swain.

'Yea,' said Stone-face, 'and what wilt thou do with the fair
day? Wilt thou to the wood?'

'Maybe, father,' said Gold-mane; 'Hall-face and some of
the swains are talking of elks up the fells which may be trapped
in the drifts, and if they go a-hunting them, I may go in
their company.'

'Ah, son,' quoth Stone-face, 'thou wilt look to see other kind
of beasts than elks. Things may ye fall in with there who may
not be impounded in the snow like to elks, but can go light-foot
on the top of the soft drift from one place to another.'

Said Gold-mane: 'Father, fear me not; I shall either refrain
me from the wood, or if I go, I shall go to hunt the wood-deer
with other hunters. But since thou hast come to me, tell me more
about the wood, for thy tales thereof are fair.'

'Yea,' said Stone-face, 'fair tales of foul things, as oft it befalleth in the world. Hearken now! if thou deemest that what thou
seekest shall come readier to thine hand because of the winter and
the snow, thou errest. For the wights that waylay the bodies and
souls of the mighty in the wild-wood heed such matters nothing;
yea and at Yule-tide are they most abroad, and most armed for
the fray. Even such an one have I seen time agone, when the
snow was deep and the wind was rough; and it was in the likeness of a woman clad in such raiment as the Bride bore last night,
and she trod the snow light-foot in thin raiment where it would

76

scarce bear the skids of a deft snow-runner. Even so she stood before me; the icy wind blew her raiment round about her, and drifted the hair from her garlanded head toward me, and she as fair and fresh as in the midsummer days. Up the fell she fared, sweetest of all things to look on, and beckoned on me to follow; on me, the Warrior, the Stout-heart; and I followed, and between us grief was born; but I it was that fostered that child and not she. Always when she would be, was she merry and lovely; and even so is she now, for she is of those that be long-lived. And I wot that thou hast seen even such an one!'

'Tell me more of thy tales, foster-father,' said Gold-mane, 'and fear not for me!'

'Ah, son,' he said, 'mayst thou have no such tales to tell to those that shall be young when thou art old. Yet hearken! We sat in the hall together and there was no third; and methought that the birds sang and the flowers bloomed, and sweet was their savour, though it was mid-winter. A rose-wreath was on her head; grapes were on the board, and fair unwrinkled summer apples on the day that we feasted together. When was the feast? sayst thou. Long ago. What was the hall, thou sayest, wherein ye feasted? I know not if it were on the earth or under it, or if we rode the clouds that even. But on the morrow what was there but the stark wood and the drift of the snow, and the iron wind howling through the branches, and a lonely man, a wanderer rising from the ground. A wanderer through the wood and up the fell, and up the high mountain, and up and up to the edges of the ice-river and the green caves of the ice-hills. A wanderer in spring, in summer, autumn and winter, with an empty heart and a burning never-satisfied desire; who hath seen in the uncouth places many an evil unmanly shape, many a foul hag and changing ugly semblance; who hath suffered hunger and thirst and wounding and fever, and hath seen many things, but hath never again seen that fair woman, or that lovely feast-hall.

'All praise and honour to the House of the Face, and the

bounteous valiant men thereof! and the like praise and honour
to the fair women whom they wed of the valiant and goodly
House of the Steer!'

'Even so say I,' quoth Gold-mane calmly; 'but now wend
we aback to the House, for it is morning indeed, and folk will be
stirring there.'

So they turned from the bridge together; and Stone-face was
kind and fatherly, and was telling his foster-son many wise
things concerning the life of a chieftain, and the giving-out of
dooms and the gathering for battle; to all which talk Face-of-
god seemed to hearken gladly, but indeed hearkened not at all;
for verily his eyes were beholding that snowy waste, and the fair
woman upon it; even such an one as Stone-face had told of.

## CHAPTER XIII. THEY FARE TO THE HUNTING OF THE ELK.

WHEN they came into the Hall, the hearth-fire had been
quickened, and the sleepers on the floor had been
wakened, and all folk were astir. So the old man sat
down by the hearth while Gold-mane busied himself in fetching
wood and water, and in sweeping out the Hall, and other such
works of the early morning. In a little while Hall-face and the
other young men and warriors were afoot duly clad, and the
Alderman came from his chamber and greeted all men kindly.
Soon meat was set upon the boards, and men broke their fast; and
day dawned while they were about it, and ere it was all done the
sun rose clear and golden, so that all men knew that the day
would be fair, for the frost seemed hard and enduring.

Then the eager young men and the hunters, and those who
knew the mountain best drew together about the hearth, and fell
to talking of the hunting of the elk; and there were three there
who knew both the woods and also the fells right up to the ice-

rivers better than any other; and these said that they who were fain of the hunting of the elk would have no likelier time than that day for a year to come. Short was the rede betwixt them, for they said they would go to the work at once and make the most of the short winter daylight. So they went each to his place, and some outside that House to their fathers' houses to fetch each man his gear. Face-of-god for his part went to his shut-bed, and stood by his chest, and opened it, and drew out of it a fine hauberk of ring-mail which his father had made for him: for though Face-of-god was a deft wright, he was not by a long way so deft as his father, who was the deftest of all men of that time and country; so that the alien merchants would give him what he would for his hauberks and helms, whenso he would chaffer with them, which was but seldom. So Face-of-god did on this hauberk over his kirtle, and over it he cast his foul-weather weed, so that none might see it: he girt a strong war-sword to his side, cast his quiver over his shoulder, and took his bow in his hand, although he had little lust to shoot elks that day, even as Stone-face had said; therewithal he took his skids, and went forth of the hall to the gate of the Burg; whereto gathered the whole company of twenty-three, and Gold-mane the twenty-fourth. And each man there had his skids and his bow and quiver, and whatso other weapon, as short-sword, or wood-knife, or axe, seemed good to him.

So they went out-a-gates, and clomb the stairway in the cliff which led to the ancient watch-tower: for it was on the lower slopes of the fells which lay near to the Weltering Water that they looked to find the elks, and this was the nighest road thereto. When they had gotten to the top they lost no time, but went their ways nearly due east, making way easily where there were but scattered trees close to the lip of the sheer cliffs.

They went merrily on their skids over the close-lying snow, and were soon up on the great shoulders of the fells that went up from the bank of the Weltering Water: at noon they came into

79

a little dale wherein were a few trees, and there they abided to eat their meat, and were very merry, making for themselves tables and benches of the drifted snow, and piling it up to windward as a defence against the wind, which had now arisen, little but bitter from the south-east; so that some, and they the wisest, began to look for foul weather: wherefore they tarried the shorter while in the said dale or hollow.

But they were scarcely on their way again before the aforesaid south-east wind began to grow bigger, and at last blew a gale, and brought up with it a drift of fine snow, through which they yet made their way, but slowly, till the drift grew so thick that they could not see each other five paces apart.

Then perforce they made stay, and gathered together under a bent which by good luck they happened upon, where they were sheltered from the worst of the drift. There they abode, till in less than an hour's space the drift abated and the wind fell, and in a little while after it was quite clear, with the sun shining brightly and the young waxing moon white and high up in the heavens; and the frost was harder than ever.

This seemed good to them; but now that they could see each other's faces they fell to telling over their company, and there was none missing save Face-of-god. They were somewhat dismayed thereat, but knew not what to do, and they deemed he might not be far off, either a little behind or a little ahead; and Hall-face said:

'There is no need to make this to-do about my brother; he can take good care of himself; neither does a warrior of the Face die because of a little cold and frost and snow-drift. Withal Gold-mane is a wilful man, and of late days hath been wilful beyond his wont; let us now find the elks.'

So they went on their ways hoping to fall in with him again. No long story need be made of their hunting, for not very far from where they had taken shelter they came upon the elks, many of them, impounded in the drifts, pretty much where the deft hunters looked to find them. There then was battle between the elks and the men, till the beasts were all slain and only one man hurt: then they made them sleighs from wood which they found in the hollows thereby, and they laid the carcasses thereon, and so turned their faces homeward, dragging their prey with them. But they met not Face-of-god either there or on the way home; and Hall-face said: 'Maybe Gold-mane will lie on the fell to-night; and I would I were with him; for adventures oft befall such folk when they abide in the wilds.'

Now it was late at night by then they reached Burgstead, so laden as they were with the dead beasts; but they heeded the night little, for the moon was well-nigh as bright as day for them. But when they came to the gate of the Thorp, there were assembled the goodmen and swains to meet them with torches and wine in their honour. There also was Gold-mane come back before them, yea for these two hours; and he stood clad in his holiday raiment and smiled on them.

Then was there some jeering at him that he was come back empty-handed from the hunting, and that he was not able to abide the wind and the drift; but he laughed thereat, for all this was but game and play, since men knew him for a keen hunter and a stout woodsman; and they had deemed it a heavy loss of him if he had been cast away, as some feared he had been: and his brother Hall-face embraced him and kissed him, and said to him: 'Now the next time that thou farest to the wood will I be with thee foot to foot, and never leave thee, and then meseemeth I shall wot of the tale that hath befallen thee, and belike it shall be no sorry one.'

Face-of-god laughed and answered but little, and they all betook them to the House of the Face and held high feast therein, for as late as the night was, in honour of this Hunting of the Elk.

No man cared to question Face-of-god closely as to how or where he had strayed from the hunt; for he had told his own tale at once as soon as he came home, to wit, that his right-foot skid-strap had broken, and even while he stopped to mend it came on

M

The true tale
of Face-of-
god.

that drift and weather; and that he could not move from that place without losing his way, and that when it had cleared he knew not whither they had gone because the snow had covered their slot. So he deemed it not unlike that they had gone back, and that he might come up with one or two on the way, and that in any case he wotted well that they could look after themselves; so he turned back, not going very swiftly. All this seemed like enough, and a little matter except to jest about, so no man made any question concerning it: only old Stone-face said to himself: 'Now were I fain to have a true tale out of him, but it is little likely that anything shall come of my much questioning; and it is ill forcing a young man to tell lies.'

So he held his peace, and the feast went on merrily and blithely.

## CHAPTER XIV.   CONCERNING FACE-OF-GOD AND THE MOUNTAIN.

BUT it must be told of Gold-mane that what had befallen him was in this wise. His skid-strap brake in good sooth, and he stayed to mend it; but when he had done what was needful, he looked up and saw no man nigh, what for the drift, and that they had gone on somewhat; so he rose to his feet, and without more delay, instead of keeping on toward the elk-ground and the way his face had been set, he turned himself north-and-by-east, and went his ways swiftly towards that airt, because he deemed that it might lead him to the Mountain-hall where he had guested. He abode not for the storm to clear, but swept off through the thick of it; and indeed the wind was somewhat at his back, so that he went the swiftlier. But when the drift was gotten to its very worst, he sheltered himself for a little in a hollow behind a thorn-bush he stumbled upon. As soon as it began to abate he went on again, and at last when it was quite clear, and the sun shone out, he found himself on a long slope of the fells covered deep with smooth white snow, and at the higher end a great crag rising bare fifty feet above the snow, and more rocks, but none so great, and broken ground as he judged (the snow being deep) about it on the hither side; and on the further, three great pine-trees all bent down and mingled together by their load of snow.

Thitherward he made, as a man might, seeing nothing else to note before him; but he had not made many strides when forth from behind the crag by the pine-trees came a man; and at first Face-of-god thought it might be one of his hunting-fellows gone astray, and he hailed him in a loud voice, but as he looked he saw the sun flash back from a bright helm on the new-comer's head; albeit he kept on his way till there was but a space of two hundred yards between them; when lo! the helm-bearer notched a shaft to his bent bow and loosed at Face-of-god, and the arrow came whistling and passed six inches by his right ear. Then Face-of-god stopped perplexed with his case; for he was on the deep snow in his skids, with his bow unbent, and he knew not how to bend it speedily. He was loth to turn his back and flee, and indeed he scarce deemed that it would help him. Meanwhile of his tarrying the archer loosed again at him, and this time the shaft flew close to his left ear. Then Face-of-god thought to cast himself down into the snow, but he was ashamed; till there came a third shaft which flew over his head amidmost and close to it. 'Good shooting on the Mountain!' muttered he; 'the next shaft will be amidst my breast, and who knows whether the Alderman's handiwork will keep it out.'

So he cried aloud: 'Thou shootest well, brother; but art thou a foe? If thou art, I have a sword by my side, and so hast thou; come hither to me, and let us fight it out friendly if we must needs fight.'

A laugh came down the wind to him clear but somewhat shrill, and the archer came swiftly towards him on his skids with no weapon in his hand save his bow; so that Face-of-god did not draw his sword, but stood wondering.

83

As they drew nearer he beheld the face of the new-comer, and
deemed that he had seen it before ; and soon, for all that it was
hooded close by the ill-weather raiment, he perceived it to be the
face of Bow-may, ruddy and smiling.

She laughed out loud again, as she stopped herself within three
feet of him, and said :

'Yea, friend Yellow-hair, we heard of the elks and looked to
see thee hereabouts, and I knew thee at once when I came out from
behind the crag and saw thee stand bewildered.'

Said Gold-mane : 'Hail to thee, Bow-may ! and glad am I
to see thee. But thou liest in saying that thou knewest me ; else
why didst thou shoot those three shafts at me ?   Surely thou art
not so quick as that with all thy friends : these be sharp greetings
of you Mountain-folk.'

'Thou lad with the sweet mouth,' she said, 'I like to see thee
and hear thee talk, but now must I hasten thy departure ; so
stand we here no longer. Let us get down into the wood where
we can do off our skids and sit down, and then will I tell thee
the tidings.   Come on !'

And she caught his hand in hers, and they went speedily
down the slopes toward the great oak-wood, the wind whistling
past their ears.

'Whither are we going ?' said he.

Said she : 'I am to show thee the way back home, which thou
wilt not know surely amidst this snow. Come, no words ! thou
shalt not have my tale from me till we are in the wood : so the
sooner we are there the sooner shalt thou be pleased.'

So Face-of-god held his peace, and they went on swiftly side
by side.   But it was not Bow-may's wont to be silent for long,
so presently she said :

'Thou art good to do as I bid thee ; but see thou, sweet playmate, for all thou art a chieftain's son, thou wert but feather-
brained to ask me why I shot at thee.   I shoot at thee ! that were
a fine tale to tell her this even !   Or dost thou think that I could

84

shoot at a big man on the snow at two hundred paces and miss him three times?  Unless I aimed to miss.'

'Yea, Bow-may,' said he, 'art thou so deft a Bow-may? Thou shalt be in my company whenso I fare to battle.'

'Indeed,' she said, 'therein thou sayest but the bare truth : nowhere else shall I be, and thou shalt find my bow no worse than a good shield.'

He laughed somewhat lightly; but she looked on him soberly and said : 'Laugh in that fashion on the day of battle, and we shall be well content with thee !'

So on they sped very swiftly, for their way was mostly down hill, so that they were soon amongst the outskirting trees of the wood, and presently after reached the edge of the thicket, beyond which the ground was but thinly covered with snow.

There they took off their skids, and went into the thick wood and sat down under a hornbeam tree ; and ere Gold-mane could open his mouth to speak Bow-may began and said :

'Well it was that I fell in with thee, Dalesman, else had there been murders of men to tell of; but ever she ordereth all things wisely, though unwisely hast thou done to seek to her. Hearken ! dost thou think that thou hast done well that thou hast me here with my tale ?  Well, hadst thou busied thyself with the slaying of elks, or with sitting quietly at home, yet shouldest thou have heard my tale, and thou shouldest have seen me in Burgstead in a day or two to tell thee concerning the flitting of the token.  And ill it is that I have missed it, for fain had I been to behold the House of the Face, and to have seen thee sitting there in thy dignity amidst the kindred of chieftains.'

And she sighed therewith.  But he said : 'Hold up thine heart, Bow-may!  On the word of a true man that shall befall thee one day.  But come, playmate, give me thy tale !'

'Yea,' she said, ' I must now tell thee in the wild-wood what else I had told thee in the Hall. Hearken closely, for this is the message :

85

'*Seek not to me again till thou hast the token; else assuredly wilt thou be slain, and I shall be sorry for many a day. Thereof as now I may not tell thee more. Now as to the token: When March is worn two weeks fail not to go to and fro on the place of the Maiden Ward for an hour before sunrise every day till thou hear tidings.*'

'Now,' quoth Bow-may, 'hast thou hearkened and understood?'

'Yea,' said he.

She said: 'Then tell me the words of my message concerning the token.' And he did so word for word. Then she said:

'It is well, there is no more to say. Now must I lead thee till thou knowest the wood; and then mayst thou get on to the smooth snow again, and so home merrily. Yet, thou grey-eyed fellow, I will have my pay of thee before I do that last work.'

Therewith she turned about to him and took his head between her hands, and kissed him well favouredly both cheeks and mouth; and she laughed, albeit the tears stood in her eyes as she said :
'Now smelleth the wood sweeter, and summer will come back again. And even thus will I do once more when we stand side by side in battle array.'

He smiled kindly on her and nodded as they both rose up from the earth: she had taken off her foul-weather gloves while they spake, and he kissed her hand, which was shapely of fashion albeit somewhat brown, and hard of palm, and he said in friendly wise:

'Thou art a merry faring-fellow, Bow-may, and belike shalt be withal a true fighting-fellow. Come now, thou shalt be my sister and I thy brother, in despite of those three shafts across the snow.'

He laughed therewith; she laughed not, but seemed glad, and said soberly:

'Yea, I may well be thy sister; for belike I also am of the people of the Gods, who have come into these Dales by many far ways. I am of the House of the Ragged Sword of the Kindred of the Wolf. Come, brother, let us toward Wildlake's Way.'

Therewith she went before him and led through the thicket

as by an assured and wonted path, and he followed hard at heel; but his thought went from her for a while; for those words of brother and sister that he had spoken called to his mind the Bride, and their kindness of little children, and the days when they seemed to have nought to do but to make the sun brighter, and the flowers fairer, and the grass greener, and the birds happier each for the other; and a hard and evil thing it seemed to him that now he should be making all these things nought and dreary to her, now when he had become a man and deeds lay before him. Yet again was he solaced by what Bow-may had said concerning battle to come; for he deemed that she must have had this from the Friend's foreseeing; and he longed sore for deeds to do, wherein all these things might be cleared up and washen clean as it were.

So passed they through the wood a long way, and it was getting dark therein, and Gold-mane said:

'Hold now, Bow-may, for I am at home here.'

She looked around and said: 'Yea, so it is: I was thinking of many things. Farewell and live merrily till March comes and the token!'

Therewith she turned and went her ways and was soon out of sight, and he went lightly through the wood, and then on skids over the hard snow along the Dale's edge till he was come to the watch-tower, when the moon was bright in heaven.

Thus was he at Burgstead and the House of the Face betimes, and before the hunters were gotten back.


CHAPTER XV.  MURDER AMONGST THE FOLK OF THE WOODLANDERS.

SO wore away midwinter tidingless. Stone-face spake no more to Face-of-god about the wood and its wights, when he saw that the young man had come back hale and merry, and seemed not to crave over-much to go back thither. As for

87

the Bride, she was sad, and more than misdoubted all ; but dauntless as she was in matters that try men's hardihood, she yet lacked
heart to ask of Face-of-god what had befallen him since the au-
tumn-tide, or where he was with her. So she put a force upon herself not to look sad or craving when she was in his company, as full
oft she was ; for he rather sought her than shunned her. For when
he saw her thus, he deemed things were changing with her as they
had changed with him, and he bethought him of what he had
spoken to Bow-may, and deemed that even so he might speak
with the Bride when the time came, and that she would not be
grieved beyond measure, and all would be well.

Now came on the thaw, and the snow went, and the grass grew
all up and down the Dale, and all waters were big. And about
this time arose rumours of strange men in the wood, uncouth,
vile, and murderous, and many of the feebler sort were made
timorous thereby.

But a little before March was born came new tidings from the
Woodlanders ; to wit : There came on a time to the house of a
woodland carle, a worthy goodman well renowned of all, two
wayfarers in the first watch of the night ; and these men said that
they were wending down to the Plain from a far-away dale, Rose-
dale to wit, which all men had heard of, and that they had strayed
from the way and were exceeding weary, and they craved a meal's
meat and lodging for the night.

This the goodman might nowise gainsay, and he saw no harm
in it, wherefore he bade them abide and be merry.

These men, said they who told the tidings, were outlanders,
and no man had seen any like them before : they were armed, and
bore short bows made of horn, and round targets, and coats-of-
fence done over with horn scales ; they had crooked swords girt
to their sides, and axes of steel forged all in one piece, right good
weapons. They were clad in scarlet and had much silver on their
raiment and about their weapons, and great rings of the same on
their arms ; and all this silver seemed brand-new.

Now the Woodland Carle gave them of such things as he had, and was kind and blithe to them : there were in his house besides himself five men of his sons and kindred, and his wife and three daughters and two other maids. So they feasted after the Wood-landers' fashion, and went to bed a little before midnight. Two hours after, the carle awoke and heard a little stir, and he looked and saw the guests on their feet amidst the hall clad in all their war-gear ; and they had betwixt them his two youngest daughters, maids of fifteen and twelve winters, and had bound their hands and done clouts over their mouths, so that they might not cry out ; and they were just at point to carry them off. Thereat the good-man, naked as he was, caught up his sword and made at these murder-carles, and or ever they were ware of him he had hewn down one and turned to face the other, who smote at him with his steel axe and gave him a great wound on the shoulder, and there-withal fled out at the open door and forth into the wood.

The Woodlander made no stay to raise the cry (there was no need, for the hall was astir now from end to end, and men getting to their weapons), but ran out after the felon even as he was ; and, in spite of his grievous hurt, overran him no long way from the house before he had gotten into the thicket. But the man was nimble and strong, and the goodman unsteady from his wound, and by then the others of the household came up with the hue and cry he had gotten two more sore wounds and was just making an end of throttling the felon with his bare hands. So he fell into their arms fainting from weakness, and for all they could do he died in two hours' time from that axe-wound in his shoulder, and another on the side of the head, and a knife-thrust in his side ; and he was a man of sixty winters.

But the stranger he had slain outright; and the one whom he had smitten in the hall died before the dawn, thrusting all help aside, and making no sound of speech.

When these tidings came to Burgstead they seemed great to all men, and to Gold-mane more than all. So he and many others took their weapons and fared up to Wildlake's Way, and so came to the Woodland Carles. But the Woodlanders had borne out the carcasses of those felons and laid them on the green before Wood-grey's door (for that was the name of the dead goodman), and they were saying that they would not bury such accursed folk, but would bear them a little way so that they should not be vexed with the stink of them, and cast them into the thicket for the wolf and the wild-cat and the stoat to deal with ; and they should lie there, weapons and silver and all ; and they deemed it base to strip such wretches, for who would wear their raiment or bear their weapons after them.

There was a great ring of folk round about them when they of Burgstead drew near, and they shouted for joy to see their neighbours, and made way before them. Then the Dalesmen cursed these murderers who had slain so good a man, and they all praised his manliness, whereas he ran out into the night naked and wounded after his foe, and had fallen like his folk of old time.

It was a bright spring afternoon in that clearing of the Wood, and they looked at the two dead men closely ; and Gold-mane, who had been somewhat silent and moody till then, became merry and wordy ; for he beheld the men and saw that they were utterly strange to him : they were short of stature, crooked-legged, long-armed, very strong for their size : with small blue eyes, snubbed-nosed, wide-mouthed, thin-lipped, very swarthy of skin, exceeding foul of favour. He and all others wondered who they were, and whence they came, for never had they seen their like ; and the Woodlanders, who often guested outlanders strayed from the way of divers kindreds and nations, said also that none such had they ever seen. But Stone-face, who stood by Gold-mane, shook his head and quoth he :

' The Wild-wood holdeth many marvels, and these be of them : the spawn of evil wights quickeneth therein, and at other whiles it melteth away again like the snow ; so may it be with these carcasses.'

And some of the older folk of the Woodlanders who stood by hearkened what he said, and deemed his words wise, for they remembered their ancient lore and many a tale of old time.

Thereafter they of Burgstead went into Wood-grey's hall, or as many of them as might, for it was but a poor place and not right great. There they saw the goodman laid on the daïs in all his war-gear, under the last tie-beam of his hall, whereon was carved amidst much goodly work of knots and flowers and twining stems the image of the Wolf of the Waste, his jaws open and gaping : the wife and daughters of the goodman and other women of the folk stood about the bier singing some old song in a low voice, and some sobbing therewithal, for the man was much beloved : and much people of the Woodlanders was in the hall, and it was somewhat dusk within.

So the Burgstead men greeted that folk kindly and humbly, and again they fell to praising the dead man, saying how his deed should long be remembered in the Dale and wide about ; and they called him a fearless man and of great worth. And the women hearkened, and ceased their crooning and their sobbing, and stood up proudly and raised their heads with gleaming eyes ; and as the words of the Burgstead men ended, they lifted up their voices and sang loudly and clearly, standing together in a row, ten of them, on the daïs of that poor hall, facing the gable and the wolf-adorned tie-beam, heeding nought as they sang what was about or behind them.

And this is some of what they sang :

Why sit ye bare in the spinning-room ?
Why weave ye naked at the loom ?

Bare and white as the moon we be,
That the Earth and the drifting night may see.

Now what is the worst of all your work ?
What curse amidst the web shall lurk ?

The worst of the work our hands shall win
Is wrack and ruin round the kin.

Shall the woollen yarn and the flaxen thread
Be gear for living men or dead?

The woollen yarn and the flaxen thread
Shall flare 'twixt living men and dead.

O what is the ending of your day?
When shall ye rise and wend away?

Our day shall end to-morrow morn,
When we hear the voice of the battle-horn.

Where first shall eyes of men behold
This weaving of the moonlight cold?

There where the alien host abides
The gathering on the Mountain-sides.

How long aloft shall the fair web fly
When the bows are bent and the spears draw nigh?

From eve to morn and morn till eve
Aloft shall fly the work we weave.

What then is this, the web ye win?
What wood-beast waxeth stark therein?

We weave the Wolf and the gift of war
From the men that were to the men that are.

So sang they: and much were all men moved at their singing,
and there was none but called to mind the old days of the Fathers,
and the years when their banner went wide in the world.

But the Woodlanders feasted them of Burgstead what they
might, and then went the Dalesmen back to their houses; but on

the morrow's morrow they fared thither again, and Wood-grey was laid in mound amidst a great assemblage of the Folk.

Many men said that there was no doubt that those two felons were of the company of those who had ransacked the steads of Penny-thumb and Harts-bane; and so at first deemed Bristler the son of Brightling: but after a while, when he had had time to think of it, he changed his mind; for he said that such men as these would have slain first and ransacked afterwards: and some who loved neither Penny-thumb nor Harts-bane said that they would not have been at the pains to choose for ransacking the two worst men about the Dale, whose loss was no loss to any but themselves.

As for Gold-mane he knew not what to think, except that his friends of the Mountain had had nought to do with it.

So wore the days awhile.


CHAPTER XVI.  THE BRIDE SPEAKETH WITH FACE-OF-GOD.

FEBRUARY had died into March, and March was now twelve days old, on a fair and sunny day an hour before noon; and Face-of-god was in a meadow a scant mile down the Dale from Burgstead.  He had been driving a bull into a goodman's byre nearby, and had had to spend toil and patience both in getting him out of the fields and into the byre; for the beast was hot with the spring days and the new grass.  So now he was resting himself in happy mood in an exceeding pleasant place, a little meadow to wit, on one side whereof was a great orchard or grove of sweet chestnuts, which went right up to the feet of the Southern Cliffs: across the meadow ran a clear brook towards the Weltering Water, free from big stones, in some places dammed up for the flooding of the deep pasture-meadow, and with the grass growing on its lips down to the very water.  There was a low bank just outside the chestnut trees, as if someone had raised a dyke about them when they were young, which had been trodden low and spreading through the lapse of years by the faring of many men and beasts. The primroses bloomed thick upon it now, and here and there along it was a low blackthorn bush in full blossom; from the mid-meadow and right down to the lip of the brook was the grass well nigh hidden by the blossoms of the meadow-saffron, with daffodils sprinkled about amongst them, and in the trees and bushes the birds, and chiefly the blackbirds, were singing their loudest.

There sat Face-of-god on the bank resting after his toil, and happy was his mood; since in two days' wearing he should be pacing the Maiden Ward awaiting the token that was to lead him to Shadowy Vale; so he sat calling to mind the Friend as he had last seen her, and striving as it were to set her image standing on the flowery grass before him, till all the beauty of the meadow seemed bare and empty to him without her. Then it fell into his mind that this had been a beloved trysting-place betwixt him and the Bride, and that often when they were little would they come to gather chestnuts in the grove, and thereafter sit and prattle on the old dyke; or in spring when the season was warm would they go barefoot into the brook, seeking its treasures of troutlets and flowers and clean-washed agate pebbles. Yea, and time not long ago had they met here to talk as lovers, and sat on that very bank in all the kindness of good days without a blemish, and both he and she had loved the place well for its wealth of blossoms and deep grass and goodly trees and clear running stream.

As he thought of all this, and how often there he had praised to himself her beauty, which he scarce dared praise to her, he frowned and slowly rose to his feet, and turned toward the chestnut-grove, as though he would go thence that way; but or ever he stepped down from the dyke he turned about again, and even therewith, like the very image and ghost of his thought, lo! the

94

Bride herself coming up from out the brook and wending toward him, her wet naked feet gleaming in the sun as they trod down the tender meadow-saffron and brushed past the tufts of daffodils. He stood staring at her discomforted, for on that day he had much to think of that seemed happy to him, and he deemed that she would now question him, and his mind pondered divers ways of answering her, and none seemed good to him. She drew near and let her skirts fall over her feet, and came to him, her gown hem dragging over the flowers: then she stood straight up before him and greeted him, but reached not forth her hand to him nor touched him. Her face was paler that its wont, and her voice trembled as she spake to him and said :

'Face-of-god, I would ask thee a gift.'

'All gifts,' he said, 'that thou mayest ask, and I may give, lie open to thee.'

She said : 'If I be alive when the time comes this gift thou mayst well give me.'

'Sweet kinswoman,' said he, 'tell me what it is that thou wouldest have of me.' And he was ill-at-ease as he waited for her answer.

She said : 'Ah, kinsman, kinsman! Woe on the day that maketh kinship accursed to me because thou desirest it !'

He held his peace and was exceeding sorry; and she said:

'This is the gift that I ask of thee, that in the days to come when thou art wedded, thou wilt give me the second man-child whom thou begettest.'

He said: 'This shalt thou have, and would that I might give thee much more. Would that we were little children together once again, as when we played here in other days.'

She said : 'I would have a token of thee that thou shalt show to the God, and swear on it to give me the gift. For the times change.'

'What token wilt thou have ?' said he.

She said : 'When next thou farest to the Wood, thou shalt bring me back, it maybe a flower from the bank ye sit upon, or

95

a splinter from the daïs of the hall wherein ye feast, or maybe a ring or some matter that the strangers are wont to wear. That shall be the token.'

She spoke slowly, hanging her head adown, but she lifted it presently and looked into his face and said:

'Woe's me, woe's me, Gold-mane! How evil is this day, when bewailing me I may not bewail thee also! For I know that thine heart is glad. All through the winter have I kept this hidden in my heart, and durst not speak to thee. But now the spring-tide hath driven me to it. Let summer come, and who shall say?'

Great was his grief, and his shame kept him silent, and he had no word to say; and again she said:

'Tell me, Gold-mane, when goest thou thither?'

He said: 'I know not surely, may happen in two days, may happen in ten. Why askest thou?'

'O friend!' she said, 'is it a new thing that I should ask thee whither thou goest and whence thou comest, and the times of thy coming and going. Farewell to-day! Forget not the token. Woe's me, that I may not kiss thy fair face!'

She spread her arms abroad and lifted up her face as one who waileth, but no sound came from her lips; then she turned about and went away as she had come.

But as for him he stood there after she was gone in all confusion, as if he were undone: for he felt his manhood lessened that he should thus and so sorely have hurt a friend, and in a manner against his will. And yet he was somewhat wroth with her, that she had come upon him so suddenly, and spoken to him with such mastery, and in so few words, and he with none to make answer to her, and that she had so marred his pleasure and his hope of that fair day. Then he sat him down again on the flowery bank, and little by little his heart softened, and he once more called to mind many a time when they had been there before, and the plays and the games they had had together there when they were little. And he bethought him of the days that were long to him then, and now seemed short to him, and as if they were all grown together into one story, and that a sweet one. Then his breast heaved with a sob, and the tears rose to his eyes and burned and stung him, and he fell a-weeping for that sweet tale, and wept as he had wept once before on that old dyke when there had been some child's quarrel between them, and she had gone away and left him.

Then after a while he ceased his weeping, and looked about him lest anyone might be coming, and then he arose and went to and fro in the chestnut-grove for a good while, and afterwards went his ways from that meadow, saying to himself: 'Yet remaineth to me the morrow of to-morrow, and that is the first of the days of the watching for the token.'

But all that day he was slow to meet the eyes of men; and in the hall that eve he was silent and moody; for from time to time it came over him that some of his manhood had departed from him.

## CHAPTER XVII.   THE TOKEN COMETH FROM THE MOUNTAIN.

THE next day wore away tidingless; and the day after Face-of-god arose betimes; for it was the first day of his watch, and he was at the Maiden Ward before the time appointed on a very fair and bright morning, and he went to and fro on that place, and had no tidings. So he came away somewhat cast down, and said within himself: 'Is it but a lie and a mocking when all is said?'

On the morrow he went thither again, and the morn was wild and stormy with drift of rain, and low clouds hurrying over the earth, though for the sunrise they lifted a little in the east, and the sun came up over the passes, amidst the red and angry rack of clouds. This morn also gave him no tidings of the token, and he

was wroth and perturbed in spirit : but towards evening he said :
' It is well : ten days she gave me, so that she might be able to
send without fail on one of them ; she will not fail me.'

So again on the morrow he was there betimes, and the morn
was windy as on the day before, but the clouds higher and of better
promise for the day.  Face-of-god walked to and fro on the
Maiden Ward, and as he turned toward Burgstead for the tenth
time, he heard, as he deemed, a bow-string twang afar off, and even
therewith came a shaft flying heavily like a winged bird, which
smote a great standing-stone on the other side of the way, where
of old some chieftain had been buried, and fell to earth at its foot.
He went up to it and handled it, and saw that there was a piece
of thin parchment wrapped about it, which indeed he was eager
to unwrap at once, but forebore ; because he was on the highway,
and people were already astir, and even then passed by him a goodman of the Dale with a man of his going afield together, and they
gave him the sele of the day.  So he went along the highway a
little till he came to a place where was a footbridge over into the
meadow.  He crossed thereby and went swiftly till he reached
a rising ground grown over with hazel-trees ; there he sat down
among the rabbit-holes, the primrose and wild-garlic blooming
about him, and three blackbirds answering one another from the
edges of the coppice.  Straightway when he had looked and seen
none coming he broke the threads that were wound about the scroll
and the arrow, and unrolled the parchment ; and there was writing
thereon in black ink of small letters, but very fair, and this is what
he read therein :

*Come thou to the Mountain Hall by the path which thou knowest
of, on the morrow of the day whereon thou readest this.  Rise betimes
and come armed, for there are other men than we in the wood, to
whom thy death should be a gain.  When thou art come to the Hall,
thou shalt find no man therein ; but a great hound only, tied to a
bench nigh the daïs.  Call him by his name, Sure-foot to wit, and
give him to eat from the meat upon the board, and give him water*

98

*to drink. If the day is then far spent, as it is like to be, abide thou*
*with the hound in the hall through the night, and eat of what thou*
*shalt find there; but see that the hound fares not abroad till the*
*morrow's morn: then lead him out and bring him to the north-east*
*corner of the Hall, and he shall lift the slot for thee that leadeth to*
*the Shadowy Vale. Follow him and all good go with thee.*

Now when he had read this, earth seemed fair indeed about him, and he scarce knew whither to turn or what to do to make the most of his joy. He presently went back to Burgstead and into the House of the Face, where all men were astir now, and the day was clearing. He hid the shaft under his kirtle, for he would not that any should see it; so he went to his shut-bed and laid it up in his chest, wherein he kept his chiefest treasures; but the writing on the scroll he set in his bosom and so hid it. He went joyfully and proudly, as one who knoweth more tidings and better than those around him. But Stone-face beheld him, and said: 'Foster-son, thou art happy. Is it that the spring-tide is in thy blood, and maketh thee blithe with all things, or hast thou some new tidings? Nay, I would not have an answer out of thee; but here is good rede: when next thou goest into the wood, it were nought so ill for thee to have a valiant old carle by thy side; one that loveth thee, and would die for thee if need were; one who might watch when thou wert seeking. Or else beware! for there are evil things abroad in the Wood, and moreover the brethren of those two felons who were slain at Carlstead.'

Then Gold-mane constrained himself to answer the old carle softly; and he thanked him kindly for his offer, and said that so it should be before long. So the talk between them fell, and Stone-face went away somewhat well-pleased.

And now was Face-of-god become wary; and he would not draw men's eyes and speech on him; so he went afield with Hall-face to deal with the lambs and the ewes, and did like other men. No less wary was he in the hall that even, and neither spake much nor little; and when his father spake to him concerning the Bride,

Face-of-god
cometh to the
Mountain-
hall again.

and made game of him as a somewhat sluggish groom, he did not change countenance, but answered lightly what came to hand.

On the morrow ere the earliest dawn he was afoot, and he clad himself and did on his hauberk, his father's work, which was fine-wrought and a stout defence, and reached down to his knees ; and over that he did on a goodly green kirtle well embroidered : he girt his war-sword to his side, and it was the work of his father's father, and a very good sword : its name was Dale-warden. He did a good helm on his head, and slung a targe at his back, and took two spears in his hand, short but strong-shafted and well-steeled. Thus arrayed he left Burgstead before the dawn, and came to Wildlake's Way and betook him to the Woodland. He made no stop or stay on the path, but ate his meat standing by an oak-tree close by the half-blind track. When he came to the little wood-lawn, where was the toft of the ancient house, he looked all round about him, for he deemed that a likely place for those ugly wood-wights to set on him ; but nought befell him, though he stooped and drank of the woodland rill warily enough. So he passed on; and there were other places also where he fared warily, because they seemed like to hold lurking felons ; though forsooth the whole wood might well serve their turn. But no evil befell him, and at last, when it yet lacked an hour to sunset, he came to the wood-lawn where Wild-wearer had made his onset that other eve.

He went straight up to the house, his heart beating, and he scarce believing but that he should find the Friend abiding him there : but when he pushed the door it gave way before him at once, and he entered and found no man therein, and the walls stripped bare and no shield or weapon hanging on the panels. But the hound he saw tied to a bench nigh the daïs, and the bristles on the beast's neck arose, and he snarled on Face-of-god, and strained on his leathern leash. Then Face-of-god went up to him and called him by his name, Sure-foot, and gave him his hand to lick, and he brought him water, and fed him with flesh from the meat on the board; so the beast became friendly and wagged his tail and whined and slobbered his hand.

Then he went all about the house, and saw and heard no living thing therein save the mice in the panels and Sure-foot. So he came back to the daïs, and sat him down at the board and ate his fill, and thought concerning his case. And it came into his mind that the Woman of the Mountain had some deed for him to do which would try his manliness and exalt his fame; and his heart rose high and he was glad, and he saw himself sitting beside her on the daïs of a very fair hall beloved and honoured of all the folk, and none had aught to say against him or owed him any grudge. Thus he pleased himself in thinking of the good days to come, sitting there till the hall grew dusk and dark and the night-wind moaned about it.

Then after a while he arose and raked together the brands on the hearth, and made light in the hall and looked to the door. And he found there were bolts and bars thereto, so he shot the bolts and drew the bars into their places and made all as sure as might be. Then he brought Sure-foot down from the daïs, and tied him up so that he might lie down athwart the door, and then lay down in his hauberk with his naked sword ready to his hand, and slept a long while.

When he awoke it was darker than when he had lain him down, for the moon had set; yet he deemed that the day was at point of breaking. So he fetched water and washed the night off him, and saw a little glimmer of the dawn. Then he ate somewhat of the meat on the board, and did on his helm and his other gear, and unbarred the door, and led Sure-foot without, and brought him to the north-east corner of the house, and in a little while he lifted the slot and they departed, the man and the hound, just as dawn broke from over the mountains.

Sure-foot led right into the heart of the pine-wood, and it was dark enough therein, with nought but a feeble glimmer for some while, and long was the way therethrough; but in two hours'

space was there something of a break, and they came to the shore
of a dark deep tarn on whose windless and green waters the daylight shone fully. The hound skirted the water, and led on un-
checked till the trees began to grow smaller and the air colder
for all that the sun was higher; for they had been going up and
up all the way.

So at last after a six hours' journey they came clean out of the
pine-wood, and before them lay the black wilderness of the bare
mountains, and beyond them, looking quite near now, the great
ice-peaks, the wall of the world. It was but an hour short of noon
by this time, and the high sun shone down on a barren boggy
moss which lay betwixt them and the rocky waste. Sure-foot
made no stay, but threaded the ways that went betwixt the quag-
mires, and in another hour led Face-of-god into a winding valley
blinded by great rocks, and everywhere stony and rough, with a
trickle of water running amidst of it. The hound fared on up the
dale to where the water was bridged by a great fallen stone, and
so over it and up a steep bent on the further side, on to a marvellously rough mountain-neck, whiles mere black sand cumbered
with scattered rocks and stones, whiles beset with mires grown
over with the cottony mire-grass; here and there a little scanty
grass growing; otherwhere nought but dwarf willow ever dying
ever growing, mingled with moss or red-blossomed sengreen; and
all blending together into mere desolation.

Few living things they saw there; up on the neck a few sheep
were grazing the scanty grass, but there was none to tend them;
yet Face-of-god deemed the sight of them good, for there must be
men anigh who owned them. For the rest, the whimbrel laughed
across the mires; high up in heaven a great eagle was hanging;
once and again a grey fox leapt up before them, and the heath-
fowl whirred up from under Face-of-god's feet. A raven who
was sitting croaking on a rock in that first dale stirred uneasily on
his perch as he saw them, and when they were passed flapped his
wings and flew after them croaking still.

102

Now they fared over that neck somewhat east, making but slow way because the ground was so broken and rocky ; and in another hour's space Sure-foot led down-hill due east to where the stony neck sank into another desolate miry heath still falling toward the east, but whose further side was walled by a rampart of crags cleft at their tops into marvellous shapes, coal-black, ungrassed and unmossed. Thitherward the hound led straight, and Gold-mane followed wondering : as he drew near them he saw that they were not very high, the tallest peak scant fifty feet from the face of the heath.

They made their way through the scattered rocks at the foot of these crags, till, just where the rock-wall seemed the closest, the way through the stones turned into a path going through it skew-wise ; and it was now so clear a path that belike it had been bettered by men's hands. Down thereby Face-of-god followed the hound, deeming that he was come to the gates of the Shadowy Vale, and the path went down steeply and swiftly. But when he had gone down a while, the rocks on his right hand sank lower for a space, so that he could look over and see what lay beneath.

There lay below him a long narrow vale quite plain at the bottom, walled on the further side as on the hither by sheer rocks of black stone. The plain was grown over with grass, but he could see no tree therein: a deep river, dark and green, ran through the vale, sometimes through its midmost, sometimes lapping the further rock-wall: and he thought indeed that on many a day in the year the sun would never shine on that valley.

Thus much he saw, and then the rocks rose again and shut it from his sight; and at last they drew so close together over head that he was in a way going through a cave with little daylight coming from above, and in the end he was in a cave indeed and mere darkness : but with the last feeble glimmer of light he thought he saw carved on a smooth space of the living rock at his left hand the image of a wolf.

This cave lasted but a little way, and soon the hound and the man were going once more between sheer black rocks, and the path grew steeper yet and was cut into steps. At last there was a sharp turn, and they stood on the top of a long stony scree, down which Sure-foot bounded eagerly, giving tongue as he went; but Face-of-god stood still and looked, for now the whole Dale lay open before him.

That river ran from north to south, and at the south end the cliffs drew so close to it that looking thence no outgate could be seen; but at the north end there was as it were a dreary street of rocks, the river flowing amidmost and leaving little foothold on either side, somewhat as it was with the pass leading from the mountains into Burgdale.

Amidmost of the Dale a little toward the north end he saw a doom-ring of black stones, and hard by it an ancient hall builded of the same black stone both wall and roof, and thitherward was Sure-foot now running. Face-of-god looked up and down the Dale and could see no break in the wall of sheer rock: toward the southern end he saw a few booths and cots built roughly of stone and thatched with turf; thereabout he saw a few folk moving about, the most of whom seemed to be women and children; there were some sheep and lambs near these cots, and a herd of fifty or so of somewhat goodly mountain-kine were feeding higher up the valley. He could look down into the river from where he stood, and he saw that it ran between rocky banks going straight down from the face of the meadow, which was rather high above the water, so that it seemed little likely that the water should rise over its banks, either in summer or winter; and in summer was it like to be highest, because the vale was so near to the high mountains and their snows.

## CHAPTER XVIII. FACE-OF-GOD TALKETH WITH THE FRIEND IN SHADOWY VALE.

IT was now about two hours after noon, and a broad band of sunlight lay upon the grass of the vale below Gold-mane's feet; he went lightly down the scree, and strode forward over the level grass toward the Doom-ring, his helm and war-gear glittering bright in the sun. He must needs go through the Doom-ring to come to the Hall, and as he stepped out from behind the last of the big upright-stones, he saw a woman standing on the threshold of the Hall-door, which was but some score of paces from him, and knew her at once for the Friend.

She was clad like himself in a green kirtle gaily embroidered and fitting close to her body, and had no gown or cloak over it; she had a golden fillet on her head beset with blue mountain stones, and her hair hung loose behind her.

Her beauty was so exceeding, and so far beyond all memory of her that his mind had held, that once more fear of her fell upon Face-of-god, and he stood still with beating heart till she should speak to him. But she came forward swiftly with both her hands held out, smiling and happy-faced, and looking very kindly on him, and she took his hands and said to him:

'Now welcome, Gold-mane, welcome, Face-of-god! and twice welcome art thou and threefold. Lo! this is the day that thou hast asked for: art thou happy in it?'

He lifted her hands to his lips and kissed them timorously, but said nought; and therewithal Sure-foot came running forth from the Hall, and fell to bounding round about them, barking noisily after the manner of dogs who have met their masters again; and still she held his hands and beheld him kindly. Then she called the hound to her, and patted him on the neck and quieted him, and then turned to Face-of-god and laughed happily and said:

'I do not bid thee hold thy peace; yet thou sayest nought. Is it well with thee?'

'Yea,' he said, 'and more than well.'

'Thou seemest to me a goodly warrior,' she said; 'hast thou met any foemen yesterday or this morning?'

'Nay,' said he, 'none hindered me; thou hast made the ways easy to me.'

She said soberly, 'Such as I might do, I did. But we may not wield everything, for our foes are many, and I feared for thee. But come thou into our house, which is ours, and far more ours than the booth before the pine-wood.'

She took his hand again and led him toward the door, but Face-of-god looked up, and above the lintel he saw carved on the dark stone that image of the Wolf, even as he had seen it carved on Wood-grey's tie-beam; and therewith such thoughts came into his mind that he stopped to look, pressing the Friend's hand hard as though bidding her note it. The stone wherein the image was carved was darker than the other building stones, and might be called black; the jaws of the wood-beast were open and gaping, and had been painted with cinnabar, but wind and weather had worn away the most of the colour.

Spake the Friend: 'So it is: thou beholdest the token of the God and Father of our Fathers, that telleth the tale of so many days, that the days which now pass by us be to them but as the drop in the sea of waters. Thou beholdest the sign of our sorrow, the memory of our wrong; yet is it also the token of our hope. Maybe it shall lead thee far.'

'Whither?' said he. But she answered not a great while, and he looked at her as she stood a-gazing on the image, and saw how the tears stole out of her eyes and ran adown her cheeks. Then again came the thought to him of Wood-grey's hall, and the women of the kindred standing before the Wolf and singing of him; and though there was little comeliness in them and she was so exceeding beauteous, he could not but deem that they were akin to her.

But after a while she wiped the tears from her face and turned to him and said : 'My friend, the Wolf shall lead thee no- They go into the Hall. whither but where I also shall be, whatsoever peril or grief may beset the road or lurk at the ending thereof. Thou shalt be no thrall, to labour while I look on.'

His heart swelled within him as she spoke, and he was at point to beseech her love that moment; but now her face had grown gay and bright again, and she said while he was gathering words to speak withal :

'Come in, Gold-mane, come into our house; for I have many things to say to thee. And moreover thou art so hushed, and so fearsome in thy mail, that I think thou yet deemest me to be a Wight of the Waste, such as Stone-face thy Fosterer told thee tales of, and forewarned thee. So would I eat before thee, and sign the meat with the sign of the Earth-god's Hammer, to show thee that he is in error concerning me, and that I am a very woman flesh and fell, as my kindred were before me.'

He laughed and was exceeding glad, and said : 'Tell me now, kind friend, dost thou deem that Stone-face's tales are mere mockery of his dreams, and that he is beguiled by empty semblances or less? Or are there such Wights in the Waste.'

'Nay,' she said, 'the man is a true man ; and of these things are there many ancient tales which we may not doubt. Yet so it is that such wights have I never yet seen, nor aught to scare me save evil men: belike it is that I have been over-much busied in dealing with sorrow and ruin to look after them : or it may be that they feared me and the wrath-breeding grief of the kindred.'

He looked at her earnestly, and the wisdom of her heart seemed to enter into his; but she said : 'It is of men we must talk, and of me and thee. Come with me, my friend.'

And she stepped lightly over the threshold and drew him in. The Hall was stern and grim and somewhat dusky, for its windows were but small: it was all of stone, both walls and roof. There was no timber-work therein save the benches and chairs, and a little about the doors at the lower end that led to the but-

tery and out-bowers; and this seemed to have been wrought of
late years; yea, the chairs against the gable on the daïs were
of stone built into the wall, adorned with carving somewhat
sparingly, the image of the Wolf being done over the midmost of
them. He looked up and down the Hall, and deemed it some
seventy feet over all from end to end; and he could see in the
dimness those same goodly hangings on the wall which he had
seen in the woodland booth.

She led him up to the daïs, and stood there leaning up against
the arm of one of those stone seats silent for a while; then she
turned and looked at him, and said:

'Yea, thou lookest a goodly warrior; yet am I glad that thou
camest hither without battle. Tell me, Gold-mane,' she said,
taking one of his spears from his hand, 'art thou deft with
the spear?'

'I have been called so,' said he.

She looked at him sweetly and said: 'Canst thou show me
the feat of spear-throwing in this Hall, or shall we wend outside
presently that I may see thee throw?'

'The Hall sufficeth,' he said. 'Shall I set this steel in the
lintel of the buttery door yonder?'

'Yea, if thou canst,' she said.

He smiled and took the spear from her, and poised it and
shook it till it quivered again, then suddenly drew back his arm
and cast, and the shaft sped whistling down the dim hall, and
smote the aforesaid door-lintel and stuck there quivering: then
he sprang down from the daïs, and ran down the hall, and put
forth his hand and pulled it forth from the wood, and was on the
daïs again in a trice, and cast again, and the second time set the
spear in the same place, and then took his other spear from the
board and cast it, and there stood the two staves in the wood side
by side; then he went soberly down the hall and drew them
both out of the wood and came back to her, while she stood
watching him, her cheek flushed, her lips a little parted.

She said: 'Good spear-casting, forsooth! and far above what our folk can do, who be no great throwers of the spear.'

Gold-mane laughed: 'Sooth is that,' said he, 'or hardly were I here to teach thee spear-throwing.'

'Wilt thou *never* be paid for that simple onslaught?' she said.

'Have I been paid then?' said he.

She reddened, for she remembered her word to him on the mountain; and he put his hand on her shoulder and kissed her cheek, but timorously; nor did she withstand him or shrink aback, but said soberly:

'Good indeed is thy spear-throwing, and meseems my brother will love thee when he hath seen thee strike a stroke or two in wrath. But, fair warrior, there be no foemen here: so get thee to the lower end of the Hall, and in the bower beyond shalt thou find fresh water; there wash the waste from off thee, and do off thine helm and hauberk, and come back speedily and eat with me; for I hunger, and so dost thou.'

He did as she bade him, and came back presently bearing in his hand both helm and hauberk, and he looked light-limbed and trim and lissome, an exceeding goodly man.

## CHAPTER XIX. THE FAIR WOMAN TELLETH FACE-OF-GOD OF HER KINDRED.

WHEN he came back to the daïs he saw that there was meat upon the board, and the Friend said to him:

'Now art thou Gold-mane indeed: but come now, sit by me and eat, though the Wood-woman giveth thee but a sorry banquet, O guest; but from the Dale it is, and we be too far now from the dwellings of men to have delicate meat on the board, though to-night when they come back thy cheer shall be better. Yet even then thou shalt have no such dainties as Stone-face hath imagined for thee at the hands of the Wood-wight.'

She laughed therewith, and he no less ; and in sooth the meat
was but simple, of curds and new cheese, meat of the herdsmen.
But Face-of-god said gaily : 'Sweet it shall be to me ; good is
all that the Friend giveth.'

Then she raised her hand and made the sign of the Hammer
over the board, and looked up at him and said :

'Hath the Earth-god changed my face, Gold-mane, to what I
verily am ?'

He held his face close to hers and looked into it, and him-
seemed it was as pure as the waters of a mountain lake, and as fine
and well-wrought every deal of it as when his father had wrought
in his stithy many days and fashioned a small piece of great mastery. He was ashamed to kiss her again, but he said to himself,
'This is the fairest woman of the world, whom I have sworn to
wed this year.' Then he spake aloud and said :

'I see the face of the Friend, and it will not change to me.'

Again she reddened a little, and the happy look in her face
seemed to grow yet sweeter, and he was bewildered with longing
and delight.

But she stood up and went to an ambrye in the wall and brought
forth a horn shod and lipped with silver of ancient fashion, and
she poured wine into it and held it forth and said :

'O guest from the Dale, I pledge thee ! and when thou hast
drunk to me in turn we will talk of weighty matters. For
indeed I bear hopes in my hands too heavy for the daughters of
men to bear ; and thou art a chieftain's son, and mayst well
help me to bear them ; so let us talk simply and without guile,
as folk that trust one another.'

So she drank and held out the horn to him, and he took the
horn and her hand both, and he kissed her hand and said :

'Here in this Hall I drink to the Sons of the Wolf, whosoever they be.' Therewith he drank and he said : 'Simply and
guilelessly indeed will I talk with thee ; for I am weary of lies,
and for thy sake have I told a many.'

'Thou shalt tell no more,' she said; 'and as for the health She asketh of thou hast drunk, it is good, and shall profit thee. Now sit we tidings. here in these ancient seats and let us talk.'

So they sat them down while the sun was westering in the March afternoon, and she said:

'Tell me first what tidings have been in the Dale.'

So he told her of the ransackings and of the murder at Carlstead.

She said: 'These tidings have we heard before, and some deal of them we know better than ye do, or can; for we were the ransackers of Penny-thumb and Harts-bane. Thereof will I say more presently. What other tidings hast thou to tell of? What oaths were sworn upon the Boar last Yule?'

So he told her of the oath of Bristler the son of Brightling. She smiled and said: 'He shall keep his oath, and yet redden no blade.'

Then he told of his father's oath, and she said:

'It is good; but even so would he do and no oath sworn. All men may trust Iron-face. And thou, my friend, what oath didst thou swear?'

His face grew somewhat troubled as he said: 'I swore to wed the fairest woman in the world, though the Dalesmen gainsaid me, and they beyond the Dale.'

'Yea,' she said, 'and there is no need to ask thee whom thou didst mean by thy "fairest woman," for I have seen that thou deemest me fair enough. My friend, maybe thy kindred will be against it, and the kindred of the Bride; and it might be that my kindred would have gainsaid it if things were not as they are. But though all men gainsay it, yet will not I. It is meet and right that we twain wed.'

She spake very soberly and quietly, but when she had spoken there was nothing in his heart but joy and gladness: yet shame of her loveliness refrained him, and he cast down his eyes before hers. Then she said in a kind voice:

'I know thee, how glad thou art of this word of mine, because

111

thou lookest on me with eyes of love, and thinkest of me as better
than I am ; though I am no ill woman and no beguiler. But
this is not all that I have to say to thee, though it be much; for
there are more folk in the world than thou and I only. But I
told thee this first, that thou mightest trust me in all things.
So, my friend, if thou canst, refrain thy joy and thy longing a
little, and hearken to what concerneth thee and me, and thy
people and mine.'

'Fair woman and sweet friend,' he said, 'thou knowest of a
gladness which is hard to bear if one must lay it aside for a
while ; and of a longing which is hard to refrain if it mingle
with another longing—knowest thou not ? '

'Yea,' she said, 'I know it.'

'Yet,' said Face-of-god, 'I will forbear as thou biddest me.
Tell me, then, what were the felons who were slain at Carlstead?
Knowest thou of them ? '

'Over well,' she said, 'they are our foes this many a year ;
and since we met last autumn they have become foes of you
Dalesmen also. Soon shall ye have tidings of them ; and it was
against them that I bade thee arm yesterday.'

Said Face-of-god : 'Is it against them that thou wouldst have
us do battle along with thy folk ? '

'So it is,' she said ; 'no other foemen have we. And now, Gold-
mane, thou art become a friend of the Wolf, and shalt before long
be of affinity with our House; that other day thou didst ask me
to tell thee of me and mine, and now will I do according to thine
asking. Short shall my tale be ; because maybe thou shalt hear
it told again, and in goodly wise, before thine whole folk.

'As thou wottest we be now outlaws and Wolves' Heads ;
and whiles we lift the gear of men, but ever if we may of ill
men and not of good ; there is no worthy goodman of the Dale
from whom we would take one hoof, or a skin of wine, or a cake
of wax.

'Wherefore are we outlaws ? Because we have been driven

112

from our own, and we bore away our lives and our weapons, and little else ; and for our lands, thou seest this Vale in the howling wilderness and how narrow and poor it is, though it hath been the nurse of warriors in time past.

'Hearken! Time long ago came the kindred of the Wolf to these Mountains of the World ; and they were in a pass in the stony maze and the utter wilderness of the Mountains, and the foe was behind them in numbers not to be borne up against. And so it befell that the pass forked, and there were two ways before our Folk ; and one part of them would take the way to the north and the other the way to the south ; and they could not agree which way the whole Folk should take. So they sundered into two companies, and one took one way and one another. Now as to those who fared by the southern road, we knew not what befell them, nor for long and long had we any tale of them.

'But we who took the northern road, we happened on this Vale amidst the wilderness, and we were weary of fleeing from the over-mastering foe ; and the dale seemed enough, and a refuge, and a place to dwell in, and no man was there before us, and few were like to find it, and we were but a few. So we dwelt here in this Vale for as wild as it is, the place where the sun shineth never in the winter, and scant is the summer sunshine therein. Here we raised a Doom-ring and builded us a Hall, wherein thou now sittest beside me, O friend, and we dwelt here many seasons.

'We had a few sheep in the wilderness, and a few neat fed down the grass of the Vale ; and we found gems and copper in the rocks about us wherewith at whiles to chaffer with the aliens, and fish we drew from our river the Shivering Flood. Also it is not to be hidden that in those days we did not spare to lift the goods of men ; yea, whiles would our warriors fare down unto the edges of the Plain and lie in wait there till the time served, and then drive the spoil from under the very walls of the

Cities. Our men were not little-hearted, nor did our women
lament the death of warriors over-much, for they were there to
bear more warriors to the Folk.

'But the seasons passed, and the Folk multiplied in Shadowy
Vale, and livelihood seemed like to fail them, and needs must
they seek wider lands. So by ways which thou wilt one day
wot of, we came into a valley that lieth north-west of Shadowy
Vale : a land like thine of Burgdale, or better ; wide it was,
plenteous of grass and trees, well watered, full of all things that
man can desire.

'Were there men before us in this Dale ? sayest thou. Yea,
but not very many, and they feeble in battle, weak of heart,
though strong of body. These, when they saw the Sons of the
Wolf with weapons in their hands, felt themselves puny before
us, and their hearts failed them ; and they came to us with gifts,
and offered to share the Dale between them and us, for they said
there was enough for both folks. So we took their offer and
became their friends ; and some of our Houses wedded wives of
the strangers, and gave them their women to wife. Therein
they did amiss ; for the blended Folk as the generations passed
became softer than our blood, and many were untrusty and
greedy and tyrannous, and the days of the whoredom fell upon us,
and when we deemed ourselves the mightiest then were we the
nearest to our fall. But the House whereof I am would never
wed with these Westlanders, and other Houses there were who
had affinity with us who chiefly wedded with us of the Wolf,
and their fathers had come with ours into that fruitful Dale ;
and these were called the Red Hand, and the Silver Arm, and
the Golden Bushel, and the Ragged Sword. Thou hast heard
those names once before, friend ?'

'Yea,' he said, and as he spoke the picture of that other
day came back to him, and he called to mind all that he had
said, and his happiness of that hour seemed the more and the
sweeter for that memory.

She went on : ' Fair and goodly is that Dale as mine own eyes The Aliens.
have seen, and plentiful of all things, and up in its mountains to the
east are caves and pits whence silver is digged abundantly; therefore
is the Dale called Silver-dale. Hast thou heard thereof, my friend ? '
' Nay,' said Face-of-god, ' though I have marvelled whence
ye gat such foison of silver.'
He looked on her and marvelled, for now she seemed as if it
were another woman : her eyes were gleaming bright, her lips
were parted ; there was a bright red flush on the pommels of her
two cheeks as she spake again and said :
' Happy lived the Folk in Silver-dale for many and many
winters and summers : the seasons were good and no lack was
there : little sickness there was and less war, and all seemed
better than well. It is strange that ye Dalesmen have not heard
of Silver-dale.'
' Nay,' said he, ' but I have not; of Rose-dale have I heard,
as a land very far away : but no further do we know of toward
that airt. Lieth Silver-dale anywhere nigh to Rose-dale ? '
She said : ' It is the next dale to it, yet is it a far journey
betwixt the two, for the ice-sea pusheth a horn in betwixt them ;
and even below the ice the mountain-neck is passable to none
save a bold crag-climber, and to him only bearing his life in his
hands. But, my friend, I am but lingering over my tale, because it grieveth me sore to have to tell it. Hearken then ! In
the days when I had seen but ten summers, and my brother was
a very young man, but exceeding strong, and as beautiful as
thou art now, war fell on us without rumour or warning ; for
there swarmed into Silver-dale, though not by the ways whereby
we had entered it, a host of aliens, short of stature, crooked of
limb, foul of aspect, but fierce warriors and armed full well :
they were men having no country to go back to, though they
had no women or children with them, as we had when we were
young in these lands, but used all women whom they took as
their beastly lust bade them, making them their thralls if they

slew them not. Soon we found that these foemen asked no more
of us than all we had, and therewithal our lives to be cast away
or used for their service as beasts of burden or pleasure. There
then we gathered our fighting-men and withstood them ; and if
we had been all of the kindreds of the Wolf and the fruit of the
wives of warriors, we should have driven back these felons and
saved the Dale, though it maybe more than half ruined : but the
most part of us were of that mingled blood, or of the generations
of the Dalesmen whom we had conquered long ago, and stout as
they were of body their hearts failed them, and they gave themselves up to the aliens to be as their oxen and asses.

'Why make a long tale of it ? We who were left, and could
brook death but not thraldom, fought it out together, women
as well as men, till the sweetness of life and a happy chance for
escape bid us flee, vanquished but free men. For at the end of
three days' fight we had been driven up to the easternmost end
of the Dale, and up anigh to the jaws of the pass whereby the
Folk had first come into Silver-dale, and we had those with us
who knew every cranny of that way, while to strangers who knew
it not it was utterly impassable ; night was coming on also, and
even those murder-carles were weary with slaying ; and, moreover, on this last day, when they saw that they had won all, they
were fighting to keep, and not to slay, and a few stubborn carles
and queens, of what use would they be, or where was the gain
of risking life to win them ?

'So they forbore us, and night came on moonless and dark ; and
it was the early spring season, when the days are not yet long, and so
by night and cloud we fled away, and back again to Shadowy Vale.

'Forsooth, we were but a few ; for when we were gotten into
this Vale, this strip of grass and water in the wilderness, and had
told up our company, we were but two hundred and thirty and five
of men and women and children. For there were an hundred and
thirty and three grown men of all ages, and of women grown seventy
and five, and one score and seven children, whereof I was one ;

116

for, as thou mayst deem, it was easier for grown men with weapons in their hands to escape from that slaughter than for women
and children.

'There sat we in yonder Doom-ring and took counsel, and to
some it seemed good that we should all dwell together in Shadowy
Vale, and beset the skirts of the foemen till the days should better;
but others deemed that there was little avail therein; and there
was a mighty man of the kindred, Stone-wolf by name, a man of
middle-age, and he said, that late in life had he tasted of war,
and though the banquet was made bitter with defeat, yet did the
meat seem wholesome to him. "Come down with me to the
Cities of the Plain," said he, "all you who are stout warriors;
and leave we here the old men and the swains and the women
and children. Hateful are the folk there, and full of malice, but
soft withal and dastardly. Let us go down thither and make ourselves strong amongst them, and sell our valour for their wealth
till we come to rule them, and they make us their kings, and we
establish the Folk of the Wolf amongst the aliens; then will we
come back hither and bring away that which we have left."

'So he spake, and the more part of the warriors yeasaid his
rede, and they went with him to the Westland, and amongst these
was my brother Folk-might (for that is his name in the kindred).
And I sorrowed at his departure, for he had borne me thither out
of the flames and the clash of swords and the press of battle, and
to me had he ever been kind and loving, albeit he hath had the
words of hard and froward used on him full oft.

'So in this Vale abode we that were left, and the seasons passed;
some of the elders died, and some of the children also; but more
children were born, for amongst us were men and women to whom
it was lawful to wed with each other. Even with this scanty remnant was left some of the life of the kindred of old days; and
after we had been here but a little while, the young men, yea and
the old also, and even some of the women, would steal through
the passes that we, and we only, knew of, and would fall upon

117

the Aliens in Silver-dale as occasion served, and lift their goods
both live and dead ; and this became both a craft and a pastime
amongst us. Nor may I hide that we sometimes went lifting
otherwhere; for in the summer and autumn we would fare west a
little and abide in the woods the season through, and hunt the
deer thereof, and whiles would we drive the spoil from the scattered folk not far from your Shepherd-Folk ; but with the Shepherds themselves and with you Dalesmen we meddled not.

'Now that little wood-lawn with the toft of an ancient dwelling in it, wherein, saith Bow-may, thou didst once rest, was one
of our summer abodes ; and later on we built the hall under the
pine-wood that thou knowest.

'Thus then grew up our young men ; and our maids were little
softer ; e'en such as Bow-may is (and kind is she withal), and it
seemed in very sooth as if the Spirit of the Wolf was with us,
and the roughness of the Waste made us fierce; and law we had
not and heeded not, though love was amongst us.'

She stopped awhile and fell a-musing, and her face softened,
and she turned to him with that sweet happy look upon it and said :

'Desolate and dreary is the Dale, thou deemest, friend ; and
yet for me I love it and its dark-green water, and it is to me as
if the Fathers of the kindred visit it and hold converse with us ;
and there I grew up when I was little, before I knew what a woman
was, and strange communings had I with the wilderness. Friend,
when we are wedded, and thou art a great chieftain, as thou wilt
be, I shall ask of thee the boon to suffer me to abide here at whiles
that I may remember the days when I was little and the love of
the kindred waxed in me.'

'This is but a little thing to ask,' said Face-of-god ; 'I would
thou hadst asked me more.'

'Fear not,' she said, 'I shall ask thee for much and many
things ; and some of them belike thou shalt deny me.'

He shook his head ; but she smiled in his face and said :

'Yea, so it is, friend ; but hearken. The seasons passed, and six years wore, and I was grown a tall slim maiden, fleet of foot and able to endure toil enough, though I never bore weapons, nor have done.  So on a fair even of midsummer when we were together, the most of us, round about this Hall and the Doom-ring, we saw a tall man in bright war-gear come forth into the Dale by the path that thou camest, and then another and another till there were two score and seven men-at-arms standing on the grass below the scree yonder; by that time had we gotten some weapons in our hands, and we stood together to meet the new-comers, but they drew no sword and notched no shaft, but came towards us laughing and joyous, and lo! it was my brother Folk-might and his men, those that were left of them, come back to us from the Westland.

'Glad indeed was I to behold him; and for him when he had taken me in his arms and looked up and down the Dale, he cried out: 'In many fair places and many rich dwellings have I been; but this is the hour that I have looked for.'

'Now when we asked him concerning Stone-wolf and the others who were missing (for ten tens of stalwarth men had fared to the Westland), he swept out his hand toward the west and said with a solemn face: "There they lie, and grass groweth over their bones, and we who have come aback, and ye who have abided, these are now the children of the Wolf: there are no more now on the earth."

'Let be! It was a fair even and high was the feast in the Hall that night, and sweet was the converse with our folk come back. A glad man was my brother Folk-might when he heard that for years past we had been lifting the gear of men, and chiefly of the Aliens in Silver-dale: and he himself was become learned in war and a deft leader of men.

'So the days passed and the seasons, and we lived on as we might; but with Folk-might's return there began to grow up in all our hearts what had long been flourishing in mine, and that was the hope of one day winning back our own again, and dying amidst the dear groves of Silver-dale. Within these years we had

119

increased somewhat in number; for if we had lost those warriors in the Westland, and some old men who had died in the Dale, yet our children had grown up (I have now seen twenty and one summers) and more were growing up. Moreover, after the first year, from the time when we began to fall upon the Dusky Men of Silver-dale, from time to time they who went on such adventures set free such thralls of our blood as they could fall in with and whom they could trust in, and they dwelt (and yet dwell) with us in the Dale: first and last we have taken in three score and twelve of such men, and a score of women-thralls withal.

' Now during these seasons, and not very long ago, after I was a woman grown, the thought came to me, and to Folk-might also, that there were kindreds of the people dwelling anear us whom we might so deal with that they should become our friends and brothers in arms, and that through them we might win back Silver-dale.

' Of Rose-dale we wotted already that the Folk were nought of our blood, feeble in the field, cowed by the Dusky Men, and at last made thralls to them; so nought was to do there. But Folk-might went to and fro to gather tidings: at whiles I with him, at whiles one or more of Wood-father's children, who with their father and mother and Bow-may have abided in the Vale ever since the Great Undoing.

' Soon he fell in with thy Folk, and first of all with the Wood-landers, and that was a joy to him; for wot ye what? He got to know that these men were the children of those of our Folk who had sundered from us in the mountain passes time long and long ago; and he loved them, for he saw that they were hardy and trusty, and warriors at heart.

' Then he went amongst the Shepherd-Folk, and he deemed them good men easily stirred, and deemed that they might soon be won to friendship; and he knew that they were mostly come from the Houses of the Woodlanders, so that they also were of the kindred.

' And last he came into Burgdale, and found there a merry

and happy Folk, little wont to war, but stout-hearted, and no-wise puny either of body or soul; he went there often and learned much about them, and deemed that they would not be hard to win to fellowship. And he found that the House of the Face was the chiefest house there; and that the Alderman and his sons were well beloved of all the folk, and that they were the men to be won first, since through them should all others be won. I also went to Burgstead with him twice, as I told thee erst; and I saw thee, and I deemed that thou wouldest lightly become our friend; and it came into my mind that I myself might wed thee, and that the House of the Face thereby might have affinity thenceforth with the Children of the Wolf.'

He said: 'Why didst thou deem thus of me, O friend?'

She laughed and said: 'Dost thou long to hear me say the words when thou knowest my thought well? So be it. I saw thee both young and fair; and I knew thee to be the son of a noble, worthy, guileless man and of a beauteous woman of great wits and good rede. And I found thee to be kind and open-handed and simple like thy father, and like thy mother wiser than thou thyself knew of thyself; and that thou wert desirous of deeds and fain of women.'

She was silent for a while, and he also: then he said: 'Didst thou draw me to the woods and to thee?'

She reddened and said: 'I am no spell-wife: but true it is that Wood-mother made a waxen image of thee, and thrust through the heart thereof the pin of my girdle-buckle, and stroked it every morning with an oak-bough over which she had sung spells. But dost thou not remember, Gold-mane, how that one day last Hay-month, as ye were resting in the meadows in the cool of the evening, there came to you a minstrel that played to you on the fiddle, and therewith sang a song that melted all your hearts, and that this song told of the Wild-wood, and what was therein of desire and peril and beguiling and death, and love unto Death itself? Dost thou remember, friend?'

R

The cause of
Folk-might's
onslaught.

'Yea,' he said, 'and how when the minstrel was done Stone-face fell to telling us more tales yet of the woodland, and the minstrel sang again and yet again, till his tales had entered into my very heart.'

'Yea,' she said, 'and that minstrel was Wood-wont; and I sent him to sing to thee and thine, deeming that if thou didst hearken, thou would'st seek the woodland and happen upon us?'

He laughed and said: 'Thou didst not doubt but that if we met, thou mightest do with me as thou wouldest?'

'So it is,' she said, 'that I doubted it little.'

'Therein wert thou wise,' said Face-of-god; 'but now that we are talking without guile to each other, mightest thou tell me wherefore it was that Folk-might made that onslaught upon me? For certain it is that he was minded to slay me.'

She said: 'It was sooth what I told thee, that whiles he groweth so battle-eager that whatso edge-tool he beareth must needs come out of the scabbard; but there was more in it than that, which I could not tell thee erst. Two days before thy coming he had been down to Burgstead in the guise of an old carle such as thou sawest him with me in the market-place. There was he guested in your Hall, and once more saw thee and the Bride together; and he saw the eyes of love wherewith she looked on thee (for so much he told me), and deemed that thou didst take her love but lightly. And he himself looked on her with such love (and this he told me not) that he deemed nought good enough for her, and would have had thee give thyself up wholly to her; for my brother is a generous man, my friend. So when I told him on the morn of that day whereon we met that we looked to see thee that eve (for indeed I am somewhat foreseeing), he said: "Look thou, Sun-beam, if he cometh, it is not unlike that I shall drive a spear through him." "Wherefore?" said I; "can he serve our turn when he is dead?" Said he: "I care little. Mine own turn will I serve. Thou sayest *Wherefore?* I tell thee this stripling beguileth to her torment the fairest woman that is in the

122

world—such an one as is meet to be the mother of chieftains, and to stand by warriors in their day of peril. I have seen her; and thus have I seen her." Then said I: "Greatly forsooth shalt thou pleasure her by slaying him!" And he answered: "I shall pleasure myself. And one day she shall thank me, when she taketh my hand in hers and we go together to the Bride-bed." Therewith came over me a clear foresight of the hours to come, and I said to him: "Yea, Folk-might, cast the spear and draw the sword; but him thou shalt not slay: and thou shalt one day see him standing with us before the shafts of the Dusky Men." So I spake; but he looked fiercely at me, and departed and shunned me all that day, and by good hap I was hard at hand when thou drewest nigh our abode. Nay, Gold-mane, what would'st thou with thy sword? Why art thou so red and wrathful? Would'st thou fight with my brother because he loveth thy friend, thine old playmate, thy kinswoman, and thinketh pity of her sorrow?'

He said, with knit brow and gleaming eyes: 'Would the man take her away from me perforce?'

'My friend,' she said, ' thou art not yet so wise as not to be a fool at whiles. Is it not so that she herself hath taken herself from thee, since she hath come to know that thou hast given thyself to another? Hath she noted nought of thee this winter and spring? Is she well pleased with the ways of thee?'

He said: 'Thou hast spoken simply with me, and I will do no less with thee. It was but four days agone that she did me to wit that she knew of me how I sought my love on the Mountain; and she put me to sore shame, and afterwards I wept for her sorrow.'

Therewith he told her all that the Bride had said to him, as he well might, for he had forgotten no word of it.

Then said the Friend: 'She shall have the token that she craveth, and it is I that shall give it to her.'

Therewith she took from her finger a ring wherein was set a very fair changeful mountain-stone, and gave it to him, and said:

123

'Thou shalt give her this and tell her whence thou hadst it;
and tell her that I bid her remember that To-morrow is a new day.'

## CHAPTER XX. THOSE TWO TOGETHER HOLD THE RING OF THE EARTH-GOD.

AND now they fell silent both of them, and sat hearkening
the sounds of the Dale, from the whistle of the plover
down by the water-side to the far-off voices of the children
and maidens about the kine in the lower meadows. At last Gold-
mane took up the word and said :

'Sweet friend, tell me the uttermost of what thou would'st have
of me. Is it not that I should stand by thee and thine in the Folk-
mote of the Dalesmen, and speak for you when ye pray us for
help against your foemen; and then again that I do my best when
ye and we are arrayed for battle against the Dusky Men? This
is easy to do, and great is the reward thou offerest me.'

'I look for this service of thee,' she said, 'and none other.'

'And when I go down to the battle,' said he, 'shalt thou be
sorry for our sundering?'

She said : 'There shall be no sundering; I shall wend with thee.'

Said he : 'And if I were slain in the battle, would'st thou
lament me?'

'Thou shalt not be slain,' she said.

Again was there silence betwixt them, till at last he said :

'This then is why thou didst draw me to thee in the Wild-wood?'

'Yea,' said she.

Again for a while no word was spoken, and Face-of-god looked
on her till she cast her eyes down before him.

Then at last he spake, and the colour came and went in his
face as he said : 'Tell me thy name what it is.'

She said : 'I am called the Sun-beam.'

Then he said, and his voice trembled therewith : 'O Sun-beam,
I have been seeking pleasant and cunning words, and can find

124

none such.  But tell me this if thou wilt: dost thou desire me as I desire thee? or is it that thou wilt suffer me to wed thee and bed thee at last as mere payment for the help that I shall give to thee and thine? Nay, doubt it not that I will take the payment, if this is what thou wilt give me and nought else.  Yet tell me.'

Her face grew troubled, and she said :

'Gold-mane, maybe that thou hast now asked me one question too many; for this is no fair game to be played between us.  For thee, as I deem, there are this day but two people in the world, and that is thou and I, and the earth is for us two alone.  But, my friend, though I have seen but twenty and one summers, it is nowise so with me, and to me there are many in the world; and chiefly the Folk of the Wolf, amidst whose very heart I have grown up.  Moreover, I can think of her whom I have supplanted, the Bride to wit; and I know her, and how bitter and empty her days shall be for a while, and how vain all our redes for her shall seem to her.  Yea, I know her sorrow, and see it and grieve for it: so canst not thou, unless thou verily see her before thee, her face unhappy, and her voice changed and hard.  Well, I will tell thee what thou askest.  When I drew thee to me on the Mountain I thought but of the friendship and brotherhood to be knitted up between our two Folks, nor did I anywise desire thy love of a young man.  But when I saw thee on the heath and in the Hall that day, it pleased me to think that a man so fair and chieftain-like should one day lie by my side; and again when I saw that the love of me had taken hold of thee, I would not have thee grieved because of me, but would have thee happy.  And now what shall I say?—I know not; I cannot tell.  Yet am I the Friend, as erst I called myself.

'And, Gold-mane, I have seen hitherto but the outward show and image of thee, and though that be goodly, how would it be if thou didst shame me with little-heartedness and evil deeds?  Let me see thee in the Folk-mote and the battle, and then may I answer thee.'

125

Then she held her peace, and he answered nothing ; and she
turned her face from him and said :

'Out on it ! have I beguiled myself as well as thee ? These are
but empty words I have been saying. If thou wilt drag the truth
out of me, this is the very truth : that to-day is happy to me as
it is to thee, and that I have longed sore for its coming. O Gold-
mane, O speech-friend, if thou wert to pray me or command me
that I lie in thine arms to-night, I should know not how to gainsay thee. Yet I beseech thee to forbear, lest thy death and mine
come of it. And why should we die, O friend, when we are so
young, and the world lies so fair before us, and the happy days
are at hand when the Children of the Wolf and the kindreds of
the Dale shall deliver the Folk, and all days shall be good and
all years ? '

They had both risen up as she spake, and now he put forth
his hands to her and took her in his arms, wondering the while, as
he drew her to him, how much slenderer and smaller and weaker
she seemed in his embrace than he had thought of her ; and when
their lips met, he felt that she kissed him as he her. Then he held
her by the shoulders at arms' length from him, and beheld her
face how her eyes were closed and her lips quivering. But before him, in a moment of time, passed a picture of the life to be
in the fair Dale, and all she would give him there, and the days
good and lovely from morn to eve and eve to morn; and though
in that moment it was hard for him to speak, at last he spoke in
a voice hoarse at first, and said :

' Thou sayest sooth, O friend ; we will not die, but live ; I will
not drag our deaths upon us both, nor put a sword in the hands
of Folk-might, who loves me not.'

Then he kissed her on the brow and said : ' Now shalt thou
take me by the hand and lead me forth from the Hall. For the
day is waxing old, and here meseemeth in this dim hall there
are words crossing in the air about us—words spoken in days long
ago, and tales of old time, that keep egging me on to do my will

126

and die, because that is all that the world hath for a valiant man; and to such words I would not hearken, for in this hour I have no will to die, nor can I think of death.'

They go forth from the Hall.

She took his hand and led him forth without more words, and they went hand in hand and paced slowly round the Doom-ring, the light air breathing upon them till their faces were as calm and quiet as their wont was, and hers especially as bright and happy as when he had first seen her that day.

The sun was sinking now, and only sent one golden ray into the valley through a cleft in the western rock-wall, but the sky overhead was bright and clear; from the meadows came the sound of the lowing of kine and the voices of children a-sporting, and it seemed to Gold-mane that they were drawing nigher, both the children and the kine, and somewhat he begrudged it that he should not be alone with the Friend.

Now when they had made half the circuit of the Doom-ring, the Sun-beam stopped him, and then led him through the Ring of Stones, and brought him up to the altar which was amidst of it; and the altar was a great black stone hewn smooth and clean, and with the image of the Wolf carven on the front thereof; and on its face lay the gold ring which the priest or captain of the Folk bore on his arm between the God and the people at all folk-motes.

So she said : ' This is the altar of the God of Earth, and often hath it been reddened by mighty men; and thereon lieth the Ring of the Sons of the Wolf; and now it were well that we swore troth on that ring before my brother cometh; for now will he soon be here.'

Then Gold-mane took the Ring and thrust his right hand through it, and took her right hand in his; so that the Ring lay on both their hands, and therewith he spake aloud :

' I am Face-of-god of the House of the Face, and I do thee to wit, O God of the Earth, that I pledge my troth to this woman, the Sun-beam of the Kindred of the Wolf, to beget my offspring

127

on her, and to live with her, and to die with her : so help me,
thou God of the Earth, and the Warrior and the God of the
Face!'

Then spake the Sun-beam : 'I, the Sun-beam of the Children
of the Wolf, pledge my troth to Face-of-god to lie in his bed and
to bear his children and none other's, and to be his speech-friend
till I die : so help me the Wolf and the Warrior and the God
of the Earth!'

Then they laid the Ring on the altar again, and they kissed each
other long and sweetly, and then turned away from the altar and
departed from the Doom-ring, going hand in hand together down
the meadow, and as they went, the noise of the kine and the children grew nearer and nearer, and presently came the whole company of them round a ness of the rock-wall ; there were some
thirty little lads and lasses driving on the milch-kine, with half
a score of older maids and grown women, one of whom was Bow-
may, who was lightly and scantily clad, as one who heeds not
the weather, or deems all months midsummer.

The children came running up merrily when they saw the
Sun-beam, but stopped short shyly when they noted the tall fair
stranger with her. They were all strong and sturdy children, and
some very fair, but brown with the weather, if not with the sun.
Bow-may came up to Gold-mane and took his hand and greeted
him kindly and said :

'So here thou art at last in Shadowy Vale ; and I hope that
thou art content therewith, and as happy as I would wish thee to
be. Well, this is the first time ; and when thou comest the second
time it may well be that the world shall be growing better.'

She held the distaff which she bore in her hand (for she had
been spinning) as if it were a spear ; her limbs were goodly and
shapely, and she trod the thick grass of the Vale with a kind of
wary firmness, as though foemen might be lurking nearby. The
Sun-beam smiled upon her kindly and said :

'That shall not fail to be, Bow-may : ye have won a new friend

128

to-day. But tell me, when dost thou look to see the men here, for I was down by the water when they went away yesterday?'

'They shall come into the Dale a little after sunset,' said Bow-may.

'Shall I abide them, my friend?' said Gold-mane, turning to the Sun-beam.

'Yea,' she said; 'for what else art thou come hither? or art thou so pressed to depart from us? Last time we met thou wert not so hasty to sunder.'

They smiled on each other; and Bow-may looked on them and laughed outright; then a flush showed in her cheeks through the tan of them, and she turned toward the children and the other women who were busied about the milking of the kine.

But those two sat down together on a bank amidst the plain meadow, facing the river and the eastern rock-wall, and the Sun-beam said:

'I am fain to speak to thee and to see thine eyes watching me while I speak; and now, my friend, I will tell thee something unasked which has to do with what e'en now thou didst ask me; for I would have thee trust me wholly, and know me for what I am. Time was I schemed and planned for this day of betrothal; but now I tell thee it has become no longer needful for bringing to pass our fellowship in arms with thy people. Yea yesterday, ere he went on a hunt, whereof he shall tell thee, Folk-might was against it, in words at least; and yet as one who would have it done if he might have no part in it. So, in good sooth, this hand that lieth in thine is the hand of a wilful woman, who desireth a man, and would keep him for her speech-friend. Now art thou fond and happy; yet bear in mind that there are deeds to be done, and the troth we have just plighted must be paid for. So hearken, I bid thee. Dost thou care to know why the wheedling of thee is no longer needful to us?'

He said: 'A little while ago I should have said, Yea, if thy lips say the words. But now, O friend, it seemeth as if thine

129    S

heart were already become a part of mine, and I feel as if the chieftain were growing up in me and the longing for deeds: so I say, Tell me, for I were fain to hear what toucheth the welfare of thy Folk and their fellowship with my Folk; for on that also have I set my heart?'

She said gravely and with solemn eyes:

'What thou sayest is good: full glad am I that I have not plighted my troth to a mere goodly lad, but rather to a chieftain and a warrior. Now then hearken! Since I saw thee first in the autumn this hath happened, that the Dusky Men, increasing both in numbers and insolence, have it in their hearts to win more than Silver-dale, and it is years since they have fallen upon Rose-dale and conquered it, rather by murder than by battle, and made all men thralls there, for feeble were the Folk thereof; and doubt it not but that they will look into Burgdale before long. They are already abroad in the woods, and were it not for the fear of the Wolf they would be thicker therein, and faring wider; for we have slain many of them, coming upon them unawares; and they know not where we dwell, nor who we be: so they fear to spread about over-much and pry into unknown places lest the Wolf howl on them. Yet beware! for they will gather in numbers that we may not meet, and then will they swarm into the Dale; and if ye would live your happy life that ye love so well, ye must now fight for it; and in that battle must ye needs join yourselves to us, that we may help each other. Herein have ye nought to choose, for now with you it is no longer a thing to talk of whether ye will help certain strangers and guests and thereby win some gain to yourselves, but whether ye have the hearts to fight for yourselves, and the wits to be the fellows of tall men and stout warriors who have pledged their lives to win or die for it.'

She was silent a little and then turned and looked fondly on Face-of-god and said:

'Therefore, Gold-mane, we need thee no longer; for thou must needs fight in our battle. I have no longer aught to do to wheedle

130

thee to love me. Yet if thou wilt love me, then am I a glad
woman.'

He said: 'Thou wottest well that thou hast all my love, neither
will I fail thee in the battle. I am not little-hearted, though I
would have given myself to thee for no reward.'

'It is well,' said the Sun-beam; 'nought is undone by that
which I have done. Moreover, it is good that we have plighted
troth to-day. For Folk-might will presently hear thereof, and he
must needs abide the thing which is done. Hearken! he cometh.'

For as she spoke there came a glad cry from the women and
children, and those two stood up and turned toward the west
and beheld the warriors of the Wolf coming down into the Dale
by the way that Gold-mane had come.

'Come,' said the Sun-beam, 'here are your brethren in arms,
let us go greet them; they will rejoice in thee.'

So they went thither, and there stood eighty and seven men on
the grass below the scree and Folk-might their captain; and besides some valiant women, and a few carles who were on watch
on the waste, and a half score who had been left in the Dale, these
were all the warriors of the Wolf. They were clad in no holiday
raiment, not even Folk-might, but were in sheep-brown gear of
the coarsest, like to husbandmen late come from the plough, but
armed well and goodly.

But when the twain drew near, the men clashed their spears on
their shields, and cried out for joy of them, for they all knew what
Face-of-god's presence there betokened of fellowship with the kindreds; but Folk-might came forward and took Face-of-god's hand
and greeted him and said:

'Hail, son of the Alderman! Here hast thou come into the
ancient abode of chieftains and warriors, and belike deeds await
thee also.'

Yet his brow was knitted as he said these words, and he spake
slowly, as one that constraineth himself; but presently his face
cleared somewhat and he said:

131

'Dalesman, it behoveth thy people to bestir them if ye would live and see good days. Hath my sister told thee what is toward? Or what sayest thou?'

'Hail to thee, son of the Wolf!' said Face-of-god. 'Thy sister hath told me all; and even if these Dusky Felons were not our foe-men also, yet could I have my way, we should have given thee all help, and should have brought back peace and good days to thy folk.'

Then Folk-might flushed red and spake, as he cast out his hand towards the warriors and up and down toward the Dale :

'These be my folk, and these only : and as to peace, only those of us know of it who are old men. Yet is it well ; and if we and ye together be strong enough to bring back good days to the feeble men whom the Dusky Ones torment in Silver-dale it shall be better yet.'

Then he turned about to his sister, and looked keenly into her eyes till she reddened, and took her hand and looked at the wrist and said :

'O sister, see I not the mark on thy wrist of the Ring of the God of the Earth? Have not oaths been sworn since yesterday?'

'True it is,' she said, 'that this man and I have plighted troth together at the altar of the Doom-ring.'

Said Folk-might : 'Thou wilt have thy will, and I may not amend it.' Therewith he turned about to Face-of-god and said :

'Thou must look to it to keep this oath, whatever other one thou hast failed in.'

Said Face-of-god somewhat wrathfully : 'I shall keep it, whether thou biddest me to keep it or break it.'

'That is well,' said Folk-might, 'and then for all that hath gone before thou mayest in a manner pay, if thou art dauntless before the foe.'

'I look to be no blencher in the battle,' said Face-of-god ; 'that is not the fashion of our kindred, whosoever may be before us. Yea, and even were it thy blade, O mighty warrior of the Wolf, I would do my best to meet it in manly fashion.'

132

As he spake he half drew forth Dale-warden from his sheath, looking steadily into the eyes of Folk-might; and the Sun-beam looked upon him happily. But Folk-might laughed and said :

'Thy sword is good, and I deem that thine heart will not fail thee; but it is by my side and not in face of me that thou shalt redden the good blade : I see not the day when we twain shall hew at each other.'

Then in a while he spake again :

'Thou must pardon us if our words are rough ; for we have stood in rough places, where we had to speak both short and loud, whereas there was much to do. But now will we twain talk of matters that concern chieftains who are going on a hard adventure. And ye women, do ye dight the Hall for the evening feast, which shall be the feast of the troth-plight for you twain. This indeed we owe thee, O guest ; for little shall be thine heritage which thou shalt have with my sister, over and above that thy sword winneth for thee.'

But the Sun-beam said : 'Hast thou any to-night?'

'Yea,' he said ; 'Spear-god, how many was it?'

There came forward a tall man bearing an axe in his right hand, and carrying over his shoulder by his left hand a bundle of silver arm-rings just such as Gold-mane had seen on the felons who were slain by Wood-grey's house. The carle cast them on the ground and then knelt down and fell to telling them over ; and then looked up and said : 'Twelve yesterday in the wood where the battle was going on ; and this morning seven by the tarn in the pine-wood and six near this eastern edge of the wood : one score and five all told. But, Folk-might, they are coming nigh to Shadowy Vale.'

'Sooth is that,' said Folk-might ; 'but it shall be looked to. Come now apart with me, Face-of-god.'

So the others went their ways toward the Hall, while Folk-might led the Burgdaler to a sheltered nook under the sheer rocks, and there they sat down to talk, and Folk-might asked

Gold-mane closely of the muster of the Dalesmen and the Shepherds and the Woodland Carles, and he was well pleased when Face-of-god told him of how many could march to a stricken field, and of their archery, and of their weapons and their goodness.

All this took some time in the telling, and now night was coming on apace, and Folk-might said :

'Now will it be time to go to the Hall ; but keep in thy mind that these Dusky Men will overrun you unless ye deal with them betimes. These are of the kind that ye must cast fear into their hearts by falling on them ; for if ye abide till they fall upon you, they are like the winter wolves that swarm on and on, how many soever ye slay. And this above all things shall help you, that we shall bring you whereas ye shall fall on them unawares and destroy them as boys do with a wasp's nest. Yet shall many a mother's son bite the dust.

'Is it not so that in four weeks' time is your spring-feast and market at Burgstead, and thereafter the great Folk-mote ? '

'So it is,' said Gold-mane.

'Thither shall I come then,' said Folk-might, 'and give myself out for the slayer of Rusty and the ransacker of Harts-bane and Penny-thumb ; and therefor shall I offer good blood-wite and theft-wite ; and thy father shall take that ; for he is a just man. Then shall I tell my tale. Yet it may be thou shalt see us before if battle betide. And now fair befall this new year ; for soon shall the scabbards be empty and the white swords be dancing in the air, and spears and axes shall be the growth of this spring-tide.'

And he leaped up from his seat and walked to and fro before Gold-mane, and now was it grown quite dark. Then Folk-might turned to Face-of-god and said :

'Come, guest, the windows of the Hall are yellow ; let us to the feast. To-morrow shalt thou get thee to the beginning of this work. I hope of thee that thou art a good sword ; else have I

134

done a folly and my sister a worse one.  But now forget that, They go into the Hall. and feast.'

Gold-mane arose, not very well at ease, for the man seemed overbearing; yet how might he fall upon the Sun-beam's kindred, and the captain of these new brethren in arms? So he spake not. But Folk-might said to him:

'Yet I would not have thee forget that I was wroth with thee when I saw thee to-day; and had it not been for the coming battle I had drawn sword upon thee.'

Then Face-of-god's wrath was stirred, and he said:

'There is yet time for that! but why art thou wroth with me? And I shall tell thee that there is little manliness in thy chiding. For how may I fight with thee, thou the brother of my plighted speech-friend and my captain in this battle?'

'Therein thou sayest sooth,' said Folk-might; 'but hard it was to see you two standing together; and thou canst not give the Bride to me as I give my sister to thee. For I have seen her, and I have seen her looking at thee; and I know that she will not have it so.'

Then they went on together toward the Hall, and Face-of-god was silent and somewhat troubled; and as they drew near to the Hall, Folk-might spake again:

'Yet time may amend it; and if not, there is the battle, and maybe the end.  Now be we merry!'

So they went into the Hall together, and there was the Sun-beam gloriously arrayed, as erst in the woodland bower, and Face-of-god sat on the daïs beside her, and the uttermost sweetness of desire entered into his soul as he noted her eyes and her mouth, that were grown so kind to him, and her hand that strayed toward his.

The Hall was full of folk, and all those warriors were there with Wood-father and his sons, and Wood-mother, and Bow-may and many other women; and Gold-mane looked down the Hall and deemed that he had never seen such stalwarth bodies of men, or

135

so bold and meet for battle: as for the women he had seen fairer
in Burgdale, but these were fair of their own fashion, shapely and
well-knit, and strong-armed and large-limbed, yet sweet-voiced
and gentle withal. Nay, the very lads of fifteen winters or so,
whereof a few were there, seemed bold and bright-eyed and keen
of wit, and it seemed like that if the warriors fared afield these
would be with them.

So wore the feast; and Folk-might as aforetime amongst the
healths called on men to drink to the Jaws of the Wolf, and the
Red Hand, and the Silver Arm, and the Golden Bushel, and the
Ragged Sword. But now had Face-of-god no need to ask what
these meant, since he knew that they were the names of the kindreds of the Wolf. They drank also to the troth-plight and to
those twain, and shouted aloud over the health and clashed their
weapons: and Gold-mane wondered what echo of that shout
would reach to Burgstead.

Then sang men songs of old time, and amongst them Wood-
wont stood with his fiddle amidst the Hall and Bow-may beside
him, and they sang in turn to it sweetly and clearly; and this is
some of what they sang:

*She singeth.*
Wild is the waste and long leagues over;
  Whither then wend ye spear and sword,
Where nought shall see your helms but the plover,
  Far and far from the dear Dale's sward?

*He singeth.*
Many a league shall we wend together
  With helm and spear and bended bow.
Hark! how the wind blows up for weather:
  Dark shall the night be whither we go.

Dark shall the night be round the byre,
  And dark as we drive the brindled kine;

136

Dark and dark round the beacon-fire,
  Dark down in the pass round our wavering line.

Turn on thy path, O fair-foot maiden,
  And come our ways by the pathless road;
Look how the clouds hang low and laden
  Over the walls of the old abode!

### She singeth.
Bare are my feet for the rough waste's wending,
  Wild is the wind, and my kirtle's thin;
Faint shall I be ere the long way's ending
  Drops down to the Dale and the grief therein.

### He singeth.
Do on the brogues of the wild-wood rover,
  Do on the byrnies' ring-close mail;
Take thou the staff that the barbs hang over,
  O'er the wind and the waste and the way to prevail.

Come, for how from thee shall I sunder?
  Come, that a tale may arise in the land;
Come, that the night may be held for a wonder,
  When the Wolf was led by a maiden's hand!

### She singeth.
Now will I fare as ye are faring,
  And wend no way but the way ye wend;
And bear but the burdens ye are bearing,
  And end the day as ye shall end.

And many an eve when the clouds are drifting
  Down through the Dale till they dim the roof,
Shall they tell in the Hall of the Maiden's Lifting,
  And how we drave the spoil aloof.

*They sing together.*

Over the moss through the wind and the weather,
   Through the morn and the eve and the death of the day,
Wend we man and maid together,
   For out of the waste is born the fray.

Then the Sun-beam spake to Gold-mane softly, and told him how this song was made by a minstrel concerning a foray in the early days of their first abode in Shadowy Vale, and how in good sooth a maiden led the fray and was the captain of the warriors :

'Erst,' she said, 'this was counted as a wonder ; but now we are so few that it is no wonder though the women will do whatsoever they may.'

So they talked, and Gold-mane was very happy ; but ere the good-night cup was drunk, Folk-might spake to Face-of-god and said :

'It were well that ye rose betimes in the morning : but thou shalt not go back by the way thou camest. Wood-wise and another shall go with thee, and show thee a way across the necks and the heaths, which is rough enough as far as toil goes, but where thy life shall be safer ; and thereby shalt thou hit the ghyll of the Weltering Water, and so come down safely into Burgdale. Now that we are friends and fellows, it is no hurt for thee to know the shortest way to Shadowy Vale. What thou shalt tell concerning us in Burgdale I leave the tale thereof to thee ; yet belike thou wilt not tell everything till I come to Burgstead at the spring market-tide. Now must I presently to bed ; for before daylight to-morrow must I be following the hunt along with two score good men of ours.'

'What beast is afield then ?' said Gold-mane.

Said Folk-might : 'The beasts that beset our lives, the Dusky Men. In these days we have learned how to find companies of them ; and forsooth every week they draw nigher to this Dale ; and some day they should happen upon us if we were not to look

138

to it, and then would there be a murder great and grim; therefore we scour the heaths round about, and the skirts of the woodland, and we fall upon these felons in divers guises, so that they
may not know us for the same men; whiles are we clad in home-
spun, as to-day, and seem like to field-working carles; whiles in
scarlet and gold, like knights of the Westland; whiles in wolf-
skins; whiles in white glittering gear, like the Wights of the
Waste : and in all guises these felons, for all their fierce hearts,
fear us, and flee from us, and we follow and slay them, and so
minish their numbers somewhat against the great day of battle.'

'Tell me,' said Gold-mane; 'when we fall upon Silver-dale
shall their thralls, the old Dale-dwellers, fight for them or for us ?'

Said Folk-might : 'The Dusky Men will not dare to put weapons into the hands of their thralls. Nay, the thralls shall help
us; for though they have but small stomach for the fight, yet joyfully when the fight is over shall they cut their masters' throats.'

'How is it with these thralls ?' said Gold-mane. 'I have never
seen a thrall.'

'But I,' said Folk-might, 'have seen a many down in the Cities.
And there were thralls who were the tyrants of thralls, and held
the whip over them; and of the others there were some who were
not very hardly entreated. But with these it is otherwise, and they
all bear grievous pains daily; for the Dusky Men are as hogs in
a garden of lilies. Whatsoever is fair there have they defiled and
deflowered, and they wallow in our fair halls as swine strayed from
the dunghill. No delight in life, no sweet days do they have for
themselves, and they begrudge the delight of others therein.
Therefore their thralls know no rest or solace; their reward of
toil is many stripes, and the healing of their stripes grievous toil.
To many have they appointed to dig and mine in the silver-yield-
ing cliffs, and of all the tasks is that the sorest, and there do stripes
abound the most. Such thralls art thou happy not to behold till
thou hast set them free; as we shall do.'

'Tell me again,' said Face-of-god; 'is there no mixed folk

between these Dusky Men and the Dalesmen, since they have no women of their own, but lie with the women of the Dale? Moreover, do not the poor folk of the Dale beget and bear children, so that there are thralls born of thralls?'

'Wisely thou askest this,' said Folk-might, 'but thereof shall I tell thee, that when a Dusky Carle mingles with a woman of the Dale, the child which she beareth shall oftenest favour his race and not hers; or else shall it be witless, a fool natural. But as for the children of these poor thralls; yea, the masters cause them to breed if so their masterships will, and when the children are born, they keep them or slay them as they will, as they would with whelps or calves. To be short, year by year these vile wretches grow fiercer and more beastly, and their thralls more hapless and down-trodden; and now at last is come the time either to do or to die, as ye men of Burgdale shall speedily find out. But now must I go sleep if I am to be where I look to be at sunrise to-morrow.'

Therewith he called for the sleeping-cup, and it was drunk, and all men fared to bed. But the Sun-beam took Gold-mane's hand ere they parted, and said:

'I shall arise betimes on the morrow; so I say not farewell to-night; yea, and after to-morrow it shall not be long ere we meet again.'

So Gold-mane lay down in that ancient hall, and it seemed to him ere he slept as if his own kindred were slipping away from him and he were becoming a child of the Wolf. 'And yet,' said he to himself, 'I am become a man; for my Friend, now she no longer telleth me to do or forbear, and I tremble. Nay, rather she is fain to take the word from me; and this great warrior and ripe man, he talketh with me as if I were a chieftain meet for converse with chieftains. Even so it is and shall be.'

And soon thereafter he fell asleep in the Hall in Shadowy Vale.

## CHAPTER XXI.  FACE-OF-GOD LOOKETH ON THE DUSKY MEN.

Morning and departure come.

WHEN he awoke again he saw a man standing over him, and knew him for Wood-wise: he was clad in his war-gear, and had his quiver at his back and his bow in his hand, for Wood-father's children were all good bowmen, though not so sure as Bow-may. He spake to Face-of-god:

'Dawn is in the sky, Dalesman; there is yet time for thee to wash the night off of thee in our bath of the Shivering Flood and to put thy mouth to the milk-bowl; but time for nought else: for I and Bow-may are appointed thy fellows for the road, and it were well that we were back home speedily.'

So Face-of-god leapt up and went forth from the Hall, and Wood-wise led to where was a pool in the river with steps cut down to it in the rocky bank.

'This,' said Wood-wise, 'is the Carle's Bath; but the Queen's is lower down, where the water is wider and shallower below the little mid-dale force.'

So Gold-mane stripped off his raiment and leapt into the ice-cold pool; and they had brought his weapons and war-gear with them; so when he came out he clad and armed himself for the road, and then turned with Wood-wise toward the outgate of the Dale; and soon they saw two men coming from lower down the water in such wise that they would presently cross their path, and as yet it was little more than twilight, so that they saw not at first who they were, but as they drew nearer they knew them for the Sun-beam and Bow-may. The Sun-beam was clad but in her white linen smock and blue gown as he had first seen her; her hair was wet and dripping with the river, her face fresh and rosy: she carried in her two hands a great bowl of milk, and stepped delicately, lest she should spill it. But Bow-may was clad in her war-gear with helm and byrny, and a quiver at her back, and a bended bow in her hand. So they greeted

each other kindly, and the Sun-beam gave the bowl to Face-of-
god and said :

'Drink, guest, for thou hast a long and thirsty road before thee.'

So Face-of-god drank, and gave her the bowl back again, and
she smiled on him and drank, and the others after her till the bowl
was empty: then Bow-may put her hand on Wood-wise's shoulder,
and they led on toward the outgate, while those twain followed
them hand in hand. But the Sun-beam said :

'This then is the new day I spoke of, and lo! it bringeth
our sundering with it ; yet shall it be no longer than a day when
all is said, and new days shall follow after. And now, my friend,
I shall see thee no later than the April market ; for doubt not
that I shall go thither with Folk-might, whether he will or not.
Also as I led thee out of the house when we last met, so shall I
lead thee out of the Dale to-day, and I will go with thee a little
way on the waste ; and therefore am I shod this morning, as thou
seest, for the ways on the waste are rough. And now I bid thee
have courage while my hand holdeth thine. For afterwards I need
not bid thee anything; for thou wilt have enough to do when thou
comest to thy Folk, and must needs think more of warriors then
than of maidens.'

He looked at her and longed for her, but said soberly : 'Thou
art kind, O friend, and thinkest kindly of me ever. But methinks it were not well done for thee to wend with me over a deal
of the waste, and come back by thyself alone, when ye have so
many foemen nearby.'

'Nay,' she said, 'they be nought so near as that yet, and I
wot that Folk-might hath gone forth toward the north-west, where
he looketh to fall in with a company of the foemen. His battle
shall be a guard unto us.'

'I pray thee turn back at the top of the outgate,' said he, 'and
be not venturesome. Thou wottest that the pitcher is not broken
the first time it goeth to the well, nor maybe the twentieth, but
at last it cometh not back.'

She said : 'Nevertheless I shall have my will herein.   And it
is but a little way I will wend with thee.'

Therewith were they come to the scree, and talk fell down between them as they clomb it ; but when they were in the darksome passage of the rocks, and could scarce see one another, Face-of-god said :

'Where then is another outgate from the Dale ?   Is it not up the water ?'

'Yea,' she said, 'and there is none other : at the lower end the rocks rise sheer from out the water, and a little further down is a great force thundering betwixt them ; so that by no boat or raft may ye come out of the Dale.   But the outgate up the water is called the Road of War, as this is named the Path of Peace. But now are all ways ways of war.'

'There is peace in my heart,' said Gold-mane.

She answered not for a while, but pressed his hand, and he felt her breath on his cheek ; and even therewithal they came out of the dark, and Gold-mane saw that her cheek was flushed ; and now she spake :

'One thing would I say to thee, my friend. Thou hast seen me amongst men of war, amongst outlaws who seek violence ; thou hast heard me bid my brother to count the slain, and I shrinking not ; thou knowest (for I have told thee) how I have schemed and schemed for victorious battle.   Yet I would not have thee think of me as a Chooser of the Slain, a warrior maiden, or as of one who hath no joy save in the battle whereto she biddeth others. O friend, the many peaceful hours that I have had on the grass down yonder, sitting with my rock and spindle in hand, the children round about my knees hearkening to some old story so well remembered by me ! or the milking of the kine in the dewy summer even, when all was still but for the voice of the water and the cries of the happy children, and there round about me were the dear and beauteous maidens with whom I had grown up, happy amidst all our troubles, since their life was free and

143

Face-of-god
telleth of the
peace of
Burgdale.

they knew no guile. In such times my heart was at peace indeed, and it seemed to me as if we had won all we needed ; as if war and turmoil were over, after they had brought about peace and good days for our little folk.

'And as for the days that be, are they not as that rugged pass, full of bitter winds and the voice of hurrying waters, that leadeth yonder to Silver-dale, as thou hast divined ? and there is nought good in it save that the breath of life is therein, and that it leadeth to pleasant places and the peace and plenty of the fair dale.'

'Sweet friend,' he said, 'what thou sayest is better than well : for time shall be, if we come alive out of this pass of battle and bitter strife, when I shall lead thee into Burgdale to dwell there. And thou wottest of our people that there is little strife and grudging amongst them, and that they are merry, and fair to look on, both men and women ; and no man there lacketh what the earth may give us, and it is a saying amongst us that there may a man have that which he desireth save the sun and moon in his hands to play with : and of this gladness, which is made up of many little matters, what story may be told ? Yet amongst it shall I live and thou with me ; and ill indeed it were if it wearied thee and thou wert ever longing for some day of victorious strife, and to behold me coming back from battle high-raised on the shields of men and crowned with bay; if thine ears must ever be tickled with the talk of men and their songs concerning my warrior deeds. For thus it shall not be. When I drive the herds it shall be at the neighbours' bidding whereso they will ; not necks of men shall I smite, but the stalks of the tall wheat, and the boles of the timber-trees which the woodreeve hath marked for felling ; the stilts of the plough rather than the hilts of the sword shall harden my hands ; my shafts shall be for the deer, and my spears for the wood-boar, till war and sorrow fall upon us, and I fight for the ceasing of war and trouble. And though I be called a chief and of the blood of chiefs, yet shall I not be masterful to the goodman of the Dale, but rather to my hound ; for my chieftainship shall be that I shall be well beloved and trusted, and that no man shall grudge against me. Canst thou learn to love such a life, which to me seemeth lovely? And thou? of whom I say that thou art as if thou wert come down from the golden chairs of the Burg of the Gods.'

They were well-nigh out of the steep path by now, and the daylight was bright about them ; there she stayed her feet a moment and turned to him and said :

'All this should I love even now, if the grief of our Folk were but healed, and hereafter shall I learn yet more of thy well-beloved face.'

Therewith she laid her face to his and kissed him fondly, and put his hand to her side and held it there, saying : ' Soon shall we be one in body and in soul.'

And he laughed with joy and pride of life, and took her hand and led her on again, and said :

'Yet feel the cold rings of my hauberk, my friend ; look at the spears that cumber my hand, and at Dale-warden hanging by my side. Thou shalt yet see me as the Slain's Chooser would see her speech-friend ; for there is much to do ere we win wheat-harvest in Burgdale.'

Therewith they stepped together on to the level ground of the waste, and saw Bow-may sitting on a stone hard by, and Wood-wise standing beside her bending his bow. Bow-may smiled on Gold-mane and rose up, and they all went on together, turning so that they went nearly alongside the wall of the Vale, but westering a little ; then the Sun-beam said :

'Many a time have I trodden this heath alongside our rock-wall ; for if ye wend a little further as our faces are turned, ye come to the crags over the place where the Shivering Flood goeth out of Shadowy Vale. There when ye have clomb a little may'st thou stand on the edge of the rock-wall, and look down and be-hold the Flood swirling and eddying in the black gorge of the rocks, and see presently the reek of the force go up, and hear the

U

thunder of the waters as they pour over it : and all this about us
now is as the garden of our house—is it not so, Bow-may ? '

'Yea,' said she, 'and there are goodly cluster-berries to be
gotten hereabout in the autumn ; many a time have the Sun-
beam and I reddened our lips with them.  Yet is it best to be
wary when war is abroad and hot withal.'

'Yea,' said the Sun-beam, 'and all this place comes into the
story of our House : lo! Gold-mane, two score paces before us a
little on our right hand those five grey stones.  They are called
the Rocks of the Elders : for there in the first days of our abiding
in Shadowy Vale the Elders were wont to come together to talk
privily upon our matters.'

Face-of-god looked thither as she spoke, but therewith saw
Bow-may, who went on the left hand of the Sun-beam, as Face-
of-god on her right hand, notch a shaft on her bent bow, and
Wood-wise, who was on his right hand, saw it also and did the
like, and therewithal Face-of-god got his target on to his arm,
and even as he did so Bow-may cried out suddenly :

'Yea, yea ! Cast thyself on to the ground, Sun-beam ! Gold-
mane, targe and spear, targe and spear ! For I see steel gleaming
yonder out from behind the Elders' Rocks.'

Scarce were the words out of her mouth ere three shafts came
flying, and the bow-strings twanged.  Gold-mane felt that one
smote his helm and glanced from it.  Therewithal he saw the Sun-
beam fall to earth, though he knew not if she had but cast herself
down as Bow-may bade.  Bow-may's string twanged at once, and
a yell came from the foemen : but Wood-wise loosed not, but
set his hand to his mouth and gave a loud wild cry—Ha ! ha !
ha ! ha !  How-ow-ow !—ending in a long and exceeding great
whoop like nought but the wolf's howl. Now Gold-mane thinking
swiftly, in a moment of time, as war-meet men do, judged that
if the Sun-beam were hurt (and she had made no cry), it were
yet wiser to fall on the foe before turning to tend her, or else all
might be lost ; so he rushed forward spear in hand and target on

arm, and saw, as he opened up the flank of the Elders' Rocks, six
men, whereof one leaned aback on the rock with Bow-may's shaft
in his shoulder, and two others were just in act of loosing at him.
In a moment, as he rushed at them, one shaft went whistling by
him, and the other glanced from off his target ; he cast a spear
as he bounded on, and saw it smite one of the shooters full in the
naked face, and saw the blood spout out and change his face and
the man roll over, and then in another moment four men were
hewing at him with their short steel axes. He thrust out his
target against them, and then let the weight of his body come on
his other spear, and drave it through the second shooter's throat,
and even therewith was smitten on the helm so hard that, though
the Alderman's work held out, he fell to his knees, holding his
target over his head and striving to draw forth Dale-warden; in
that nick of time a shaft whistled close by his ear, and as he
rose to his feet again he saw his foeman rolling over and over,
clutching at the ling with both hands. Then rang out again the
terrible wolf-whoop from Wood-wise's mouth, and both he and
Bow-may loosed a shaft, for the two other foes had turned their
backs and were fleeing fast. Again Bow-may hit the clout, and
the Dusky Man fell dead at once, but Wood-wise's arrow flew
over the felon's shoulder as he ran. Then in a trice was Gold-
mane bounding after him like the hare just roused from her form ;
for it came into his head that these felons had beheld them coming
up out of the Vale, and that if even this one man escaped, he
would bring his company down upon the Vale-dwellers.

Strong and light-foot as any was Face-of-god, and though he
was cumbered with his hauberk, yet was Iron-face's handiwork
far lighter than the war-coat of the Dusky Man, and the race
was soon over. The felon turned breathless to meet Gold-mane,
who drave his target against him and cast him to earth, and as
he strove to rise smote off his head at one stroke; for Dale-
warden was a good sword and the Dalesman as fierce of mood
as might be. There he let the felon lie, and, turning, walked

147

back swiftly toward the Elders' Rocks, and found there Wood-
wise and the dead foemen, for the carle had slain the wounded,
and he was now drawing the silver arm-rings off the slain men;
for all these Dusky Felons bore silver arm-rings. But Bow-may
was walking towards the Sun-beam, and thitherward followed
Gold-mane speedily.

He found her sitting on a tussock of grass close by where she
had fallen, her face pale, her eyes eager and gleaming; she looked
up at him as he drew nigher and said:

'Friend, art thou hurt?'

'Nay,' he said, 'and thou? Thou art pale.'

'I am not hurt,' she said. Then she smiled and said again:
'Did I not tell thee that I am no warrior like Bow-may here?
Such deeds make maidens pale.'

Said Bow-may: 'If ye will have the truth, Gold-mane, she is
not wont to grow pale when battle is nigh her. Look you, she
hath had the gift of a new delight, and findeth it sweeter and
softer than she had any thought of; and now hath she feared lest
it should be taken from her.'

'Bow-may saith but the sooth,' said the Sun-beam simply,
'and kind it is of her to say it. I saw thee, Bow-may, and good
was thy shooting, and I love thee for it.'

Said Bow-may: 'I never shoot otherwise than well. But
those idle shooters of the Dusky Ones, whereabouts nigh to thee
went their shafts?'

Said the Sun-beam: 'One just lifted the hair by my left ear, and
that was not so ill-aimed; as for the other, it pierced my raiment
by my right knee, and pinned me to the earth, so that I tottered
and fell, and my gown and smock are grievously wounded, both
of them.'

And she took the folds of the garments in her hands to show
the rents therein; and her colour was come again, and she was glad.

'What were best to do now?' she said.

Said Face-of-god: 'Let us tarry a little; for some of thy

148

carles shall surely come up from the Vale: because they will have heard Wood-wise's whoop, since the wind sets that way.'

'Yea, they will come,' said the Sun-beam.

'Good is that,' said Face-of-god; 'for they shall take the dead felons and cast them where they be not seen if perchance any more stray hereby. For if they wind them, they may well happen on the path down to the Vale. Also, my friend, it were well if thou wert to bid a good few of the carles that are in the Vale to keep watch and ward about here, lest there be more foemen wandering about the waste.'

She said: 'Thou art wise in war, Gold-mane; I will do as thou biddest me. But soothly this is a perilous thing that the Dusky Men are gotten so close to the Vale.'

Said Face-of-god: 'This will Folk-might look to when he cometh home; and it is most like that he will deem it good to fall on them somewhere a good way aloof, so as to draw them off from wandering over the waste. Also I will do my best to busy them when I am home in Burgdale.'

Therewith came up Wood-wise, and fell to talk with them; and his mind it was that these foemen were but a band of strayers, and had had no inkling of Shadowy Vale till they had heard them talking together as they came up the path from the Vale, and that then they had made that ambush behind the Elders' Rocks, so that they might slay the men, and then bear off the woman. He said withal that it would be best to carry their corpses further on, so that they might be cast over the cliffs into the fierce stream of the Shivering Flood.

Amidst this talk came up men from the Vale, a score of them, well armed; and they ran to meet the wayfarers; and when they heard what had befallen, they rejoiced exceedingly, and were above all glad that Face-of-god had shown himself doughty and deft; and they deemed his rede wise, to set a watch thereabouts till Folk-might came home, and said that they would do even so.

Then spake the Sun-beam and said:

' Now must ye wayfarers depart ; for the road is but rough,
and the day not over-long.'

Then she turned to Face-of-god and put her hand on his
shoulder, and brought her face close to his and spake to him softly :
' Doth this second parting seem at all strange to thee, and that I
am now so familiar to thee, I whom thou didst once deem to be
a very goddess ?   And now thou hast seen me redden before thine
eyes because of thee ;  and thou hast seen me grow pale with fear
because of thee ;  and thou hast felt my caresses which I might
not refrain ;  even as if I were altogether such a maiden as ye
warriors hang about for a nine days' wonder, and then all is over
save an aching heart—wilt thou do so with me ?   Tell me, have
I not belittled myself before thee as if I asked thee to scorn me ?
For thus desire dealeth both with maid and man.'

He said : ' In all this there is but one thing for me to say, and
that is that I love thee ; and surely none the less, but rather the
more, because thou lovest me, and art of my kind, and mayest
share in my deeds and think well of them.   Now is my heart
full of joy, and one thing only weigheth on it ; and that is that
my kinswoman the Bride begrudgeth our love together.   For
this is the thing that of all things most misliketh me, that any
should bear a grudge against me.'

She said : ' Forget not the token, and my message to her.'

' I will not forget it,' said he.   ' And now I bid thee to kiss
me even before all these that are looking on ; for there is nought
to belittle us therein, since we be troth-plight.'

And indeed those folk stood all round about them gazing on
them, but a little aloof, that they might not hear their words if
they were minded to talk privily.   For they had long loved the
Sun-beam, and now the love of Face-of-god had begun to spring
up in their hearts.

So the twain embraced and kissed one another, and made no
haste thereover ; and those men deemed that but meet and right,
and clashed their weapons on their shields in token of their joy.

Then Face-of-god turned about and strode out of the ring of men, with Bow-may and Wood-wise beside him, and they went on their journey over the necks towards Burgstead. But the Sun-beam turned slowly from that place toward the Vale, and two of the stoutest carles went along with her to guard her from harm, and she went down into the Vale pondering all these things in her heart.

Then the other carles dragged off the corpses of the Dusky Men till they had brought them to the sheer rocks above the Shivering Flood, and there they tossed them over into the boiling caldron of the force, and so departed taking with them the silver arm-rings of the slain to add to the tale.

But when they came back into the Vale the Sun-beam duly ordered that watch and ward to keep the ingate thereto, and note all that should befall till Folk-might came home.


## CHAPTER XXII. FACE-OF-GOD COMETH HOME TO BURGSTEAD.

BUT Face-of-god with Bow-may and Wood-wise fared over the waste, going at first alongside the cliffs of the Shivering Flood, and then afterwards turning somewhat to the west. They soon had to climb a very high and steep bent going up to a mountain-neck ; and the way over the neck was rough indeed when they were on it, and they toiled out of it into a barren valley, and out of the valley again on to a rough neck ; and such-like was their journey the day long, for they were going athwart all those great dykes that went from the ice-mountains toward the lower dales like the outspread fingers of a hand or the roots of a great tree. And the ice-mountains they had on their left hands and whiles at their backs.

They went very warily, with their bows bended and spear in hand, but saw no man, good or bad, and but few living things.

151

At noon they rested in a valley where was a stream, but no grass,
nought but stones and sand; but where they were at least sheltered
from the wind, which was mostly very great in these high wastes;
and there Bow-may drew meat and wine from a wallet she bore,
and they ate and drank, and were merry enough; and Bow-
may said:

'I would I were going all the way with thee, Gold-mane; for
I long sore to let my eyes rest a while on the land where I shall
one day live.'

'Yea,' said Face-of-god, 'art thou minded to dwell there?
We shall be glad of that.'

'Whither are thy wits straying?' said she; 'whether I am
minded to it or not, I shall dwell there.'

And Wood-wise nodded a yea to her. But Face-of-god said:
'Good will be thy dwelling; but wherefore must it be so?'

Then Wood-wise laughed and said: 'I shall tell thee in fewer
words than she will, and time presses now: Wood-father and
Wood-mother, and I and my two brethren and this woman have
ever been about and anigh the Sun-beam; and we deem that war
and other troubles have made us of closer kin to her than we were
born, whether ye call it brotherhood or what not, and never shall
we sunder from her in life or in death. So when thou goest to
Burgdale with her, there shall we be.'

Then was Face-of-god glad when he found that they deemed
his wedding so settled and sure; but Wood-wise fell to making
ready for the road. And Face-of-god said to him:

'Tell me one thing, Wood-wise; that whoop that thou gavest
forth when we were at handy-strokes e'en now—is it but a cry of
thine own or is it of thy Folk, and shall I hear it again?'

'Thou may'st look to hear it many a time,' said Wood-wise,
'for it is the cry of the Wolf. Seldom indeed hath battle been
joined where men of our blood are, but that cry is given forth.
Come now, to the road!'

So they went their ways and the road worsened upon them, and

toilsome was the climbing up steep bents and the scaling of doubtful paths in the cliff-sides, so that the journey, though the distance
of it were not so long to the fowl flying, was much eked out for
them, and it was not till near nightfall that they came on the
ghyll of the Weltering Water some six miles above Burgstead.
Forsooth Wood-wise said that the way might be made less toilsome though far longer by turning back eastward a little past the
vale where they had rested at midday; and that seemed good to
Gold-mane, in case they should be wending hereafter in a great
company between Burgdale and Shadowy Vale.

But now those two went with Face-of-god down a path in the
side of the cliff whereby him-seemed he had gone before; and they
came down into the ghyll and sat down together on a stone by
the water-side, and Face-of-god spake to them kindly, for he
deemed them good and trusty faring-fellows.

'Bow-may,' said he, 'thou saidst a while ago that thou wouldst
be fain to look on Burgdale; and indeed it is fair and lovely, and
ye may soon be in it if ye will. Ye shall both be more than welcome to the house of my father, and heartily I bid you thither.
For night is on us, and the way back is long and toilsome and beset with peril. Sister Bow-may, thou wottest that it would be a
sore grief to me if thou camest to any harm, and thou also, fellow
Wood-wise. Daylight is a good faring-fellow over the waste.'

Said Bow-may: 'Thou art kind, Gold-mane, and that is thy
wont, I know; and fain were I to-night of the candles in thine hall.
But we may not tarry; for thou wottest how busy we be at home;
and Sun-beam needeth me, if it were only to make her sure that no
Dusky Man is bearing off thine head by its lovely locks. Neither
shall we journey in the mirk night; for look you, the moon yonder.'

'Well,' said Face-of-god, 'parting is ill at the best, and I
would I could give you twain a gift, and especially to thee, my
sister Bow-may.'

Said Wood-wise: 'Thou may'st well do that; or at least promise
the gift; and that is all one as if we held it in our hands.'

'Yea,' said Bow-may, 'Wood-wise and I have been thinking in one way belike; and I was at point to ask a gift of thee.'

'What is it?' said Gold-mane. 'Surely it is thine, if it were but a guerdon for thy good shooting.'

She laughed and handled the skirts of his hauberk as she said: 'Show us the dint in thine helm that the steel axe made this morning.'

'There is no such great dint,' said he; 'my father forged that helm, and his work is better than good.'

'Yea,' said Bow-may, 'and might I have hauberk and helm of his handiwork, and Wood-wise a good sword of the same, then were I a glad woman, and this man a happy carle.'

Said Gold-mane: 'I am well pleased at thine asking, and so shall Iron-face be when he heareth of thine archery; and how that Hall-face were now his only son but for thy close shooting. But now must I to the way; for my heart tells me that there may have been tidings in Burgstead this while I have been aloof.'

So they rose all three, and Bow-may said:

'Thou art a kind brother, and soon shall we meet again; and that will be well.'

Then he put his hands on her shoulders and kissed both her cheeks; and he kissed Wood-wise, and turned and went his ways, threading the stony tangle about the Weltering Water, which was now at middle height, and running clear and strong; so turning once he beheld Wood-wise and Bow-may climbing the path up the side of the ghyll, and Bow-may turned to him also and waved her bow as token of farewell. Then he went upon his way, which was rough enough to follow by night, though the moon was shining brightly high aloft. Yet as he knew his road he made but little of it all, and in somewhat more than an hour and a half was come out of the pass into the broken ground at the head of the Dale, and began to make his way speedily under the bright moonlight toward the Gate, still going close by the water. But as he went he heard of a sudden cries and rumour not far from him,

154

unwonted in that place, where none dwelt, and where the only folk he might look to see were those who cast an angle into the pools and eddies of the Water. Moreover, he saw about the place whence came the cries torches moving swiftly hither and thither; so that he looked to hear of new tidings, and stayed his feet and looked keenly about him on every side; and just then, between his rough path and the shimmer of the dancing moonlit water, he saw the moon smite on something gleaming; so, as quietly as he could, he got his target on his arm, and shortened his spear in his right hand, and then turned sharply toward that gleam. Even therewith up sprang a man on his right hand, and then another in front of him just betwixt him and the water; an axe gleamed bright in the moon, and he caught a great stroke on his target, and therewith drave his left shoulder straight forward, so that the man before him fell over into the water with a mighty splash; for they were at the very edge of the deepest eddy of the Water. Then he spun round on his heel, heeding not that another stroke had fallen on his right shoulder, yet ill-aimed, and not with the full edge, so that it ran down his byrny and rent it not. So he sent the thrust of his spear crashing through the face and skull of the smiter, and looked not to him as he fell, but stood still, brandishing his spear and crying out, 'For the Burg and the Face! For the Burg and the Face!'

No other foe came against him, but like to the echo of his cry rose a clear shout not far aloof, 'For the Face, for the Face! For the Burg and the Face!' He muttered, 'So ends the day as it begun,' and shouted loud again, 'For the Burg and the Face!' And in a minute more came breaking forth from the stone-heaps into the moonlit space before the water the tall shapes of the men of Burgstead, the red torchlight and the moonlight flashing back from their war-gear and weapons; for every man had his sword or spear in hand.

Hall-face was the first of them, and he threw his arms about his brother and said: 'Well met, Gold-mane, though thou comest

155

amongst us like Stone-fist of the Mountain. Art thou hurt? With whom hast thou dealt? Where be they? Whence comest thou?'

'Nay, I am not hurt,' said Face-of-god. 'Stint thy questions then, till thou hast told me whom thou seekest with spear and sword and candle.'

'Two felons were they,' said Hall-face, ' even such as ye saw lying dead at Wood-grey's the other day.'

'Then may ye sheathe your swords and go home,' said Gold-mane, 'for one lieth at the bottom of the eddy, and the other, thy feet are well-nigh treading on him, Hall-face.'

Then arose a rumour of praise and victory, and they brought the torches nigh and looked at the fallen man, and found that he was stark dead ; so they even let him lie there till the morrow, and all turned about toward the Thorp ; and many looked on Face-of-god and wondered concerning him, whence he was and what had befallen him. Indeed, they would have asked him thereof, but could not get at him to ask; but whoso could, went as nigh to Hall-face and him as they might, to hearken to the talk between the brothers.

So as they went along Hall-face did verily ask him whence he came : 'For was it not so,' said he, 'that thou didst enter into the wood seeking some adventure early in the morning the day before yesterday?'

'Sooth is that,' said Face-of-god, ' and I came to Shadowy Vale, and thence am I come this morning.'

Said Hall-face: 'I know not Shadowy Vale, nor doth any of us. This is a new word. How say ye, friends, doth any man here know of Shadowy Vale?'

They all said, 'Nay.'

Then said Hall-face : 'Hast thou been amongst mere ghosts and marvels, brother, or cometh this tale of thy minstrelsy?'

'For all your words,' said Gold-mane, 'to that Vale have I been ; and, to speak shortly (for I desire to have your tale, and am waiting for it), I will tell thee that I found there no marvels

156

or strange wights, but a folk of valiant men ; a folk small in numbers, but great of heart ; a folk come, as we be, from the Fathers and the Gods. And this, moreover, is to be said of them, that they are the foes of these felons of whom ye were chasing these twain. And these same Dusky Men of Silver-dale would slay them every man if they might ; and if we look not to it they will soon be doing the same by us ; for they are many, and as venomous as adders, as fierce as bears, and as foul as swine. But these valiant men, who bear on their banner the image of the Wolf, should be our fellows in arms, and they have good will thereto ; and they shall show us the way to Silver-dale by blind paths, so that we may fall upon these felons while they dwell there torment-ing the poor people of the land, and thus may we destroy them as lads a hornet's nest. Or else the days shall be hard for us.'

The men who hung about them drank in his words greedily. But Hall-face was silent a little while, and then he said : 'Brother Gold-mane, these be great tidings. Time was when we might have deemed them but a minstrel's tale; for Silver-dale we know not, of which thou speakest so glibly, nor the Dusky Men, any more than the Shadowy Vale. Howbeit, things have befallen these two last days so strange and new, that putting them together with the murder at Wood-grey's, and thy words which seem somewhat wild, it may well seem to us that tidings unlooked for are coming our way.'

'Come, then,' said Face-of-god, 'give me what thou hast in thy scrip, and trust me, I shall not jeer at thy tale.'

Said Hall-face : 'I also will be short with the tale ; and that the more, as meseemeth it is not yet done, and that thou thyself shalt share in the ending of it. It was the day before yesterday, that is the day when thou departedst into the woods on that ad-venture whereof thou shalt one day tell me more, wilt thou not ?'

'Yea, in good time,' said Face-of-god.

'Well,' quoth Hall-face, 'we went into the woods that day and in the morning, but after sunrise, to the number of a score :

157

we looked to meet a bear and a she-bear with cubs in a certain place ; for one of the Woodlanders, a keen hunter, had told us of their lair. Also we were wishful to slay some of the wild-swine, the yearlings, if we might. Therefore, though we had no helms or shields or coats of fence, we had bowshot a plenty, and good store of casting-weapons, besides our wood-knives and an axe or so ; and some of us, of whom I was one, bore our battle-swords, as we are wont ever to do, be the foe beast or man.

' Thus armed we went up Wildlake's Way and came to Carl-stead, where half-a-score Woodlanders joined themselves to us, so that we became a band. We went up the half-cleared places past Carlstead for a mile, and then turned east into the wood, and went I know not how far, for the Woodlanders led us by crooked paths, but two hours wore away in our going, till we came to the place where they looked to find the bears. It is a place that may well be noted, for it is unlike the wood round about. There is a close thicket some two furlongs about of thorn and briar and ill-grown ash and oak and other trees, planted by the birds belike ; and it stands as it were in an island amidst of a wide-spreading wood-lawn of fine turf, set about in the most goodly fashion with great tall straight-boled oak-trees, that seem to have been planted of set purpose by man's hand. Yea, dost thou know the place?'

' Methinks I do,' said Gold-mane, ' and I seem to have heard the Woodlanders give it a name and call it Boars-bait.'

' That may be,' said Hall-face. ' Well, there we were, the dogs and the men, and we drew nigh the thicket and beset it, and doubted not to find prey therein : but when we would set the dogs at the thicket to enter it, they were uneasy, and would not take up the slot, but growled and turned about this way and that, so that we deemed that they winded some fierce beast at our flanks or backs.

' Even so it was, and fierce enough and deadly was the beast ; for suddenly we heard bow-strings twang, and shafts came flying ; and Iron-shield of the Upper Dale, who was close beside me, leapt

158

up into the air and fell down dead with an arrow through his back.
Then I bethought me in the twinkling of an eye, and I cried out,
"The foe are on us! take the cover of the tree-boles and be wary!
For the Burg and the Face! For the Burg and the Face!"

'So we scattered and covered ourselves with the oak-boles, but
besides Iron-shield, who was slain outright, two goodmen were
sorely hurt, to wit Bald-face, a man of our house, and Stonyford
of the Lower Dale.

'I looked from behind my tree-bole, a great one; and far off down
the glades I saw men moving, clad in gay raiment; but nearer
to me, not a hundred yards from my cover, I saw an arm clad in
scarlet come out from behind a tree-bole, so I loosed at it, and
missed not; for straight there tottered out from behind the tree
one of those dusky foul-favoured men like to those that were slain
by Wood-grey. I had another shaft ready notched, so I loosed
and set the shaft in his throat, and he fell.

'Straightway was a yelling and howling about us like the cries
of scalded curs, and the oak-wood swarmed thick with these felons
rushing on us; for it seems that the man whom I had slain was a
chief amongst them, or we judged so by his goodly raiment.

'Methought then our last day was come. What could we do
but run together again after we had loosed at a venture, and so
withstand them sword and spear in hand? Some fell beneath our
shot, but not many, for they came on very swiftly.

'So they fell on us; but for all their fierceness and their numbers they might not break our array, and we slew four and hurt
many by sword-hewing and spear-casting and push of spear; and
five of us were hurt and one slain by their dart-casting. So they
drew off from us a little, and strove to spread out and fall to shooting at us again; but this we would not suffer, but pushed on as
they fell back, keeping as close together as we might for the trees.
For we said that we would all die together if needs must; and
verily the stour was hard.

'Yet hearken! In that nick of time rose up a strange cry not
159

far from us, Ha! ha! ha! ha! How-ow-ow! ending like the howl
of a wolf, and then another and another and another, till the
whole wood rang again.

'At first we deemed that here were come fresh foemen, and
that we were undone indeed; but when they heard it, the foemen before us faltered and gave way, and at last turned their
backs and fled, and we followed, keeping well together still:
thereby the more part of these men escaped us, for they fled
wildly here and there from those who bore that cry with them;
so we knew that our work was being done for us; therefore we
stood, and saw tall men clad in sheep-brown weed running through
the glades pursuing those felons and smiting them down, till both
fleers and pursuers passed out of our sight like men in a dream,
or as when ye roll up a pictured cloth to lay it in the coffer.

'But to Stone-face's mind those brown-clad men were the
Wights of the Wood that be of the Fathers' blood, and our very
friends; and when some of us would yet have gone forward and
foregathered with them, and followed the chase along with them,
Stone-face gainsaid it, bidding us not to run into the arms of a
second death, when we had but just escaped from the first. Sooth
to say, moreover, we had divers hurt men that needed looking to.

'So what with one thing, what with another, we turned back:
but War-cliff's brother, a tall man, had felled two of those felons
with an oak sapling which he had torn from the thicket; but he had
not slain them, and by now they were just awakening from their
swoon, and were sitting up looking round them with fierce rolling eyes, expecting the stroke, for Raven of Longscree was standing over them with a naked war-sword in his hand. But now
that our blood was cool, we were loth to slay them as they lay
in our hands; so we bound them and brought them away with
us; and our own dead we carried also on such biers as we might
lightly make there, and with them three that were so grievously
hurt that they might not go afoot, these we left at Carlstead:
they were Tardy the Son of the Untamed, and Swan of Bull-

meadow, both of the Lower Dale, and a Woodlander, Undoomed to wit. But the dead were Iron-shield aforesaid, and Wool-sark, and the Hewer, a Woodlander.

'So came we sadly at eventide to Burgstead with the two dead Burgdalers, and the captive felons, and the wounded of us that might go afoot; and ye may judge that they of Burgdale and our father deemed these tidings great enough, and wotted not what next should befall. Stone-face would have had those two felons slain there and then; for no true tale could we get out of them, nor indeed any word at all. But the Alderman would not have it so; and he deemed they might serve our turn as hostages if any of our folk should be taken: for one and all we deemed, and still deem, that war is on us and that new folk have gathered on our skirts.

'So the captives were shut up in the red out-bower of our house; and our father was minded that thou mightest tell us somewhat of them when thou wert come home. But about dusk to-day the word went that they had broken out and gotten them weapons and fled up the Dale; and so it was.

'But to-morrow morning will a Gate-thing be holden, and there it will be looked for of thee that thou tell us a true tale of thy goings. For it is deemed, and it is my deeming especially, that thou may'st tell us more of these men than thou hast yet told us. Is it not so?'

'Yea, surely,' said Gold-mane, 'I can make as many words as ye will about it; yet when all is said, it will come to much the same tale as I have already told thee. Yet belike, if ye are minded to take up the sword to defend you, I may tell you in what wise to lay hold on the hilts.'

'And that is well,' said Hall-face, 'and no less do I look for of thee. But lo! here are we come to the Gate of the Burg that abideth battle.'

## CHAPTER XXIII. TALK IN THE HALL OF THE HOUSE OF THE FACE.

Men hearken in the Hall.

IN sooth they were come to the very Gate of Burgstead, and the great gates were shut, and only a wicket was open, and a half score of stout men in all their war-gear were holding ward thereby. They gave place to Hall-face and his company, albeit some of the warders followed them through the wicket that they might hear the story told.

The street was full of folk, both men and women, talking together eagerly concerning all these tidings, and when they saw the men of the Hue-and-cry they came thronging about them, so that they might scarce get to the door of the House of the Face because of the press; so Hall-face (who was a very tall man) cried out:

'Good people, all is well! the runaways are slain, and Face-of-god is come back with us; give place a little, that we may come into our house.'

Then the throng set up a shout, and made way a little, so that Hall-face and Gold-mane and the others could get to the door. And they entered into the Hall, and saw much folk therein; and men were sitting at table, for supper was not yet over. But when they saw the new-comers they mostly rose up from the board and stood silent to hear the tale, for they had been talking many together each to each, so that the Hall was full of confused noise. So Hall-face again cried out: 'Men in this hall, good is the tidings. The runaways are slain; and it was Face-of-god who slew them as he came back safe from the waste.'

Then they shouted for joy, and the brethren and Stone-face with them (for he had entered with them from the street) went up on to the daïs, while the others of the Hue-and-cry gat them seats where they might at the endlong tables.

But when Face-of-god came up on to the daïs, there sat Iron-face looking down on the thronged Hall with a ruddy cheerful countenance, and beside him sat the Bride; for he had caused her to be brought thither when he had heard of the tidings of battle. She was daintily clad in a flame-coloured kirtle embroidered with gold about the bosom and sleeves, and there was a fillet of golden roses on her ruddy hair. Her eyes shone bright and eager, and the pommels of her cheeks were flushed and red contrary to their wont. Needs must Gold-mane sit by her, and when he came close to her he knew not what to do, but he put forth his hand to her, yet with a troubled countenance; for he feared her grief mingled with her beauty: as for her, she wavered in her mind whether she should forbear to touch him or not; but she saw that men about were looking at them, and especially was Iron-face looking on her: therefore she stood up and took Gold-mane's hand and kissed his face as she had been wont to do, and by then was her face as white as paper; and her anguish pierced his heart, so that he well-nigh groaned for grief of her. But Iron-face looked on her and said kindly:

'Kinswoman, thou art pale; thou hast feared for thy mate amidst all these tidings of war, and still fearest for him. But pluck up a heart; for the man is a deft warrior for all his fair face, which thou lovest as a woman should, and his hands may yet save his head. And if he be slain, yet are there other men of the kindred, and the earth will not be a desert to thee even then.'

She looked at Iron-face, and the colour was come back to her face somewhat, and she said:

'It is true; I have feared for him; for he goeth into perilous places. But for thee, thou art kind, and I thank thee for it.'

And therewith she kissed Iron-face and sat down in her place, and strove to overmaster her grief, that her face might not be changed by it; for now were thoughts of battle, and valiant hopes arising in men's hearts; and it seemed to her too grievous if she should mar that feast on the eve of battle.

But Iron-face kissed and embraced his son and said: 'Art thou late come from the waste? Hast thou seen new things?

163

We look to have a notable tale from thee; though here also have been tidings, and it is not unlike that we shall presently have new work on our hands.'

'Father,' quoth Face-of-god, 'I deem that when thou hast heard my tale thou wilt think no less of it than that there are valiant folk to be holpen, poor folk to be delivered, and evil folk to be swept from off the face of the earth.'

'It is well, son,' said Iron-face. 'I see that thy tale is long; let it alone for to-night. To-morrow shall we hold a Gate-thing, and then shall we hear all that thou hast to tell. Now eat thy meat and drink a bowl of wine, and comfort thy troth-plight maiden.'

So Gold-mane sat down by the Bride, and ate and drank as he needs must; but he was ill at ease and he durst not speak to her. For, on the one hand, he thought concerning his love for the Sun-beam, and how sweet and good a thing it was that she should take him by the hand and lead him into noble deeds and great fame, caressing him so softly and sweetly the while; and, on the other hand, there sat the Bride beside him, sorrowful and angry, begrudging all that sweetness of love, as though it were something foul and unseemly; and heavy on him lay the weight of that grudge, for he was a man of a friendly heart.

Stone-face sat outward from him on the other side of the Bride; and he leaned across her towards Gold-mane and said:

'Fair shall be thy tale to-morrow, if thou tellest us all thine adventure. Or wilt thou tell us less than all?'

Said Face-of-god: 'In good time shalt thou know it all, fos-ter-father; but it is not unlike that by the time that thou hast heard it, there shall be so many other things to tell of, that my tale shall seem of little account to thee—even as the saw saith that one nail driveth out the other.'

'Yea,' said Stone-face, 'but one tale belike shall be knit up with the others, as it fareth with the figures that come one after other on the weaver's cloth; though one maketh not the other, yet one cometh of the other.'

164

Said Face-of-god : 'Wise art thou now, foster-father, but thou shalt be wiser yet in this matter by then a month hath worn : and to-morrow shalt thou know enough to set thine hands a-work.'

So the talk fell between them ; and the night wore, and the men of Burgdale feasted in their ancient hall with merry hearts, little weighed down by thought of the battle that might be and the trouble to come ; for they were valorous and kindly folk.

## CHAPTER XXIV.  FACE-OF-GOD GIVETH THAT TOKEN TO THE BRIDE.

NOW on the morrow, when Face-of-god arose and other men with him, and the Hall was astir and there was no little throng therein, the Bride came up to him ; for she had slept in the House of the Face by the bidding of the Alderman ; and she spake to him before all men, and bade him come forth with her into the garden, because she would speak to him apart. He yeasaid her, though with a heavy heart ; and to the folk about that seemed meet and due, since those twain were deemed to be troth-plight, and they smiled kindly on them as they went out of the Hall together.

So they came into the garden, where the pear-trees were blossoming over the spring lilies, and the cherries were showering their flowers on the deep green grass, and everything smelled sweetly on the warm windless spring morning.

She led the way, going before him till they came by a smooth grass path between the berry bushes, to a square space of grass about which were barberry trees, their first tender leaves bright green in the sun against the dry yellowish twigs.  There was a sundial amidmost of the grass, and betwixt the garden-boughs one could see the long grey roof of the ancient hall ; and sweet familiar sounds of the nesting birds and men and women going on their errands were all about in the scented air.  She turned

165

about at the sundial and faced Face-of-god, her hand lightly
laid on the scored brass, and spake with no anger in her voice :

'I ask thee if thou hast brought me the token whereon thou
shalt swear to give me that gift.'

'Yea,' said he; and therewith drew the ring from his bosom,
and held it out to her. She reached out her hand to him slowly
and took it, and their fingers met as she did so, and he noted that
her hand was warm and firm and wholesome as he well remembered it.

She said : 'Whence hadst thou this fair finger-ring ? '

Said Face-of-god : 'My friend there in the mountain-valley drew
it from off her finger for thee, and bade me bear thee a message.'

Her face flushed red : 'Yea,' she said, 'and doth she send me
a message ? Then doth she know of me, and ye have talked of
me together.—Well, give the message ! '

Said Face-of-god : 'She saith, that thou shalt bear in mind,
That to-morrow is a new day.'

'Yea,' she said, 'for her it is so, and for thee ; but not for me.
But now I have brought thee here that thou mightest swear thine
oath to me ; lay thine hand on this ring and on this brazen plate
whereby the sun measures the hours of the day for happy folk,
and swear by the spring-tide of the year and all glad things that
find a mate, and by the God of the Earth that rejoiceth in the
life of man.'

Then he laid his hand on the finger-ring as it lay on the dial-
plate and said :

'By the spring-tide and the live things that long to multiply
their kind ; by the God of the Earth that rejoiceth in the life of
man, I swear to give to my kinswoman the Bride the second
man-child that I beget; to be hers, to leave or cherish, to love or
hate, as her will may bid her.' Then he looked on her soberly
and said : 'It is duly sworn ; is it enough ? '

'Yea,' she said ; but he saw how the tears ran out of her eyes
and wetted the bosom of her kirtle, and she hung her head for

166

shame of her grief. And Gold-mane was all abashed, and had no word to say; for he knew that no word of his might comfort her; and he deemed it ill done to stay there and behold her sorrow; and he knew not how to get him gone, and be glad elsewhere, and leave her alone.

Then, as if she had read his thought, she looked up at him and said smiling a little amidst of her tears:

'I bid thee stay by me till the flood is over; for I have yet a word to say to thee.'

So he stood there gazing down on the grass in his turn, and not daring to raise his eyes to her face, and the minutes seemed long to him: till at last she said in a voice scarcely yet clear of weeping:

'Wilt thou say anything to me, and tell me what thou hast done, and why, and what thou deemest will come of it?'

He said: 'I will tell the truth as I know it, because thou askest it of me, and not because I would excuse myself before thee. What have I done? Yesterday I plighted my troth to wed the woman that I met last autumn in the wood. And why? I wot not why, but that I longed for her. Yet I must tell thee that it seemed to me, and yet seemeth, that I might do no otherwise—that there was nothing else in the world for me to do. What do I deem will come of it, sayest thou? This, that we shall be happy together, she and I, till the day of our death.'

She said: 'And even so long shall I be sorry: so far are we sundered now. Alas! who looked for it? And whither shall I turn to now?'

Said Gold-mane: 'She bade me tell thee that to-morrow is a new day: meseemeth I know her meaning.'

'No word of hers hath any meaning to me,' said the Bride.

'Nay,' said he, 'but hast thou not heard these rumours of war that are in the Dale? Shall not these things avail thee? Much may grow out of them; and thou with the mighty heart, so faithful and compassionate!'

167

She said : ' What sayest thou ?   What may grow out of them ?
Yea, I have heard those rumours as a man sick to death heareth
men talk of their business down in the street while he lieth on his
bed; and already he hath done with it all, and hath no world to
mend or mar.  For me nought shall grow out of it.  What meanest
thou ? '

Said Gold-mane : ' Is there nought in the fellowship of Folks,
and the aiding of the valiant, and the deliverance of the hapless?'

' Nay,' she said, ' there is nought to me.  I cannot think of it
to-day nor yet to-morrow belike.  Yet true it is that I may mingle
in it, though thinking nought of it.  But this shall not avail me.'

She was silent a little, but presently spake and said : ' Thou
sayest right ; it is not thou that hast done this, but the woman who
sent me the ring and the message of an old saw.  O that she
should be born to sunder us !  How hath it befallen that I am now
so little to thee and she so much ? '

And again she was silent ; and after a while Face-of-god spake
kindly and softly and said : ' Kinswoman, wilt thou for ever begrudge our love ? this grudge lieth heavy on my soul, and it is I
alone that have to bear it.'

She said : ' This is but a light burden for thee to bear, when
thou hast nought else to bear !  But do I begrudge thee thy love,
Gold-mane ?  I know not that.  Rather meseemeth I do not believe in it—nor shall do ever.'

Then she held her peace a long while, nor did he speak one word :
and they were so still, that a robin came hopping about them,
close to the hem of her kirtle, and a starling pitched in the apple-
tree hard by and whistled and chuckled, turning about and about,
heeding them nought.  Then at last she lifted up her face from
looking on the grass and said : ' These are idle words and avail
nothing: one thing only I know, that we are sundered.  And now
it repenteth me that I have shown thee my tears and my grief
and my sickness of the earth and those that dwell thereon.  I am
ashamed of it, as if thou hadst smitten me, and I had come and

168

shown thee the stripes, and said, See what thou hast done! hast The Bride will declare the sundering of the troth-plight. thou no pity? Yea, thou pitiest me, and wilt try to forget thy pity. Belike thou art right when thou sayest, To-morrow is a new day; belike matters will arise that will call me back to life, and I shall once more take heed of the joy and sorrow of my people. Nay, it is most like that this I shall feign to do even now. But if to-morrow be a new day, it is to-day now and not to-morrow, and so shall it be for long. Hereof belike we shall talk no more, thou and I. For as the days wear, the dealings between us shall be that thou shalt but get thee away from my life, and I shall be nought to thee but the name of a kinswoman. Thus should it be even wert thou to strive to make it otherwise; and thou shalt *not* strive. So let all this be; for this is not the word I had to say to thee. But hearken! now are we sundered, and it irketh me beyond measure that folk know it not, and are kind, and rejoice in our love, and deem it a happy thing for the folk; and this burden I may bear no longer. So I shall declare unto men that I will not wed thee; and belike they may wonder why it is, till they see thee wedded to the Woman of the Mountain. Art thou content that so it shall be?'

Said Face-of-god: 'Nay, thou shalt not take this all upon thyself; I also shall declare unto the Folk that I will wed none but her, the Mountain-Woman.'

She said: 'This shalt thou not do; I forbid it thee. And I *will* take it all upon myself. Shall I have it said of me that I am unmeet to wed thee, and that thou hast found me out at last and at latest? I lay this upon thee, that wheresoever I declare this and whatsoever I may say, thou shalt hold thy peace. This at least thou may'st do for me. Wilt thou?'

'Yea,' he said, 'though it shall put me to shame.'

Again she was silent for a little; then she said:

'O Gold-mane, this would I take upon myself not soothly for any shame of seeming to be thy cast-off; but because it is I who needs must bear all the sorrow of our sundering; and I have the

169

Face-of-god
is sorry for
past days.

will to bear it greater and heavier, that I may be as the women
of old time, and they that have come from the Gods, lest I belittle
my life with malice and spite and confusion, and it become
poisonous to me. Be at peace! be at peace! And leave all to the
wearing of the years; and forget not that which thou hast sworn!'

Therewith she turned and went from that green place toward
the House of the Face, walking slowly through the garden amongst
the sweet odours, beneath the fair blossoms, a body most dainty
and beauteous of fashion, but the casket of grievous sorrow, which
all that goodliness availed not.

But Face-of-god lingered in that place a little, and for that
little while the joy of his life was dulled and overworn; and the
days before his wandering on the mountain seemed to him free and
careless and happy days that he could not but regret. He was
ashamed, moreover, that this so unquenchable grief should come
but of him, and the pleasure of his life, which he himself had found
out for himself, and which was but such a little portion of the Earth
and the deeds thereof. But presently his thought wandered from
all this, and as he turned away from the sundial and went his ways
through the garden, he called to mind his longing for the day of
the spring market, when he should see the Sun-beam again and be
cherished by the sweetness of her love.

## CHAPTER XXV. OF THE GATE-THING AT BURGSTEAD.

BUT now must he hasten, for the Gate-thing was to be
holden two hours before noon; so he betook him speedily
to the Hall, and took his shield and did on a goodly helm
and girt his sword to his side, for men must needs go to all folk-
motes with their weapons and clad in war-gear. Thus he went
forth to the Gate with many others, and there already were many
folk assembled in the space aforesaid betwixt the Gate of the Burg
and the sheer rocks on the face of which were the steps that led

up to the ancient Tower on the height. The Alderman was Men gather to the Gate-thing. sitting on the great stone by the Gate-side which was his appointed place, and beside him on the stone bench were the six Wardens of the Burg; but of the six Wardens of the Dale there were but three, for the others had not yet heard tell of the battle or had got the summons to the Thing, since they had been about their business down the Dale.

Face-of-god took his place silently amongst the neighbours, but men made way for him, so that he must needs stand in front, facing his father and the Wardens; and there went up a murmur of expectation round about him, both because the word had gone about that he had a tale of new tidings to tell, and also because men deemed him their best and handiest man, though he was yet so young.

Now the Alderman looked around and beheld a great throng gathered together, and he looked on the shadow of the Gate which the southering sun was casting on the hard white ground of the Thing-stead, and he saw that it had just taken in the standing-stone which was in the midst of the place. On the face of the said stone was carven the image of a fighting man with shield on arm and axe in hand; for it had been set there in old time in memory of the man who had bidden the Folk build the Gate and its wall, and had showed them how to fashion it: for he was a deft house-smith as well as a great warrior; and his name was Iron-hand. So when the Alderman saw that this stone was wholly within the shadow of the Gate he knew that it was the due time for the hallowing-in of the Thing. So he bade one of the wardens who sat beside him and had a great slug-horn slung about him, to rise and set the horn to his mouth.

So that man arose and blew three great blasts that went bellowing about the towers and down the street, and beat back again from the face of the sheer rocks and up them and over into the wild-wood; and the sound of it went on the light west-wind along the lips of the Dale toward the mountain wastes. And many a

171

goodman, when he heard the voice of the horn in the bright spring
morning, left spade or axe or plough-stilts, or the foddering of the
ewes and their younglings, and turned back home to fetch his
sword and helm and hasten to the Thing, though he knew not
why it was summoned: and women wending over the meadows,
who had not yet heard of the battle in the wood, hearkened and
stood still on the green grass or amidst the ripples of the ford, and
the threat of coming trouble smote heavy on their hearts, for they
knew that great tidings must be towards if a Thing must needs
be summoned so close to the Great Folk-mote.

But now the Alderman stood up and spake amidst the silence
that followed the last echoes of the horn:

'Now is hallowed in this Gate-thing of the Burgstead Men
and the Men of the Dale, wherein they shall take counsel concerning matters late befallen, that press hard upon them. Let no man
break the peace of the Holy Thing, lest he become a man accursed
in holy places from the plain up to the mountain, and from the
mountain down to the plain; a man not to be cherished of any
man of good will, not be holpen with victuals or edge-tool or
draught-beast; a man to be sheltered under no roof-tree, and
warmed at no hearth of man: so help us the Warrior and the
God of the Earth, and Him of the Face, and all the Fathers!'

When he had spoken men clashed their weapons in token of
assent; and he sat down again, and there was silence for a space.
But presently came thrusting forward a goodman of the Dale, who
seemed as if he had come hurriedly to the Thing; for his face was
running down with sweat, his wide-rimmed iron cap sat awry
over his brow, and he was girt with a rusty sword without a
scabbard, and the girdle was ill-braced up about his loins. So
he said:

'I am Red-coat of Waterless of the Lower Dale. Early this
morning as I was going afield I met on the way a man akin to me,
Fox of Upton to wit, and he told me that men were being summoned to a Gate-thing. So I turned back home, and caught up

172

any weapon that came handy, and here I am, Alderman, asking thee of the tidings which hath driven thee to call this Thing so hard on the Great Folk-mote, for I know them not.'

Then stood up Iron-face the Alderman and said: ' This is well asked, and soon shall ye be as wise as I am on this matter. Know ye, O men of Burgstead and the Dale, that we had not called this Gate-thing so hard on the Great Folk-mote had not great need been to look into troublous matters. Long have ye dwelt in peace, and it is years on years now since any foeman hath fallen on the Dale : but, as ye will bear in mind, last autumn were there ransackings in the Dale and amidst of the Shepherds after the manner of deeds of war; and it troubleth us that none can say who wrought these ill deeds. Next, but a little while agone, was Wood-grey, a valiant goodman of the Woodlanders, slain close to his own door by evil men. These men we took at first for mere gangrel felons and outcasts from their own folk : though there were some who spoke against that from the beginning.

' But thirdly are new tidings again : for three days ago, while some of the folk were hunting peaceably in the Wild-wood and thinking no evil, they were fallen upon of set purpose by a host of men-at-arms, and nought would serve but mere battle for dear life, so that many of our neighbours were hurt, and three slain outright; and now mark this, that those who there fell upon our folk were clad and armed even as the two felons that slew Wood-grey, and moreover were like them in aspect of body. Now stand forth Hall-face my son, and answer to my questions in a loud voice, so that all may hear thee.'

So Hall-face stood forth, clad in gleaming war-gear, with an axe over his shoulder, and seemed a doughty warrior. And Iron-face said to him :

' Tell me, son, those whom ye met in the wood, and of whom ye brought home two captives, how much like were they to the murder-carles at Wood-grey's ?'

Said Hall-face : ' As like as peas out of the same cod, and to

173

our eyes all those whom we saw in the wood might have been sons of one father and one mother, so much alike were they.'

'Yea,' said the Alderman; 'now tell me how many by thy deeming fell upon you in the wood?'

Said Hall-face: 'We deemed that if they were any less than threescore, they were little less.'

'Great was the odds,' said the Alderman. 'Or how many were ye?'

'One score and seven,' said Hall-face.

Said the Alderman: 'And yet ye escaped with life all save those three?'

Hall-face said: 'I deem that scarce one should have come back alive, had it not been that as we fought came a noise like the howling of wolves, and thereat the foemen turned and fled, and there followed on the fleers tall men clad in sheep-brown raiment, who smote them down as they fled.'

'Here then is the story, neighbours,' said the Alderman, 'and ye may see thereby that if those slayers of Wood-grey were outcast, their band is a great one; but it seemeth rather that they were men of a folk whose craft it is to rob with the armed hand, and to slay the robbed; and that they are now gathering on our borders for war. Yet, moreover, they have foemen in the woods who should be fellows-in-arms of us. How sayest thou, Stoneface? Thou art old, and hast seen many wars in the Dale, and knowest the Wild-wood to its innermost.

'Alderman,' said Stone-face, 'and ye neighbours of the Dale, maybe these foes whom ye have met are not of the race of man, but are trolls and wood-wights. Now if they be trolls it is ill, for then is the world growing worser, and the wood shall be right perilous for those who needs must fare therein. Yet if they be men it is a worse matter; for the trolls would not come out of the waste into the sunlight of the Dale. But these foes, if they be men, are lusting after our fair Dale to eat it up, and it is most like that they are gathering a huge host to fall upon us at home.

174

Such things I have heard of when I was young, and the aspect of the evil men who overran the kindreds of old time, according to all tales and lays that I have heard, is even such as the aspect of those whom we have seen of late.  As to those wolves who saved the neighbours and chased their foemen, there is one here who belike knoweth more of all this than we do, and that, O Alderman, is thy son whom I have fostered, Face-of-god to wit. Bid him answer to thy questioning, and tell us what he hath seen and heard of late; then shall we verily know the whole story as far as it can be known.'

The dead felons: Face-of-god questioned.

Then men pressed round, and were eager to hear what Face-of-god would be saying.  But or ever the Alderman could begin to question him, the throng was cloven by new-comers, and these were the men who had been sent to bring home the corpses of the Dusky Men: so they had cast loaded hooks into the Weltering Water, and had dragged up him whom Face-of-god had shoved into the eddy, and who had sunk like a stone just where he fell, and now they were bringing him on a bier along with him who had been slain a-land.  They were set down in the place before the Alderman, and men who had not seen them before looked eagerly on them that they might behold the aspect of their foemen; and nought lovely were they to look on; for the drowned man was already bleached and swollen with the water, and the other, his face was all wryed and twisted with that spear-thrust in the mouth.

Then the Alderman said: 'I would question my son Face-of-god.  Let him stand forth!'

And therewith he smiled merrily in his son's face, for he was standing right in front of him; and he said:

'Ask of me, Alderman, and I will answer.'

'Kinsman,' said Iron-face, 'look at these two dead men, and tell me, if thou hast seen any such besides those two murder-carles who were slain at Carlstead; or if thou knowest aught of their folk?'

175

Said Face-of-god: 'Yesterday I saw six others like to these both in array and of body, and three of them I slew, for we were in battle with them early in the morning.'

There was a murmur of joy at this word, since all men took these felons for deadly foemen; but Iron-face said: 'What meanest thou by "we"?'

'I and the men who had guested me overnight,' said Face-of-god, 'and they slew the other three; or rather a woman of them slew the felons.'

'Valiant she was; all good go with her hand!' said the Alderman. 'But what be these people, and where do they dwell?'

Said Face-of-god: 'As to what they are, they are of the kindred of the Gods and the Fathers, valiant men, and guest-cherishing: rich have they been, and now are poor: and their poverty cometh of these same felons, who mastered them by numbers not to be withstood. As to where they dwell: when I say the name of their dwelling-place men mock at me, as if I named some valley in the moon: yet came I to Burgdale thence in one day across the mountain-necks led by sure guides, and I tell thee that the name of their abode is Shadowy Vale.'

'Yea,' said Iron-face, 'knoweth any man here of Shadowy Vale, or where it is?'

None answered for a while; but there was an old man who was sitting on the shafts of a wain on the outskirts of the throng, and when he heard this word he asked his neighbour what the Alderman was saying, and he told him. Then said that elder:

'Give me place; for I have a word to say hereon.' Therewith he arose, and made his way to the front of the ring of men, and said: 'Alderman, thou knowest me?'

'Yea,' said Iron-face, 'thou art called the Fiddle, because of thy sweet speech and thy minstrelsy; whereof I mind me well in the time when I was young and thou no longer young.'

'So it is,' said the Fiddle. 'Now hearken! When I was very young I heard of a vale lying far away across the mountain-

176

necks; a vale where the sun shone never in winter and scantily in summer; for my sworn foster-brother, Fight-fain, a bold man and a great hunter, had happened upon it; and on a day in full midsummer he brought me thither; and even now I see the Vale before me as in a picture; a marvellous place, well grassed, treeless, narrow, betwixt great cliff-walls of black stone, with a green river running through it towards a yawning gap and a huge force. Amidst that Vale was a doom-ring of black stones, and nigh thereto a feast-hall well builded of the like stones, over whose door was carven the image of a wolf with red gaping jaws, and within it (for we entered into it) were stone benches on the daïs. Thence we came away, and thither again we went in late autumn, and so dusk and cold it was at that season, that we knew not what to call it save the valley of deep shade. But its real name we never knew; for there was no man there to give us a name or tell us any tale thereof; but all was waste there; the wimbrel laughed across its water, the raven croaked from its crags, the eagle screamed over it, and the voices of its waters never ceased; and thus we left it. So the seasons passed, and we went thither no more: for Fight-fain died, and without him wandering over the waste was irksome to me; so never have I seen that valley again, or heard men tell thereof.

'Now, neighbours, have I told you of a valley which seemeth to be Shadowy Vale; and this is true and no made-up story.'

The Alderman nodded kindly to him, and then said to Face-of-god: 'Kinsman, is this word according with what thou knowest of Shadowy Vale?'

'Yea, on all points,' said Face-of-god; 'he hath put before me a picture of the valley. And whereas he saith, that in his youth it was waste, this also goeth with my knowledge thereof. For once was it peopled, and then was waste, and now again is it peopled.'

'Tell us then more of the folk thereof,' said the Alderman; 'are they many?'

'Nay,' said Face-of-god, 'they are not. How might they be

many, dwelling in that narrow Vale amid the wastes? But they
are valiant, both men and women, and strong and well-liking.
Once they dwelt in a fair dale called Silver-dale, the name whereof
will be to you as a name in a lay; and there were they wealthy and
happy. Then fell upon them this murderous Folk, whom they call
the Dusky Men; and they fought and were overcome, and many
of them were slain, and many enthralled, and the remnant of them
escaped through the passes of the mountains and came back to
dwell in Shadowy Vale, where their forefathers had dwelt long and
long ago; and this overthrow befell them ten years agone. But
now their old foemen have broken out from Silver-dale and have
taken to scouring the wood seeking prey; so they fall upon these
Dusky Men as occasion serves, and slay them without pity, as if
they were adders or evil dragons; and indeed they be worse.
And these valiant men know for certain that their foemen are
now of mind to fall upon this Dale and destroy it, as they have
done with others nigher to them. And they will slay our men,
and lie with our women against their will, and enthrall our children,
and torment all those that lie under their hands till life shall be
worse than death to them. Therefore, O Alderman and Wardens,
and ye neighbours all, it behoveth you to take counsel what we
shall do, and that speedily.'

There was again a murmur, as of men nothing daunted, but
intent on taking some way through the coming trouble. But no
man said aught till the Alderman spake:

'When didst thou first happen upon this Earl-folk, son?'

'Late last autumn,' said Face-of-god.

Said Iron-face: 'Then mightest thou have told us of this tale
before.'

'Yea,' said his son, 'but I knew it not, or but little of it, till
two days agone. In the autumn I wandered in the woodland, and
on the fell I happened on a few of this folk dwelling in a booth
by the pine-wood; and they were kind and guest-fain with me,
and gave me meat and drink and lodging, and bade me come to

178

Shadowy Vale in the spring, when I should know more of them.
And that was I fain of; for they are wise and goodly men. But
I deemed no more of those that I saw there save as men who had
been outlawed by their own folk for deeds that were unlawful belike, but not shameful, and were biding their time of return, and
were living as they might meanwhile. But of the whole Folk
and their foemen knew I no more than ye did, till two days
agone, when I met them again in Shadowy Vale. Also I think
before long ye shall see their chieftain in Burgstead, for he hath
a word for us. Lastly, my mind it is that those brown-clad men
who helped Hall-face and his company in the wood were nought
but men of this Earl-kin seeking their foemen; for indeed they
told me that they had come upon a battle in the woodland wherein they had slain their foemen. Now have I told you all that ye
need to know concerning these matters.'

Again was there silence as Iron-face sat pondering a question
for his son; then a goodman of the Upper Dale, Gritgarth to wit,
spake and said:

'Gold-mane mine, tell us how many is this folk; I mean their
fighting-men?'

'Well asked, neighbour,' said Iron-face.

Said Face-of-god: 'Their fighting-men of full age may be
five score; but besides that there shall be some two or three
score of women that will fight, whoever says them nay; and
many of these are little worse in the field than men; or no worse,
for they shoot well in the bow. Moreover, there will be a full
score of swains not yet twenty winters old whom ye may not
hinder to fight if anything is a-doing.'

'This is no great host,' said the Alderman; 'yet if they deem
there is little to lose by fighting, and nought to gain by sitting
still, they may go far in winning their desire; and that more
especially if they may draw into their quarrel some other valiant
Folk more in number than they be. I marvel not, though, they
were kind to thee, son Gold-mane, if they knew who thou wert.'

179

'They knew it,' said Face-of-god.

'Neighbours,' said the Alderman, 'have ye any rede hereon, and aught to say to back your rede?'

Then spake the Fiddle: 'As ye know and may see, I am now very old, and, as the word goes, unmeet for battle: yet might I get me to the field, either on mine own legs or on the legs of some four-foot beast, I would strike, if it were but one stroke, on these pests of the earth. And, Alderman, meseemeth we shall do amiss if we bid not the Earl-folk of Shadowy Vale to be our fellows in arms in this adventure. For look you, how few soever they be, they will be sure to know the ways of our foemen, and the mountain passes, and the surest and nighest roads across the necks and the mires of the waste; and though they be not a host, yet shall they be worth a host to us?'

When men heard his words they shouted for joy of them; for hatred of the Dusky Men who should so mar their happy life in the Dale was growing up in them, and the more that hatred waxed, the more waxed their love of those valiant ones.

Now Red-coat of Waterless spake again: he was a big man, both tall and broad, ruddy-faced and red-haired, some forty winters old. He said:

'Life hath been well with us of the Lower Dale, and we deem that we have much to lose in losing it. Yet ill would the bargain be to buy life with thralldom: we have been over-merry hitherto for that. Therefore I say, to battle! And as to these men, these well-wishers of Face-of-god, if they also are minded for battle with our foes, we were fools indeed if we did not join them to our company, were they but one score instead of six.'

Men shouted again, and they said that Red-coat had spoken well.

Then one after other the goodmen of the Dale came and gave their word for fellowship in arms with the Men of Shadowy Vale, if there were such as Face-of-god had said, which they doubted not; and amongst them that spake were Fox of Nethertown, and Warwell, and Gritgarth, and Bearswain, and Warcliff, and

Hart of Highcliff, and Worm of Willowholm, and Bullsbane, and Highneb of the Marsh : all these were stout men-at-arms and men of good counsel.

Last of all the Alderman spake and said :

'As to the war, that must we needs meet if all be sooth that we have heard, and I doubt it not.

'Now therefore let us look to it like wise men while time yet serves. Ye shall know that the muster of the Dalesmen will bring under shield eight long hundreds of men well-armed, and of the Shepherd-Folk four hundreds, and of the Woodlanders two hundreds ; and this is a goodly host if it be well ordered and wisely led. Now am I your Alderman and your Doomster, and I can heave up a sword as well as another maybe, nor do I think that I shall blench in the battle ; yet I misdoubt me that I am no leader or orderer of men-of-war : therefore ye will do wisely to choose a wiser man-at-arms than I be for your War-leader ; and if at the Great Folk-mote, when all the Houses and Kindreds are gathered, men yeasay your choosing, then let him abide ; but if they naysay it, let him give place to another. For time presses. Will ye so choose ? '

'Yea, yea!' cried all men.

'Good is that, neighbours,' said the Alderman. 'Whom will ye have for War-leader ? Consider well.'

Short was their rede, for every man opened his mouth and cried out 'Face-of-god!' Then said the Alderman :

'The man is young and untried ; yet though he is so near akin to me, I will say that ye will do wisely to take him; for he is both deft of his hands and brisk ; and moreover, of this matter he knoweth more than all we together. Now therefore I declare him your War-leader till the time of the Great Folk-mote.'

Then all men shouted with great glee and clashed their weapons; but some few put their heads together and spake apart a little while, and then one of them, Red-coat of Waterless to wit, came forward and said : 'Alderman, some of us deem it good that

Stone-face, the old man wise in war and in the ways of the Wood,
should be named as a counsellor to the War-leader; and Hall-face,
a very brisk and strong young man, to be his right hand and
sword-bearer.'

'Good is that,' said Iron-face. 'Neighbours, will ye have it so?'

This also they yeasaid without delay, and the Alderman declared Stone-face and Hall-face the helpers of Face-of-god in
this business. Then he said:

'If any hath aught to say concerning what is best to be done
at once, it were good that he said it now before all and not to
murmur and grudge hereafter.'

None spake save the Fiddle, who said: 'Alderman and War-
leader, one thing would I say: that if these foemen are anywise
akin to those overrunners of the Folks of whom the tales went in
my youth (for I also as well as Stone-face mind me well of those
tales concerning them), it shall not avail us to sit still and await
their onset. For then may they not be withstood, when they
have gathered head and burst out and over the folk that have
been happy, even as the waters that overtop a dyke and cover
with their muddy ruin the deep green grass and the flower-buds
of spring. Therefore my rede is, as soon as may be to go seek
these folk in the woodland and wheresoever else they may be
wandering. What sayest thou, Face-of-god?'

'My rede is as thine,' said he; 'and to begin with, I do now
call upon ten tens of good men to meet me in arms at the beginning of Wildlake's Way to-morrow morning at daybreak; and I
bid my brother Hall-face to summon such as are most meet thereto.
For this I deem good, that we scour the wood daily at present
till we hear fresh tidings from them of Shadowy Vale, who are
nigher than we to the foemen. Now, neighbours, are ye ready
to meet me?'

Then all shouted, 'Yea, we will go, we will go!'

Said the Alderman: 'Now have we made provision for the war
in that which is nearest to our hands. Yet have we to deal with

182

the matter of the fellowship with the Folk whom Face-of-god A fair-clad warrior. hath seen. This is a matter for thee, son, at least till the Great Folk-mote is holden. Tell me then, shall we send a messenger to Shadowy Vale to speak with this folk, or shall we abide the chieftain's coming?'

'By my rede,' said Face-of-god, 'we shall abide his coming: for first, though I might well make my way thither, I doubt if I could give any the bearings, so that he could come there without me; and belike I am needed at home, since I am become War-leader. Moreover, when your messenger cometh to Shadowy Vale, he may well chance to find neither the chieftain there, nor the best of his men; for whiles are they here, and whiles there, as they wend following after the Dusky Men.'

'It is well, son,' said the Alderman, 'let it be as thou sayest: soothly this matter must needs be brought before the Great Folk-mote. Now will I ask if any other hath any word to say, or any rede to give before this Gate-thing sundereth?'

But no man came forward, and all men seemed well content and of good heart; and it was now well past noontide.

CHAPTER XXVI.   THE ENDING OF THE GATE-THING.

BUT just as the Alderman was on the point of rising to declare the breaking-up of the Thing, there came a stir in the throng and it opened, and a warrior came forth into the innermost of the ring of men, arrayed in goodly glittering war-gear; clad in such wise that a tunicle of precious gold-wrought web covered the hauberk all but the sleeves thereof, and the hem of it beset with blue mountain-stones smote against the ankles and well-nigh touched the feet, shod with sandals gold-embroidered and gemmed. This warrior bore a goodly gilded helm on the head, and held in hand a spear with gold-garlanded shaft, and was girt with a sword whose hilts and scabbard both were adorned with gold and gems: beardless, smooth-cheeked, exceeding fair of face was the warrior, but pale and somewhat haggard-eyed : and those who were nearby beheld and wondered ; for they saw that there was come the Bride arrayed for war and battle, as if she were a messenger from the House of the Gods, and the Burg that endureth for ever.

Then she fell to speech in a voice which at first was somewhat hoarse and broken, but cleared as she went on, and she said :

'There sittest thou, O Alderman of Burgdale ! Is Face-of-god thy son anywhere nigh, so that he can hear me ? '

But Iron-face wondered at her word, and said : 'He is beside thee, as he should be.' For indeed Face-of-god was touching her, shoulder to shoulder. But she looked not to the right hand nor the left, but said :

'Hearken, Iron-face ! Chief of the House of the Face, Alderman of the Dale, and ye also, neighbours and goodmen of the Dale : I am a woman called the Bride, of the House of the Steer, and ye have heard that I have plighted my troth to Face-of-god to wed with him, to love him, and lie in his bed. But it is not so: we are not troth-plight ; nor will I wed with him, nor any other, but will wend with you to the war, and play my part therein according to what might is in me ; nor will I be worser than the wives of Shadowy Vale.'

Face-of-god heard her words with no change of countenance ; but Iron-face reddened over all his face, and stared at her, and knit his brows and said :

'Maiden, what are these words ? What have we done to thee ? Have I not been to thee as a father, and loved thee dearly ? Is not my son goodly and manly and deft in arms ? Hath it not ever been the wont of the House of the Face to wed in the House of the Steer ? and in these two Houses there hath never yet been a goodlier man and a lovelier maiden than are ye two. What have we done then ? '

'Ye have done nought against me,' she said, 'and all that thou sayest is sooth ; yet will I not wed with Face-of-god.'

Yet fiercer waxed the face of the Alderman, and he said in a loud voice :

'But how if I tell thee that I will speak with thy kindred of the Steer, and thou shalt do after my bidding whether thou wilt or whether thou wilt not?'

'And how will ye compel me thereto?' she said. 'Are there thralls in the Dale? Or will ye make me an outlaw? Who shall heed it? Or I shall betake me to Shadowy Vale and become one of their warrior-maidens.'

Now was the Alderman's face changing from red to white, and belike he forgat the Thing, and what he was doing there, and he cried out :

'This is an evil day, and who shall help me? Thou, Face-of-god, what hast thou to say? Wilt thou let this woman go without a word? What hath bewitched thee?'

But never a word spake his son, but stood looking straight forward, cold and calm by seeming. Then turned Iron-face again to the Bride, and said in a softer voice :

'Tell me, maiden, whom I erst called daughter, what hath befallen, that thou wilt leave my son; thou who wert once so kind and loving to him; whose hand was always seeking his, whose eyes were ever following his; who wouldst go where he bade, and come when he called. What hath betid that ye have cast him out, and flee from our House?'

She flushed red beneath her helm and said :

'There is war in the land, and I have seen it coming, and that things shall change around us. I have looked about me and seen men happy and women content, and children weary for mere mirth and joy. And I have thought, in a day, or two days or three, all this shall be changed, and the women shall be, some anxious and wearied with waiting, some casting all hope away; and the men, some shall come back to the garth no more, and some shall come back maimed and useless, and there shall be loss of friends and fellows, and mirth departed, and dull days and empty hours,

B B

and the children wandering about marvelling at the sorrow of
the house. All this I saw before me, and grief and pain and
wounding and death; and I said: Shall I be any better than
the worst of the folk that loveth me? Nay, this shall never be;
and since I have learned to be deft with mine hands in all the play
of war, and that I am as strong as many a man, and as hardy-
hearted as any, I will give myself to the Warrior and the God
of the Face; and the battle-field shall be my home, and the after-
grief of the fight my banquet and holiday, that I may bear the
burden of my people, in the battle and out of it; and know every
sorrow that the Dale hath; and cast aside as a grievous and ugly
thing the bed of the warrior that the maiden desires, and the toying
of lips and hands and soft words of desire, and all the joy that
dwelleth in the Castle of Love and the Garden thereof; while the
world outside is sick and sorry, and the fields lie waste and the
harvest burneth. Even so have I sworn, even so will I do.'

Her eyes glittered and her cheek was flushed, and her voice was
clear and ringing now; and when she ended there arose a murmur of
praise from the men round about her. But Iron-face said coldly:

'These are great words; but I know not what they mean. If
thou wilt to the field and fight among the carles (and that I would
not naysay, for it hath oft been done and praised aforetime), why
shouldest thou not go side by side with Face-of-god and as his
plighted maiden?'

The light which the sweetness of speech had brought into her
face had died out of it now, and she looked weary and hapless as
she answered him slowly:

'I will not wed with Face-of-god, but will fare afield as a
virgin of war, as I have sworn to the Warrior.'

Then waxed Iron-face exceeding wroth, and he rose up before
all men and cried loudly and fiercely:

'There is some lie abroad, that windeth about us as the gos-
samers in the lanes of an autumn morning.'

And therewith he strode up to Face-of-god as though he had

nought to do with the Thing; and he stood before him and cried out at him while all men wondered : Iron-face would break the peace of the Thing.

'Thou! what hast thou done to turn this maiden's heart to stone? Who is it that is devising guile with thee to throw aside this worthy wedding in a worthy House, with whom our sons are ever wont to wed? Speak, tell the tale!'

But Face-of-god held his peace and stood calm and proud before all men.

Then the blood mounted to Iron-face's head, and he forgat folk and kindred and the war to come, and he cried so that all the place rang with the words of his anger :

'Thou dastard! I see thee now; it is thou that hast done this, and not the maiden; and now thou hast made her bear a double burden, and set her on to speak for thee, whilst thou standest by saying nought, and wilt take no scruple's weight of her shame upon thee!'

But his son spake never a word, and Iron-face cried: 'Out on thee! I know thee now, and why thou wouldest not to the Westland last winter. I am no fool; I know thee. Where hast thou hidden the stranger woman?'

Therewith he drew forth his sword and hove it aloft as if to hew down Face-of-god, who spake not nor flinched nor raised a hand from his side. But the Bride threw herself in front of Gold-mane, while there arose an angry cry of 'The Peace of the Holy Thing! Peace-breaking, peace-breaking!' and some cried, 'For the War-leader, the War-leader!' and as men could for the press they drew forth their swords, and there was tumult and noise all over the Thing-stead.

But Stone-face caught hold of the Alderman's right arm and dragged down the sword, and the big carle, Red-coat of Waterless, came up behind him and cast his arms about his middle and drew him back; and presently he looked around him, and slowly sheathed his sword, and went back to his place and sat him down; and in a little while the noise abated and swords were sheathed,

187

and men waxed quiet again, and the Alderman arose and said in
a loud voice, but in the wonted way of the head man of the Thing:

'Here hath been trouble in the Holy Thing; a violent man
hath troubled it, and drawn sword on a neighbour; will the neighbours give the dooming hereof into the hands of the Alderman?'

Now all knew Iron-face, and they cried out, 'That will we.'
So he spake again:

'I doom the troubler of the Peace of the Holy Thing to pay a
fine, to wit double the blood-wite that would be duly paid for a
full-grown freeman of the kindreds.'

Then the cry went up and men yeasaid his doom, and all said
that it was well and fairly doomed; and Iron-face sat still.

But Stone-face stood forth and said:

'Here have been wild words in the air; and dreams have taken
shape and come amongst us, and have bewitched us, so that friends
and kin have wrangled. And meseemeth that this is through the
wizardry of these felons, who, even dead as they are, have cast
spells over us. Good it were to cast them into the Death Tarn,
and then to get to our work; for there is much to do.'

All men yeasaid that; and Forkbeard of Lea went with
those who had borne the corpses thither to cast them into the
black pool.

But the Fiddle spake and said:

'Stone-face sayeth sooth. O Alderman, thou art no young man,
yet am I old enough to be thy father; so will I give thee a rede,
and say this: Face-of-god thy son is no liar or dastard or beguiler, but he is a young man and exceeding goodly of fashion,
well-spoken and kind; so that few women may look on him and
hear him without desiring his kindness and love, and to such men
as this many things happen. Moreover, he hath now become our
captain, and is a deft warrior with his hands, and as I deem, a sober
and careful leader of men; therefore we need him and his courage
and his skill of leading. So rage not against him as if he had
done an ill deed not to be forgiven—whatever he hath done,

188

whereof we know not—for life is long before him, and most like we shall still have to thank him for many good deeds towards us. As for the maiden, she is both lovely and wise. She hath a sorrow at her heart, and we deem that we know what it is. Yet hath she not lied when she said that she would bear the burden of the griefs of the people. Even so shall she do; and whether she will, or whether she will not, that shall heal her own griefs. For to-morrow is a new day. Therefore, if thou do after my rede, thou wilt not meddle betwixt these twain, but wilt remember all that we have to do, and that war is coming upon us. And when that is over, we shall turn round and behold each other, and see that we are not wholly what we were before; and then shall that which were hard to forgive, be forgotten, and that which is remembered be easy to forgive.'

So he spake; and Iron-face sat still and put his left hand to his beard as one who pondereth; but the Bride looked in the face of the old man the Fiddle, and then she turned and looked at Gold-mane, and her face softened, and she stood before the Alderman, and bent down before him and held out both her hands to him the palms upward. Then she said: 'Thou hast been wroth with me, and I marvel not; for thy hope, and the hope which we all had, hath deceived thee. But kind indeed hast thou been to me ere now: therefore I pray thee take it not amiss if I call to thy mind the oath which thou swearedst on the Holy Boar last Yule, that thou wouldst not gainsay the prayer of any man if thou couldest perform it; therefore I bid thee naysay not mine: and that is, that thou wilt ask me no more about this matter, but wilt suffer me to fare afield like any swain of the Dale, and to deal so with my folk that they shall not hinder me. Also I pray thee that thou wilt put no shame upon Face-of-god my playmate and my kinsman, nor show thine anger to him openly, even if for a little while thy love for him be abated. No more than this will I ask of thee.'

All men who heard her were moved to the heart by her kind-

189

ness and the sweetness of her voice, which was like to the robin singing suddenly on a frosty morning of early winter. But as for Gold-mane, his heart was smitten sorely by it, and her sorrow and her friendliness grieved him out of measure.

But Iron-face answered after a little while, speaking slowly and hoarsely, and with the shame yet clinging to him of a man who has been wroth and has speedily let his wrath run off him. So he said:

'It is well, my daughter. I have no will to forswear myself; nor hast thou asked me a thing which is over-hard. Yet indeed I would that to-day were yesterday, or that many days were worn away.'

Then he stood up and cried in a loud voice over the throng: 'Let none forget the muster; but hold him ready against the time that the Warden shall come to him. Let all men obey the War-leader, Face-of-god, without question or delay. As to the fine of the peace-breaker, it shall be laid on the altar of the God at the Great Folk-mote. Herewith is the Thing broken up.'

Then all men shouted and clashed their weapons, and so sundered, and went about their business.

And the talk of men it was that the breaking of the troth-plight between those twain was ill; for they loved Face-of-god, and as for the Bride they deemed her the Dearest of the kindreds and the Jewel of the Folk, and as if she were the fairest and the kindest of all the Gods. Neither did the wrath of Iron-face mislike any; but they said he had done well and manly both to be wroth and to let his wrath run off him. As to the war which was to come, they kept a good heart about it, and deemed it as a game to be played, wherein they might show themselves deft and valiant, and so get back to their merry life again.

So wore the day through afternoon to even and night.

## CHAPTER XXVII. FACE-OF-GOD LEADETH A BAND THROUGH THE WOOD.

NEXT morning tryst was held faithfully, and an hundred and a half were gathered together on Wildlake's Way; and Face-of-god ordered them into three companies. He made Hall-face leader over the first one, and bade him hold on his way northward, and then to make for Boars-bait and see if he should meet with anything thereabout where the battle had been. Red-coat of Waterless he made captain of the second band; and he had it in charge to wend eastward along the edge of the Dale, and not to go deep into the wood, but to go as far as he might within the time appointed, toward the Mountains. Furthermore, he bade both Hall-face and Red-coat to bring their bands back to Wildlake's Way by the morrow at sunset, where other goodmen should be come to take the places of their men; and then if he and his company were back again, he would bid them further what to do; but if not, as seemed likely, then Hall-face's band to go west toward the Shepherd country half a day's journey, and so back, and Red-coat's east along the Dale's lip again for the like time, and then back, so that there might be a constant watch and ward of the Dale kept against the Felons.

All being ordered Gold-mane led his own company north-east through the thick wood, thinking that he might so fare as to come nigh to Silver-dale, or at least to hear tidings thereof. This intent he told to Stone-face, but the old man shook his head and said:

'Good is this if it may be done; but it is not for everyone to go down to Hell in his lifetime and come back safe with a tale thereof. However, whither thou wilt lead, thither will I follow, though assured death waylayeth us.'

And the old carle was joyous and proud to be on this adventure, and said, that it was good indeed that his foster-son had with

191

him a man well stricken in years, who had both seen many things, and learned many, and had good rede to give to valiant men.

So they went on their ways, and fared very warily when they were gotten beyond those parts of the wood which they knew well. By this time they were strung out in a long line; and they noted their road carefully, blazing the trees on either side when there were trees, and piling up little stone-heaps where the trees failed them. For Stone-face said that oft it befell men amidst the thicket and the waste to be misled by wights that begrudged men their lives, so that they went round and round in a ring which they might not depart from till they died; and no man doubted his word herein.

All day they went, and met no foe, nay, no man at all; nought but the wild things of the wood; and that day the wood changed little about them from mile to mile. There were many thickets across their road which they had to go round about; so that to the crow flying over the tree-tops the journey had not been long to the place where night came upon them, and where they had to make the wood their bedchamber.

That night they lighted no fire, but ate such cold victual as they might carry with them; nor had they shot any venison, since they had with them more than enough; they made little noise or stir therefore and fell asleep when they had set the watch.

On the morrow they arose betimes, and broke their fast and went their ways till noon: by then the wood had thinned somewhat, and there was little underwood betwixt the scrubby oak and ash which were pretty nigh all the trees about: the ground also was broken, and here and there rocky, and they went into and out of rough little dales, most of which had in them a brook of water running west and south-west; and now Face-of-god led his men somewhat more easterly; and still for some while they met no man.

At last, about four hours after noon, when they were going less warily, because they had hitherto come across nothing to

hinder them, rising over the brow of a somewhat steep ridge, They come
they saw down in the valley below them a half score of men upon the foe.
sitting by the brook-side eating and drinking, their weapons lying
beside them, and along with them stood a woman with her hands
tied behind her back.

They saw at once that these men were of the Felons, so they
that had their bows bent, loosed at them without more ado, while
the others ran in upon them with sword and spear. The felons
leapt up and ran scattering down the dale, such of them as were
not smitten by the shafts; but he who was nighest to the woman,
ere he ran, turned and caught up a sword from the ground and
thrust it through her, and the next moment fell across the brook
with an arrow in his back.

No one of the felons was nimble enough to escape from the
fleet-foot hunters of Burgdale, and they were all slain there to
the number of eleven.

But when they came back to the woman to tend her, she breathed
her last in their hands: she was a young and fair woman, black-
haired and dark-eyed. She had on her body a gown of rich web,
but nought else: she had been bruised and sore mishandled, and
the Burgdale carles wept for pity of her, and for wrath, as they
straightened her limbs on the turf of the little valley. They let
her lie there a little, whilst they searched round about, lest there
should be any other poor soul needing their help, or any felon
lurking thereby; but they found nought else save a bundle wherein
was another rich gown and divers woman's gear, and sundry rings
and jewels, and therewithal the weapons and war-gear of a knight,
delicately wrought after the Westland fashion: these seemed to
them to betoken other foul deeds of these murder-carles. So when
they had abided a while, they laid the dead woman in mould by
the brook-side, and buried with her the other woman's attire and
the knight's gear, all but his sword and shield, which they had
away with them: then they cast the carcasses of the felons into the
brake, but brought away their weapons and the silver rings from

C C

their arms, which they wore like all the others of them whom they
had fallen in with; and so went on their way to the north-east,
full of wrath against those dastards of the Earth.

It was hard on sunset when they left the valley of murder, and
they went no long way thence before they must needs make stay
for the night; and when they had arrayed their sleeping-stead
the moon was up, and they saw that before them lay the close
wood again, for they had made their lair on the top of a little ridge.

There then they lay, and nought stirred them in the night, and
betimes on the morrow they were afoot, and entered the abovesaid thicket, wherein two of them, keen hunters, had been aforetime, but had not gone deep into it. Through this wood they
went all day toward the north-east, and met nought but the wild
things therein. At last, when it was near sunset, they came out
of the thicket into a small plain, or shallow dale rather, with no
great trees in it, but thorn-brakes here and there where the ground
sank into hollows; a little river ran through the midst of it, and
winded round about a height whose face toward the river went
down sheer into the water, but away from it sank down in a long
slope to where the thick wood began again: and this height or
burg looked well-nigh west.

Thitherward they went; but as they were drawing nigh to the
river, and were on the top of a bent above a bushy hollow between
them and the water, they espied a man standing in the river near
the bank, who saw them not, because he was stooping down intent
on something in the bank or under it: so they gat them speedily
down into the hollow without noise, that they might get some
tidings of the man.

Then Face-of-god bade his men abide hidden under the bushes
and stole forward quietly up the further bank of the hollow, his
target on his arm and his spear poised. When he was behind
the last bush on the top of the bent he was within half a spear-
cast of the water and the man; so he looked on him and saw
that he was quite naked except for a clout about his middle.

194

Face-of-god saw at once that he was not one of the Dusky Men; he was a black-haired man, but white-skinned, and of fair stature, though not so tall as the Burgdale folk. He was busied in tickling trouts, and just as Face-of-god came out from the bush into the westering sunlight, he threw up a fish on to the bank, and looked up therewithal, and beheld the weaponed man glittering, and uttered a cry, but fled not when he saw the spear poised for casting.

Then Face-of-god spake to him and said: 'Come hither, Woodsman! we will not harm thee, but we desire speech of thee : and it will not avail thee to flee, since I have bowmen of the best in the hollow yonder.'

The man put forth his hands towards him as if praying him to forbear casting, and looked at him hard, and then came dripping from out the water, and seemed not greatly afeard; for he stooped down and picked up the trouts he had taken, and came towards Face-of-god stringing the last-caught one through the gills on to the withy whereon were the others: and Face-of-god saw that he was a goodly man of some thirty winters.

Then Face-of-god looked on him with friendly eyes and said: 'Art thou a foeman? or wilt thou be helpful to us?'

He answered in the speech of the kindreds with the hoarse voice of a much weather-beaten man :

'Thou seest, lord, that I am naked and unarmed.'

'Yet mayst thou bewray us,' said Face-of-god. 'What man art thou?'

Said the man: 'I am the runaway thrall of evil men; I have fled from Rose-dale and the Dusky Men. Hast thou the heart to hurt me?'

'We are the foemen of the Dusky Men,' said Face-of-god; 'wilt thou help us against them?'

The man knit his brows and said : 'Yea, if ye will give me your word not to suffer me to fall into their hands alive. But whence art thou, to be so bold?'

Said Face-of-god : 'We are of Burgdale ; and I will swear
to thee on the edge of the sword that thou shalt not fall alive into
the hands of the Dusky Men.'

'Of Burgdale have I heard,' said the man ; 'and in sooth
thou seemest not such a man as would bewray a hapless man.
But now had I best bring you to some lurking-place where ye
shall not be easily found of these devils, who now oft-times scour
the woods hereabout.'

Said Face-of-god : 'Come first and see my fellows ; and then
if thou thinkest we have need to hide, it is well.'

So the man went side by side with him towards their lair, and
as they went Gold-mane noted marks of stripes on his back and
sides, and said : 'Sorely hast thou been mishandled, poor man ! '

Then the man turned on him and said somewhat fiercely :
'Said I not that I had been a thrall of the Dusky Men ? how
then should I have escaped tormenting and scourging, if I had
been with them for but three days ? '

As he spake they came about a thorn-bush, and there were the
Burgdale men down in the hollow ; and the man said : 'Are
these thy fellows ?  Call to mind that thou hast sworn by the
edge of the sword not to hurt me.'

'Poor man ! ' said Face-of-god ; 'these are thy friends, unless
thou bewrayest us.'

Then he cried aloud to his folk : 'Here is now a good hap !
this is a runaway thrall of the Dusky Men ; of him shall we hear
tidings ; so cherish him all ye may.'

So the carles thronged about him and bestirred themselves to
help him, and one gave him his surcoat for a kirtle, and another
cast a cloak about him ; and they brought him meat and drink,
such as they had ready to hand : and the man looked as if he
scarce believed in all this, but deemed himself to be in a dream.
But presently he turned to Face-of-god and said :

'Now I see so many men and weapons I deem that ye have
no need to skulk in caves to-night, though I know of good ones :

yet shall ye do well not to light a fire till moon-setting; for the flame ye may lightly hide, but the smoke may be seen from far aloof.'

But they bade him to meat, and he needed no second bidding but ate lustily, and they gave him wine, and he drank a great draught and sighed as for joy. Then he said in a trembling voice, as though he feared a naysay:

'If ye are from Burgdale ye shall be faring back again presently; and I pray you to take me with you.'

Said Face-of-god: 'Yea surely, friend, that will we do, and rejoice in thee.'

Then he drank another cup which Warcliff held out to him, and spake again: 'Yet if ye would abide here till about noon to-morrow, or mayhappen a little later, I would bring other runaways to see you; and them also might ye take with you: ye may think when ye see them that ye shall have small gain of their company; for poor wretched folk they be, like to myself. Yet since ye seek for tidings, herein might they do you more service than I; for amongst them are some who came out of the hapless Dale within this moon; and it is six months since I escaped. Moreover, though they may look spent and outworn now, yet if ye give them a little rest, and feed them well, they shall yet do many a day's work for you: and I tell you that if ye take them for thralls, and put collars on their necks, and use them no worse than a goodman useth his oxen and his asses, beating them not save when they are idle or at fault, it shall be to them as if they were come to heaven out of hell, and to such goodhap as they have not thought of, save in dreams, for many and many a day. And thus I entreat you to do because ye seem to me to be happy and merciful men, who will not begrudge us this happiness.'

The carles of Burgdale listened eagerly to what he said, and they looked at him with great eyes and marvelled; and their hearts were moved with pity towards him; and Stone-face said:

197

'Herein, O War-leader, need I give thee no rede, for thou mayst see clearly that all we deem that we should lose our manhood and become the dastards of the Warrior if we did not abide the coming of these poor men, and take them back to the Dale, and cherish them.'

'Yea,' said Wolf of Whitegarth, 'and great thanks we owe to this man that he biddeth us this: for great will be the gain to us if we become so like the Gods that we may deliver the poor from misery. Now must I needs think how they shall wonder when they come to Burgdale and find out how happy it is to dwell there.'

'Surely,' said Face-of-god, 'thus shall we do, whatever cometh of it. But, friend of the wood, as to thralls, there be none such in the Dale, but therein are all men friends and neighbours, and even so shall ye be.'

And he fell a-musing, when he bethought him of how little he had known of sorrow.

But that man, when he beheld the happy faces of the Burgdalers, and hearkened to their friendly voices, and understood what they said, and he also was become strong with the meat and drink, he bowed his head adown and wept a long while; and they meddled not with him, till he turned again to them and said:

'Since ye are in arms, and seem to be seeking your foemen, I suppose ye wot that these tyrants and man-quellers will fall upon you in Burgdale ere the summer is well worn.'

'So much we deem indeed,' said Face-of-god, 'but we were fain to hear the certainty of it, and how thou knowest thereof.'

Said the man: 'It was six moons ago that I fled, as I have told you; and even then it was the common talk amongst our masters that there were fair dales to the south which they would overrun. Man would say to man: We were over many in Silverdale, and we needed more thralls, because those we had were lessening, and especially the women; now are we more at ease

198

in Rose-dale, though we have sent thralls to Silver-dale; but yet we can bear no more men from thence to eat up our stock from us: let them fare south to the happy dales, and conquer them, and we will go with them and help therein, whether we come back to Rose-dale or no. Such talk did I hear then with mine own ears: but some of those whom I shall bring to you to-morrow shall know better what is doing, since they have fled from Rose-dale but a few days. Moreover, there is a man and a woman who have fled from Silver-dale itself, and are but a month from it, journeying all the time save when they must needs hide; and these say that their masters have got to know the ways to Burgdale, and are minded for it before the winter, as I said; and nought else but the ways thither do they desire to know, since they have no fear.'

By then was night come, and though the moon was high in heaven, and lighted all that waste, the Burgdalers must needs light a fire for cooking their meat, whatsoever that woodsman might say; moreover, the night was cold and somewhat frosty. A little before they had come to that place they had shot a fat buck and some smaller deer, but of other meat they had no great store, though there was wine enough. So they lit their fire in the thickest of the thorn-bush to hide it all they might, and thereat they cooked their venison and the trouts which the runaway had taken, and they fell to, and ate and drank and were merry, making much of that poor man till him-seemed he was gotten into the company of the kindest of the Gods.

But when they were full, Face-of-god spake to him, and asked him his name; and he named himself Dallach; but said he: 'Lord, this is according to the naming of men in Rose-dale before we were enthralled: but now what names have thralls? Also I am not altogether of the blood of them of Rose-dale, but of better and more warrior-like kin.'

Said Face-of-god: 'Thou hast named Silver-dale; knowest thou it?'

199

Dallach answered : 'I have never seen it. It is far hence ; in
a week's journey, making all diligence, and not being forced to
hide and skulk like those runaways, ye shall come to the mouth
thereof lying west, where its rock-walls fall off toward the plain.'

'But,' said Face-of-god, 'is there no other way into that
Dale ? '

'Nay, none that folk wot of,' said Dallach, 'except to bold
cragsmen with their lives in their hands.'

'Knowest thou aught of the affairs of Silver-dale ? ' said
Face-of-god.

Said Dallach : 'Somewhat I know : we wot that but a few
years ago there was a valiant folk dwelling therein, who were
lords of the whole dale, and that they were vanquished by the
Dusky Men : but whether they were all slain and enthralled we
wot not ; but we deem it otherwise. As for me it is of their blood
that I am partly come ; for my father's father came thence to
settle in Rose-dale, and wedded a woman of the Dale, who was
my father's mother.'

'When was it that ye fell under the Dusky Men ? ' said
Face-of-god.

Said Dallach : 'It was five years ago. They came into the
Dale a great company, all in arms.'

'Was there battle betwixt you ? ' said Face-of-god.

'Alas ! not so,' said Dallach. 'We were a happy folk there ;
but soft and delicate : for the Dale is exceeding fertile, and beareth
wealth in abundance, both corn and oil and wine and fruit, and
of beasts for man's service the best that may be. Would that
there had been battle, and that I had died therein with those that
had a heart to fight ; and even so saith now every man, yea, every
woman in the Dale. But it was not so when the elders met in
our Council-House on the day when the Dusky Men bade us pay
them tribute and give them houses to dwell in and lands to live
by. Then had we weapons in our hands, but no hearts to
use them.'

200

'What befell then?' said the goodman of Whitegarth.

Said Dallach: 'Look ye to it, lords, that it befall not in Burgdale! We gave them all they asked for, and deemed we had much left. What befell, sayst thou? We sat quiet; we went about our work in fear and trembling, for grim and hideous were they to look on. At first they meddled not much with us, save to take from our houses what they would of meat and drink, or raiment, or plenishing. And all this we deemed we might bear, and that we needed no more than to toil a little more each day so as to win somewhat more of wealth. But soon we found that it would not be so; for they had no mind to till the teeming earth or work in the acres we had given them, or to sit at the loom, or hammer in the stithy, or do any manlike work; it was we that must do all that for their behoof, and it was altogether for them that we laboured, and nought for ourselves; and our bodies were only so much our own as they were needful to be kept alive for labour. Herein were our tasks harder than the toil of any mules or asses, save for the younger and goodlier of the women, whom they would keep fair and delicate to be their bed-thralls.

'Yet not even so were our bodies safe from their malice: for these men were not only tyrants, but fools and madmen. Let alone that there were few days without stripes and torments to satiate their fury or their pleasure, so that in all streets and nigh any house might you hear wailing and screaming and groaning; but moreover, though a wise man would not willingly slay his own thrall any more than his own horse or ox, yet did these men so wax in folly and malice, that they would often hew at man or woman as they met them in the way from mere grimness of soul; and if they slew them it was well. Thereof indeed came quarrels enough betwixt master and master, for they are much given to man-slaying amongst themselves: but what profit to us thereof? Nay, if the dead man were a chieftain, then woe betide the thralls! for thereof must many an one be slain on his grave-mound to serve him on the hell-road. To be short: we have heard of men who

be fierce, and men who be grim ; but these we may scarce believe
to be men at all, but trolls rather ; and ill will it be if their race
waxeth in the world.'

The Burgdale men hearkened with all their ears, and wondered
that such things could befall ; and they rejoiced at the work that
lay before them, and their hearts rose high at the thought of battle
in that behalf, and the fame that should come of it.   As for the
runaway, they made so much of him that the man marvelled ; for
they dealt with him like a woman cherishing a son, and knew not
how to be kind enough to him.

## CHAPTER XXVIII. THE MEN OF BURGDALE MEET THE RUNAWAYS.

NOW ere the night was far spent, Dallach arose and said :
'Kind folk, ye will presently be sleeping ; but I bid you
keep a good watch, and if ye will be ruled by me, ye will
kindle no fire on the morrow, for the smoke riseth thick in the
morning air, and is as a beacon.   As for me, I shall leave you
here to rest, and I myself will fare on mine errand.'

They bade him sleep and rest him after so many toils and hard-
ships, saying that they were not tied to an hour to be back in
Burgdale ; but he said : 'Nay, the moon is high, and it is as good
as daylight to me, who could find my way even by starlight ; and
your tarrying here is nowise safe.   Moreover, if I could find those
folk and bring them part of the way by night and cloud it were
well ; for if we were taken again, burning quick would be the best
death by which we should die.   As for me, now am I strong with
meat and drink and hope ; and when I come to Burgdale there
will be time enough for resting and slumber.'

Said Face-of-god : 'Shall I not wend with thee to see these
people and the lairs wherein they hide ?'

The man smiled : 'Nay, earl,' said he, 'that shall not be.

For wot ye what? If they were to see me in company of a man-at-arms they would deem that I was bringing the foe upon them, and would flee, or mayhappen would fall upon us. For as for me, when I saw thee, thou wert close anigh me, so I knew thee to be no Dusky Man; but they would see the glitter of thine arms from afar, and to them all weaponed men are foemen. Thou, lord, knowest not the heart of a thrall, nor the fear and doubt that is in it. Nay, I myself must cast off these clothes that ye have given me, and fare naked, lest they mistrust me. Only I will take a spear in my hand, and sling a knife round my neck, if ye will give them to me; for if the worst happen, I will not be taken alive.'

Therewith he cast off his raiment, and they gave him the weapons and wished him good speed, and he went his way twixt moonlight and shadow; but the Burgdalers went to sleep when they had set a watch.

Early in the morning they awoke, and the sun was shining and the thrushes singing in the thorn-brake, and all seemed fair and peaceful, and a little haze still hung about the face of the burg over the river. So they went down to the water and washed the night from off them; and thence the most part of them went back to their lair among the thorn-bushes: but four of them went up the dale into the oak-wood to shoot a buck, and five more they sent out to watch their skirts around them; and Face-of-god with old Stone-face went over a ford of the stream, and came on to the lower slope of the burg, and so went up it to the top. Thence they looked about to see if aught were stirring, but they saw little save the waste and the wood, which on the north-east was thick of big trees stretching out a long way. Their own lair was clear to see over its bank and the bushes thereof, and that misliked Face-of-god, lest any foe should climb the burg that day. The morning was clear, and Face-of-god looking north-and-by-west deemed he saw smoke rising into the air over the tree-covered ridges that hid the further distance toward that airt, though further east uphove the black shoulders of the Great

The elves that
love the van-
quished wane
with them.
Waste and the snowy peaks behind them. The said smoke was
not such as cometh from one great fire, but was like a thin veil
staining the pale blue sky, as when men are burning ling on the
heath-side and it is seen aloof.

He showed that smoke to Stone-face, who smiled and said :
'Now will they be lighting the cooking fires in Rose-dale : would
I were there with a few hundreds of axes and staves at my back!'

'Yea,' said Face-of-god, smiling in his face, ' but where I pray
thee are these elves and wood-wights, that we meet them not?
Grim things there are in the woods, and things fair enough also :
but meseemeth that the trolls and the elves of thy young years
have been frighted away.'

Said Stone-face : ' Maybe, foster-son ; that hath been seen ere
now, that when one race of man overrunneth the land inhabited
by another, the wights and elves that love the vanquished are
seen no more, or get them away far off into the outermost wilds,
where few men ever come.'

' Yea,' said Face-of-god, 'that may well be. But deemest
thou by that token that we shall be vanquished ? '

' As for us, I know not,' said Stone-face ; ' but thy friends of
Shadowy Vale have been vanquished. Moreover, concerning
these felons whom now we are hunting, are we all so sure that they
be men ? Certain it is, that when I go into battle with them,
I shall smite with no more pity than my sword, as if I were
smiting things that may not feel the woes of man.'

Said Face-of-god : ' Yea, even so shall it be with me. But
what thinkest thou of these runaways ? Shall we have tidings of
them, or shall Dallach bring the foe upon us ? It was for the sake
of that question that I have clomb the burg : and that we might
watch the land about us.'

' Nay,' said Stone-face, ' I have seen many men, and I deem of
Dallach that he is a true man. I deem we shall soon have tidings
of his fellows ; and they may have seen the elves and wood-wights :
I would fain ask them thereof, and am eager to see them.'

204

Said Face-of-god : 'And I somewhat dread to see them, and They see the their rags and their misery and the weals of their stripes. It irked new-comers me to see Dallach when he first fell to his meat last night, how from the he ate like a dog for fear and famine. How shall it be, moreover, Burg. when we have them in the Dale, and they fall to the deed of kind there, as they needs must. Will they not bear us evil and thrall-like men ?'

'Maybe,' said Stone-face, 'and maybe not ; for they have been thralls but for a little while : and I deem that in no long time shall ye see them much bettered by plenteous meat and rest. And after all is said, this Dallach bore him like a valiant man ; also it was valiant of him to flee ; and of the others may ye say the like. But look you ! there are men going down yonder towards our lair : belike those shall be our guests, and there be no Dusky Men amongst them. Come, let us home !'

So Face-of-god looked and beheld from the height of the burg shapes of men grey and colourless creeping toward the lair from sunshine to shadow, like wild creatures shy and fearful of the hunter, or so he deemed of them.

So he turned away, angry and sad of heart, and the twain went down the burg and across the water to their camp, having seen little to tell of from the height.

When they came to their campment there were their folk standing in a ring round about Dallach and the other runaways. They made way for the War-leader and Stone-face, who came amongst them and beheld the Runaways, that they were many more than they looked to see ; for they were of carles one score and three, and of women eighteen, all told save Dallach. When they saw those twain come through the ring of men and perceived that they were chieftains, some of them fell down on their knees before them and held out their joined hands to them, and kissed the Burgdalers' feet and the hems of their garments, while the tears streamed out of their eyes : some stood moving little and staring before them stupidly : and some kept glancing from face to face of the well-

205

liking happy Burgdale carles, though for a while even their faces
were sad and downcast at the sight of the poor men : some also
kept murmuring one or two words in their country tongue, and
Dallach told Face-of-god that these were crying out for victual.

It must be said of these poor folk that they were of divers conditions, and chiefly of three : and first there were seven of Rose-
dale and five of Silver-dale late come to the wood (of these Silver-
dalers Dallach had told but of two, for the other three were
but just come). Of these twelve were seven women, and all, save
two of the women, were clad in one scanty kirtle or shirt only ;
for such was the wont of the Dusky Men with their thralls. They
had brought away weapons, and had amongst them six axes and
a spear, and a sword, and five knives, and one man had a shield.

Yet though these were clad and armed, yet in some wise were
they the worst of all ; they were so timorous and cringing, and
most of them heavy-eyed and sullen and down-looking. Many
of them had been grievously mishandled : one man had had his
left hand smitten off ; another was docked of three of his toes,
and the gristle of his nose slit up ; one was halt, and four had
been ear-cropped, nor did any lack weals of whipping. Of the
Silver-dale new-comers the three men were the worst of all
the Runaways, with wild wandering eyes, but sullen also, and
cringing if any drew nigh, and would not look anyone in the
face, save presently Face-of-god, on whom they were soon fond
to fawn, as a dog on his master. But the women who were
with them, and who were well-nigh as timorous as the men, were
those two gaily-clad ones, and they were soft-handed and white-
skinned, save for the last days of weather in the wood ; for they
had been bed-thralls of the Dusky Men.

Such were the new-comers to the wood. But others had been,
like Dallach, months therein ; it may be said that there were
eighteen of these, carles and queens together. Little raiment
they had amongst them, and some were all but stark naked, so
that on these might well be seen as on Dallach the marks of old

stripes, and of these also were there men who had been shorn of some member or other, and they were all burnt and blackened by the weather of the woodland; yet for all their nakedness, they bore themselves bolder and more manlike than the later comers, nor did they altogether lack weapons taken from their foemen, and most of them had some edge-tool or another. Of these folk were four from Silver-dale, though Dallach knew it not.

Besides these were a half score and one who had been years in the wood instead of months; weather-beaten indeed were these, shaggy and rough-skinned like wild men of kind. Some of them had made themselves skin breeches or clouts, some went stark naked; of weapons of the Dale had they few, but they bore bows of hazel or wych-elm strung with deer-gut, and shafts headed with flint stones; staves also of the same fashion, and great clubs of oak or holly: some of them also had made them targets of skin and willow-twigs, for these were the warriors of the Runaways: they had a few steel knives amongst them, but had mostly learned the craft of using sharp flints for knives: but four of these were women.

Three of these men were of the kindreds of the Wolf from Silver-dale, and had been in the wood for hard upon ten years, and wild as they were, and without hope of meeting their fellows again, they went proudly and boldly amongst the others, over-topping them by the head and more. For the greater part of these men were somewhat short of stature, though by nature strong and stout of body.

It must be told that though Dallach had thus gotten all these many Runaways together, yet had they not been dwelling together as one folk; for they durst not, lest the Dusky Men should hear thereof and fall upon them, but they had kept themselves as best they could in caves and in brakes three to-gether or two, or even faring alone as Dallach did: only as he was a strong and stout-hearted man, he went to and fro and wandered about more than the others, so that he foregathered

with most of them and knew them. He said also that he doubted
not but that there were more Runaways in the wood, but these
were all he could come at. Divers who had fled had died from
time to time, and some had been caught and cruelly slain by their
masters. They were none of them old ; the oldest, said Dallach,
scant of forty winters, though many from their aspect might have
been old enough.

So Face-of-god looked and beheld all these poor people ; and
said to himself, that he might well have dreaded that sight. For
here was he brought face to face with the Sorrow of the Earth,
whereof he had known nought heretofore, save it might be as a
tale in a minstrel's song. And when he thought of the minutes
that had made the hours, and the hours that had made the days
that these men had passed through, his heart failed him, and he
was dumb and might not speak, though he perceived that the
men of Burgdale looked for speech from him ; but he waved
his hand to his folk, and they understood him, for they had
heard Dallach say that some of them were crying for victual.
So they set to work and dighted for them such meat as they had,
and they set them down on the grass and made themselves their
carvers and serving-men, and bade them eat what they would of
such as there was. Yet, indeed, it grieved the Burgdalers again to
note how these folk were driven to eat ; for they themselves, though
they were merry folk, were exceeding courteous at table, and of
great observance of manners : whereas these poor Runaways ate,
some of them like hungry dogs, and some hiding their meat as if
they feared it should be taken from them, and some cowering over
it like falcons, and scarce any with a manlike pleasure in their
meal. And, their eating over, the more part of them sat dull and
mopish, and as if all things were forgotten for the time present.

Albeit presently Dallach bestirred him and said to Face-of-
god : ' Lord of the Earl-folk, if I might give thee rede, it were
best to turn your faces to Burgdale without more tarrying. For
we are over-nigh to Rose-dale, being but thus many in com-

208

pany. But when we come to our next resting-place, then shall I They turn about to Burgdale. bring thee to speech with the last-comers from Silver-dale; for there they talk with the tongue of the kindreds; but we of Rose-dale for the more part talk otherwise; though in my house it came down from father to son.'

'Yea,' said Face-of-god, gazing still on that unhappy folk, as they sat or lay upon the grass at rest for a little while: but him-seemed as he gazed that some memories of past time stirred in some of them; for some, they hung their heads and the tears stole out of their eyes and rolled down their cheeks. But those older Runaways of Silver-dale were not crouched down like most of the others, but strode up and down like beasts in a den; yet were the tears on the face of one of these. Then Face-of-god constrained himself, and spake to the folk, and said: 'We are now over-nigh to our foes of Rose-dale to lie here any longer, being too few to fall upon them. We will come hither again with a host when we have duly questioned these men who have sought refuge with us: and let us call yonder height the Burg of the Runaways, and it shall be a landmark for us when we are on the road to Rose-dale.'

Then the Burgdalers bade the Runaways courteously and kindly to arise and take the road with them; and by that time were their men all come in; and four of them had venison with them, which was needful, if they were to eat that night or the morrow, as the guests had eaten them to the bone.

So they tarried no more, but set out on the homeward way; and Face-of-god bade Dallach walk beside him, and asked him much concerning Rose-dale and its Dusky Men. Dallach told him that these were not so many as they were masterful, not being above eight hundreds of men, all fighting-men. As to women, they had none of their own race, but lay with the Daleswomen at their will, and begat children of them; and all or most of the said children favoured the race of their begetters. Of the men-children they reared most, but the women-children they slew at once; for

209                                         E E

Dallach tells
of the griefs
of Rose-dale.

they valued not women of their own blood : but besides the women of the Dale, they would go at whiles in bands to the edges of the Plain and beguile wayfarers, and bring back with them thence women to be their bed-thralls ; albeit some of these were bought with a price from the Westland men.

As to the number of the folk of Rose-dale, its own folk, he said they would number some five thousand souls, one with another ; of whom some thousand might be fit to bear arms if they had the heart thereto, as they had none. Yet being closely questioned, he deemed that they might fall on their masters from behind, if battle were joined.

He said that the folk of Rose-dale had been a goodly folk before they were enthralled, and peaceable with one another, but that now it was a sport of the Dusky Men to set a match between their thralls to fight it out with sword and buckler or otherwise ; and the vanquished man, if he were not sore hurt, they would scourge, or shear some member from him, or even slay him outright, if the match between the owners were so made. And many other sad and grievous tales he told to Face-of-god, more than need be told again ; so that the War-leader went along sorry and angry, with his teeth set, and his hand on the sword-hilt.

Thus they went till night fell on them, and they could scarce see the signs they had made on their outward journey. Then they made stay in a little valley, having set a watch duly ; and since they were by this time far from Rose-dale, and were a great company as regarded scattered bands of the foe, they lighted their fires and cooked their venison, and made good cheer to the Runaways, and so went to sleep in the wild-wood.

When morning was come they gat them at once to the road ; and if the Burgdalers were eager to be out of the wood, their eagerness was as nought to the eagerness of the Runaways, most of whom could not be easy now, and deemed every minute lost unless they were wending on to the Dale ; so that this day they were willing to get over the more ground, whereas they had not set out on their road till afternoon yesterday.

Howsoever, they rested at noontide, and Face-of-god bade Dallach bring him to speech with others of the Runaways, and first that he might talk with those three men of the kindreds who had fled from Silver-dale in early days. So Dallach brought them to him; but he found that though they spake the tongue, they were so few-spoken from wildness and loneliness, at least at first, that nought could come from them that was not dragged from them.

These men said that they had been in the wood more than nine years, so that they knew but little of the conditions of the Dale in that present day. However, as to what Dallach had said concerning the Dusky Men, they strengthened his words; and they said that the Dusky Men took no delight save in beholding torments and misery, and that they doubted if they were men or trolls. They said that since they had dwelt in the wood they had slain not a few of the foemen, waylaying them as occasion served, but that in this warfare they had lost two of their fellows. When Face-of-god asked them of their deeming of the numbers of the Dusky Men, they said that before those bands had broken into Rose-dale, they counted them, as far as they could call to mind, at about three thousand men, all warriors; and that somewhat less than one thousand had gone up into Rose-dale, and some had died, and many had been cast away in the wild-wood, their fellows knew not how. Yet had not their numbers in Silver-dale diminished; because two years after they (the speakers) had fled, came three more Dusky Companies or Tribes into Silver-dale, and each of these tribes was of three long hundreds; and with their coming had the cruelty and misery much increased in the Dale, so that the thralls began to die fast; and that drave the Dusky Men beyond the borders of Silver-dale, so that they fell upon Rose-dale. When asked how many of the kindreds might yet be abiding in Silver-dale, their faces clouded, and they seemed exceeding wroth, and answered, that they would willingly hope that most of those that had not been slain at the time of the over-throw were now dead, yet indeed they feared there were yet some alive, and mayhappen not a few women.

By then must they get on foot again, and so the talk fell between them; but when they made stay for the night, after they had done their meat, Face-of-god prayed Dallach bring to him some of the latest-come folk from Silver-dale, and he brought to him the man and the woman who had been in the Dale within that moon. As to the man, if those of the Earl-folk had been few-spoken from fierceness and wildness, he was no less so from mere dulness and weariness of misery; but the woman's tongue went glibly enough, and it seemed to pleasure her to talk about her past miseries. As aforesaid, she was better clad than most of those of Rose-dale, and indeed might be called gaily clad, and where her raiment was befouled or rent, it was from the roughness of the wood and its weather, and not from the thralldom. She was a young and fair woman, black-haired and grey-eyed. She had washed herself that day in a woodland stream which they had crossed on the road, and had arrayed her garments as trimly as she might, and had plucked some fumitory, wherewith she had made a garland for her head. She sat down on the grass in front of Face-of-god, while the man her mate stood leaning against a tree and looked on her greedily. The Burgdale carles drew near to her to hearken her story, and looked kindly on the twain. She smiled on them, but especially on Face-of-god, and said:

'Thou hast sent for me, lord, and I wot well thou wouldst hear my tale shortly, for it would be long to tell if I were to tell it fully, and bring into it all that I have endured, which has been bitter enough, for all that ye see me smooth of skin and well-liking of body. I have been the bed-thrall of one of the chief-tains of the Dusky Men, at whose house many of their great men would assemble, so that ye may ask me whatso ye will; as I have heard much talk and may call it to mind. Now if ye ask me whether I have fled because of the shame that I, a free woman

come of free folk, should be a mere thrall in the bed of the foes of
my kin, and with no price paid for me, I must needs say it is not
so; since over long have we of the Dale been thralls to be ashamed
of such a matter. And again, if ye deem that I have fled because
I have been burdened with grievous toil and been driven thereto
by the whip, ye may look on my hands and my body and ye will
see that I have toiled little therewith : nor again did I flee because I could not endure a few stripes now and again ; for such
usage do thralls look for, even when they are delicately kept for
the sake of the fairness of their bodies, and this they may well
endure ; yea also, and the mere fear of death by torment now and
again. But before me lay death both assured and horrible ; so I
took mine own counsel, and told none for fear of bewrayal, save him
who guarded me ; and that was this man ; who fled not from fear,
but from love of me, and to him I have given all that I might
give. So we got out of the house and down the Dale by night
and cloud, and hid for one whole day in the Dale itself, where I
trembled and feared, so that I deemed I should die of fear ; but this
man was well pleased with my company, and with the lack of toil
and beating even for the day. And in the night again we fled and
reached the wild-wood before dawn, and well-nigh fell into the
hands of those who were hunting us, and had outgone us the day
before, as we lay hid. Well, what is to say ? They saw us not,
else had we not been here, but scattered piece-meal over the land.
This carle knew the passes of the wood, because he had followed
his master therein, who was a great hunter in the wastes, contrary to the wont of these men, and he had lain a night on the
burg yonder ; therefore he brought me thither, because he knew
that thereabout was plenty of prey easy to take, and he had a
bow with him ; and there we fell in with others of our folk who
had fled before, and with Dallach ; who e'en now told us what
was hard to believe, that there was a fair young man like one of
the Gods leading a band of goodly warriors, and seeking for us
to bring us into a peaceful and happy land ; and this man would

213

not have gone with him because he feared that he might fall into thralldom of other folk, who would take me away from him; but for me, I said I would go in any case, for I was weary of the wood and its roughness and toil, and that if I had a new master he would scarcely be worse than my old one was at his best, and him I could endure. So I went, and glad and glad I am, whatever ye will do with me. And now will I answer whatso ye may ask of me.'

She laid her limbs together daintily and looked fondly on Face-of-god, and the carle scowled at her somewhat at first, but presently, as he watched her, his face smoothed itself out of its wrinkles.

But Face-of-god pondered a little while, and then asked the woman if she had heard any words to remember of late days concerning the affairs of the Dusky Men and their intent; and he said:

'I pray thee, sister, be truthful in thine answer, for somewhat lieth on it.'

She said: 'How could I speak aught but the sooth to thee, O lovely lord? The last word spoken hereof I mind me well: for my master had been mishandling me, and I was sullen to him after the smart, and he mocked and jeered me, and said: Ye women deem we cannot do without you, but ye are fools, and know nothing; we are going to conquer a new land where the women are plenty, and far fairer than ye be; and we shall leave you to fare afield like the other thralls, or work in the digging of silver; and belike ye wot what that meaneth. Also he said that they would leave us to the new tribe of their folk, far wilder than they, whom they looked for in the Dale in about a moon's wearing; so that they needs must seek to other lands. Also this same talk would we hear whenever it pleased any of them to mock us their bed-thralls. Now, my sweet lord, this is nought but the very sooth.'

Again spake Face-of-god after a while:

'Tell me, sister, hast thou heard of any of the Dusky Men being slain in the wood?'

214

'Yea,' she said, and turned pale therewith and caught her breath as one choking; but said in a little while :

'This alone was it hard for me to tell thee amongst all the griefs I have borne, whereof I might have told thee many tales, and will do one day if thou wilt suffer it; but fear makes this hard for me. For in very sooth this was the cause of my fleeing, that my master was brought in slain by an arrow in the wood; and he was to be borne to bale and burned in three days' wearing; and we three bed-thralls of his, and three of the best of the men-thralls, were to be burned quick on his bale-fire after sore torments; therefore I fled, and hid a knife in my bosom, that I might not be taken alive; but sweet was life to me, and belike I should not have smitten myself.'

And she wept sore for pity of herself before them all. But Face-of-god said :

'Knowest thou, sister, by whom the man was slain ? '

'Nay,' she said, still sobbing; 'but I heard nought thereof, nor had I noted it in my terror. The death of others, who were slain before him, and the loss of many, we knew not how, made them more bitterly cruel with us.'

And again was she weeping; but Face-of-god said kindly to her : 'Weep no more, sister, for now shall all thy troubles be over : I feel in my heart that we shall overcome these felons, and make an end of them, and there then is Burgdale for thee in its length and breadth, or thine own Dale to dwell in freely.'

'Nay,' she said, 'never will I go back thither!' and she turned round to him and kissed his feet, and then arose and turned a little toward her mate; and the carle caught her by the hand and led her away, and seemed glad so to do.

So once again they fell asleep in the woods, and again the next morning fared on their way early that they might come into Burg-dale before nightfall. When they stayed a while at noontide and ate, Face-of-god again had talk with the Runaways, and this time with those of Rose-dale, and he heard much the same story

215

from them that he had heard before, told in divers ways, till his heart was sick with the hearing of it.

On this last day Face-of-god led his men well athwart the wood, so that he hit Wildlake's Way without coming to Carlstead; and he came down into the Dale some four hours after noon on a bright day of latter March. At the ingate to the Dale he found watches set, the men whereof told him that the tidings were not right great. Hall-face's company had fallen in with a band of the Felons three score in number in the oak-wood nigh to Boars-bait, and had slain some and chased the rest, since they found it hard to follow them home as they ran for the tangled thicket: of the Burgdalers had two been slain and five hurt in this battle.

As for Red-coat's company, they had fallen in with no foemen.


## CHAPTER XXIX. THEY BRING THE RUNAWAYS TO BURGSTEAD.

SO now being out of the wood, they went peaceably and safely along the Portway, the Runaways mingling with the Dalesmen. Strange showed amidst the health and wealth of the Dale the rags and misery and nakedness of the thralls, like a dream amidst the trim gaiety of spring; and whomsoever they met, or came up with on the road, whatso his business might be, could not refrain himself from following them, but mingled with the men-at-arms, and asked them of the tidings; and when they heard who these poor people were, even delivered thralls of the Foemen, they were glad at heart and cried out for joy; and many of the women, nay, of the men also, when they first came across that misery from out the heart of their own pleasant life, wept for pity and love of the poor folk, now at last set free, and blessed the swords that should do the like by the whole people.

They went slowly as men began to gather about them; yea,

some of the good folk that lived hard by must needs fare home to their houses to fetch cakes and wine for the guests; and they made them sit down and rest on the green grass by the side of the Portway, and eat and drink to cheer their hearts; others, women and young swains, while they rested went down into the meadows and plucked of the spring flowers, and twined them hastily with deft and well-wont fingers into chaplets and garlands for their heads and bodies. Thus indeed they covered their nakedness, till the lowering faces and weather-beaten skins of those hardly-entreated thralls looked grimly out from amidst the knots of cowslip and oxlip, and the branches of the milk-white blackthorn bloom, and the long trumpets of the daffodils, of the hue that wrappeth round the quill which the webster takes in hand when she would pleasure her soul with the sight of the yellow growing upon the dark green web.

So they went on again as the evening was waning, and when they were gotten within a furlong of the Gate, lo! there was come the minstrelsy, the pipe and the tabor, the fiddle and the harp, and the folk that had learned to sing the sweetest, both men and women, and Redesman at the head of them all.

Then fell the throng into an ordered company; first went the music, and then a score of Face-of-god's warriors with drawn swords and uplifted spears; and then the flower-bedecked misery of the Runaways, men and women going together, gaunt, befouled, and hollow-eyed, with here and there a flushed cheek or gleaming eye, or tear-bedewed face, as the joy and triumph of the eve pierced through their wonted weariness of grief; then the rest of the warriors, and lastly the mingled crowd of Dalesfolk, tall men and fair women gaily arrayed, clean-faced, clear-skinned, and sleek-haired, with glancing eyes and ruddy lips.

And now Redesman turned about to the music and drew his bow across his fiddle, and the other bows ran out in concert, and the harps followed the story of them, and he lifted up his voice and sang the words of an old song, and all the singers joined him

F F

and blended their voices with his.  And these are some of the
words which they sang :

Lo! here is Spring, and all we are living,
    We that were wan with Winter's fear ;
Reach out your hands to her hands that are giving,
    Lest ye lose her love and the light of the year.

Many a morn did we wake to sorrow,
    When low on the land the cloud-wrath lay ;
Many an eve we feared to-morrow,
    The unbegun unfinished day.

Ah we—we hoped not, and thou wert tardy ;
    Nought wert thou helping ; nought we prayed.
Where was the eager heart, the hardy ?
    Where was the sweet-voiced unafraid ?

But now thou lovest, now thou leadest,
    Where is gone the grief of our minds ?
What was the word of the tale, that thou heedest
    E'en as the breath of the bygone winds ?

Green and green is thy garment growing
    Over thy blossoming limbs beneath ;
Up o'er our feet rise the blades of thy sowing,
    Pierced are our hearts with thine odorous breath.

But where art thou wending, thou new-comer ?
    Hurrying on to the Courts of the Sun ?
Where art thou now in the House of the Summer ?
    Told are thy days and thy deed is done.

Spring has been here for us that are living
    After the days of Winter's fear ;

Here in our hands is the wealth of her giving,
    The Love of the Earth, and the Light of the Year.

Thus came they to the Gate, and lo! the Bride thereby, leaning
against a buttress, gazing with no dull eyes at the coming throng.
She was now clad in her woman's attire again, to wit a light
flame-coloured gown over a green kirtle; but she yet bore a gilded
helm on her head and a sword girt to her side in token of her
oath to the God. She had been in Hall-face's company in that
last battle, and had done a man's service there, fighting very
valiantly, but had not been hurt, and had come back to Burgstead
when the shift of men was.

Now she drew herself up and stood a little way before the Gate
and looked forth on the throng, and when her eyes beheld the
Runaways amidst of the weaponed carles of Burgdale, her face
flushed, and her eyes filled with tears as she stood, partly wondering, partly deeming what they were. She waited till Stone-
face came by her, and then she took the old man by the sleeve,
and drew him apart a little and said to him: 'What meaneth this
show, my friend? Who hath clad these folk thus strangely; and
who be these three naked tall ones, so fierce-looking, but somewhat noble of aspect?'

For indeed those three men of the kindreds, when they had
gotten into the Dale, and had rested them, and drunk a cup of
wine, and when they had seen the chaplets and wreaths of the
spring-flowers wherewith they were bedecked, and had smelt the
sweet savour of them, fell to walking proudly, heeding not their
nakedness; for no rag had they upon them save breech-clouts of
deer-skin: they had changed weapons with the Burgdale carles;
and one had gotten a great axe, which he bore over his shoulder,
and the shaft thereof was all done about with copper; and another
had shouldered a long heavy thrusting-spear, and the third, an exceeding tall man, bore a long broad-bladed war-sword. Thus they
went, brown of skin beneath their flower-garlands, their long hair

219

bleached by the sun falling about their shoulders; high they strode amongst the shuffling carles and tripping women of the later-come thralls. But when they heard the music, and saw that they were coming to the Gate in triumph, strange thoughts of old memories swelled up in their hearts, and they refrained them not from weeping, for they felt that the joy of life had come back to them.

Nor must it be deemed that these were the only ones amongst the Runaways whose hearts were cheered and softened: already were many of them coming back to life, as they felt their worn bodies caressed by the clear soft air of Burgdale, and the sweetness of the flowers that hung about them, and saw all round about the kind and happy faces of their well-willers.

So Stone-face looked on the Bride as she stood with face yet tear-bedewed, awaiting his answer, and said:

'Daughter, thou sayest who clad these folk thus? It was misery that hath so dight them; and they are the images of what we shall be if we love foul life better than fair death, and so fall into the hands of the Felons, who were the masters of these men. As for the tall naked men, they are of our own blood, and kinsmen to Face-of-god's new friends; and they are of the best of the vanquished: it was in early days that they fled from thralldom; as we may have to do. Now, daughter, I bid thee be as joyous as thou art valiant, and then shall all be well.'

Therewith she smiled on him, and he departed, and she stood a little while, as the throng moved on and was swallowed by the Gate, and looked after them; and for all her pity for the other folk, she thought chiefly of those fearless tall men who were of the blood of those with whom it was lawful to wed.

There she stood as the wind dried the tears upon her cheeks, thinking of the sorrow which these folk had endured, and their stripes and mocking, their squalor and famine; and she wondered and looked on her own fair and shapely hands with the precious finger-rings thereon, and on the dainty cloth and trim broidery of her sleeve; and she touched her smooth cheek with the back of her hand, and smiled, and felt the spring sweet in her mouth, and its savour goodly in her nostrils; and therewith she called to mind the aspect of her lovely body, as whiles she had seen it imaged, all its full measure, in the clear pool at midsummer, or piece-meal, in the shining steel of the Westland mirror. She thought also with what joy she drew the breath of life, yea, even amidst of grief, and of how sweet and pure and well-nurtured she was, and how well beloved of many friends and the whole folk, and she set all this beside those woeful bodies and lowering faces, and felt shame of her sorrow of heart, and the pain it had brought to her; and ever amidst shame and pity of all that misery rose up before her the images of those tall fierce men, and it seemed to her as if she had seen something like to them in some dream or imagination of her mind.

So came the Burgdalers and their guests into the street of Burgstead amidst music and singing; and the throng was great there. Then Face-of-god bade make a ring about the strangers, and they did so, and he and the Runaways alone were in the midst of it; and he spake in a loud voice and said:

'Men of the Dale and the Burg, these folk whom here ye see in such a sorry plight are they whom our deadly foes have rejoiced to torment; let us therefore rejoice to cherish them. Now let those men come forth who deem that they have enough and more, so that they may each take into their houses some two or three of these friends such as would be fain to be together. And since I am War-leader, and have the right hereto, I will first choose them whom I will lead into the House of the Face. And lo you! will I have this man (and he laid his hand on Dallach), who is he whom I first came across, and who found us all these others, and next I will have yonder tall carles, the three of them, because I perceive them to be men meet to be with a War-leader, and to follow him in battle.'

Therewith he drew the three Men of the Wolf towards him, but Dallach already was standing beside him. And folk rejoiced in Face-of-god.

221

But the Bride came forward next, and spake to him meekly and simply :

'War-leader, let me have of the women those who need me most, that I may bring them to the House of the Steer, and try if there be not some good days yet to be found for them, wherein they shall but remember the past grief as an ugly dream.'

Then Face-of-god looked on her, and him-seemed he had never seen her so fair ; and all the shame wherewith he had beheld her of late was gone from him, and his heart ran over with friendly love towards her as she looked into his face with kindly eyes ; and he said :

'Kinswoman, take thy choice as thy kindness biddeth, and happy shall they be whom thou choosest.'

She bowed her head soberly, and chose from among the guests four women of the saddest and most grievous, and no man of their kindred spake for going along with them ; then she went her ways home, leading one of them by the hand, and strange was it to see those twain going through sun and shade together, that poor wretch along with the goodliest of women.

Then came forward one after other of the worthy goodmen of the Dale, and especially such as were old, and they led away one one man, and another two, and another three, and often would a man crave to go with a woman or a woman with a man, and it was not gainsaid them.  So were all the guests apportioned, and ill-content were those goodmen that had to depart without a guest ; and one man would say to another : 'Such-an-one, be not downcast ; this guest shall be between us, if he will, and shall dwell with thee and me month about ; but this first month with me, since I was first comer.'  And so forth was it said.

Now to prevent the time to come, it may be said about the Runaways, that when they had been a little while amongst the Burgdalers, well fed and well clad and kindly cherished, it was marvellous how they were bettered in aspect of body, and it began

222

to be seen of them that they were well-favoured people, and
divers of the women exceeding goodly, black-haired and grey-
eyed, and very clear-skinned and white-skinned; most of them
were young, and the oldest had not seen above forty winters.
They of Rose-dale, and especially such as had first fled away
to the wood, were very soon seen to be merry and kindly folk;
but they who had been longest in captivity, and notably those
from Silver-dale who were not of the kindreds, were for a long
time sullen and heavy, and it availed little to trust to them for
the doing of work; albeit they would follow about their friends
of Burgdale with the love of a dog; also they were, divers of
them, somewhat thievish, and if they lacked anything would
liefer take it by stealth than ask for it; which forsooth the Burgdale men took not amiss, but deemed of it as a jest rather.

Very few of the Runaways had any will to fare back to their
old homes, or indeed could be got to go into the wood, or, after
a day or two, to say any word of Rose-dale or Silver-dale. In
this and other matters the Burgdalers dealt with them as with
children who must have their way; for they deemed that their
guests had much time to make up; also they were well content
when they saw how goodly they were, for these Dalesmen loved
to see men goodly of body and of a cheerful countenance.

As for Dallach and the three Silver-dale men of the kindred,
they went gladly whereas the Burgdale men would have them;
and half a score others took weapons in their hands when the
war was foughten: concerning which more hereafter.

But on the even whereof the tale now tells, Face-of-god and
Stone-face and their company met after nightfall in the Hall
of the Face clad in glorious raiment, and therewith were Dallach
and the men of Silver-dale, washen and docked of their long hair,
after the fashion of warriors who bear the helm; and they were
clad in gay attire, with battle-swords girt to their sides and gold
rings on their arms. Somewhat stern and sad-eyed were those
Silver-dalers yet, though they looked on those about them kindly

223

Face-of-god
leadeth those
three into the
Hall.

and courteously when they met their eyes; and Face-of-god yearned towards them when he called to mind the beauty and wisdom and loving-kindness of the Sun-beam. They were, as aforesaid, strong men and tall, and one of them taller than any amidst that house of tall men. Their names were Wolf-stone, the tallest, and God-swain, and Spear-fist; and God-swain the youngest was of thirty winters, and Wolf-stone of forty. They came into the Hall in such wise, that when they were washed and attired, and all men were assembled in the Hall, and the Alderman and the chieftains sitting on the daïs, Face-of-god brought them in from the out-bower, holding Dallach by the right hand and Wolf-stone by the left; and he looked but a stripling beside that huge man.

And when the men in the Hall beheld such goodly warriors, and remembered their grief late past, they all stood up and shouted for joy of them. But Face-of-god passed up the Hall with them, and stood before the daïs and said:

'O Alderman of the Dale and Chief of the House of the Face, here I bring to you the foes of our foemen, whom I have met in the Wild-wood, and bidden to our House; and meseemeth they will be our friends, and stand beside us in the day of battle. Therefore I say, take these guests and me together, or put us all to the door together; and if thou wilt take them, then show them to such places as thou deemest meet.'

Then stood up the Alderman and said:

'Men of Silver-dale and Rose-dale, I bid you welcome! Be ye our friends, and abide here with us as long as seemeth good to you, and share in all that is ours. Son Face-of-god, show these warriors to seats on the daïs beside thee, and cherish them as well as thou knowest how.'

Then Face-of-god brought them up on to the daïs and sat down on the right hand of his father, with Dallach on his right hand, and then Wolf-stone out from him; then sat Stone-face, that there might be a man of the Dale to talk with them and

224

serve them; and on his right hand first Spear-fist and then God-swain. And when they were all sat down, and the meat was on the board, Iron-face turned to his son Face-of-god and took his hand, and said in a loud voice, so that many might hear him :

'Son Face-of-god, son Gold-mane, thou bearest with thee both ill luck and good. Erewhile, when thou wanderedst out into the Wild-wood, seeking thou knewest not what from out of the Land of Dreams, thou didst but bring aback to us grief and shame; but now that thou hast gone forth with the neighbours seeking thy foemen, thou hast come aback to us with thine hands full of honour and joy for us, and we thank thee for thy gifts, and I call thee a lucky man. Herewith, kinsman, I drink to thee and the lasting of thy luck.'

Therewith he stood up and drank the health of the War-leader and the Guests : and all men were exceeding joyous thereat, when they called to mind his wrath at the Gate-thing, and they shouted for gladness as they drank that health, and the feast became exceeding merry in the House of the Face ; and as to the war to come, it seemed to them as if it were over and done in all triumph.


CHAPTER XXX. HALL-FACE GOETH TOWARD ROSE-DALE.

ON the morrow Face-of-god took counsel with Hall-face and Stone-face as to what were best to be done, and they sat on the daïs in the Hall to talk it over.

Short was the time that had worn since that day in Shadowy Vale, for it was but eight days since then ; yet so many things had befallen in that time, and, to speak shortly, the outlook for the Burgdalers had changed so much, that the time seemed long to all the three, and especially to Face-of-god.

It was yet twenty days till the Great Folk-mote should be holden, and to Hall-face the time seemed long enough to do somewhat, and he deemed it were good to gather force and fall on the Dusky Men in Rose-dale, since now they had gotten men who could lead them the nighest way and by the safest passes, and who knew all the ways of the foemen. But to Stone-face this rede seemed not so good; for they would have to go and come back, and fight and conquer, in less time than twenty days, or be belated of the Folk-mote, and meanwhile much might happen.

'For,' said Stone-face, 'we may deem the fighting-men of Rose-dale to be little less than one thousand, and however we fall on them, even if it be unawares at first, they shall fight stubbornly; so that we may not send against them many less than they be, and that shall strip Burgdale of its fighting-men, so that whatever befalls, we that be left shall have to bide at home.'

Now was Face-of-god of the same mind as Stone-face; and he said moreover: 'When we go to Rose-dale we must abide there a while unless we be overthrown. For if ye conquer it and come away at once, presently shall the tidings come to the ears of the Dusky Men in Silver-dale, and they shall join themselves to those of Rose-dale who have fled before you, and between them they shall destroy the unhappy people therein; for ye cannot take them all away with you: and that shall they do all the more now, when they look to have new thralls in Burgdale, both men and women. And this we may not suffer, but must abide till we have met all our foemen and have overcome them, so that the poor folk there shall be safe from them till they have learned how to defend their dale. Now my rede is, that we send out the War-arrow at once up and down the Dale, and to the Shepherds and Woodlanders, and appoint a day for the Muster and Weapon-show of all our Folk, and that day to be the day before the Spring Market, that is to say, four days before the Great Folk-mote, and meantime that we keep sure watch about the border of the wood, and now and again scour the wood, so as to clear the Dale of their wandering bands.'

226

'Yea,' said Hall-face; 'and I pray thee, brother, let me have Hall-face to seek toward Rose-dale. an hundred of men and thy Dallach, and let us go somewhat deep into the wood towards Rose-dale, and see what we may come across; peradventure it might be something better than hart or wild-swine.'

Said Face-of-god: 'I see no harm therein, if Dallach goeth with thee freely; for I will have no force put on him or any other of the Runaways. Yet meseemeth it were not ill for thee to find the road to Rose-dale; for I have it in my mind to send a company thither to give those Rose-dale man-quellers somewhat to do at home when we fall upon Silver-dale. Therefore go find Dallach, and get thy men together at once; for the sooner thou art gone on thy way the better. But this I bid thee, go no further than three days out, that ye may be back home betimes.'

At this word Hall-face's eyes gleamed with joy, and he went out from the Hall straightway and sought Dallach, and found him at the Gate. Iron-face had given him a new sword, a good one, and had bidden him call it Thicket-clearer, and he would not leave it any moment of the day or night, but would lay it under his pillow at night as a child does with a new toy; and now he was leaning against a buttress and drawing the said sword half out of the scabbard and poring over its blade, which was indeed fair enough, being wrought with dark grey waving lines like the eddies of the Weltering Water.

So Hall-face greeted him, and smiled and said:

'Guest, if thou wilt, thou may'st take that new blade of my father's work which thou lovest so, a journey which shall rejoice it.'

'Yea,' said Dallach, 'I suppose that thou wouldest fare on thy brother's footsteps, and deemest that I am the man to lead thee on the road, and even farther than he went; and though it might be thought by some that I have seen enough of Rose-dale and the parts thereabout for one while, yet will I go with thee; for now am I a man again, body and soul.'

And therewith he drew Thicket-clearer right out of his sheath

227

and waved him in the air. And Hall-face was glad of him
and said he was well apaid of his help. So they went away together to gather men, and on the morrow Hall-face departed
and went into the Wild-wood with Dallach and an hundred and
two score men.

But as for Face-of-god, he fared up and down the Dale
following the War-arrow, and went into all houses, and talked
with the folk, both young and old, men and women, and told
them closely all that had betid and all that was like to betide;
and he was well pleased with that which he saw and heard; for all
took his words well, and were nought afeard or dismayed by the
tidings; and he saw that they would not hang aback. Meantime the days wore, and Hall-face came not back till the seventh
day, and he brought with him twelve more Runaways, of whom
five were women. But he had lost four men, and had with him
Dallach and five others of the Dalesmen borne upon litters sore
hurt; and this was his story:

They got to the Burg of the Runaways on the forenoon of the
third day, and thereby came on five carles of the Runaways—men
who had missed meeting Dallach that other day, but knew what
had been done; for one of them had been sick and could not come
with him, and he had told the others: so now they were hanging
about the Burg of the Runaways hoping somewhat that he might
come again; and they met the Burgdalers full of joy, and brought
them trouts that they had caught in the river.

As for the other runaways, namely, five women and two more
carles—they had gotten them close to the entrance into Silver-dale,
where by night and cloud they came on a campment of the Dusky
Men, who were leading home these seven poor wretches, runaways
whom they had caught, that they might slay them most evilly in
Rose-stead. So Hall-face fell on the Dusky Men, and delivered
their captives, but slew not all the foe, and they that fled brought
pursuers on them who came up with them the next day, so near
was Rose-dale, though they made all diligence homeward. The

228

Burgdalers must needs turn and fight with those pursuers, and at last they drave them aback so that they might go on their ways home.  They let not the grass grow beneath their feet thereafter, till they were assured by meeting a band of the Woodlanders, who had gone forth to help them, and with whom they rested a little.  But neither so were they quite done with the foemen, who came upon them next day a very many : these however they and the Woodlanders, who were all fresh and unwounded and very valiant, speedily put to the worse ; and so they came on to Burg-stead, leaving those of them who were sorest hurt to be tended by the Woodlanders at Carlstead, who, as might be looked for, dealt with them very lovingly.

It was in the first fight that they suffered that loss of slain and wounded; and therein the newly delivered thralls fought valiantly against their masters : as for Dallach, it was no marvel, said Hall-face, that he was hurt ; but rather a marvel that he was not slain, so little he recked of point and edge, if he might but slay the foemen.

Such was Hall-face's tale ; and Face-of-god deemed that he had done unwisely to let him go that journey ; for the slaying of a few Dusky Men was but a light gain to set against the loss of so many Burgdalers ; yet was he glad of the deliverance of those Runaways, and deemed it a gain indeed.  But henceforth would he hold all still till he should have tidings of Folk-might; so nought was done thereafter save the warding of the Dale, from the country of the Shepherds to the Waste above the Eastern passes.

But Face-of-god himself went up amongst the Shepherds, and abode with a goodman hight Hound-under-Greenbury, who gathered to him the folk from the country-side, and they went up on to Greenbury, and sat on the green grass while he spoke with them and told them, as he had told the others, what had been done and what should be done.  And they heard him gladly, and he deemed that there would be no blenching in them, for they were all in one tale to live and die with their friends of Burgdale, and they said that they would have no other word save that to bear to the Great Folk-mote.

So he went away well-pleased, and he fared on thence to the Woodlanders, and guested at the house of a valiant man hight Wargrove, who on the morrow morn called the folk together to a green lawn of the Wild-wood, so that there was scarce a soul of them that was not there. Then he laid the whole matter before them; and if the Dalesmen had been merry and ready, and the Shepherds stout-hearted and friendly, yet were the Woodlanders more eager still, so that every hour seemed long to them till they stood in their war-gear; and they told him that now at last was the hour drawing nigh which they had dreamed of, but had scarce dared to hope for, when the lost way should be found, and the crooked made straight, and that which had been broken should be mended; that their meat and drink, and sleeping and waking, and all that they did were now become to them but the means of living till the day was come whereon the two remnants of the children of the Wolf should meet and become one Folk to live or die together.

Then went Face-of-god back to Burgstead again, and as he stood anigh the Thing-stead once more, and looked down on the Dale as he had beheld it last autumn, he bethought him that with all that had been done and all that had been promised, the earth was clearing of her trouble, and that now there was nought betwixt him and the happy days of life which the Dale should give to the dwellers therein, save the gathering hosts of the battle-field and the day when the last word should be spoken and the first stroke smitten. So he went down on to the Portway well content.

Thereafter till the day of the Weapon-show there is nought to tell of, save that Dallach and the other wounded men began to grow whole again; and all men sat at home, or went on the woodland ward, expecting great tidings after the holding of the Folk-mote.

## CHAPTER XXXI. OF THE WEAPON-SHOW OF THE MEN OF BURGDALE AND THEIR NEIGHBOURS.

NOW on the day appointed for the Weapon-show came the Folk flock-meal to the great and wide meadow that was cleft by Wildlake as it ran to join the Weltering Water. Early in the morning, even before sunrise, had the wains full of women and children begun to come thither. Also there came little horses and asses from the Shepherd country with one or two or three damsels or children sitting on each, and by wain-side or by beast strode the men of the house, merry and fair in their war-gear. The Woodlanders, moreover, man and woman, elder and swain and young damsel, streamed out of the wood from Carl-stead, eager to make the day begin before the sunrise, and end before his setting.

Then all men fell to pitching of tents and tilting over of wains; for the April sun was hot in the Dale, and when he arose the meads were gay with more than the spring flowers; for the tents and the tilts were stained and broidered with many colours, and there was none who had not furbished up his war-gear so that all shone and glittered. And many wore gay surcoats over their armour, and the women were clad in all their bravery, and the Houses mostly of a suit; for one bore blue and another corn-colour, and another green, and another brazil, and so forth, and all gleaming and glowing with broidery of gold and bright hues. But the women of the Shepherds were all clad in white, embroidered with green boughs and red blossoms, and the Woodland women wore dark red kirtles. Moreover, the women had set garlands of flowers on their heads and the helms of the men, and for the most part they were slim of body and tall and light-limbed, and as dainty to look upon as the willow-boughs that waved on the brook-side.

Thither had the goodmen who were guesting the Runaways brought their guests, even now much bettered by their new soft days; and much the poor folk marvelled at all this joyance, and

they scarce knew where they were; but to some it brought back
to their minds days of joyance before the thralldom and all that
they had lost, so that their hearts were heavy a while, till they saw
the warriors of the kindreds streaming into the mead and bethought
them why they carried steel.

Now by then the sun was fully up there was a great throng on
the Portway, and this was the folk of the Burg on their way to
the Weapon-mead. The men-at-arms were in the midst of the
throng, and at the head of them was the War-leader, with the
banner of the Face before him, wherein was done the image of the
God with the ray-ringed head. But at the rearward of the warriors
went the Alderman and the Burg-wardens, before whom was borne
the banner of the Burg pictured with the Gate and its Towers;
but in the midst betwixt those two was the banner of the Steer,
a white beast on a green field.

So when the Dale-wardens who were down in the meadow heard
the music and beheld who were coming, they bade the companies
of the Dale and the Shepherds and the Woodlanders who were
down there to pitch their banners in a half circle about the ingle
of the meadow which was made by the streams of Wildlake and
the Weltering Water, and gather to them to be ordered there
under their leaders of scores and half-hundreds and hundreds; and
even so they did. But the banners of the Dale without the Burg
were the Bridge, and the Bull, and the Vine, and the Sickle. And
the Shepherds had three banners, to wit Greenbury, and the Fleece,
and the Thorn.

As for the Woodlanders, they said that they were abiding their
great banner, but it should come in good time; 'and meantime,'
said they, 'here are the war-tokens that we shall fight under; for
they are good enough banners for us poor men, the remnant of the
valiant of time past.' Therewith they showed two great spears,
and athwart the one was tied an arrow, its point dipped in blood,
its feathers singed with fire; and they said, 'This is the banner
of the War-shaft.'

On the other spear there was nought; but the head thereof was great and long, and they had so burnished the steel that the sun smote out a ray of light from it, so that it might be seen from afar. And they said: 'This is the Banner of the Spear! Down yonder where the ravens are gathering ye shall see a banner flying over us. There shall fall many a mother's son.'

Smiled the Dale-wardens, and said that these were good banners to fight under; and those that stood nearby shouted for the valiancy of the Woodland Carles.

Now the Dale-wardens went to the entrance from the Portway to the meadow, and there met the Men of the Burg, and two of them went one on either side of the War-leader to show him to his seat, and the others abode till the Alderman and Burg-wardens came up, and then joined themselves to them, and the horns blew up both in the meadow and on the road, and the new-comers went their ways to their appointed places amidst the shouts of the Dalesmen; and the women and children and old men from the Burg followed after, till all the mead was covered with bright raiment and glittering gear, save within the ring of men at the further end.

So came the War-leader to his seat of green turf raised in the ingle aforesaid; and he stood beside it till the Alderman and Wardens had taken their places on a seat behind him raised higher than his; below him on the step of his seat sat the Scrivener with his pen and ink-horn and scroll of parchment, and men had brought him a smooth shield whereon to write.

On the left side of Face-of-god stood the men of the Face all glittering in their arms, and amongst them were Wolf-stone and his two fellows, but Dallach was not yet whole of his hurts. On his right were the folk of the House of the Steer: the leader of that House was an old white-bearded man, grandfather of the Bride, for her father was dead; and who but the Bride herself stood beside him in her glorious war-gear, looking as if she were new come from the City of the Gods, thought most men; but

H H

those who beheld her closely deemed that she looked heavy-eyed
and haggard, as if she were aweary.   Nevertheless, wheresoever
she passed, and whosoever looked on her (and all men looked on
her), there arose a murmur of praise and love; and the women,
and especially the young ones, said how fair her deed was, and
how meet she was for it; and some of them were for doing on
war-gear and faring to battle with the carles; and of these some
were sober and solemn, as was well seen afterwards, and some
spake lightly : some also fell to boasting of how they could run
and climb and swim and shoot in the bow, and fell to baring of
their arms to show how strong they were : and indeed they were
no weaklings, though their arms were fair.

There then stood the ring of men, each company under its
banner ; and beyond them stood the women and children and
men unmeet for battle ; and beyond them again the tilted wains
and the tents.

Now Face-of-god sat him down on the turf-seat with his bright
helm on his head and his naked sword across his knees, while
the horns blew up loudly, and when they had done, the elder of
the Dale-wardens cried out for silence.   Then again arose Face-
of-god and said :

'Men of the Dale, and ye friends of the Shepherds, and ye, O
valiant Woodlanders ; we are not assembled here to take counsel, for in three days' time shall the Great Folk-mote be holden,
whereat shall be counsel enough.   But since I have been appointed your Chief and War-leader, till such time as the Folk-
mote shall either yeasay or naysay my leadership, I have sent
for you that we may look each other in the face and number our
host and behold our weapons, and see if we be meet for battle and
for the dealing with a great host of foemen.   For now no longer
can it be said that we are going to war, but rather that war is
on our borders, and we are blended with it ; as many have learned
to their cost ; for some have been slain and some sorely hurt.
Therefore I bid you now, all ye that are weaponed, wend past us

234

that the tale of you may be taken. But first let every hundred-leader and half-hundred-leader and score-leader make sure that he hath his tale aright, and give his word to the captain of his banner that he in turn may give it out to the Scrivener with his name and the House and Company that he leadeth.'

So he spake and sat him adown; and the horns blew again in token that the companies should go past; and the first that came was Hall-ward of the House of the Steer, and the first of those that went after him was the Bride, going as if she were his son.

So he cried out his name, and the name of his House, and said, 'An hundred and a half,' and passed forth, his men following him in most goodly array. Each man was girt with a good sword and bore a long heavy spear over his shoulder, save a score who bare bows; and no man lacked a helm, a shield, and a coat of fence.

Then came a goodly man of thirty winters, and stayed before the Scrivener and cried out:

'Write down the House of the Bridge of the Upper Dale at one hundred, and War-well their leader.'

And he strode on, and his men followed clad and weaponed like those of the Steer, save that some had axes hanging to their girdles instead of swords; and most bore casting-spears instead of the long spears, and half a score were bowmen.

Then came Fox of Upton leading the men of the Bull of Mid-dale, an hundred and a half lacking two; very great and tall were his men, and they also bore long spears, and one score and two were bowmen.

Then Fork-beard of Lea, a man well on in years, led on the men of the Vine, an hundred and a half and five men thereto; two score of them bare bow in hand and were girt with sword; the rest bore their swords naked in their right hands, and their shields (which were but small bucklers) hanging at their backs, and in the left hand each bore two casting-spears. With these went two doughty women-at-arms among the bowmen, tall and well-knit, already growing brown with the spring sun, for their

235

work lay among the stocks of the vines on the southward-look-ing bents.

Next came a tall young man, yellow-haired, with a thin red beard, and gave himself out for Red-beard of the Knolls; he bore his father's name, as the custom of their house was, but the old man, who had long been head man of the House of the Sickle, was late dead in his bed, and the young man had not seen twenty winters. He bade the Scrivener write the tale of the Men of the Sickle at an hundred and a half, and his folk fared past the War-leader joyously, being one half of them bowmen; and fell shooters they were; the other half were girt with swords, and bore withal long ashen staves armed with great blades curved inwards, which weapon they called heft-sax.

All these bands, as the name and the tale of them was declared, were greeted with loud shouts from their fellows and the by-standers; but now arose a greater shout still, as Stone-face, clad in goodly glittering array, came forth and said:

'I am Stone-face of the House of the Face, and I bring with me two hundreds of men with their best war-gear and weapons: write it down, Scrivener!'

And he strode on like a young man after those who had gone past, and after him came the tall Hall-face and his men, a gallant sight to see: two score bowmen girt with swords, and the others with naked swords waving aloft, and each bearing two casting-spears in his left hand.

Then came a man of middle age, broad-shouldered, yellow-haired, blue-eyed, of wide and ruddy countenance, and after him a goodly company; and again great was the shout that went up to the heavens; for he said:

'Scrivener, write down that Hound-under-Greenbury, from amongst the dwellers in the hills where the sheep feed, leadeth the men who go under the banner of Greenbury, to the tale of an hundred and four score.'

Therewith he passed on, and his men followed, stout, stark,

and merry-faced, girt with swords, and bearing over their shoulders long-staved axes, and spears not so long as those which the Dalesmen bore ; and they had but a half score of arrow-shot with them.

Now go by the Fleece, the Thorn, the War-shaft, and the Spear.

Next came a young man, blue-eyed also, with hair the colour of flax on the distaff, broad-faced and short-nosed, low of stature, but very strong-built, who cried out in a loud, cheerful voice :

'I am Strongitharm of the Shepherds, and these valiant men are of the Fleece and the Thorn blended together, for so they would have it ; and their tale is one hundred and two score and ten.'

Then the men of those kindreds went past merry and shouting, and they were clad and weaponed like to them of Greenbury, but had with them a score of bowmen. And all these Shepherd-folk wore over their hauberks white woollen surcoats broidered with green and red.

Now again uprose the cry, and there stood before the War-leader a very tall man of fifty winters, dark-faced and grey-eyed, and he spake slowly and somewhat softly, and said :

'War-leader, this is Red-wolf of the Woodlanders leading the men who go under the sign of the War-shaft, to the number of an hundred and two.'

Then he passed on, and his men after him, tall, lean, and silent amidst the shouting. All these men bare bows, for they were keen hunters ; each had at his girdle a little axe and a wood-knife, and some had long swords withal. They wore, everyone of the carles, short green surcoats over their coats of fence ; but amongst them were three women who bore like weapons to the men, but were clad in red kirtles under their hauberks, which were of good ring-mail gleaming over them from throat to knee.

Last came another tall man, but young, of twenty-five winters, and spake :

'Scrivener, I am Bears-bane of the Woodlanders, and these that come after me wend under the sign of the Spear, and they are of the tale of one hundred and seven.'

237

And he passed by at once, and his men followed him, clad and weaponed no otherwise than they of the War-shaft, and with them were two women.

Now went all those companies back to their banners, and stood there; and there arose among the bystanders much talk concerning the Weapon-show, and who were the best arrayed of the Houses. And of the old men, some spake of past weapon-shows which they had seen in their youth, and they set them beside this one, and praised and blamed. So it went on a little while till the horns blew again, and once more there was silence. Then arose Face-of-god and said:

' Men of Burgdale, and ye Shepherd-folk, and ye of the Woodland, now shall ye wot how many weaponed men we may bring together for this war. Scrivener, arise and give forth the tale of the companies, as they have been told unto you.'

Then the Scrivener stood up on the turf-bench beside Face-of-god, and spake in a loud voice, reading from his scroll:

' Of the Men of Burgdale there have passed by me nine hundreds and six; of the Shepherds three hundreds and eight and ten; and of the Woodlanders two hundreds and nine; so that all told our men are fourteen hundreds and thirty and three.'

Now in those days men reckoned by long hundreds, so that the whole tale of the host was one thousand, five hundred, and four score and one, telling the tale in short hundreds.

When the tale had been given forth and heard, men shouted again, and they rejoiced that they were so many. For it exceeded the reckoning which the Alderman had given out at the Gate-thing. But Face-of-god said:

' Neighbours, we have held our Weapon-show; but now hold you ready, each man, for the Hosting toward very battle; for belike within seven days shall the leaders of hundreds and twenties summon you to be ready in arms to take whatso fortune may befall. Now is sundered the Weapon-show. Be ye as merry to-day as your hearts bid you to be.'

238

Therewith he came down from his seat with the Alderman and the Wardens, and they mingled with the good folk of the Dale and the Shepherds and the Woodlanders, and merry was their converse there.  It yet lacked an hour of noon ;  so presently they fell to and feasted in the green meadow, drinking from wain to wain and from tent to tent ; and thereafter they played and sported in the meads, shooting at the butts and wrestling, and trying other masteries.  Then they fell to dancing one and all, and so at last to supper on the green grass in great merriment. Nor might you have known from the demeanour of any that any threat of evil overhung the Dale.  Nay, so glad were they, and so friendly, that you might rather have deemed that this was the land whereof tales tell, wherein people die not, but live for ever, without growing any older than when they first come thither, unless they be born into the land itself, and then they grow into fair manhood, and so abide.  In sooth, both the land and the folk were fair enough to be that land and the folk thereof.

But a little after sunset they sundered, and some fared home ; but many of them abode in the tents and tilted wains, because the morrow was the first day of the Spring Market : and already were some of the Westland chapmen come ;  yea, two of them were with the bystanders in the meadow ;  and more were looked for ere the night was far spent.


CHAPTER XXXII.  THE MEN OF SHADOWY VALE COME TO THE SPRING MARKET AT BURGSTEAD.

ON the morrow betimes in the morning the Westland chapmen, who were now all come, went out from the House of the Face, where they were ever wont to be lodged, and set up their booths adown the street betwixt gate and bridge. Gay was the show ; for the booths were tilted over with painted cloths, and the merchants themselves were clad in long gowns of fine cloth; scarlet, and blue, and white, and green, and black, with broidered welts of gold and silver; and their knaves were gaily attired in short coats of divers hues, with silver rings about their arms, and short swords girt to their sides. People began to gather about these chapmen at once when they fell to opening their bales and their packs, and unloading their wains. There had they iron, both in pigs and forged scrap and nails; steel they had, and silver, both in ingots and vessel; pearls from over sea; cinnabar and other colours for staining, such as were not in the mountains: madder from the marshes, and purple of the sea, and scarlet grain from the holm-oaks by its edge, and woad from the deep clayey fields of the plain; silken thread also from the outer ocean, and rare webs of silk, and jars of olive oil, and fine pottery, and scented woods, and sugar of the cane. But gold they had none with them, for that they took there; and for weapons, save a few silver-gilt toys, they had no market.

So presently they fell to chaffer; for the carles brought them little bags of the river-borne gold, so that the weights and scales were at work; others had with them scrolls and tallies to tell the number of the beasts which they had to sell, and the chapmen gave them wares therefor without beholding the beasts; for they wotted that the Dalesmen lied not in chaffer. While the day was yet young withal came the Dalesmen from the mid and nether Dale with their wares and set up their booths; and they had with them flasks and kegs of the wine which they had to sell; and bales of the good winter-woven cloth, some grey, some dyed, and pieces of fine linen; and blades of swords, and knives, and axes of such fashion as the Westland men used; and golden cups and chains, and fair rings set with mountain-blue stones, and copper bowls, and vessels gilt and parcel-gilt, and mountain-blue for staining. There were men of the Shepherds also with such fleeces as they could spare from the daily chaffer with the neighbours. And of the Woodlanders were four carles and a woman with peltries and dressed deer-skins, and a few pieces

of well-carven wood-work for bedsteads and chairs and such
like.

Soon was the Burg thronged with folk in all its open places, and all were eager and merry, and it could not have been told from their demeanour and countenance that the shadow of a grievous trouble hung over them. True it was that every man of the Dale and the neighbours was girt with his sword, or bore spear or axe or other weapon in his hand, and that most had their bucklers at their backs and their helms on their heads; but this was ever their custom at all meetings of men, not because they dreaded war or were fain of strife, but in token that they were free men, from whom none should take the weapons without battle.

Such were the folk of the land : as for the chapmen, they were well-spoken and courteous, and blithe with the folk, as they well might be, for they had good pennyworths of them ; yet they dealt with them without using measureless lying, as behoved folk dealing with simple and proud people ; and many was the tale they told of the tidings of the Cities and the Plain.

There amongst the throng was the Bride in her maiden's attire, but girt with the sword, going from booth to booth with her guests of the Runaways, and doing those poor people what pleasure she might, and giving them gifts from the goods there, such as they set their hearts on. And the more part of the Runaways were about among the people of the Fair; but Dallach, being still weak, sat on a bench by the door of the House of the Face looking on well-pleased at all the stir of folk.

Hall-face was gone on the woodland ward ; while Face-of-god went among the folk in his most glorious attire ; but he soon betook him to the place of meeting without the Gate, where Stone-face and some of the elders were sitting along with the Alderman, beside whom sat the head man of the merchants, clad in a gown of fine scarlet embroidered with the best work of the Dale, with a golden chaplet on his head, and a good sword, golden-hilted, by his side, all which the Alderman had given to

The chiefs sit
in the Gate
and talk.
him that morning. These chiefs were talking together concerning
the tidings of the Plain, and many a tale the guest told to the
Dalesmen, some true, some false. For there had been battles
down there, and the fall of kings, and destruction of people, as
oft befalleth in the guileful Cities. He told them also, in answer
to their story of the Dusky Men, of how men even such-like, but
riding on horses, or drawn in wains, an host not to be numbered,
had erewhile overthrown the hosts of the Cities of the Plain, and
had wrought evils scarce to be told of; and how they had piled up
the skulls of slaughtered folk into great hills beside the city-gates,
so that the sun might no longer shine into the streets; and how
because of the death and the rapine, grass had grown in the
kings' chambers, and the wolves had chased deer in the Temples
of the Gods.

'But,' quoth he, 'I know you, bold tillers of the soil, valiant
scourers of the Wild-wood, that the worst that can befall you will
be to die under shield, and that ye shall suffer no torment of the
thrall. May the undying Gods bless the threshold of this Gate,
and oft may I come hither to taste of your kindness! May your
race, the uncorrupt, increase and multiply, till your valiant men
and clean maidens make the bitter sweet and purify the earth!'

He spake smooth-tongued and smiling, handling the while the
folds of his fine scarlet gown, and belike he meant a full half of
what he said; for he was a man very eloquent of speech, and had
spoken with kings, uncowed and pleased with his speaking;
and for that cause and his riches had he been made chief of the
chapmen. As he spake the heart of Face-of-god swelled within
him, and his cheek flushed; but Iron-face sat up straight and proud,
and a light smile played about his face, as he said gravely:

'Friend of the Westland, I thank thee for the blessing and the
kind word. Such as we are, we are; nor do I deem that the very
Gods shall change us. And if they will be our friends, it is well;
for we desire nought of them save their friendship; and if they
will be our foes, that also shall we bear; nor will we curse them for
242

doing that which their lives bid them to do.   What sayest thou, They hear a horn winded.
Face-of-god, my son ? '

'Yea, father,' said Face-of-god, 'I say that the very Gods, though they slay me, cannot unmake my life that has been.   If they do deeds, yet shall we also do.'

The Outlander smiled as they spake, and bowed his head to Iron-face and Face-of-god, and wondered at their pride of heart, marvelling what they would say to the great men of the Cities if they should meet them.

But as they sat a-talking, there came two men running to them from the Portway, their weapons all clattering upon them, and they heard withal the sound of a horn winded not far off very loud and clear ; and the Chapman's cheek paled : for in sooth he doubted that war was at hand, after all he had heard of the Dalesmen's dealings with the Dusky Men.   And all battle was loathsome to him, nor for all the gain of his chaffer had he come into the Dale, had he known that war was looked for.

But the chiefs of the Dalesmen stirred not, nor changed countenance ; and some of the goodmen who were in the street nigh the Gate came forth to see what was toward; for they also had heard the voice of the horn.

Then one of those messengers came up breathless, and stood before the chiefs, and said :

'New tidings, Alderman ; here be weaponed strangers come into the Dale ? '

The Alderman smiled on him and said :   'Yea, son, and are they a great host of men ? '

'Nay,' said the man, 'not above a score as I deem, and there is a woman with them.'

'Then shall we abide them here,' said the Alderman, 'and thou mightest have saved thy breath, and suffered them to bring tidings of themselves ; since they may scarce bring us war.   For no man desireth certain and present death ; and that is all that such a band may win at our hands in battle to-day ; and all who

come in peace are welcome to us. What like are they to behold?'

Said the man: 'They are tall men gloriously attired, so that
they seem like kinsmen of the Gods; and they bear flowering
boughs in their hands.'

The Alderman laughed, and said: 'If they be Gods they are
welcome indeed; and they shall grow the wiser for their coming;
for they shall learn how guest-fain the Burgdale men may be.
But if, as I deem, they be like unto us, and but the children of
the Gods, then are they as welcome, and it may be more so, and
our greeting to them shall be as their greeting to us would be.'

Even as he spake the horn was winded nearer yet, and more
loudly, and folk came pouring out of the Gate to learn the tidings.
Presently the strangers came from off the Portway into the space
before the Gate; and their leader was a tall and goodly man of some
thirty winters, in glorious array, helm on head and sword by side,
his surcoat green and flowery like the spring meads. In his right
hand he held a branch of the blossomed black-thorn (for some
was yet in blossom), and his left had hold of the hand of an exceeding fair woman who went beside him: behind him was a
score of weaponed men in goodly attire, some bearing bows, some
long spears, but each bearing a flowering bough in hand.

The tall man stopped in the midst of the space, and the Alderman and they with him stirred not; though, as for Face-of-god,
it was to him as if summer had come suddenly into the midst of
winter, and for the very sweetness of delight his face grew pale.

Then the new-comer drew nigh to the Alderman and said:
'Hail to the Gate and the men of the Gate! Hail to the kindred of the children of the Gods!'

But the Alderman stood up and spake: 'And hail to thee,
tall man! Fair greeting to thee and thy company! Wilt thou
name thyself with thine own name, or shall I call thee nought
save Guest? Welcome art thou, by whatsoever name thou wilt
be called. Here may'st thou and thy folk abide as long as ye will.'

244

Said the new-comer : 'Thanks have thou for thy greeting Folk-might and for thy bidding! And that bidding shall we take, what- would give up soever may come of it; for we are minded to abide with thee for his sword. a while. But know thou, O Alderman of the Dalesmen, that I am not sackless toward thee and thine. My name is Folk-might of the Children of the Wolf, and this woman is the Sun-beam, my sister, and these behind me are of my kindred, and are well beloved and trusty. We are no evil men or wrong-doers ; yet have we been driven into sore straits, wherein men must needs at whiles do deeds that make their friends few and their foes many. So it may be that I am thy foeman. Yet, if thou doubtest of me that I shall be a baneful guest, thou shalt have our weapons of us, and then mayest thou do thy will upon us without dread ; and here first of all is my sword ! '

Therewith he cast down the flowering branch he was bearing, and pulled his sword from out his sheath, and took it by the point, and held out the hilt to Iron-face.

But the Alderman smiled kindly on him and said :

' The blade is a good one, and I say it who know the craft of sword-forging ; but I need it not, for thou seest I have a sword by my side. Keep your weapons, one and all ; for ye have come amongst many and those no weaklings : and if so be that thy guilt against us is so great that we must needs fall on you, ye will need all your war-gear. But hereof is no need to speak till the time of the Folk-mote, which will be holden in three days' wear- ing ; so let us forbear this matter till then ; for I deem we shall have enough to say of other matters. Now, Folk-might, sit down beside me, and thou also, Sun-beam, fairest of women.'

Therewith he looked into her face and reddened, and said :

' Yet belike thou hast a word of greeting for my son, Face-of- god, unless it be so that ye have not seen him before ? '

Then Face-of-god came forward, and took Folk-might by the hand and kissed him ; and he stood before the Sun-beam and took her hand, and the world waxed a wonder to him as he kissed her cheeks; and in no wise did she change countenance, save that her eyes softened, and she gazed at him full kindly from the happiness of her soul.

Then Face-of-god said: 'Welcome, Guests, who erewhile guested me so well: now beginneth the day of your well-doing to the men of Burgdale; therefore will we do to you as well as we may.'

Then Folk-might and the Sun-beam sat them down with the chieftains, one on either side of the Alderman, but Face-of-god passed forth to the others, and greeted them one by one: of them was Wood-father and his three sons, and Bow-may; and they rejoiced exceedingly to see him, and Bow-may said:

' Now it gladdens my heart to look upon thee alive and thriving, and to remember that day last winter when I met thee on the snow, and turned thee back from the perilous path to thy pleasure, which the Dusky Men were besetting, of whom thou knewest nought. Yea, it was merry that tide; but this is better. Nay, friend,' she said, ' it availeth thee nought to strive to look out of the back of thine head: let it be enough to thee that she is there. Thou art now become a great chieftain, and she is no less; and this is a meeting of chieftains, and the folk are looking on and expecting demeanour of them as of the Gods; and she is not to be dealt with as if she were the daughter of some little goodman with whom one hath made tryst in the meadows. There! hearken to me for a while; at least till I tell thee that thou seemest to me to hold thine head higher than when last I saw thee; though that is no long time either. Hast thou been in battle again since that day?'

' Nay,' he said, ' I have stricken no stroke since I slew two felons within the same hour that we parted. And thou, sister, what hast thou done?'

She said: ' The grey goose hath been on the wing thrice since that, bearing on it the bane of evil things.'

Then said Wood-wise: ' Kinswoman, tell him of that battle, since thou art deft with thy tongue.'

246

She said : 'Weary on battles! it is nought save this : twelve days agone needs must every fighting-man of the Wolf, carle or queen, wend away from Shadowy Vale, while those unmeet for battle we hid away in the caves at the nether end of the Dale : but Sun-beam would not endure that night, and fared with us, though she handled no weapon. All this we had to do because we had learned that a great company of the Dusky Men were over-nigh to our Dale, and needs must we fall upon them, lest they should learn too much, and spread the story. Well, so wise was Folk-might that we came on them unawares by night and cloud at the edge of the Pine-wood, and but one of our men was slain, and of them not one escaped ; and when the fight was over we counted four score and ten of their arm-rings.'

He said : 'Did that or aught else come of our meeting with them that morning ?'

'Nay,' she said, 'nought came of it : those we slew were but a straying band. Nay, the four score and ten slain in the Pine-wood knew not of Shadowy Vale belike, and had no intent for it : they were but scouring the wood seeking their warriors that had gone out from Silver-dale and came not aback.'

'Thou art wise in war, Bow-may,' said Face-of-god, and he smiled withal.

Bow-may reddened and said : 'Friend Gold-mane, dost thou perchance deem that there is aught ill in my warring ? And the Sun-beam, she naysayeth the bearing of weapons ; though I deem that she hath little fear of them when they come her way.'

Said Face-of-god : 'Nay, I deem no ill of it, but much good. For I suppose that thou hast learned overmuch of the wont of the Dusky Men, and hast seen their thralls ?'

She knitted her brows, and all the merriment went out of her face at that word, and she answered : 'Yea, thou hast it ; for I have both seen their thralls and been in the Dale of thralldom ; and how then can I do less than I do ? But for thee, I perceive that thou hast been nigh unto our foes and hast fallen in with

247

their thralls ; and that is well ; for whatso tales we had told thee thereof it is like thou wouldst not have trowed in, as now thou must do, since thou thyself hast seen these poor folk.  But now I will tell thee, Gold-mane, that my soul is sick of these comings and goings for the slaughter of a few wretches ; and I long for the Great Day of Battle, when it will be seen whether we shall live or die ; and though I laugh and jest, yet doth the wearing of the days wear me.'

He looked kindly on her and said : ' I am War-leader of this Folk, and trust me that the waiting-tide shall not be long ; wherefore now, sister, be merry to-day, for that is but meet and right ; and cast aside thy care, for presently shalt thou behold many new friends.  But now meseemeth overlong have ye been standing before our Gate, and it is time that ye should see the inside of our Burg and the inside of our House.'

Indeed by this time so many men had come out of the street that the place before the Gate was all thronged, and from where he stood Face-of-god could scarce see his father, or Folk-might and the Sun-beam and the chieftains.

So he took Wood-father by the hand, and close behind him came Wood-wise and Bow-may, and he cried out for way that he might speak with the Alderman, and men gave way to them, and he led those new-comers close up to the gate-seats of the Elders, and as he clove the press smiling and bright-eyed and happy, all gazed on him ; but the Sun-beam, who was sitting between Iron-face and the Westland Chapman, and who heretofore had been agaze with eyes beholding little, past whose ears the words went unheard, and whose mind wandered into thoughts of things unfashioned yet, when she beheld him close to her again, then, taken unawares, her eyes caressed him, and she turned as red as a rose, as she felt all the sweetness of desire go forth from her to meet him.  So that, he perceiving it, his voice was the clearer and sweeter for the inward joy he felt, as he said :

' Alderman, meseemeth it is now time that we bring our Guests

248

into the House of our Fathers; for since they are in warlike array, and we are no longer living in peace, and I am now War-leader of the Dale, I deem it but meet that I should have the guesting of them.  Moreover, when we are come into our House, I will bid thee look into thy treasury, that thou may'st find therein somewhat which it may pleasure us to give to our Guests.'

Said Iron-face : 'Thou sayest well, son, and since the day is now worn past noon, and these folk are but just come from the Waste, therefore such as we have of meat and drink abideth them. And surely there is within our house a coffer which belongeth to thee and me ;  and forsooth I know not why we keep the treasures hoarded therein, save that it be for this cause : that if we were to give to our friends that which we ourselves use and love, which would be of all things pleasant to us, if we gave them such goods, they would be worn and worsened by our use of them. For this reason, therefore, do we keep fair things which we use not, so that we may give them to our friends.

'Now, Guests, both of the Waste and the Westland, since here is no Gate-thing or meeting of the Dale-wardens, and we sit here but for our pleasure, let us go take our pleasure within doors for a while, if it seem good to you.'

Therewith he arose, and the folk made way for him and his Guests ; and Folk-might went on the right hand of Iron-face, and beside him went the Chapman, who looked on him with a half-smile, as though he knew somewhat of him.  But on the other side of Iron-face went the Sun-beam, whose hand he held, and after these came Face-of-god, leading in the rest of the New-comers, who yet held the flowery branches in their hands.

Now so much had Face-of-god told the Dalesmen, that they deemed they all knew these men for their battle-fellows of whom they had heard tell ; and this the more as the men were so goodly and manly of aspect, especially Folk-might, so that they seemed as if they were nigh akin to the Gods.  As for the Sun-beam, they knew not how to praise her beauty enough, but they said that they had never known before how fair the Gods might be. So they raised a great shout of welcome as the men came through the Gate into the Burg, and all men turned their backs on the booths, so eager were they to behold closely these new friends.

But as the Guests went from the Gate to the House of the Face, going very slowly because of the press, there in the front of the throng stood the Bride with the women of the Runaways, whom she had caused to be clad very fairly; and she was fain to do them a pleasure by bringing them to sight of these new-comers, of whom she had not heard who they were, though she had heard the cry that strangers were at hand. So there she stood smiling a little, with the pleasure of showing a fair sight to the poor people, as folk do with children. But when she saw those twain going on each side of the Alderman she knew them at once; and when the Sun-beam, who was on his left side, passed so close to her that she could see the very smoothness and dainty fashion of her skin, then was she astonied, and the world seemed strange to her, and till they were gone by, and for a while afterwards, she knew not where she was nor what she did, though it seemed to her as if she still saw the face of that fair woman as in a picture.

But the Sun-beam had noted her at first, even amongst the fair women of Burgstead, and she so steady and bright beside the wandering timorous eyes and lowering faces of the thralls. But suddenly, as eye met eye, she saw her face change; she saw her cheek whiten, her eyes stare, and her lips quiver, and she knew at once who it was; for she had not seen her before as Folk-might had. Then the Sun-beam cast her eyes adown, lest her compassion might show in her face, and be a fresh grief to her that had lost the wedding and the love; and so she passed on.

As for Folk-might, he had seen her at once amongst all that folk as he came into the street, and in sooth he was looking for her; and when he saw her face change, as the sight of the Sun-beam smote upon her heart, his own face burned with shame and anger, and he looked back at her as he went toward the House.

250

But she saw him not, nor noted him ; and none deemed it strange that he looked long on the Bride, the treasure of Burgstead. But for some while Folk-might was few-spoken and sharp-spoken amongst the chieftains ; for he was slow to master his longing and his wrath.

So when all the Guests had entered the door of the House of the Face, the Alderman turned back, and, standing on the threshold of his House, spake unto the throng :

'Men of the Dale, and ye Outlanders who may be here, know that this is a happy day ; for hither have come to us Guests, men of the kindred of the Gods, and they are even those of whom Face-of-god my son hath told you. And they are friends of our friends and foes of our foes. These men are now in my House, as is but right ; but when they come forth I look to you to cherish them in the best way ye know, and make much of them, as of those who may help us and who may by us be holpen.'

Therewith he went in again and into the Hall, and bade show the New-comers to the daïs ; and wine of the best, and meat such as was to hand, was set before them. He bade men also get ready high feast as great as might be against the evening ; and they did his bidding straightway.

## CHAPTER XXXIII. THE ALDERMAN GIVES GIFTS TO THEM OF SHADOWY VALE.

IN the Hall of the Face Folk-might sat on the daïs at the right hand of the Alderman, and the Sun-beam on his left hand. But Iron-face also had beheld the Bride how her face changed, and he knew the cause, and was grieved and angry and ashamed thereof : also he bethought him how this stranger was sitting in the very place where the Bride used to sit, and of all the love, as of a very daughter, that he had had for her ; howbeit he constrained himself to talk courteously and kindly both to Folk-might and

the Sun-beam, as behoved the Chief of the House and the Alderman of the Dale. Moreover, he was not a little moved by the
goodliness and wisdom of the Sun-beam and the manliness of
Folk-might, who was the most chieftain-like of men.

But while they sat there Face-of-god went from man to man
of the Guests, and made much of each, but especially of Wood-
father and his sons and Bow-may, and they loved him, and praised
him, and deemed him the best of hall-mates. Nor might the
Sun-beam altogether refrain her from looking lovingly on him, and
it could be seen of her that she deemed he was doing well, and
like a wise leader and chieftain.

So wore away a while, and men were fulfilled of meat and drink;
so then the Alderman arose and spake, and said:

'Is it not so, Guests, that ye would now gladly behold our
market, and the goodly wares which the chapmen have brought
us from the Cities?'

Then most men cried out 'Yea, yea!' and Iron-face said:
'Then shall ye go, nor be holden by me from your pleasure.
And ye kinsmen who are the most guest-fain and the wisest, go ye
with our friends, and make all things easy and happy for them.
But first of all, Guests, I were well pleased if ye would take
some small matters out of our abundance; for it were well that
ye see them ere ye stand before the chapmen's booths, lest ye
chaffer with them for what ye have already.'

They all praised his bounty and thanked him for his goodwill:
so he arose to go to his treasury, and bade certain of his folk
go along with him to bear in the gifts. But ere he had taken
three steps down the hall, Face-of-god prevented him and said:

'Kinsman, if thou hast anywhere a hauberk somewhat better
than folk are wont to bear, such as thine own hand fashioneth,
and a sword of the like stuff, I would have thee give them, the
sword to my brother-in-arms Wood-wise here, and the war-coat
to my sister Bow-may, who shooteth so well in the bow that none
may shoot closer, and very few as close; and her shaft it was

252

that delivered me when my skull was amongst the axes of the Dusky Men : else had I not been here.'

Thereat Bow-may reddened and looked down, like a scholar who hath been over-praised for his learning and diligence ; but the Alderman smiled on her and said :

'I thank thee, son, that thou hast let me know what these our two friends may be fain of : and as for this damsel-at-arms, it is a little thing that thou askest for her, and we might have found her something more worthy of her goodliness ; yet forsooth, since we are all bound for the place where shafts and staves shall be good cheap, a greater treasure might be of less avail to her.'

Thereat men laughed, and the Alderman went down the Hall with those bearers of gifts, and was away for a space while they drank and made merry : but presently back they came from the treasury bearing loads of goodly things which were laid on one of the endlong boards. Then began the gift-giving : and first he gave unto Folk-might six golden cups marvellously fashioned, the work of four generations of wrights in the Dale, and he himself had wrought the last two thereof. To Sun-beam he gave a girdle of gold, fashioned with great mastery, whereon were images of the Gods and the Fathers, and warriors, and beasts of the field and fowls of the air ; and as he girt it about her loins, he said in a soft voice so that few heard :

'Sun-beam, thou fair woman, time has been when thou wert to us as the edge of the poisonous sword or the midnight torch of the murderer ; but now I know not how it will be, or if the grief which thou hast given me will ever wear out or not. And now that I have beheld thee, I have little to do to blame my son ; for indeed when I look on thee I cannot deem that there is any evil in thee. Yea, however it may be, take thou this gift as the reward of thine exceeding beauty.'

She looked on him with kind eyes, and said meekly :
'Indeed, if I have hurt thee unwittingly, I grieve to have hurt so good a man. Hereafter belike we may talk more of this, but

253

now I will but say, that whereas at first I needed but to win thy son's goodwill, so that our Folk might come to life and thriving again, now it is come to this, that he holdeth my heart in his hand and may do what he will with it; therefore I pray thee withhold not thy love either from him or from me.'

He looked on her wondering, and said: 'Thou art such an one as might make the old man young, and the boy grow into manhood suddenly; and thy voice is as sweet as the voice of the song-birds singing in the dawn of early summer soundeth to him who hath been sick unto death, but who hath escaped it and is mending. And yet I fear thee.'

Therewith he kissed her hand and turned unto the others, and he gave unto Bow-may a hauberk of ring-mail of his own fashioning, a sure defence and a wonderful work, and the collar thereof was done with gold and gems.

But he said to her: 'Fair damsel-at-arms, faithful is thy face, and the fashion of thee is goodly: now art thou become one of the best of our friends, and this is little enough to give thee; yet would we fain ward thy body against the foeman; so grieve us not by gainsaying us.'

And Bow-may was exceeding glad, and scarce knew how to cease handling that marvel of ring-mail.

Then to Wood-wise Iron-face gave a most goodly sword, the blade all marked with dark lines like the stream of an eddying river, the hilts of steel and gold marvellously wrought; and all the work of a smith who had dwelt in the house of his father's father, and was a great warrior.

Unto Wood-father he gave a very goodly helm parcel-gilded; and to his sons and the other folk fair gifts of weapons and jewels and girdles and cups and other good things; so that their hearts were full of joy, and they all praised his open hand.

Then some of the best and merriest of the kinsmen of the Face, and Face-of-god with them, brought the Guests out into the street and among the booths. There Face-of-god beheld the Bride again; and she was standing by the booth of a chapman and dealing with him for a piece of goodly silken cloth to be a gown for one of her guests, and she was talking and smiling as she chaffered with him, as her wont was; for she was ever very friendly of demeanour with all men. But he noted that she was yet exceeding pale, and he was right sorry thereof, for he loved her friendly; yet now had he no shame for all that had befallen, when he bethought him of the Sun-beam and the love she had for him. And also he had a deeming that the Bride would better of her grief.

Face-of-god cometh in to the Council.

## CHAPTER XXXIV. THE CHIEFTAINS TAKE COUNSEL IN THE HALL OF THE FACE.

THEN turned Face-of-god back into the Hall, and saw where Iron-face sat at the daïs, and with him Folk-might and Stone-face and the Elder of the Dale-wardens, and Sun-beam withal; so he went soberly up to the board, and sat himself down thereat beside Stone-face, over against Folk-might and his father, beside whom sat the Sun-beam; and Folk-might looked on him gravely, as a man powerful and trustworthy, yet was his look somewhat sour.

Then the Alderman said: 'My son, I said not to thee come back presently, because I wotted that thou wouldst surely do so, knowing that we have much to speak of. For, whatever these thy friends may have done, or whatsoever thou hast done with them to grieve us, all that must be set aside at this present time, since the matter in hand is to save the Dale and its folk. What sayest thou hereon? Since, young as thou mayst be, thou art our War-leader, and doubtless shalt so be after the Folk-mote hath been holden.'

Face-of-god answered not hastily: indeed, as he sat thinking for a minute or two, the fair spring day seemed to darken about

255

them or to glare into the light of flames amidst the night-tide;
and the joyous clamour without doors seemed to grow hoarse and
fearful as the sound of wailing and shrieking. But he spake
firmly and simply in a clear voice, and said:

'There can be no two words concerning what we have to aim
at; these Dusky Men we must slay everyone, though we be
fewer than they be.'

Folk-might smiled and nodded his head; but the others sat
staring down the hall or into the hangings.

Then spake Folk-might: 'Thou wert a boy methought when
I cast my spear at thee last autumn, Face-of-god, but now hast
thou grown into a man. Now tell me, what deemest thou we
must do to slay them all?'

Said Face-of-god: 'Once again it is clear that we must fall
upon them at home in Rose-dale and Silver-dale.'

Again Folk-might nodded: but Iron-face said:

'Needeth this? May we not ward the Dale and send many
bands into the wood to fall upon them when we meet them? Yea,
and so doing these our guests have already slain many, as this
valiant man hath told me e'en now. Will ye not slay so many
at last, that they shall learn to fear us, and abide at home and
leave us at peace?'

But Face-of-god said: 'Meseemeth, father, that this is not
thy rede, and that thou sayest this but to try me: and perchance
ye have been talking about me when I was without in the street
e'en now. Even if it might be that we should thus cow these
felons into abiding at home and tormenting their own thralls at
their ease, yet how then are our friends of the Wolf holpen to
their own again? And I shall tell thee that I have promised to
this man and this woman that I will give them no less than a
man's help in this matter. Moreover, I have spoken in every
house of the Dale, and to the Shepherds and the Woodlanders,
and there is no man amongst them but will follow me in the
quarrel. Furthermore, they have heard of the thralldom that is

256

done on men no great way from their own houses; yea, they have seen it; and they remember the old saw, "Grief in thy neighbour's hall is grief in thy garth," and sure it is, father, that whether thou or I gainsay them, go they will to deliver the thralls of the Dusky Men, and will leave us alone in the Dale.'

'This is no less than sooth,' said the Dale-warden, 'never have men gone forth more joyously to a merry-making than all men of us shall wend to this war.'

'But,' said Face-of-god, 'of one thing ye may be sure, that these men will not abide our pleasure till we cut them all off in scattered bands, nor will they sit deedless at home. Nor indeed may they; for we have heard from their thralls that they look to have fresh tribes of them come to hand to eat their meat and waste their servants, and these and they must find new abodes and new thralls; and they are now warned by the overthrows and slayings that they have had at our hands that we are astir, and they will not delay long, but will fall upon us with all their host; it might even be to-day or to-morrow.'

Said Folk-might: 'In all this thou sayest sooth, brother of the Dale; and to cut this matter short, I will tell you all, that yesterday we had with us a runaway from Silver-dale (it is over-long to tell how we fell in with her; for it was a woman). But she told us that this very moon is a new tribe come into the Dale, six long hundreds in number, and twice as many more are looked for in two eights of days, and that ere this moon hath waned, that is, in twenty-four days, they will wend their ways straight for Burg-dale, for they know the ways thereto. So I say that Face-of-god is right in all wise. But tell me, brother, hast thou thought of how we shall come upon these men?'

'How many men wilt thou lead into battle?' said Face-of-god.

Folk-might reddened, and said: 'A few, a few; maybe two hundreds all told.'

'Yea,' said Face-of-god, 'but some special gain wilt thou be to us.'

They talk of
the two Dales
of the
Foemen.

'So I deem at least,' said Folk-might.

Said Face-of-god: 'Good is that. Now have we held our Weapon-show in the Dale, and we find that we together with you be sixteen long hundreds of men; and the tale of the foemen that be now in Silver-dale, new-comers and all, shall be three thousands or thereabout, and in Rose-dale hard on a thousand.'

'Scarce so many,' said Folk-might; 'some of the felons have died; we told over our silver arm-rings yesterday, and the tale was three hundred and eighty and six. Besides, they were never so many as thou deemest.'

'Well,' said Face-of-god, 'yet at least they shall outnumber us sorely. We may scarce leave the Dale unguarded when our host is gone; therefore I deem that we shall have but one thousand of men for our onslaught on Silver-dale.'

'How come ye to that?' said Stone-face.

Said Face-of-god: 'Abide a while, fosterer! Though the odds between us be great, it is not to be hidden that I wot how ye of the Wolf know of privy passes into Silver-dale; yea, into the heart thereof; and this is the special gain ye have to give us. Therefore we, the thousand men, falling on the foe unawares, shall make a great slaughter of them; and if the murder be but grim enough, those thralls of theirs shall fear us and not them, as already they hate them and not us, so that we may look to them for rooting out these sorry weeds after the overthrow. And what with one thing, what with another, we may cherish a good hope of clearing Silver-dale at one stroke with the said thousand men.

'There remaineth Rose-dale, which will be easier to deal with, because the Dusky Men therein are fewer and the thralls as many: that also would I fall on at the same time as we fall on Silver-dale with the men that are left over from the Silver-dale onslaught. Wherefore my rede is, that we gather all those unmeet for battle in the field into this Burg, with ten tens of men to strengthen them; which shall be enough for them, along with the old men, and lads, and sturdy women, to defend themselves till help comes, if aught

258

of evil befall, or to flee into the mountains, or at the worst to die valiantly. Then let the other five hundreds fare up to Rose-dale, and fall on the Dusky Men therein about the same time, but not before our onslaught on Silver-dale : thus shall hand help foot, so that stumbling be not falling ; and we may well hope that our rede shall thrive.'

Then was he silent, and the Sun-beam looked upon him with gleaming eyes and parted lips, waiting eagerly to hear what Folk-might would say. He held his peace a while, drumming on the board with his fingers, and none else spake a word. At last he said :

'War-leader of Burgdale, all that thou hast spoken likes me well, and even so must it be done, saving that parting of our host and sending one part to fall upon Rose-dale. I say, nay ; let us put all our might into that one stroke on Silver-dale, and then we are undone indeed if we fail ; but so shall we be if we fail any-wise ; but if we win Silver-dale, then shall Rose-dale lie open before us.'

' My brother,' said Face-of-god, 'thou art a tried warrior, and I but a lad : but dost thou not see this, that whatever we do, we shall not at one onslaught slay all the Dusky Men of Silver-dale, and those that flee before us shall betake them to Rose-dale, and tell all the tale, and what shall hinder them then from falling on Burgdale (since they are no great way from it) after they have murdered what they will of the unhappy people under their hands ? '

Said Folk-might : ' I say not but that there is a risk thereof, but in war we must needs run such risks, and all should be risked rather than that our blow on Silver-dale be light. For we be the fewer ; and if the foemen have time to call that to mind, then are we all lost.'

Said Stone-face : 'Meseemeth, War-leader, that there is nought so much to dread in leaving Rose-dale to itself for a while ; for not only may we follow hard on the fleers if they flee to Rose-dale, and be there no long time after them, before they have time to stir

259

their host ; but also after the overthrow we shall be free to send men back to Burgdale by way of Shadowy Vale. I deem that herein Folk-might hath the right of it.'

' Even so say I,' said the Alderman ; 'besides, we might then leave more folk behind us for the warding of the Dale. So, son, the risk whereof thou speakest groweth the lesser the longer it is looked on.'

Then spake the Dale-warden : 'Yet saving your wisdom, Alderman, the risk is there yet. For if these felons come into the Dale at all, even if the folk left behind hold the Burg and keep themselves unmurdered, yet may they not hinder the foe from spoiling our homesteads; so that our folk coming back in triumph shall find ruin at home, and spend weary days in hunting their foemen, who shall, many of them, escape into the Wild-wood.'

' Yea,' said the Sun-beam, 'sooth is that; and Face-of-god is wise to think of it and of other matters. Yet one thing we must bear in mind, that all may not go smoothly in our day's work in Silver-dale ; so we must have force there to fall back on, in case we miss our stroke at first. Therefore, I say, send we no man to Rose-dale, and leave we no able man-at-arms behind in the Burg, so that we have with us every blade that may be gathered.'

Iron-face smiled and said : 'Thou art wise, damsel ; and I marvel that so fair-fashioned a thing as thou can think so hardly of the meeting of the fallow blades. But hearken! will not the Dusky Men hear that we have stripped the Dale of fighting-men, and may they not then give our host the go-by and send folk to ruin us ?'

There was silence while Face-of-god looked down on the board ; but presently he lifted up his face and said :

' Folk-might was right when he said that all must be risked. Let us leave Rose-dale till we have overcome them of Silver-dale. Moreover, my father, thou must not deem of these felons as if they were of like wits to us, to forecast the deeds to come, and weigh the chances nicely, and unravel tangled clews. Rather they move like to the stares in autumn, or the winter wild-geese, and will all be thrust forward by some sting that entereth into their imagina- tions. Therefore, if they have appointed one moon to wear before they fall upon us, they will not stir till then, and we have time enough to do what must be done. Wherefore am I now of one mind with the rest of you. Now meseemeth it were well that these things which we have spoken here, and shall speak, should not be noised abroad openly; nay, at the Folk-mote it would be well that nought be said about the day or the way of our onslaught on Silver-dale, lest the foe take warning and be on their guard. Though, sooth to say, did I deem that if they had word of our intent they of Rose-dale would join themselves to them of Silver-dale, and that we should thus have all our foes in one net, then were I fain if the word would reach them. For my soul loathes the hunting that shall befall up and down the wood for the slaying of a man here, and two or three there, and the wearing of the days in wandering up and down with weapons in the hand, and the spinning out of hatred and delaying of peace.'

Then Iron-face reached his hand across the board and took his son's hand, and said:

'Hail to thee, son, for thy word! Herein thou speakest as if from my very soul, and fain am I of such a War-leader.'

And desire drew the eyes of the Sun-beam to Face-of-god, and she beheld him proudly. But he said:

'All hath been spoken that the others of us may speak; and now it falleth to the part of Folk-might to order our goings for the tryst for the onslaught, and the trysting-place shall be in Shadowy Vale. How sayest thou, Chief of the Wolf?'

Said Folk-might: 'I have little to say; and it is for the War-leader to see to this closely and piecemeal. I deem, as we all deem, that there should be no delay; yet were it best to wend not all to-gether to Shadowy Vale, but in divers bands, as soon as ye may after the Folk-mote, by the sure and nigh ways that we shall show you. And when we are gathered there, short is the rede, for all

261

is ready there to wend by the passes which we know throughly,
and whereby it is but two days' journey to the head of Silver-
dale, nigh to the caves of the silver, where the felons dwell the
thickest.'

He set his teeth, and his colour came and went : for as con-
stantly as the onslaught had been in his mind, yet whenever he
spake of the great day of battle, hope and joy and anger wrought
a tumult in his soul ; and now that it was so nigh withal, he
could not refrain his joy.

But he spake again: 'Now therefore, War-leader, it is for thee
to order the goings of thy folk. But I will tell thee that they
shall not need to take aught with them save their weapons and
victual for the way, that is, for thirty hours ; because all is ready
for them in Shadowy Vale, though it be but a poor place as to
victual. Canst thou tell us, therefore, what thou wilt do ? '

Face-of-god had knit his brows and become gloomy of countenance ; but now his face cleared, and he set his hand to his
pouch, and drew forth a written parchment, and said :

' This is the order whereof I have bethought me. Before the
Folk-mote I and the Wardens shall speak to the leaders of hundreds, who be mostly here at the Fair, and give them the day and
the hour whereon they shall, each hundred, take their weapons
and wend to Shadowy Vale, and also the place where they shall
meet the men of yours who shall lead them across the Waste.
These hundred-leaders shall then go straightway and give the
word to the captains of scores, and the captains of scores to the
captains of tens ; and if, as is scarce doubtful, the Folk-mote yea-
says the onslaught and the fellowship with you of the Wolf, then
shall those leaders of tens bring their men to the trysting-place,
and so go their ways to Shadowy Vale. Now here I have the
roll of our Weapon-show, and I will look to it that none shall be
passed over ; and if ye ask me in what order they had best get
on the way, my rede is that a two hundred should depart on the
very evening of the day of the Folk-mote, and these to be of our

folk of the Upper Dale; and on the morning of the morrow of the Folk-mote another two hundreds from the Dale; and in the evening of the same day the folk of the Shepherds, three hundreds or more, and that will be easy to them; again on the next day two more bands of the Lower Dale, one in the morning, one in the evening. Lastly, in the earliest dawn of the third day from the Folk-mote shall the Woodlanders wend their ways. But one hundred of men let us leave behind for the warding of the Burg, even as we agreed before. As for the place of tryst for the faring over the Waste, let it be the end of the knolls just by the jaws of the pass yonder, where the Weltering Water comes into the Dale from the East. How say ye?'

They all said, and Folk-might especially, that it was right well devised, and that thus it should be done.

Then turned Face-of-god to the Dale-warden, and said:

'It were good, brother, that we saw the other wardens as soon as may be, to do them to wit of this order, and what they have to do.'

Therewith he arose and took the Elder of the Dale-wardens away with him, and the twain set about their business straightway. Neither did the others abide long in the Hall, but went out into the Burg to see the chapmen and their wares. There the Alderman bought what he needed of iron and steel and other matters; and Folk-might cheapened him a dagger curiously wrought, and a web of gold and silk for the Sun-beam, for which wares he paid in silver arm-rings, new-wrought and of strange fashion.

But amidst of the chaffer was now a great ring of men; and in the midst of the ring stood Redesman, fiddle and bow in hand, and with him were four damsels wondrously arrayed; for the first was clad in a smock so craftily wrought with threads of green and many colours, that it seemed like a piece of the green field beset with primroses and cowslips and harebells and windflowers, rather than a garment woven and sewn; and in her hand she bore a

263

naked sword, with golden hilts and gleaming blade. But the
second bore on her roses done in like manner, both blossoms and
green leaves, wherewith her body was covered decently, which
else had been naked. The third was clad as though she were
wading the wheat-field to the waist, and above was wrapped in
the leaves and bunches of the wine-tree. And the fourth was
clad in a scarlet gown flecked with white wool to set forth
the winter's snow, and broidered over with the burning brands
of the Holy Hearth; and she bore on her head a garland of
mistletoe. And these four damsels were clearly seen to image
the four seasons of the year—Spring, Summer, Autumn, and
Winter. But amidst them stood a fountain or conduit of gilded
work cunningly wrought, and full of the best wine of the Dale,
and gilded cups and beakers hung about it.

So now Redesman fell to caressing his fiddle with the bow till
it began to make sweet music, and therewith the hearts of all
danced with it; and presently words come into his mouth, and he
fell to singing; and the damsels answered him:

Earth-wielders, that fashion the Dale-dwellers' treasure,
   Soft are ye by seeming, yet hardy of heart!
No warrior amongst us withstandeth your pleasure;
   No man from his meadow may thrust you apart.

Fresh and fair are your bodies, but far beyond telling
   Are the years of your lives, and the craft ye have stored.
Come give us a word, then, concerning our dwelling,
   And the days to befall us, the fruit of the sword.

*Winter saith:*
When last in the feast-hall the Yule-fire flickered,
   The foot of no foeman fared over the snow,
And nought but the wind with the ash-branches bickered:
   Next Yule ye may deem it a long time ago.

*Autumn saith :*

Loud laughed ye last year in the wheat-field a-smiting ;
    And ye laughed as your backs drave the beam of the press.
When the edge of the war-sword the acres are lighting
    Look up to the Banner and laugh ye no less.


*Summer saith :*

Ye called and I came, and how good was the greeting,
    When ye wrapped me in roses both bosom and side !
Here yet shall I long, and be fain of our meeting,
    As hidden from battle your coming I bide.


*Spring saith :*

I am here for your comfort, and lo ! what I carry ;
    The blade with the bright edges bared to the sun.
To the field, to the work then, that e'en I may tarry
    For the end of the tale in my first days begun !


Therewith the throng opened, and a young man stepped lightly
into the ring, clad in very fair armour, with a gilded helm on his
head ; and he took the sword from the hand of the Maiden of
Spring, and waved it in the air till the westering sun flashed
back from it. Then each of the four damsels went up to the
swain and kissed his mouth ; and Redesman drew the bow across
the strings, and the four damsels sang together, standing round
about the young warrior :

It was but a while since for earth's sake we trembled,
    Lest the increase our life-days had won for the Dale,
All the wealth that the moons and the years had assembled,
    Should be but a mock for the days of your bale.

But now we behold the sun smite on the token
    In the hand of the Champion, the heart of a man ;

M M

We look down the long years and see them unbroken ;
  Forth fareth the Folk by the ways it began.

So bid ye these chapmen in autumn returning,
  To bring iron for ploughshares and steel for the scythe,
And the over-sea oil that hath felt the sun's burning,
  And fair webs for your women soft-spoken and blithe ;

And pledge ye your word in the market to meet them,
  As many a man and as many a maid,
As eager as ever, as guest-fain to greet them,
  And bide till the booth from the waggon is made.

Come, guests of our lovers ! for we, the year-wielders,
  Bid each man and all to come hither and take
A cup from our hands midst the peace of our shielders,
  And drink to the days of the Dale that we make.

Then went the damsels to that wine-fountain, and drew thence
cups of the best and brightest wine of the Dale, and went round
about the ring, and gave drink to whomsoever would, both of the
chapmen and the others ; while the weaponed youth stood in the
midst bearing aloft his sword and shield like an image in a holy
place, and Redesman's bow still went up and down the strings,
and drew forth a sweet and merry tune.

Great game it was now to see the stark Burgdale carles dragging the Men of the Plain, little loth, up to the front of the
ring, that they might stretch out their hands for a cup, and how
many a one, as he took it, took as much as he might of the damsel's hand withal. As for the damsels, they played the Holy Play
very daintily, neither reddening nor laughing, but faring so
solemnly, and withal so sweetly and bright-faced, that it might well
have been deemed that they were in very sooth Maidens of the God
of Earth sent from the ever-enduring Hall to cheer the hearts of men.

So simply and blithely did the Men of Burgdale disport them

after the manner of their fathers, trusting in their valour and be-

So wore the evening, and when night was come, men feasted
throughout the Burg from house to house, and every hall was full.
But the Guests from Shadowy Vale feasted in the Hall of the
Face in all glee and goodwill; and with them were the chief of the
chapmen and two others; but the rest of them had been laid hold
of by goodmen of the Burg, and dragged into their feast-halls,
for they were fain of those guests and their tales. One of the
chapmen in the House of the Face knew Folk-might, and hailed
him by the name he had borne in the Cities, Regulus to wit;
indeed, the chief chapman knew him, and even somewhat over-
well, for he had been held to ransom by Folk-might in those past
days, and even yet feared him, because he, the chapman, had
played somewhat of a dastard's part to him. But the other was
an open-hearted and merry fellow, and no weakling; and Folk-
might was fain of his talk concerning times bygone, and the fields
they had foughten in, and other adventures that had befallen
them, both good and evil.

As for Face-of-god, he went about the Hall soberly, and spake
no more than behoved him, so as not to seem a mar-feast; for
the image of the slaughter to be yet abode with him, and his
heart foreboded the after-grief of the battle. He had no speech
with the Sun-beam till men were sundering after the feast, and
then he came close to her amidst of the turmoil, and said:

'Time presses on me these days; but if thou wouldest speak
with me to-morrow as I would with thee, then mightest thou go
on the Bridge of the Burg about sunrise, and I will be there,
and we two only.'

Her face, which had been somewhat sad that evening (for she
had been watching his), brightened at that word, and she took
his hand as folk came thronging round about them, and said:
'Yea, friend, I shall be there, and fain of thee.' And therewithal
they sundered for that night.

267

And all men went to sleep throughout the Burg : howbeit they
set a watch at the Burg-Gate; and Hall-face, when he was coming
back from the woodland ward about sunset, fell in with Red-
coat of Waterless and four score men on the Portway coming to
meet him and take his place. All which was clean contrary to
the wont of the Burgdalers, who at most whiles held no watch
and ward, not even in Fair-time.


## CHAPTER XXXV. FACE-OF-GOD TALKETH WITH THE SUN-BEAM.

FACE-OF-GOD was at the Bridge on the morrow before
sun-rising, and as he turned about at the Bridge-foot he
saw the Sun-beam coming down the street; and his heart
rose to his mouth at the sight of her, and he went to meet her
and took her by the hand ; and there were no words between
them till they had kissed and caressed each other, for there was
no one stirring about them. So they went over the Bridge into
the meadows, and eastward of the beaten path thereover.

The grass was growing thick and strong, and it was full of
flowers, as the cowslip and the oxlip, and the chequered daffodil,
and the wild tulip: the black-thorn was well-nigh done blooming, but the hawthorn was in bud, and in some places growing
white. It was a fair morning, warm and cloudless, but the night
had been misty, and the haze still hung about the meadows of
the Dale where they were wettest, and the grass and its flowers
were heavy with dew, so that the Sun-beam went barefoot in
the meadow. She had a dark cloak cast over her kirtle, and
had left her glittering gown behind her in the House.

They went along hand in hand exceeding fain of each other,
and the sun rose as they went, and the long beams of gold shone
through the tops of the tall trees across the grass they trod, and
a light wind rose up in the north, as Face-of-god stayed a mo-

ment and turned toward the Face of the Sun and prayed to Him, while the Sun-beam's hand left the War-leader's hand and stole up to his golden locks and lay amongst them.

Presently they went on, and the feet of Face-of-god led him unwitting toward the chestnut grove by the old dyke where he had met the Bride such a little while ago, till he bethought whither he was going and stopped short and reddened; and the Sun-beam noted it, but spake not; but he said : ' Hereby is a fair place for us to sit and talk till the day's work beginneth.'

So then he turned aside, and soon they came to a hawthorn brake out of which arose a great tall-stemmed oak, showing no green as yet save a little on its lower twigs; and anigh it, yet with room for its boughs to grow freely, was a great bird-cherry tree, all covered now with sweet-smelling white blossoms. There they sat down on the trunk of a tree felled last year, and she cast off her cloak, and took his face between her two hands and kissed him long and fondly, and for a while their joy had no word. But when speech came to them, it was she that spake first and said :

' Gold-mane, my dear, sorely I wonder at thee and at me, how we are changed since that day last autumn when I first saw thee. Whiles I think, didst thou not laugh when thou wert by thyself that day, and mock at me privily, that I must needs take such wisdom on myself, and lesson thee standing like a stripling before me. Dost thou not call it all to mind and make merry over it, now that thou art become a great chieftain and a wise warrior, and I am yet what I always was, a young maiden of the kindred; save that now I abide no longer for my love ? '

Her face was exceeding bright and rippled with joyous smiles, and he looked at her and deemed that her heart was overflowing with happiness, and he wondered at her indeed that she was so glad of him, and he said :

' Yea, indeed, oft do I see that morning in the woodland hall and thee and me therein, as one looketh on a picture; yea verily,

269

and I laugh, yet is it for very bliss; neither do I mock at all.
Did I not deem thee a God then? and am I not most happy now
when I can call it thus to mind? And as to thee, thou wert wise
then, and yet art thou wise now. Yea, I thought thee a God;
and if we are changed, is it not rather that thou hast lifted me
up to thee, and not come down to me?'

Yet therewithal he knit his brows somewhat and said:

'Yet thou hast not to tell me that all thy love for thy Folk,
and thy yearning hope for its recoverance, was but a painted
show. Else why shouldst thou love me the better now that I
am become a chieftain, and therefore am more meet to under-
stand thy hope and thy sorrow? Did I not behold thee as we
stood before the Wolf of the Hall of Shadowy Vale, how the
tears stood in thine eyes as thou beheldest him, and thine hand
in mine quivered and clung to me, and thou wert all changed in
a moment of time? Was all this then but a seeming and a
beguilement?'

'O young man,' she said, 'hast thou not said it, that we stood
there close together, and my hand in thine and desire growing up
in me? Dost thou not know how this also quickeneth the story
of our Folk, and our goodwill towards the living, and remembrance of the dead? Shall they have lived and desired, and we
deny desire and life? Or tell me: what was it made thee so
chieftain-like in the Hall yesterday, so that thou wert the master
of all our wills, for as self-willed as some of us were? Was it
not that I, whom thou deemest lovely, was thereby watching thee
and rejoicing in thee? Did not the sweetness of thy love quicken
thee? Yet because of that was thy warrior's wisdom and thy
foresight an empty show? Heedest thou nought the Folk of the
Dale? Wouldest thou sunder from the children of the Fathers,
and dwell amongst strangers?'

He kissed her and smiled on her and said: 'Did I not say of
thee that thou wert wiser than the daughters of men? See how
wise thou hast made me!'

She spake again: 'Nay, nay, there was no feigning in my Face-of-god love for my people. How couldest thou think it, when the made wise Fathers and the kindred have made this body that thou lovest, by love. and the voice of their songs is in the speech thou deemest sweet?'

He said: 'Sweet friend, I deemed not that there was feigning in thee: I was but wondering what I am and how I was fashioned, that I should make thee so glad that thou couldst for a while forget thy hope of the days before we met.'

She said: 'O how glad, how glad! Yet was I nought hapless. In despite of all trouble I had no down-weighing grief, and I had the hope of my people before me. Good were my days; but I knew not till now how glad a child of man may be.'

Their words were hushed for a while amidst their caresses. Then she said:

'Gold-mane, my friend, I mocked not my past self because I deem that I was a fool then, but because I see now that all that my wisdom could do, would have come about without my wisdom; and that thou, deeming thyself something less than wise, didst accomplish the thing I craved, and that which thou didst crave also; and withal wisdom embraced thee, along with love.'

Therewith she cast her arms about him and said:

'O friend, I mock myself of this: that erst thou deemedst me a God and fearedst me, but now thou seemest to me to be a God, and I fear thee. Yea, though I have longed so sore to be with thee since the day of Shadowy Vale, and though I have wearied of the slow wearing of the days, and it hath tormented me; yet now that I am with thee, I bless the torment of my longing; for it is but my longing that compelleth me to cast away my fear of thee and caress thee, because I have learned how sweet it is to love thee thus.'

He wound his arms about her, and sweeter was their longing than mere joy; and though their love was beyond measure, yet was therein no shame to aught, not even to the lovely Dale and that fair season of spring, so goodly they were among the children of men.

271

In a while they arose and turned homeward, and went over the open meadow, and it was yet early, and the dew was as heavy on the grass as before, though the wide sunlight was now upon it, glittering on the wet blades, and shining through the bells of the chequered daffodils till they looked like gouts of blood.

'Look,' said Sun-beam, as they went along by the same way whereas they came, 'deemest thou not that other speech-friends besides us have been abroad to talk together apart on this morning of the eve of battle. It is nought unwonted, that we do, even though we forget the trouble of the people to think of our own joy for a while.'

The smile died out of her face as she spoke, and she said: 'O friend, this much may I say for myself in all sooth, that indeed I would die for the kindred and its good days, nor falter therein; but if I am to die, might I but die in thine arms!'

He looked very lovingly on her, and put his arm about her and kissed her and said: 'What ails us to stand in the doom-ring and bear witness against ourselves before the kindred? Now I will say, that whatsoever the kindred may or can call upon me to do, that will I do, nor grudge the deed: I am sackless before them. But that is true which I spake to thee when we came together up out of Shadowy Vale, to wit, that I am no strifeful man, but a peaceful; and I look to it to win through this war, and find on the other side either death, or life amongst a happy folk; and I deem that this is mostly the mind of our people.'

She said: 'Thou shalt not die, thou shalt not die!'

'Mayhappen not,' he said; 'yet yesterday I could not but look into the slaughter to come, and it seemed to me a grim thing, and darkened the day for me; and I grew acold as a man walking with the dead. But tell me: thou sayest I shall not die; dost thou say this only because I am become dear to thee, or dost thou speak it out of thy foresight of things to come?'

She stopped and looked silently a while over the meadows towards the houses of the Thorp: they were standing now on the border of a shallow brook that ran down toward the Wel- tering Water; it had a little strand of fine sand like the sea-shore, driven close together, and all moist, because that brook was used to flood the meadow for the feeding of the grass; and the last evening the hatches which held up the water had been drawn, so that much had ebbed away and left the strand aforesaid.

After a while the Sun-beam turned to Face-of-god, and she was become somewhat pale; she said:

'Nay, I have striven to see, and can see nought save the picture of hope and fear that I make for myself. So it oft befalleth foreseeing women, that the love of a man cloudeth their vision. Be content, dear friend; it is for life or death; but whichso it be, the same for me and thee together?'

'Yea,' he said, 'and well content I am; so now let each of us trust in the other to be both good and dear, even as I trusted in thee the first hour that I looked on thee.'

'It is well,' she said; 'it is well. How fair thou art; and how fair is the morn, and this our Dale in the goodly season; and all this abideth us when the battle is over.'

Once more her voice became sweet and wheedling, and the smile lit up her face again, and she pointed down to the sand with her finger, and said:

'See thou! Here indeed have other lovers passed by across the brook. Shall we wish them good luck?'

He laughed and looked down on the sand, and said:

'Thou art in haste to make a story up. Indeed I see that these first footprints are of a woman, for no carle of the Dale has a foot as small; for we be tall fellows; and these others withal are a man's footprints; and if they showed that they had been walking side by side, simple had been thy tale; but so it is not. I cannot say that these two pairs of feet went over the brook within five minutes of each other; but sure it is that they could not have been faring side by side. Well, belike they were lovers bickering, and we may wish them luck out of that. Truly

273                                        N N

it is well seen that Bow-may hath done thine hunting for thee,
dear friend; or else wouldest thou have lacked venison; for thou
hast no hunter's eye.'

'Well,' she said, 'but wish them luck, and give me thine hand
upon it.'

He took her hand, and fondled it, and said: 'By this hand
of my speech-friend, I wish these twain all luck, in love and in
leisure, in faring and fighting, in sowing and samming, in getting
and giving. Is it well enough wished? If so it be, then come
thy ways, dear friend; for the day's work is at hand.'

'It is well wished,' she said. 'Now hearken: by the valiant
hand of the War-leader, by the hand that shall unloose my girdle,
I wish these twain to be as happy as we be.'

He made as if to draw her away, but she hung aback to set
the print of her foot beside the woman's foot, and then they went
on together, and soon crossed the Bridge, and came home to the
House of the Face.

When they had broken their fast, Face-of-god would straight
get to his business of ordering matters for the warfare, and was
wishful to speak with Folk-might; but found him not, either in
the House or the street. But a man said:

'I saw the tall Guest come abroad from the House and go
toward the Bridge very early in the morning.'

The Sun-beam, who was anigh when that was spoken, heard
it and smiled, and said: 'Gold-mane, deemest thou that it was
my brother whom we blessed?'

'I wot not,' he said; 'but I would he were here, for this gear
must speedily be looked to.'

Nevertheless it was nigh an hour before Folk-might came home
to the House. He strode in lightly and gaily, and shaking the
crest of his war-helm as he went. He looked friendly on Face-
of-god, and said to him:

'Thou hast been seeking me, War-leader; but grudge it not
that I have caused thee to tarry. For as things have gone, I am

274

twice the man for thine helping that I was yester-eve ; and thou art so ready and deft, that all will be done in due time.'

He looked as if he would have had Face-of-god ask of him what made him so fain, but Face-of-god said only :

'I am glad of thy gladness ; but now let us dally no longer, for I have many folk to see to-day and much to set a-going.'

So therewith they spake together a while, and then went their ways together toward Carlstead and the Woodlanders.


## CHAPTER XXXVI. FOLK-MIGHT SPEAKETH WITH THE BRIDE.

IT must be told that those footprints which Face-of-god and the Sun-beam had blessed betwixt jest and earnest had more to do with them than they wotted of. For Folk-might, who had had many thoughts and longings since he had seen the Bride again, rose up early about sunrise, and went out-a-doors, and wandered about the Burg, letting his eyes stray over the goodly stone houses and their trim gardens, yet noting them little, since the Bride was not there.

At last he came to where there was an open place, straight-sided, longer than it was wide, with a wall on each side of it, over which showed the blossomed boughs of pear and cherry and plum-trees : on either hand before the wall was a row of great lindens, now showing their first tender green, especially on their lower twigs, where they were sheltered by the wall. At the nether end of this place Folk-might saw a grey stone house, and he went towards it betwixt the lindens, for it seemed right great, and presently was but a score of paces from its door, and as yet there was no man, carle or queen, stirring about it.

It was a long low house with a very steep roof ; but belike the hall was built over some undercroft, for many steps went up to the door on either hand ; and the doorway was low, with a

275

straight lintel under its arch. This house, like the House of the
Face, seemed ancient and somewhat strange, and Folk-might
could not choose but take note of it. The front was all of
good ashlar work, but it was carven all over, without heed being
paid to the joints of the stones, into one picture of a flowery
meadow, with tall trees and bushes in it, and fowl perched in
the trees and running through the grass, and sheep and kine and
oxen and horses feeding down the meadow ; and over the door
at the top of the stair was wrought a great steer bigger than all
the other neat, whose head was turned toward the sun-rising and
uplifted with open mouth, as though he were lowing aloud.
Exceeding fair seemed that house to Folk-might, and as though
it were the dwelling of some great kindred.

But he had scarce gone over it with his eyes, and was just
about to draw nigher yet to it, when the door at the top of those
steps opened, and a woman came out of the house clad in a green
kirtle and a gown of brazil, with a golden-hilted sword girt to
her side. Folk-might saw at once that it was the Bride, and
drew aback behind one of the trees so that she might not see
him, if she had not already seen him, as it seemed not that she
had ; for she stayed but for a moment on the top of the stair,
looking out down the tree-rows, and then came down the stair
and went soberly along the road, passing so close to Folk-might
that he could see the fashion of her beauty closely, as one looks
into the work of some deftest artificer. Then it came suddenly
into his head that he would follow her and see whither she was
wending. ' At least,' said he to himself, ' if I come not to speech
with her, I shall be nigh unto her, and shall see somewhat of
her beauty.'

So he came out quietly from behind the tree, and followed her
softly ; and he was clad in no garment save his kirtle, and bare
no weapons to clash and jingle, though he had his helm on his
head for lack of a softer hat. He kept her well in sight, and she
went straight onward and looked not back. She went by the way

276

whereas he had come, till they were in the main street, wherein as yet was no one afoot ; she made her way to the Bridge, and passed over it into the meadows ; but when she had gone but a few steps, she stayed a little and looked on the ground, and as she did so turned a little toward Folk-might, who had drawn back into the last of the refuges over the up-stream buttresses. He saw that there was a half-smile on her face, but he could not tell whether she were glad or sorry. A light wind was beginning to blow, that stirred her raiment and raised a lock of hair that had strayed from the golden fillet round about her head, and she looked most marvellous fair.

Now she looked along the grass that glittered under the beams of the newly-risen sun, and noted belike how heavy the dew lay on it ; and the grass was high already, for the spring had been hot, and haysel would be early in the Dale. So she put off her shoes, that were of deerskin and broidered with golden threads, and turned somewhat from the way, and hung them up amidst the new green leaves of a hawthorn bush that stood nearby, and so went thwart the meadow somewhat eastward straight from that bush, and her feet shone out like pearls amidst the deep green grass.

Folk-might followed presently, and she stayed not again, nor turned, nor beheld him ; he recked not if she had, for then would he have come up with her and hailed her, and he knew that she was no foolish maiden to start at the sight of a man who was the friend of her Folk.

So they went their ways till she came to the strand of the water-meadow brook aforesaid, and she went through the little ripples of the shallow without staying, and on through the tall deep grass of the meadow beyond, to where they met the brook again ; for it swept round the meadow in a wide curve, and turned back toward itself ; so it was some half furlong over from water to water.

She stood a while on the brink of the brook here, which was brim-full and nigh running into the grass, because there was a dam

just below the place; and Folk-might drew nigher to her under
cover of the thorn-bushes, and looked at the place about her and
beyond her. The meadow beyond stream was very fair and
flowery, but not right great; for it was bounded by a grove of
ancient chestnut trees, that went on and on toward the southern
cliffs of the Dale: in front of the chestnut wood stood a broken row
of black-thorn bushes, now growing green and losing their blossom, and he could see betwixt them that there was a grassy bank
running along, as if there had once been a turf-wall and ditch
round about the chestnut trees.—For indeed this was the old place
of tryst between Gold-mane and the Bride, whereof the tale hath
told before.

The Bride stayed scarce longer than gave him time to note all
this; but he deemed that she was weeping, though he could not
rightly see her face; for her shoulders heaved, and she hung her
face adown and put up her hands to it. But now she went a
little higher up the stream, where the water was shallower, and
waded the stream and went up over the meadow, still weeping,
as he deemed, and went between the black-thorn bushes, and sat
her down on the grassy bank with her back to the chestnut trees.

Folk-might was ashamed to have seen her weeping, and was
half-minded to turn him back again at once; but love constrained
him, and he said to himself, 'Where shall I see her again privily
if I pass by this time and place?' So he waited a little till he
deemed she might have mastered the passion of tears, and then
came forth from his bush, and went down to the water and crossed
it, and went quietly over the meadow straight towards her.
But he was not half-way across, when she lifted up her face from
between her hands and beheld the man coming. She neither started
nor rose up; but straightened herself as she sat, and looked right
into Folk-might's eyes as he drew near, though the tears were not
dry on her cheeks.

Now he stood before her, and said: 'Hail to the Daughter of
a mighty House! Mayst thou live happy!'

She answered : 'Hail to thee also, Guest of our Folk! Hast She greeteth thou been wandering about our meadows, and happened on me him friendly. perchance ?'

'Nay,' he said; 'I saw thee come forth from the House of the Steer, and I followed thee hither.'

She reddened a little, and knit her brow, and said :

'Thou wilt have something to say to me ?'

'I have much to say to thee,' he said ; 'yet it was sweet to me to behold thee, even if I might not speak with thee.'

She looked on him with her deep simple eyes, and neither reddened again, nor seemed wroth ; then she said :

'Speak what thou hast in thine heart, and I will hearken without anger whatsoever it may be ; even if thou hast but to tell me of the passing folly of a mighty man, which in a month or two he will not remember for sorrow or for joy. Sit here beside me, and tell me thy thought.'

So he sat him adown and said : 'Yea, I have much to say to thee, but it is hard to me to say it. But this I will say : to-day and yesterday make the third time I have seen thee. The first time thou wert happy and calm, and no shadow of trouble was on thee ; the second time thine happy days were waning, though thou scarce knewest it ; but to-day and yesterday thou art constrained by the bonds of grief, and wouldest loosen them if thou mightest.'

She said : 'What meanest thou ? How knowest thou this ? How may a stranger partake in my joy and my sorrow ?'

He said : 'As for yesterday, all the people might see thy grief and know it. But when I beheld thee the first time, I saw thee that thou wert more fair and lovely than all other women ; and when I was away from thee, the thought of thee and thine image were with me, and I might not put them away ; and oft at such and such a time I wondered and said to myself, what is she doing now ? though god wot I was dealing with tangles and troubles and rough deeds enough. But the second time I beheld thee, when I had looked to have great joy in the sight of thee, my heart was

279

smitten with a pang of grief; for I saw thee hanging on the words and the looks of another man, who was light-minded toward thee, and that thou wert troubled with the anguish of doubt and fear. And he knew it not, nor saw it, though I saw it.'

Her face grew troubled, and the tearful passion stirred within her. But she held it aback, and said, as anyone might have said it :

' How wert thou in the Dale, mighty man ? We saw thee not.'

He said : ' I came hither hidden in other semblance than mine own. But meddle not therewith ; it availeth nought. Let me say this, and do thou hearken to it. I saw thee yesterday in the street, and thou wert as the ghost of thine old gladness ; although belike thou hast striven with sorrow ; for I see thee with a sword by thy side, and we have been told that thou, O fairest of women, hast given thyself to the Warrior to be his damsel.'

' Yea,' she said, ' that is sooth.'

He went on : ' But the face which thou bearedst yesterday against thy will, amidst all the people, that was because thou hadst seen my sister the Sun-beam for the first time, and Face-of-god with her, hand clinging to hand, lip longing for lip, desire unsatisfied, but glad with all hope.'

She laid hand upon hand in the lap of her gown, and looked down, and her voice trembled as she said :

' Doth it avail to talk of this ? '

He said : ' I know not : it may avail ; for I am grieved, and shall be whilst thou art grieved ; and it is my wont to strive with my griefs till I amend them.'

She turned to him with kind eyes and said :

' O mighty man, canst thou clear away the tangle which besetteth the soul of her whose hope hath bewrayed her ? Canst thou make hope grow up in her heart ? Friend, I will tell thee that when I wed, I shall wed for the sake of the kindred, hoping for no joy therein. Yea, or if by some chance the desire of man came again into my heart, I should strive with it to rid myself of it, for I should know of it that it was but a wasting folly, that

280

should but beguile me, and wound me, and depart, leaving me empty of joy and heedless of life.'

He shook his head and said: 'Even so thou deemest now; but one day it shall be otherwise. Or dost thou love thy sorrow? I tell thee, as it wears thee and wears thee, thou shalt hate it, and strive to shake it off.'

'Nay, nay,' she said; 'I love it not; for not only it grieveth me, but also it beateth me down and belittleth me.'

'Good is that,' said he. 'I know how strong thine heart is. Now, wilt thou take mine hand, which is verily the hand of thy friend, and remember what I have told thee of my grief which cannot be sundered from thine? Shall we not talk more concerning this? For surely I shall soon see thee again, and often; since the Warrior, who loveth me belike, leadeth thee into fellowship with me. Yea, I tell thee, O friend, that in that fellowship shalt thou find both the seed of hope, and the sun of desire that shall quicken it.'

Therewith he arose and stood before her, and held out to her his hand all hardened with the sword-hilt, and she took it, and stood up facing him, and said:

'This much will I tell thee, O friend; that what I have said to thee this hour, I thought not to have said to any man; or to talk with a man of the grief that weareth me, or to suffer him to see my tears; and marvellous I deem it of thee, for all thy might, that thou hast drawn this speech from out of me, and left me neither angry nor ashamed, in spite of these tears; and thou whom I have known not, though thou knewest me!

'But now it were best that thou depart, and get thee home to the House of the Face, where I was once so frequent; for I wot that thou hast much to do; and as thou sayest, it will be in warfare that I shall see thee. Now I thank thee for thy words and the thought thou hast had of me, and the pain which thou hast taken to heal my hurt: I thank thee, I thank thee, for as grievous as it is to show one's hurts even to a friend.'

O O

He said : 'O Bride, I thank thee for hearkening to my tale ;
and one day shall I thank thee much more. Mayest thou fare
well in the Field and amidst the Folk ! '

Therewith he kissed her hand, and turned away, and went
across the meadow and the stream, glad at heart and blithe with
everyone ; for kindness grew in him as gladness grew.

## CHAPTER XXXVII. OF THE FOLK-MOTE OF THE DALES-MEN, THE SHEPHERD-FOLK, AND THE WOODLAND CARLES: THE BANNER OF THE WOLF DISPLAYED.

NOW came the day of the Great Folk-mote, and there was
much thronging from everywhere to the Mote-stead, but
most from Burgstead itself, whereas few of the Dale-
dwellers who had been at the Fair had gone back home. Albeit
some of the Shepherds and of the Dalesmen of the westernmost
Dale had brought light tents, and tilted themselves in in the night
before the Mote down in the meadows below the Mote-stead.
From early morning there had been a stream of folk on the Portway setting westward ; and many came thus early that they
might hold converse with friends and well-wishers ; and some
that they might disport them in the woods. Men went in no
ordered bands, as the Burgstead men at least had done on the day
of the Weapon-show, save that a few of them who were arrayed
the bravest gathered about the banners, and went with them to the
Mote-stead; for all the banners must needs be there.

The Folk-mote was to be hallowed-in three hours before noon,
as all men knew ; therefore an hour before that time were all men
of the Dale and the Shepherds assembled that might be looked
for, save the Alderman and the chieftains with the banner of the
Burg, and these were not like to come many minutes before the
Hallowing. Folk were gathered on the Field in such wise, that
the men-at-arms made a great ring round about the Doom-ring

(albeit there were many old men there, girt with swords that they Here cometh
should never heave up again in battle), so that without that ring in the Alder-
there was nought save women and children.  But when all the man.
other Houses were assembled, men looked around, and beheld
the place of the Woodlanders that it was empty; and they marvelled that they were thus belated.  For now all was ready, and
a watcher had gone up to the Tower on the height, and had with
him the great Horn of Warning, which could be heard past the
Mote-stead and a great way down the Dale : and if he saw foes
coming from the East he should blow one blast; if from the South,
two; if from the West, three; if from the North, four.

So half an hour from the appointed time of Hallowing rose the
rumour that the Alderman was on the road, and presently they
of the women who were on the outside of the throng, by drawing
nigh to the edge of the sheer rock, could behold the Banner of
the Burg on the Portway, and soon after could see the wain,
done about with green boughs, wherein sat the chieftains in their
glittering war-gear.  Speedily they spread the tidings, and a confused shout went up into the air ; and in a little while the wain
stayed on Wildlake's Way at the bottom of the steep slope that
went up to the Mote-stead, and the banner of the Burg came on
proudly up the hill.  Soon all men beheld it, and saw that the
tall Hall-face bore it in front of his brother Face-of-god, who
came on gleaming in war-gear better than most men had seen;
which was indeed of his father's fashioning, and his father's gift
to him that morning.

After Face-of-god came the Alderman, and with him Folk-
might leading the Sun-beam by the hand, and then Stone-face
and the Elder of the Dale-wardens ; and then the six Burg-
wardens : as to the other Dale-wardens, they were in their places
on the Field.

So now those who had been standing up turned their faces toward the Altar of the Gods, and those who had been sitting down
sprang to their feet, and the confused rumour of the throng rose

into a clear shout as the chieftains went to their places, and sat
them down on the turf-seats amidst the Doom-ring facing the
Speech-hill and the Altar of the Gods. Amidmost sat the Alderman, on his right hand Face-of-god, and out from him Hall-face,
and then Stone-face and three of the Wardens; but on his left
hand sat first the two Guests, then the Elder of the Dale-wardens,
and then the other three Burg-wardens; as for the Banner of the
Burg, its staff was stuck into the earth behind them, and the
Banner raised itself in the morning wind and flapped and rippled
over their heads.

There then they sat, and folk abided, and it still lacked some
minutes of the due time, as the Alderman wotted by the shadow
of the great standing-stone betwixt him and the Altar. Therewithal came the sound of a great horn from out of the wood on
the north side, and men knew it for the horn of the Woodland
Carles, and were glad; for they could not think why they should
be belated; and now men stood up a-tiptoe and on other's
shoulders to look over the heads of the women and children to
behold their coming; but their empty place was at the south-
west corner of the ring of men.

So presently men beheld them marching toward their place,
cleaving the throng of the women and children, a great company; for besides that they had with them two score more of
men under weapons than on the day of the Weapon-show, all
their little ones and women and outworn elders were with them,
some on foot, some riding on oxen and asses. In their forefront
went the two signs of the Battle-shaft and the War-spear. But
moreover, in front of all was borne a great staff with the cloth
of a banner wrapped round about it, and tied up with a hempen
yarn that it might not be seen.

Stark and mighty men they looked; tall and lean, broad-
shouldered, dark-faced. As they came amongst the throng the
voice of their horn died out, and for a few moments they fared
on with no sound save the tramp of their feet; then all at once

the man who bare the hidden banner lifted up one hand, and
straightway they fell to singing, and with that song they came
to their place.  And this is some of what they sang:

O white, white Sun, what things of wonder
  Hast thou beheld from thy wall of the sky!
All the Roofs of the Rich and the grief thereunder,
  As the fear of the Earl-folk flitteth by!

Thou hast seen the Flame steal forth from the Forest
  To slay the slumber of the lands,
As the Dusky Lord whom thou abhorrest
  Clomb up to thy Burg unbuilt with hands.

Thou lookest down from thy door the golden,
  Nor batest thy wide-shining mirth,
As the ramparts fall, and the roof-trees olden
  Lie smouldering low on the burning earth.

When flitteth the half-dark night of summer
  From the face of the murder great and grim,
'Tis thou thyself and no new-comer
  Shines golden-bright on the deed undim.

Art thou our friend, O Day-dawn's Lover?
  Full oft thine hand hath sent aslant
Bright beams athwart the Wood-bear's cover,
  Where the feeble folk and the nameless haunt.

Thou hast seen us quail, thou hast seen us cower,
  Thou hast seen us crouch in the Green Abode,
While for us wert thou slaying slow hour by hour,
  And smoothing down the war-rough road.

285

Yea, the rocks of the Waste were thy Dawns upheaving,
  To let the days of the years go through ;
And thy Noons the tangled brake were cleaving
  The slow-foot seasons' deed to do.

Then gaze adown on this gift of our giving,
  For the WOLF comes wending frith and ford,
And the Folk fares forth from the dead to the living,
  For the love of the Lief by the light of the Sword.

Then ceased the song, and the whole band of the Woodlanders came pouring tumultuously into the space allotted them, like the waters pouring over a river-dam, their white swords waving aloft in the morning sunlight ; and wild and strange cries rose up from amidst them, with sobbing and weeping of joy. But soon their troubled front sank back into ordered ranks, their bright blades stood upright in their hands before them, and folk looked on their company, and deemed it the very Terror of battle and Render of the ranks of war. Right well were they armed ; for though many of their weapons were ancient and somewhat worn, yet were they the work of good smiths of old days ; and moreover, if any of them lacked good war-gear of his own, that had the Alderman and his sons made good to them.

But before the hedge of steel stood the two tall men who held in their hands the war-tokens of the Battle-shaft and the War-spear, and betwixt them stood one who was indeed the tallest man of the whole assembly, who held the great staff of the hidden banner. And now he reached up his hand, and plucked at the yarn that bound it, which of set purpose was but feeble, and tore it off, and then shook the staff aloft with both hands, and shouted, and lo ! the Banner of the Wolf with the Sun-burst behind him, glittering-bright, new-woven by the women of the kindred, ran out in the fresh wind, and flapped and rippled before His warriors there assembled.

Then from all over the Mote-stead arose an exceeding great shout, and all men waved aloft their weapons ; but the men of Shadowy Vale who were standing amidst the men of the Face knew not how to demean themselves, and some of them ran forth into the Field and leapt for joy, tossing their swords into the air, and catching them by the hilts as they fell : and amidst it all the Woodlanders now stood silent, unmoving, as men abiding the word of onset.

As for that brother and sister : the Sun-beam flushed red all over her face, and pressed her hands to her bosom, and then the passion of tears over-mastered her, and her breast heaved, and the tears gushed out of her eyes, and her body was shaken with weeping. But Folk-might sat still, looking straight before him, his eyes glittering, his teeth set, his right hand clutching hard at the hilts of his sword, which lay naked across his knees. And the Bride, who stood clad in her begemmed and glittering war-array in the forefront of the Men of the Steer, nigh unto the seats of the chieftains, beheld Folk-might, and her face flushed and brightened, and still she looked upon him. The Alderman's face was as of one pleased and proud ; yet was its joy shadowed as it were by a cloud of compassion. Face-of-god sat like the very image of the War-god, and stirred not, nor looked toward the Sun-beam ; for still the thought of the after-grief of battle, and the death of friends and folk that loved him, lay heavy on his heart, for all that it beat wildly at the shouting of the men.

CHAPTER XXXVIII. OF THE GREAT FOLK-MOTE : ATONEMENTS GIVEN, AND MEN MADE SACKLESS.

AMIDST the clamour uprose the Alderman; for it was clear to all men that the Folk-mote should be holden at once, and the matters of the War, and the Fellowship, and the choosing of the War-leader, speedily dealt with. So the Alderman fell

to hallowing in the Folk-mote : he went up to the Altar of the
Gods, and took the Gold-ring off it, and did it on his arm ; then he
drew his sword and waved it toward the four airts, and spake; and
the noise and shouting fell, and there was silence but for him :

'Herewith I hallow in this Folk-mote of the Men of the Dale
and the Sheepcotes and the Woodland, in the name of the Warrior and the Earth-god and the Fathers of the kindreds.  Now
let not the peace of the Mote be broken.  Let not man rise against
man, or bear blade or hand, or stick or stone against any.  If any
man break the Peace of the Holy Mote, let him be a man accursed,
a wild-beast in the Holy Places ; an outcast from home and hearth,
from bed and board, from mead and acre ;  not to be holpen with
bread, nor flesh, nor wine ;  nor flax, nor wool, nor any cloth ;  nor
with sword, nor shield, nor axe, nor plough-share ;  nor with horse,
nor ox, nor ass;  with no saddle-beast nor draught-beast ;  nor with
wain, nor boat, nor way-leading;  nor with fire nor water;  nor with
any world's wealth.  Thus let him who hath cast out man be cast
out by man.  Now is hallowed-in the Folk-mote of the Men of
the Dale and the Sheepcotes and the Woodlands.'

Therewith he waved his sword again toward the four airts,
and went and sat down in his place.  But presently he arose
again, and said :

'Now if man hath aught to say against man, and claimeth
boot of any, or would lay guilt on any man's head, let him come
forth and declare it ;  and the judges shall be named, and the case
shall be tried this afternoon or to-morrow.  Yet first I shall tell
you that I, the Alderman of the Dalesmen, doomed one Iron-face
of the House of the Face to pay a double fine, for that he drew
a sword at the Gate-thing of Burgstead with the intent to break
the peace thereof.  Thou, Green-sleeve, bring forth the peace-
breaker's fine, that Iron-face may lay the same on the Altar.'

Then came forth a man from the men of the Face bearing a
bag, and he brought it to Iron-face, who went up to the Altar and
poured forth weighed gold from the bag thereon, and said :

288

'Warden of the Dale, come thou and weigh it!' Penny-thumb cometh forth.
'Nay,' quoth the Warden, 'it needeth not, no man here doubteth thee, Alderman Iron-face.'

A murmur of yeasay went up, and none had a word to say against the Alderman, but they praised him rather : also men were eager to hear of the war, and the fellowship, and to be done with these petty matters. Then the Alderman rose again and said :

'Hath any man a grief against any other of the Kindreds of the Dale, or the Sheepcotes, or the Woodlands?'

None answered or stirred; so after he had waited a while, he said :

'Is there any who hath any guilt to lay against a Stranger, an Outlander, being such a man as he deems we can come at?'

Thereat was a stir amongst the Men of the Fleece of the Shepherds, and their ranks opened, and there came forth an ill-favoured lean old man, long-nebbed, blear-eyed, and bent, girt with a rusty old sword, but not otherwise armed. And all men knew Penny-thumb, who had been ransacked last autumn. As he came forth, it seemed as if his neighbours had been trying to hold him back ; but a stout, broad-shouldered man, black-haired and red-bearded, made way for the old man, and led him out of the throng, and stood by him ; and this man was well armed at all points, and looked a doughty carle. He stood side by side with Penny-thumb, right in front of the men of his house, and looked about him at first somewhat uneasily, as though he were ashamed of his fellow ; but though many smiled, none laughed aloud ; and they forbore, partly because they knew the man to be a good man, partly because of the solemn tide of the Folk-mote, and partly in sooth because they wished all this to be over, and were as men who had no time for empty mirth.

Then said the Alderman: 'What wouldest thou, Penny-thumb, and thou, Bristler, son of Brightling?'

Then Penny-thumb began to speak in a high squeaky voice :

P P

'Alderman, and Lord of the Folk!'—But therewithal Bristler pulled him back, and said:

'I am the man who hath taken this quarrel upon me, and have sworn upon the Holy Boar to carry this feud through; and we deem, Alderman, that if they who slew Rusty and ransacked Penny-thumb be not known now, yet they soon may be.'

As he spake, came forth those three men of the Shepherds and the two Dalesmen who had sworn with him on the Holy Boar. Then up stood Folk-might, and came forth into the field, and said:

'Bristler, son of Brightling, and ye other good men and true, it is but sooth that the ransackers and the slayer may soon be known; and here I declare them unto you: I it was and none other who slew Rusty; and I was the leader of those who ransacked Penny-thumb, and cowed Harts-bane of Greentofts. As for the slaying of Rusty, I slew him because he chased me, and would not forbear, so that I must either slay or be slain, as hath befallen me erewhile, and will befall again, methinks. As for the ransacking of Penny-thumb, I needed the goods that I took, and he needed them not, since he neither used them, nor gave them away, and, they being gone, he hath lived no worser than aforetime. Now I say, that if ye will take the outlawry off me, which, as I hear, ye laid upon me, not knowing me, then will I handsel self-doom to thee, Bristler, if thou wilt bear thy grief to purse, and I will pay thee what thou wilt out of hand; or if perchance thou wilt call me to Holm, thither will I go, if thou and I come unslain out of this war. As to the ransacking and cowing of Harts-bane, I say that I am sackless therein, because the man is but a ruffler and a man of violence, and hath cowed many men of the Dale; and if he gainsay me, then do I call him to the Holm after this war is over; either him or any man who will take his place before my sword.'

Then he held his peace, and man spake to man, and a murmur arose, as they said for the more part that it was a fair and manly offer. But Bristler called his fellows and Penny-thumb to him,

and they spake together; and sometimes Penny-thumb's shrill
squeak was heard above the deep-voiced talk of the others; for
he was a man that harboured malice. But at last Bristler spake
out and said:

'Tall man, we know that thou art a chieftain and of good will
to the men of the Dale and their friends, and that want drave
thee to the ransacking, and need to the manslaying, and neither
the living nor the dead to whom thou art guilty are to be called
good men; therefore will I bring the matter to purse, if thou wilt
handsel me self-doom.'

'Yea, even so let it be,' quoth Folk-might; and stepped forward and took Bristler by the hand, and handselled him self-doom.
Then said Bristler:

'Though Rusty was no good man, and though he followed
thee to slay thee, yet was he in his right therein, since he was
following up his goodman's gear; therefore shalt thou pay a full
blood-wite for him, that is to say, the worth of three hundreds in
weed-stuff in whatso goods thou wilt. As for the ransacking of
Penny-thumb, he shall deem himself well paid if thou give him four
hundreds in weed-stuff for that which thou didst borrow of him.'

Then Penny-thumb set up his squeak again, but no man hearkened to him, and each man said to his neighbour that it was
well doomed of Bristler, and neither too much nor too little.
But Folk-might bade Wood-wont to bring thither to him that
which he had borne to the Mote; and he brought forth a big sack,
and Folk-might emptied it on the earth, and lo! the silver rings of
the slain felons, and they lay in a heap on the green field, and they
were the best of silver. Then the Elder of the Dale-wardens
weighed out from the heap the blood-wite for Rusty, according
to the due measure of the hundred in weed-stuff, and delivered it
unto Bristler. And Folk-might said:

'Draw nigh now, Penny-thumb, and take what thou wilt of
this gear, which I need not, and grudge not at me henceforward.'

But Penny-thumb was afraid, and abode where he was; and

Bristler laughed, and said : 'Take it, goodman, take it ; spare
not other men's goods as thou dost thine own.'

And Folk-might stood by, smiling faintly : so Penny-thumb
plucked up a heart, and drew nigh trembling, and took what he
durst from that heap; and all that stood by said that he had gotten
a full double of what had been awarded to him.   But as for him,
he went his ways straight from the Mote-stead, and made no stay
till he had gotten him home, and laid the silver up in a strong
coffer ; and thereafter he bewailed him sorely that 'he had not
taken the double of that which he took, since none would have
said him nay.

When he was gone, the Alderman arose and said :

' Now, since the fines have been paid duly and freely, according
to the dooming of Bristler, take we off the outlawry from Folk-
might and his fellows, and account them to be sackless before us.'

Then he called for other cases ; but no man had aught more to
bring forward against any man, either of the kindreds or the
Strangers.


CHAPTER XXXIX.   OF THE GREAT FOLK-MOTE : MEN
TAKE REDE OF THE WAR-FARING, THE FELLOWSHIP,
AND   THE   WAR-LEADER.   FOLK-MIGHT   TELLETH
WHENCE HIS PEOPLE CAME.   THE FOLK-MOTE SUN-
DERED.

NOW a great silence fell upon the throng, and they stood
as men abiding some new matter.   Unto them arose the
Alderman, and said :

' Men of the Dale, and ye Shepherds and Woodlanders ; it is
well known to you that we have foemen in the wood and beyond
it ; and now have we gotten sure tidings, that they will not abide
at home or in the wood, but are minded to fall upon us at home.
Now therefore I will not ask you whether ye will have peace

or war; for with these foemen ye may have peace no otherwise save by war. But if ye think with me, three things have ye to determine: first, whether ye will abide your foes in your own houses, or will go meet them at theirs; next, whether ye will take to you as fellows in arms a valiant folk of the children of the Gods, who are foemen to our foemen; and lastly, what man ye will have to be your War-leader. Now, I bid all those here assembled, to speak hereof, any man of them that will, either what they may have conceived in their own minds, or what their kindred may have put into their mouths to speak.'

Therewith he sat down, and in a little while came forth old Hall-ward of the House of the Steer, and stood before the Alderman, and said: 'O Alderman, all we say: Since war is awake we will not tarry, but will go meet our foes while it is yet time. The valiant men of whom thou tellest shall be our fellows, were there but three of them. We know no better War-leader than Face-of-god of the House of the Face. Let him lead us.'

Therewith he went his ways; and next came forth War-well, and said: 'The House of the Bridge would have Face-of-god for War-leader, these tall men for fellows, and the shortest way to meet the foe.' And he went back to his place.

Next came Fox of Upton, and said: 'Time presses, or much might be spoken. Thus saith the House of the Bull: Let us go meet the foe, and take these valiant strangers for way-leaders, and Face-of-god for War-leader.' And he also went back again.

Then came forth two men together, an old man and a young, and the old man spake as soon as he stood still: 'The Men of the Vine bid me say their will: They will not stay at home to have their houses burned over their heads, themselves slain on their own hearths, and their wives haled off to thralldom. They will take any man for their fellow in arms who will smite stark strokes on their side. They know Face-of-god, and were liefer of him for War-leader than any other, and they will follow him whereso-ever he leadeth. Thus my kindred biddeth me say, and I hight

293

Fork-beard of Lea. If I live through this war, I shall have lived through five.'

Therewith he went back to his place ; but the young man lifted up his voice and said : ' To all this I say yea, and so am I bidden by the kindred of the Sickle. I am Red-beard of the Knolls, the son of my father.' And he went to his place again.

Then came forth Stone-face, and said : ' The House of the Face saith : Lead us through the wood, O Face-of-god, thou War-leader, and ye warriors of the Wolf. I am Stone-face, as men know, and this word hath been given to me by the kindred.' And he took his place again.

Then came forth together the three chiefs of the Shepherds, to wit Hound-under-Greenbury, Strongitharm, and the Hyllier ; and Strongitharm spake for all three, and said :

' The Men of Greenbury, and they of the Fleece and the Thorn, are of one accord, and bid us say that they are well pleased to have Face-of-god for War-leader ; and that they will follow him and the warriors of the Wolf to live or die with them ; and that they are ready to go meet the foe at once, and will not skulk behind the walls of Greenbury.'

Therewith the three went back again to their places.

Then came forth that tall man that bare the Banner of the Wolf, when he had given the staff into the hands of him who stood next. He came and stood over against the seat of the chieftains ; and for a while he could say no word, but stood struggling with the strong passion of his joy ; but at last he lifted his hands aloft, and cried out in a loud voice :

' O war, war ! O death ! O wounding and grief ! O loss of friends and kindred ! let all this be rather than the drawing back of meeting hands and the sundering of yearning hearts ! ' and he went back hastily to his place. But from the ranks of the Woodlanders ran forth a young man, and cried out :

' As is the word of Red-wolf, so is my word, Bears-bane of Carlstead ; and this is the word which our little Folk hath put

294

into our mouths; and O! that our hands may show the mean-ing of our mouths; for nought else can.'

Then indeed went up a great shout, though many forebore to cry out; for now were they too much moved for words or sounds. And in special was Face-of-god moved; and he scarce knew which way to look, lest he should break out into sobs and weep-ing; for of late he had been much among the Woodlanders, and loved them much.

Then all the noise and clamour fell, and it was to men as if they who had come thither a folk, had now become an host of war.

But once again the Alderman rose up and spake:

'Now have ye yeasaid three things: That we take Face-of-god of the House of the Face for our War-leader; that we fare under weapons at once against them who would murder us; and that we take the valiant Folk of the Wolf for our fellows in arms.'

Therewith he stayed his speech, and this time the shout arose clear and most mighty, with the tossing up of swords and the clashing of weapons on shields.

Then he said: 'Now, if any man will speak, here is the War-leader, and here is the chief of our new friends, to answer to whatso any of the kindred would have answered.'

Thereon came forth the Fiddle from amongst the Men of the Sickle, and drew somewhat nigh to the Alderman, and said: 'Alderman, we would ask of the War-leader if he hath devised the manner of our assembling, and the way of our war-faring, and the day of our hosting. More than this I will not ask of him, because we wot that in so great an assembly it may be that the foe may have some spy of whom we wot not; and though this be not likely, yet some folk may babble; therefore it is best for the wise to be wise everywhere and always. Therefore my rede it is, that no man ask any more concerning this, but let it lie with the War-leader to bring us face to face with the foe as speedily as he may.'

All men said that this was well counselled. But Face-of-god

Folk-might is asked concerning whence and what he is. arose and said : ' Ye Men of the Dale, ye Shepherds and Wood-landers, meseemeth the Fiddle hath spoken wisely. Now therefore I answer him and say, that I have so ordered everything since the Gate-thing was holden at Burgstead, that we may come face to face with the foemen by the shortest of roads. Every man shall be duly summoned to the Hosting, and if any man fail, let it be accounted a shame to him for ever.'

A great shout followed on his words, and he sat down again. But Fox of Upton came forth and said :

'O Alderman, we have yeasaid the fellowship of the valiant men who have come to us from out of the waste ; but this we have done, not because we have known them, otherwise than by what our kinsman Face-of-god hath told us concerning them, but because we have seen clearly that they will be of much avail to us in our warfare. Now, therefore, if the tall chieftain who sitteth beside thee were to do us to wit what he is, and whence he and his are come, it were well, and fain were we thereof ; but if he listeth not to tell us, that also shall be well.'

Then arose Folk-might in his place ; but or ever he could open his mouth to speak, the tall Red-wolf strode forward bearing with him the Banner of the Wolf and the Sun-burst, and came and stood beside him ; and the wind ran through the folds of the banner, and rippled it out above the heads of those twain. Then Folk-might spake and said :

' O Men of the Dale and the Sheepcotes, I will do as ye bid me do ;
And fain were ye of the story if every deal ye knew.
But long, long were its telling, were I to tell it all :
Let it bide till the Cup of Deliverance ye drink from hall to hall.

' Like you we be of the kindreds, of the Sons of the Gods we come,
Midst the Mid-earth's mighty Woodland of old we had our home ;
But of older time we abided 'neath the mountains of the Earth,
O'er which the Sun ariseth to waken woe and mirth.

296

Great were we then and many; but the long days wore us thin, Folk-might
And war, wherein the winner hath weary work to win. telleth how
And the woodland wall behind us e'en like ourselves was worn, his kindred
And the tramp of the hosts of the foemen adown its glades was borne came to those
On the wind that bent our wheat-fields. So in the morn we rose, mountains.
And left behind the stubble and the autumn-fruited close,
And went our ways to the westward, nor turned aback to see
The glare of our burning houses rise over brake and tree.
But the foe was fierce and speedy, nor long they tarried there,
And through the woods of battle our laden wains must fare;
And the Sons of the Wolf were minished, and the maids of the
      Wolf waxed few,
As amidst the victory-singing we fared the wild-wood through.

' So saith the ancient story, that west and west we went,
And many a day of battle we had in brake, on bent;
Whilst here a while we tarried, and there we hastened on,
And still the battle-harvest from many a folk we won.

' Of the tale of the days who wotteth? Of the years what man
      can tell,
While the Sons of the Wolf were wandering, and knew not where
      to dwell?
But at last we clomb the mountains, and mickle was our toil,
As high the spear-wood clambered of the drivers of the spoil;
And tangled were the passes and the beacons flared behind,
And the horns of gathering onset came up upon the wind.
So saith the ancient story, that we stood in a mountain-cleft,
Where the ways and the valleys sundered to the right hand and
      the left.
There in the place of sundering all woeful was the rede;
We knew no land before us, and behind was heavy need.
As the sword cleaves through the byrny, so there the mountain flank
Cleft through the God-kin's people; and ne'er again we drank

The wine of war together, or feasted side by side
In the Feast-hall of the Warrior on the fruit of the battle-tide.
For there we turned and sundered; unto the North we went
And up along the waters, and the clattering stony bent;
And unto the South and the Sheepcotes down went our sister's sons;
And O for the years passed over since we saw those valiant ones!'

He ceased, and laid his right hand on the banner-staff a little
below the left hand of Red-wolf; and men were so keen to hear
each word that he spake, that there was no cry nor sound of
voices when he had done, only the sound of the rippling banner
of the Wolf over the heads of those twain. The Sun-beam
bowed her head now, and wept silently. But the Bride, she had
drawn her sword, and held it upright in her hand before her, and
the sun smote fire from out of it.

Then it was but a little while before Red-wolf lifted up his
voice, and sang:

'Hearken a wonder, O Folk of the Field,
How they that did sunder stand shield beside shield!

Lo! the old wont and manner by fearless folk made,
On the Bole of the Banner the brothers' hands laid.

Lo! here the token of what hath betid!
Grown whole is the broken, found that which was hid.

Now one way we follow whate'er shall befall;
As seeketh the swallow his yesteryear's hall.

Seldom folk fewer to fight-stead hath fared;
Ne'er have men truer the battle-reed bared.

Grey locks now I carry, and old am I grown,
Nor looked I to tarry to meet with mine own.

For we who remember the deeds of old days
Were nought but the ember of battle ablaze.

For what man might aid us? what deed and what day
Should come where Weird laid us aloof from the way?

What man save that other of Twain rent apart,
Our war-friend, our Brother, the piece of our heart.

Then hearken the wonder how shield beside shield
The twain that did sunder wend down to the Field!'

How the Sons
of the Wolf
came to Silver-
dale.

Now when he had made an end, men could no longer fore-
bear the shout; and it went up into the heavens, and was borne
by the west-wind down the Dale to the ears of the stay-at-home
women and men unmeet to go abroad, and it quickened their
blood and the spirits within them as they heard it, and they
smiled and were fain; for they knew that their kinsfolk were glad.
But when there was quiet on the Mote-field again, Folk-might
spake again and said;

'It is sooth that my Brother sayeth, and that now again we wend,
All the Sons of the Wolf together, till the trouble hath an end.
But as for that tale of the Ancients, it saith that we who went
To the northward, climbed and stumbled o'er many a stony bent,
Till we happed on that isle of the waste-land, and the grass of
    Shadowy Vale,
Where we dwelt till we throve a little, and felt our might avail.
Then we fared abroad from the shadow and the little-lighted hold,
And the increase fell to the valiant, and the spoil to the battle-bold,
And never a man gainsaid us with the weapons in our hands;
And in Silver-dale the happy we gat us life and lands.

'So wore the years o'er-wealthy; and meseemeth that ye know
How we sowed and reaped destruction, and the Day of the overthrow:

How we leaned on the staff we had broken, and put our lives in
        the hand
Of those whom we had vanquished and the feeble of the land ;
And these were the stone of stumbling, and the burden not to be borne,
When the battle-blast fell on us and our day was over-worn.
Thus then did our wealth bewray us, and left us wise and sad ;
And to you, bold men, it falleth once more to make us glad,
If so your hearts are bidding, and ye deem the deed of worth.
Such were we ; what we shall be, 'tis yours to say henceforth.'

He said furthermore : ' How great we have been I have told
you already ; and ye shall see for yourselves how little we be now.
Is it enough, and will ye have us for friends and brothers ? How
say ye ? '

They answered with shout upon shout, so that all the place
and the wild-wood round about was full of the voice of their crying; but when the clamour fell, then spake the Alderman and said :

' Friend, and chieftain of the Wolf, thou mayst hear by this
shouting of the people that we have no mind to naysay our yeasay. And know that it is not our use and manner to seek the
strong for friends, and to thrust aside the weak ; but rather to
choose for our friends them who are of like mind to us, men in
whom we put our trust. From henceforth then there is brotherhood between us ; we are yours, and ye are ours; and let this
endure for ever ! '

Then were all men full of joy; and now at last the battle
seemed at hand, and the peace beyond the battle.

Then men brought the hallowed beasts all garlanded with
flowers into the Doom-ring, and there were they slain and offered
up unto the Gods, to wit the Warrior, the Earth-god, and the
Fathers; and thereafter was solemn feast holden on the Field of the
Folk-mote, and all men were fain and merry. Nevertheless, not
all men abode there the feast through ; for or ever the afternoon
was well worn, were many men wending along the Portway

eastward toward the Upper Dale, each man in his war-gear and with a scrip hung about him; and these were they who were bound for the trysting-place and the journey over the waste.

So the Folk-mote was sundered; and men went to their houses, and there abode in peace the time of their summoning; since they wotted well that the Hosting was afoot.

But as for the Woodlanders, who were at the Mote-stead with all their folk, women, children, and old men, they went not back again to Carlstead; but prayed the neighbours of the Middle Dale to suffer them to abide there awhile, which they yeasaid with a good will. So the Woodlanders tilted themselves in, the more part of them, down in the meadows below the Mote-stead, along either side of Wildlake's Way; but their ancient folk, and some of the women and children, the neighbours would have into their houses, and the rest they furnished with victual and all that they needed without price, looking upon them as their very guests. For indeed they deemed that they could see that these men would never return to Carlstead, but would abide with the Men of the Wolf in Silver-dale, once it were won. And this they deemed but meet and right, yet were they sorry thereof; for the Woodlanders were well beloved of all the Dalesmen; and now that they had gotten to know that they were come of so noble a kindred, they were better beloved yet, and more looked upon.

## CHAPTER XL. OF THE HOSTING IN SHADOWY VALE.

IT was on the evening of the fourth day after the Folk-mote that there came through the Waste to the rocky edge of Shadowy Vale a band of some fifteen score of men-at-arms, and with them a multitude of women and children and old men, some afoot, some riding on asses and bullocks; and with them were sumpter asses and neat laden with household goods, and a few goats and kine. And this was the whole folk of the Woodlanders come

to the Hosting in Shadowy Vale and the Home of the Children
of the Wolf. Their leaders of the way were Wood-father and
Wood-wont and two other carles of Shadowy Vale ; and Red-
wolf the tall, and Bears-bane and War-grove were the captains
and chieftains of their company.

Thus then they entered into the narrow pass aforesaid, which
was the ingate to the Vale from the Waste, and little by little
its dimness swallowed up their long line. As they went by the
place where the lowering of the rock-wall gave a glimpse of the
valley, they looked down into it as Face-of-god had done, but
much change was there in little time. There was the black wall
of crags on the other side stretching down to the ghyll of the
great Force ; there ran the deep green waters of the Shivering
Flood ; but the grass which Face-of-god had seen naked of everything but a few kine, thereon now the tents of men stood thick.
Their hearts swelled within them as they beheld it, but they forebore the shout and the cry till they should be well within the Vale,
and so went down silently into the darkness. But as their eyes
caught that dim image of the Wolf on the wall of the pass, man
pointed it out to man, and not a few turned and kissed it hurriedly ;
and to them it seemed that many a kiss had been laid on that
dear token since the days of old, and that the hard stone had been
worn away by the fervent lips of men, and that the air of the
mirk place yet quivered with the vows sworn over the sword-blade.

But down through the dark they went, and so came on to the
stony scree at the end of the pass and into the Vale ; and the whole
Folk save the three chieftains flowed over it and stood about it
down on the level grass of the Vale. But those three stood yet
on the top of the scree, bearing the war-signs of the Shaft and
the Spear, and betwixt them the banner of the Wolf and the Sun-
burst newly displayed to the winds of Shadowy Vale.

Up and down the Vale they looked, and saw before the tents
of men the old familiar banners of Burgdale rising and falling in
the evening wind. But amidst of the Doom-ring was pitched a

great banner, whereon was done the image of the Wolf with red gaping jaws on a field of green; and about him stood other banners, to wit, The Silver Arm on a red field, the Red Hand on a white field, and on green fields both, the Golden Bushel and the Ragged Sword.

All about the plain shone glittering war-gear of men as they moved hither and thither, and a stream of folk began at once to draw toward the scree to look on those new-comers; and amidst the helmed Burgdalers and the white-coated Shepherds went the tall men of the Wolf, bare-headed and unarmed save for their swords, mingled with the fair strong women of the kindred, treading barefoot the soft grass of their own Vale.

Presently there was a great throng gathered round about the Woodlanders, and each man as he joined it waved hand or weapon toward them, and the joy of their welcome sent a confused clamour through the air. Then forth from the throng stepped Folk-might, unarmed save his sword, and behind him was Face-of-god, in his war-gear save his helm, hand in hand with the Sunbeam, who was clad in her goodly flowered green kirtle, her feet naked like her sisters of the kindred.

Then Folk-might cried aloud: 'A full and free greeting to our brothers! Well be ye, O Sons of our Ancient Fathers! And today are ye the dearer to us because we see that ye have brought us a gift, to wit, your wives and children, and your grandsires unmeet for war. By this token we see how great is your trust in us, and that it is your meaning never to sunder from us again. O well be ye; well be ye!'

Then spake Red-wolf, and said: 'Ye Sons of the Wolf, who parted from us of old time in that cleft of the mountains, it is our very selves that we give unto you; and these are a part of ourselves; how then should we leave them behind us? Bear witness, O men of Burgdale and the Sheepcotes, that we have become one Folk with the men of Shadowy Vale, never to be sundered again!'

303

Then all that multitude shouted with a loud voice; and when
the shout had died away, Folk-might spake again :

' O Warriors of the Sundering, here shall your wives and children abide, while we go a little journey to rejoice our hearts with
the hard handplay, and take to us that which we have missed :
and to-morrow morn is appointed for this same journey, unless ye
be over foot-weary with the ways of the Waste.'

Red-wolf smiled as he answered : 'This ye say in jest, brother ;
for ye may see that our day's journey hath not been over-much for
our old men ; how then should it weary those who may yet bear
sword ?  We are ready for the road and eager for the handplay.'

' This is well,' said Folk-might, ' and what was to be looked
for.  Therefore, brother, do ye and your counsel-mates come
straightway to the Hall of the Wolf ; wherein, after ye have
eaten and drunken, shall we take counsel with our brethren
of Burgdale and the Sheepcotes, so that all may be ordered
for battle !'

Said Red-wolf : ' Good is that, if we must needs abide till to-
morrow ; for verily we came not hither to eat and drink and rest
our bodies ; but it must be as ye will have it.'

Then the Sun-beam left the hand of Face-of-god and came forward, and held out both her palms to the Woodland-folk, and spake
in a voice that was heard afar, though it were a woman's, so clear
and sweet it was ; and she said :

' O Warriors of the Sundering, ye who be not needed in the
Hall, and ye our sisters with your little ones and your fathers,
come now to us and down to the tents which we have arrayed for
you, and there think for a little that we are all at our very home
that we long for and have yet to win, and be ye merry with us
and make us merry.'

Therewith she stepped forward daintily and entered into their
throng, and took an old man of the Woodlanders by the hand, and
kissed his cheek and led him away, and the coming rest seemed
sweet to him.  And then came other women of the Vale, kind and

304

fair and smiling, and led away, some an old mother of the Woodlanders, some a young wife, some a pair of lads; and not a few
forsooth kissed and embraced the stark warriors, and went away
with them toward the tents, which stood along the side of the
Shivering Flood where it was at its quietest; for there was the
grass the softest and most abundant. There on the green grass
were tables arrayed, and lamps were hung above them on spears,
to be litten when the daylight should fail. And the best of the
victual which the Vale could give was spread on the boards, along
with wine and dainties, bought in Silver-dale, or on the edges of
the Westland with sword-strokes and arrow-flight.

There then they feasted and were merry; and the Sun-beam
and Bow-may and the other women of the Vale served them at
table, and were very blithe with them, caressing them with soft
words, and with clipping and kissing, as folk who were grown exceeding dear to them; so that that eve of battle was softer and
sweeter to them than any hour of their life. With these feasters
were God-swain and Spear-fist of the delivered thralls of Silver-
dale as glad as glad might be; but Wolf-stone their eldest was
gone with Dallach to the Council in the Hall.

The men of Burgdale and the Shepherds feasted otherwhere
in all content, nor lacked folk of the Vale to serve them. Amongst
the men of the Face were the ten delivered thralls who had heart
to meet their masters in arms: seven of them were of Rose-dale
and three of Silver-dale.

The Bride was with her kindred of the Steer, with whom were
many men of Shadowy Vale, and she served her friends and fellows
clad in her war-gear, save helm and hauberk, bearing herself as
one who is serving dear guests. And men equalled her for her
beauty to the Gods of the High Place and the Choosers of the
Slain; and they who had not beheld her before marvelled at her,
and her loveliness held all men's hearts in a net of desire, so that
they forebore their meat to gaze upon her; and if perchance her
hand touched some young man, or her cheek or sweet-breathed

mouth came nigh to his face, he became bewildered and wist not
where he was, nor what to do. Yet was she as lowly and simple
of speech and demeanour as if she were a gooseherd of fourteen winters.

In the Hall was a goodly company, and all the leaders of the
Folk were therein, and Folk-might and the War-leader sitting
in the midst of those stone seats on the daïs. There then they
agreed on the whole ordering of the battle and the wending of the
host, as shall be told later on ; and this matter was long a-doing,
and when it was done, men went to their places to sleep, for the
night was well worn.

But when men had departed and all was still, Folk-might,
light-clad and without a weapon, left the Hall and walked briskly
toward the nether end of the Vale. He passed by all the tents,
the last whereof were of the House of the Steer, and came to a
place where was a great rock rising straight up from the plain
like sheaves of black staves standing close together ; and it was
called Staff-stone, and tales of the elves had been told concerning
it, so that Stone-face had beheld it gladly the day before.

The moon was just shining into Shadowy Vale, and the grass
was bright wheresoever the shadows of the high cliffs were not,
and the face of Staff-stone shone bright grey as Folk-might came
within sight of it, and he beheld someone sitting at the base of
the rock, and as he drew nigher he saw that it was a woman,
and knew her for the Bride ; for he had prayed her to abide
him there that night, because it was nigh to the tents of the
House of the Steer; and his heart was glad as he drew nigh to her.

She sat quietly on a fragment of the black rock, clad as she
had been all day, in her glittering kirtle, but without hauberk
or helm, a wreath of wind-flowers about her head, her feet crossed
over each other, her hands laid palm uppermost in her lap. She
moved not as he drew nigh, but said in a gentle voice when he
was close to her :

' Chief of the Wolf, great warrior, thou wouldest speak with me ; and good it is that friends should talk together on the eve of battle, when they may never meet alive again.'

He said : ' My talk shall not be long ; for thou and I both must sleep to-night, since there is work to hand to-morrow. Now since, as thou sayest, O fairest of women, we may never meet again alive, I ask thee now at this hour, when we both live and are near to one another, to suffer me to speak to thee of my love of thee and desire for thee. Surely thou, who art the sweetest of all things the Gods and the kindreds have made, wilt not gainsay me this?'

She said very sweetly, yet smiling : ' Brother of my father's sons, how can I gainsay thee thy speech? Nay, hast thou not said it? What more canst thou add to it that will have fresh meaning to mine ears?'

He said : ' Thou sayest sooth : might I then but kiss thine hand?'

She said, no longer smiling : ' Yea surely, even so may all men do who can be called my friends—and thou art much my friend.'

He took her hand and kissed it, and held it thereafter ; nor did she draw it away. The moon shone brightly on them ; but by its light he could not see if she reddened, but he deemed that her face was troubled. Then he said : ' It were better for me if I might kiss thy face, and take thee in mine arms.'

Then said she : ' This only shall a man do with me when I long to do the like with him. And since thou art so much my friend, I will tell thee that as for this longing, I have it not. Bethink thee what a little while it is since the lack of another man's love grieved me sorely.'

' The time is short,' said Folk-might, 'if we tell up the hours thereof ; but in that short space have a many things betid.'

She said : ' Dost thou know, canst thou guess, how sorely ashamed I went amongst my people? I durst look no man in the face for the aching of mine heart, which methought all might see through my face.'

'I knew it well,' he said; 'yet of me wert thou not ashamed
but a little while ago, when thou didst tell me of thy grief.'

She said: 'True it is; and thou wert kind to me. Thou didst
become a dear friend to me, methought.'

'And wilt thou hurt a dear friend?' said he.

'O no,' she said, 'if I might do otherwise. Yet how if I might
not choose? Shall there be no forgiveness for me then?'

He answered nothing; and still he held her hand that strove
not to be gone from his, and she cast down her eyes. Then he
spake in a while:

'My friend, I have been thinking of thee and of me; and now
hearken: if thou wilt declare that thou feelest no sweetness
embracing thine heart when I say that I desire thee sorely, as
now I say it; or when I kiss thine hand, as now I kiss it; or
when I pray thee to suffer me to cast mine arms about thee and
kiss thy face, as now I pray it: if thou wilt say this, then will
I take thee by the hand straightway, and lead thee to the tents
of the House of the Steer, and say farewell to thee till the battle
is over. Canst thou say this out of the truth of thine heart?'

She said: 'What then if I cannot say this word? What
then?'

But he answered nothing; and she sat still a little while, and
then arose and stood before him, looking him in the eyes, and said:

'I cannot say it.'

Then he caught her in his arms and strained her to him, and
then kissed her lips and her face again and again, and she strove
not with him. But at last she said:

'Yet after all this shalt thou lead me back to my folk straightway; and when the battle is done, if both we are living, then shall
we speak more thereof.'

So he took her hand and led her on toward the tents of the
Steer, and for a while he spake nought; for he doubted himself,
what he should say; but at last he spake:

'Now is this better for me than if it had not been, whether I

live or whether I die.  Yet thou hast not said that thou lovest
me and desirest me.'

'Wilt thou compel me?' she said.  'To-night I may not say
it.  Who shall say what words my lips shall fashion when we
stand together victorious in Silver-dale; then indeed may the time
seem long from now.'

He said: 'Yea, true is that; yet once again I say that so
measured long and long is the time since first I saw thee in Burgdale before thou knewest me.  Yet now I will not bicker with
thee, for be sure that I am glad at heart.  And lo you! our feet
have brought us to the tents of thy people.  All good go with thee!'

'And with thee, sweet friend,' she said.  Then she lingered a
little, turning her head toward the tents, and then turned her
face toward him and laid her hand on his neck, and drew his
head adown to her and kissed his cheek, and therewith swiftly
and lightly departed from him.

Now the night wore and the morning came; and Face-of-god
was abroad very early in the morning, as his custom was; and
he washed the night from off him in the Carles' Bath of the Shivering Flood, and then went round through the encampment of the
host, and saw none stirring save here and there the last watchmen
of the night.  He spake with one or two of these, and then went
up to the head of the Vale, where was the pass that led to Silver-
dale; and there he saw the watch, and spake with them, and
they told him that none had as yet come forth from the pass, and
he bade them to blow the horn of warning to rouse up the Host
as soon as the messengers came thence.  For forerunners had been
sent up the pass, and had been set to hold watch at divers places
therein to pass on the word from place to place.

Thence went Face-of-god back toward the Hall; but when
he was yet some way from it, he saw a slender glittering warrior
come forth from the door thereof, who stood for a moment looking
round about, and then came lightly and swiftly toward him;
and lo! it was the Sun-beam, with a long hauberk over her kirtle

309

falling below her knees, a helm on her head and plated shoes on
her feet. She came up to him, and laid her hand to his cheek
and the golden locks of his head (for he was bare-headed), and
said to him, smiling :

'Gold-mane! thou badest me bear arms, and Folk-might also
constrained me thereto. Lo thou!'

Said Face-of-god: 'Folk-might is wise then, even as I am;
and forsooth as thou art. For bethink thee if the bow drawn at
a venture should speed the eyeless shaft against thy breast, and
send me forth a wanderer from my Folk! For how could I bear
the sight of the fair Dale, and no hope to see thee again therein?'

She said : 'The heart is light within me to-day. Deemest
thou that this is strange? Or dost thou call to mind that which
thou spakest the other day, that it was of no avail to stand in
the Doom-ring of the Folk and bear witness against ourselves?
This will I not. This is no light-mindedness that thou beholdest
in me, but the valiancy that the Fathers have set in mine heart.
Deem not, O Gold-mane, fear not, that we shall die before they
dight the bride-bed for us.'

He would have kissed her mouth, but she put him away with
her hand, and doffed her helm and laid it on the grass, and said :

'This is not the last time that thou shalt kiss me, Gold-mane,
my dear ; and yet I long for it as if it were, so high as the
Fathers have raised me up this morn above fear and sadness.'

He said nought, but drew her to him, and wonder so moved
him, that he looked long and closely at her face before he kissed
her ; and forsooth he could find no blemish in it : it was as if it
were but new come from the smithy of the Gods, and exceeding
longing took hold of him. But even as their lips met, from the
head of the Vale came the voice of the great horn ; and it was
answered straightway by the watchers all down the tents ; and
presently arose the shouts of men and the clash of weapons as
folk armed themselves, and laughter therewith, for most men
were battle-merry, and the cries of women shrilly-clear as they

hastened about, busy over the morning meal before the departure of the Host. But Face-of-god said softly, still caressing the Sun-beam, and she him:

'Thus then we depart from this Valley of the Shadows, but as thou saidst when first we met therein, there shall be no sundering of thee and me, but thou shalt go down with me to the battle.'

And he led her by the hand into the Hall of the Wolf, and there they ate a morsel, and thereafter Face-of-god tarried not, but busied himself along with Folk-might and the other chieftains in arraying the Host for departure.

CHAPTER XLI. THE HOST DEPARTETH FROM SHADOWY VALE: THE FIRST DAY'S JOURNEY.

IT was about three hours before noon that the Host began to enter into the pass out of Shadowy Vale by the river-side; and the women and children, and men unfightworthy, stood on the higher ground at the foot of the cliffs to see the Host wend on the way. Of these a many were of the Woodlanders, who were now one folk with them of Shadowy Vale. And all these had chosen to abide tidings in the Vale, deeming that there was little danger therein, since that last slaughter which Folk-might had made of the Dusky Men; albeit Face-of-god had offered to send them all to Burgstead with two score and ten men-at-arms to guard them by the way and to eke out the warders of the Burg.

Now the fighting-men of Shadowy Vale were two long hun-dreds lacking five; of whom two score and ten were women, and three score and ten lads under twenty winters; but the women, though you might scarce see fairer of face and body, were doughty in arms, all good shooters in the bow; and the swains were eager and light-foot, cragsmen of the best, wont to scaling the cliffs of the Vale in search of the nests of gerfalcons

and such-like fowl, and swimming the strong streams of the
Shivering Flood; tough bodies and wiry, stronger than most
grown men, and as fearless as the best.

The order of the Departure of the Host was this:

The Woodlanders went first into the pass, and with them
were two score of the ripe Warriors of the Wolf. Then came
of the kindreds of Burgdale, the Men of the Steer, the Bridge,
and the Bull; then the Men of the Vine and the Sickle; then the
Shepherd-folk; and lastly, the Men of the Face led by Stone-
face and Hall-face. With these went another two score of the
dwellers in Shadowy Vale, and the rest were scattered up and
down the bands of the Host to guide them into the best paths
and to make the way easier to them. Face-of-god was sundered
from his kindred, and went along with Folk-might in the forefront of the Host, while his father the Alderman went as a
simple man-at-arms with his House in the rearward. The Sun-
beam followed her brother and Face-of-god amidst the Warriors
of the Wolf, and with her were Bow-may clad in the Alderman's gift, and Wood-father and his children. Bow-may had
caused her to doff her hauberk for that day, whereon they looked
to fall in with no foeman. As for the Bride, she went with her
kindred in all her war-gear; and the morning sun shone in the
gems of her apparel, and her jewelled feet fell like flowers upon
the deep grass of the upper Vale, and shone strange and bright
amongst the black stones of the pass. She bore a quiver at her
back and a shining yew bow in her hand, and went amongst the
bowmen, for she was a very deft archer.

So fared they into the pass, leaving peace behind them, with
all their banners displayed, and the banner of the Red-mouthed
Wolf went with the Wolf and the Sun-burst in the forefront
of their battle next after the two captains.

As for their road, the grassy space between the rock-wall and
the water was wide and smooth at first, and the cliffs rose up
like bundles of spear-shafts high and clear from the green grass

with no confused litter of fallen stones; so that the men strode on briskly, their hearts high-raised and full of hope. And as they went, the sweetness of song stirred in their souls, and at last Bow-may fell to singing in a loud clear voice, and her cousin Wood-wise answered her, and all the warriors of the Wolf who were in their band fell into the song at the ending, and the sound of their melody went down the water and reached the ears of those that were entering the pass, and of those who were abiding till the way should be clear of them: and this is some of what they sang:

*Bow-may singeth:*

Hear ye never a voice come crying
    Out from the waste where the winds fare wide?
'Sons of the Wolf, the days are dying,
    And where in the clefts of the rocks do ye hide?

'Into your hands hath the Sword been given,
    Hard are the palms with the kiss of the hilt;
Through the trackless waste hath the road been riven
    For the blade to seek to the heart of the guilt.

'And yet ye bide and yet ye tarry;
    Dear deem ye the sleep 'twixt hearth and board,
And sweet the maiden mouths ye marry,
    And bright the blade of the bloodless sword.'

*Wood-wise singeth:*

Yea, here we dwell in the arms of our Mother
    The Shadowy Queen, and the hope of the Waste;
Here first we came, when never another
    Adown the rocky stair made haste.

Far is the foe, and no sword beholdeth
    What deed we work and whither we wend;

Dear are the days, and the Year enfoldeth
  The love of our life from end to end.

Voice of our Fathers, why will ye move us,
  And call up the sun our swords to behold?
Why will ye cry on the foeman to prove us?
  Why will ye stir up the heart of the bold?

*Bow-may singeth :*
Purblind am I, the voice of the chiding ;
  Then tell me what is the thing ye bear ?
What is the gift that your hands are hiding,
  The gold-adorned, the dread and dear ?

*Wood-wise singeth :*
Dark in the sheath lies the Anvil's Brother,
  Hid is the hammered Death of Men.
Would ye look on the gift of the green-clad Mother ?
  How then shall ye ask for a gift again ?

*The Warriors sing :*
Show we the Sunlight the Gift of the Mother,
  As foot follows foot to the foeman's den !
Gleam Sun, breathe Wind, on the Anvil's Brother,
  For bare is the hammered Death of Men.

Therewith they shook their naked swords in the air, and fared
on eagerly, and as swiftly as the pass would have them fare. But
so it was, that when the rearward of the Host was entering the
first of the pass, and was going on the wide smooth sward, the
vanward was gotten to where there was but a narrow space clear
betwixt water and cliff; for otherwise was a litter of great
rocks and small, hard to be threaded even by those who knew the
passes well; so that men had to tread along the very verge of the
Shivering Flood, and wary must they be, for the water ran swift

314

and deep betwixt banks of sheer rock half a fathom below their very foot-soles, which had but bare space to go on the narrow way. So it held on for a while, and then got safer, and there was more space for going betwixt cliff and flood; albeit it was toil-some enough, since for some way yet there was a drift of stones to cumber their feet, some big and some little, and some very big. After a while the way grew better, though here and there, where the cliffs lowered, were wide screes of loose stones that they must needs climb up and down. Thereafter for a space was there an end of the stony cumber, but the way betwixt the river and the cliffs narrowed again, and the black crags grew higher, and at last so exceeding high, and the way so narrow, that the sky overhead was to them as though they were at the bottom of a well, and men deemed that thence they could see the stars at noontide. For some time withal had the way been mounting up and up, though the cliffs grew higher over it; till at last they were but going on a narrow shelf, the Shivering Flood swirling and rattling far below them betwixt sheer rock-walls grown ex-ceeding high; and above them the cliffs going up towards the heavens as black as a moonless starless night of winter. And as the flood thundered below, so above them roared the ceaseless thunder of the wind of the pass, that blew exceeding fierce down that strait place; so that the skirts of their garments were wrapped about their knees by it, and their feet were well-nigh stayed at whiles as they breasted the push thereof.

But as they mounted higher and higher yet, the noise of the waters swelled into a huge roar that drowned the bellowing of the prisoned wind, and down the pass came drifting a fine rain that fell not from the sky, for between the clouds of that drift could folk see the heavens bright and blue above them. This rain was but the spray of the great force up to whose steps they were climbing.

Now the way got rougher as they mounted; but this toil was caused by their gain; for the rock-wall, which thrust out a buttress

there as if it would have gone to the very edge of the gap wherethrough the flood ran, and so have cut the way off utterly, was
here somewhat broken down, and its stones scattered down the
steep bent, so that there was a passage, though a toilsome one.

Thus then through the wind-borne drift of the great force,
through which men could see the white waters tossing down
below, amidst the clattering thunder of the Shivering Flood
and the rumble of the wind of the gap, that tore through their
garments and hair as if it would rend all to rags and bear it
away, the banners of the Wolf won their way to the crest of the
midmost height of the pass, and the long line of the Host came
clambering after them ; and each band of warriors as it reached
the top cast an unheard shout from amidst the tangled fury of
wind and waters.

A little further on and all that turmoil was behind them ; the
sun, now grown low, smote the wavering column of spray from
the force at their backs, till the rainbows lay bright across it ;
and the sunshine lay wide over a little valley that sloped somewhat steeply to the west right up from the edge of the river ; and
beyond these western slopes could men see a low peak spreading
down on all sides to the plain, till it was like to a bossed shield,
and the name of it was Shield-broad. Dark grey was the valley
everywhere, save that by the side of the water was a space of
bright green-sward hedged about toward the mountain by a wall
of rocks tossed up into wild shapes of spires and jagged points.
The river itself was spread out wide and shallow, and went rattling about great grey rocks scattered here and there amidst it, till
it gathered itself together to tumble headlong over three slant steps
into the mighty gap below.

From the height in the pass those grey slopes seemed easy to
traverse ; but the warriors of the Wolf knew that it was far otherwise, for they were but the molten rock-sea that in time long past
had flowed forth from Shield-broad and filled up the whole valley
endlong and overthwart, cooling as it flowed, and the tumbled

316

hedge of rock round about the green plain by the river was where the said rock-sea had been stayed by meeting with soft ground, and had heaped itself up round about the green-sward. And that great rock-flood as it cooled split in divers fashions; and the rain and weather had been busy on it for ages, so that it was worn into a maze of narrow paths, most of which, after a little, brought the way-farer to a dead stop, or else led him back again to the place whence he had started; so that only those who knew the passes throughly could thread that maze without immeasurable labour.

Now when the men of the Host looked from the high place whereon they stood toward the green plain by the river, they saw on the top of that rock-wall a red pennon waving on a spear, and beside it three or four weaponed men gleaming bright in the even-ing sun; and they waved their swords to the Host, and made light-ning of the sunbeams, and the men of the Host waved swords to them in turn. For these were the outguards of the Host; and the place whereon they were was at whiles dwelt in by those who would drive the spoil in Silver-dale, and midmost of the green-sward was a booth builded of rough stones and turf, a refuge for a score of men in rough weather.

So the men of the vanward gat them down the hill, and made the best of their way toward the grassy plain through that rocky maze which had once been as a lake of molten glass; and as short as the way looked from above, it was two hours or ever they came out of it on to the smooth turf, and it was moonlight and night ere the House of the Face had gotten on to the green-sward.

There then the Host abode for that night, and after they had eaten lay down on the green grass and slept as they might. Bow-may would have brought the Sun-beam into the booth with some others of the women, but she would not enter it, because she deemed that otherwise the Bride would abide without; and the Bride, when she came up, along with the House of the Steer, beheld the Sun-beam, that Wood-father's children had made a lair for her without like a hare's form; and forsooth many a time had she lain

317

under the naked heaven in Shadowy Vale and the waste about it,
even as the Bride had in the meadows of Burgdale. So when the
Bride was bidden thereto, she went meekly into the booth, and lay
there with others of the damsels-at-arms.

## CHAPTER XLII. THE HOST COMETH TO THE EDGES OF SILVER-DALE.

SO wore the night, and when the dawn was come were the two
captains afoot, and they went from band to band to see that
all was ready, and all men were astir betimes, and by the
time that the sun smote the eastern side of Shield-broad ruddy,
they had broken their fast and were dight for departure. Then
the horns blew up beside the banners, and rejoiced the hearts of
men. But by the command of the captains this was the last time
that they should sound till they blew for onset in Silver-dale, because now would they be drawing nigher and nigher to the foemen, and they wotted not but that wandering bands of them might
be hard on the lips of the pass, and might hear the horns' voice,
and turn to see what was toward.

Forth then went the banners of the Wolf, and the men of the
vanward fell to threading the rock-maze toward the north, and
in two hours' time were clear of the Dale under Shield-broad.
All went in the same order as yesterday; but on this day the
Sun-beam would bear her hauberk, and had a sword girt to her
side, and her heart was high and her speech merry.

When they left the Dale under Shield-broad the way was easy
and wide for a good way, the river flowing betwixt low banks,
and the pass being more like a string of little valleys than a mere
gap, as it had been on the other side of the Dale. But when one
third of the day was past, the way began to narrow on them
again, and to rise up little by little; and at last the rock-walls
drew close to the river, and when men looked toward the north they

318

saw no way, and nought but a wall. For the gap of the Shivering Flood turned now to the east, and the Flood came down from the east in many falls, as it were over a fearful stair, through a gap where there was no path between the cliffs and the water, nought but the boiling flood and its turmoil; so that they who knew not the road wondered what they should do. They turn from the Shivering Flood.

But Folk-might led the banners to where a great buttress of the cliffs thrust itself into the way, coming well-nigh down to the water, just at the corner where the river turned eastward, and they got them about it as they might, and on the other side thereof lo! another gap exceeding strait, scarce twenty foot over, wall-sided, rugged beyond measure, going up steeply from the great valley: a little water ran through it, mostly filling up the floor of it from side to side; but it was but shallow. This was now the battle-road of the Host, and the vanward entered it at once, turning their backs upon the Shivering Flood.

Full toilsome and dreary was that strait way; often great stones hung above their heads, bridging the gap and hiding the sky from them; nor was there any path for them save the stream itself; so that whiles were they wading its waters to the knee or higher, and whiles were they striding from stone to stone amidst the rattle of the waters, and whiles were they stepping warily along the ledges of rock above the deeper pools, and in all wise labouring in overcoming the rugged road amidst the twilight of the gap.

Thus they toiled till the afternoon was well worn, and so at last they came to where the rock-wall was somewhat broken down on the north side, and great rocks had fallen across the gap, and dammed up the waters, which fell scantily over the dam from stone to stone into a pool at the bottom of it. Up this breach, then, below the force they scrambled and struggled, for rough indeed was the road for them; and so came they up out of the gap on to the open hill-side, a great shoulder of the heath sloping down from the north, and littered over with big stones, borne thither

319

belike by some ice-river of the earlier days; and one great rock
was in special as great as the hall of a wealthy goodman, and
shapen like to a hall with hipped gables, which same the men
of the Wolf called House-stone.

There then the noise and clatter of the vanward rose up on the
face of the heath, and men were exceeding joyous that they had
come so far without mishap. Therewith came weaponed men out
from under House-stone, and they came toward the men of the
vanward, and they were a half-score of the forerunners of the
Wolf; therefore Folk-might and Face-of-god fell at once into
speech with them, and had their tidings; and when they had
heard them, they saw nought to hinder the host from going on
their road to Silver-dale forthright; and there were still three
hours of daylight before them. So the vanward of the host tarried
not, and the captains left word with the men from under House-
stone that the rest of the Host should fare on after them speedily,
and that they should give this word to each company, as men
came up from out the gap. Then they fared speedily up the hill-
side, and in an hour's wearing had come to the crest thereof, and to
where the ground fell steadily toward the north, and hereabout
the scattered stones ceased, and on the other side of the crest
the heath began to be soft and boggy, and at last so soft, that if
they had not been wisely led, they had been bemired oftentimes.
At last they came to where the flows that trickled through the
mires drew together into a stream, so that men could see it running;
and thereon some of the Woodlanders cried out joyously that
the waters were running north; and then all knew that they were
drawing nigh to Silver-dale.

No man they met on the road, nor did they of Shadowy Vale
look to meet any; because the Dusky Men were not great hunters
for the more part, except it were of men, and especially of women;
and, moreover, these hill-slopes of the mountain-necks led no-
whither and were utterly waste and dreary, and there was nought
to be seen there but snipes and bitterns and whimbrel and plover,

320

and here and there a hill-fox, or the great erne hanging over the
heath on his way to the mountain.

When sunset came, they were getting clear of the miry ground,
and the stream which they had come across amidst of the mires
had got clearer and greater, and rattled down between wide stony
sides over the heath; and here and there it deepened as it cleft its
way through little knolls that rose out of the face of the mountain-neck. As the Host climbed one of these and was come to
its topmost (it was low enough not to turn the stream), Face-of-
god looked and beheld dark-blue mountains rising up far off
before him, and higher than these, but away to the east, the snowy
peaks of the World-mountains. Then he called to mind what he
had seen from the Burg of the Runaways, and he took Folk-
might by the arm, and pointed toward those far-off mountains.

'Yea,' said Folk-might, 'so it is, War-leader. Silver-dale lieth
between us and yonder blue ridges, and it is far nigher to us than
to them.'

But the Sun-beam came close to those twain, and took Face-of-
god by the hand and said: 'O Gold-mane, dost thou see?' and
he turned about and beheld her, and saw how her cheeks flamed
and her eyes glittered, and he said in a low voice: 'To-morrow
for mirth or silence, for life or death.'

But the whole vanward as they came up stayed to behold
the sight of the mountains on the other side of Silver-dale, and
the banners of the Folk hung over their heads, moving but little
in the soft air of the evening: so went they on their ways.

The sun sank, and dusk came on them as they followed down
the stream, and night came, and was clear and starlit, though the
moon was not yet risen. Now was the ground firm and the
grass sweet and flowery, and wind-worn bushes were scattered
round about them, as they began to go down into the ghyll that
cleft the wall of Silver-dale, and the night-wind blew in their
faces from the very Dale and place of the Battle to be. The
path down was steep at first, but the ghyll was wide, and the

sides of it no longer straight walls, as in the gaps of their earlier
journey, but broken, sloping back, and (as they might see on the
morrow) partly of big stones and shaly grit, partly grown over
with bushes and rough grass, with here and there a little stream
trickling down their sides. As they went, the ghyll widened out,
till at last they were in a valley going down to the plain, in places
steep, in places flat and smooth, the stream ever rattling down
the midst of it, and they on the west side thereof. The vale
was well grassed, and oak-trees and ash and holly and hazel grew
here and there about it; and at last the Host had before it a
wood which filled the vale from side to side, not much tangled
with undergrowth, and quite clear of it nigh to the stream-side.
Thereinto the vanward entered, but went no long way ere the
leaders called a halt and bade pitch the banners, for that there
should they abide the daylight. Thus it had been determined at the
Council of the Hall of the Wolf; for Folk-might had said: 'With
an Host as great as ours, and mostly of men come into a land of
which they know nought at all, an onslaught by night is perilous:
yea, and our foes should be over-much scattered, and we should
have to wander about seeking them. Let us rather abide in the
wood of Wood-dale till the morning, and then display our banners
on the hill-side above Silver-dale, so that they may gather together
to fall upon us: in no case shall they keep us out of the Dale.'
There then they stayed, and as each company came up to the
wood, they were marshalled into their due places, so that they
might set the battle in array on the edge of Silver-dale.

CHAPTER XLIII.  FACE-OF-GOD LOOKETH ON SILVER-
DALE: THE BOWMEN'S BATTLE.

THERE then they rested, as folk wearied with the toilsome
journey, when they had set sure watches round about their
campment; and they ate quietly what meat they had

with them, and so gat them to sleep in the wood on the eve of battle.

But not all slept; for the two captains went about amongst the companies, Folk-might to the east, Face-of-god to the west, to look to the watches, and to see that all was ordered duly. Also the Sun-beam slept not, but she lay beside Bow-may at the foot of an oak-tree; she watched Face-of-god as he went away amidst the men of the Host, and watched and waked abiding his returning footsteps.

The night was well worn by then he came back to his place in the vanward, and on his way back he passed through the folk of the Steer laid along on the grass, all save those of the watch, and the light of the moon high aloft was mingled with the light of the earliest dawn; and as it happed he looked down, and lo! close to his feet the face of the Bride as she lay beside her grand-sire, her head pillowed on a bundle of bracken. She was sleeping soundly like a child who has been playing all day, and whose sleep has come to him unsought and happily. Her hands were laid together by her side; her cheek was as fair and clear as it was wont to be at her best; her face looked calm and happy, and a lock of her dark-red hair strayed from her uncovered head over her breast and lay across her wrists, so peacefully she slept.

Face-of-god turned his eyes from her at once, and went by swiftly, and came to his own company. The Sun-beam saw him coming, and rose straightway to her feet from beside Bow-may, who lay fast asleep, and she held out her hands to him; and he took them and kissed them, and he cast his arms about her and kissed her mouth and her face, and she his in like wise; and she said:

'O Gold-mane, if this were but the morrow of to-morrow! Yet shall all be well; shall it not?'

Her voice was low, but it waked Bow-may, who sat up at once broad awake, after the manner of a hunter of the waste ever ready for the next thing to betide, and moreover the Sun-beam had been in her thoughts these two days, and she feared for her,

lest she should be slain or maimed. Now she smiled on the
Sun-beam and said :

'What is it ? Does thy mind forebode evil ? That needeth not.
I tell thee it is not so ill for us of the sword to be in Silver-dale.
Thrice have I been there since the Overthrow, and never more
than a half-score in company, and yet am I whole to-day.'

'Yea, sister,' said Face-of-god, 'but in past times ye did your
deed and then fled away ; but now we come to abide here, and
this night is the last of lurking.'

'Ah,' she said, 'a little way from this I saw such things that
we had good will to abide here longer, few as we were, but that
we feared to be taken alive.'

'What things were these ?' said Face-of-god.

'Nay,' she said, 'I will not tell thee now ; but mayhap in the
lighted winter feast-hall, when the kindred are so nigh us and
about us that they seem to us as if they were all the world, I may
tell it thee ; or mayhap I never shall.'

Said the Sun-beam, smiling : 'Thou wilt ever be talking,
Bow-may. Now let the War-leader depart, for he will have
much to do.'

And she was well at ease that she had seen Face-of-god again ;
but he said :

'Nay, not so much ; all is well-nigh done ; in an hour it will
be broad day, and two hours thereafter shall the Banner be displayed on the edge of Silver-dale.'

The cheek of the Sun-beam flushed, and paled again, as she
said : 'Yea, we shall stand even as our Fathers stood on the day
when, coming from off the waste, they beheld it, and knew it would
be theirs. Ah me! how have I longed for this morn. But now
—Tell me, Gold-mane, dost thou deem that I am afraid ? And
I whom thou hast deemed to be a God.'

Quoth Bow-may : 'Thou shalt deem her twice a God ere noontide, brother Gold-mane. But come now ! the hour of deadly
battle is at hand, and we may not laugh that away ; and there-

324

fore I bid thee remember, Gold-mane, how thou didst promise to kiss me once more on the verge of deadly battle.'

Therewith she stood up before him, and he tarried not, but kind and smiling took her face between his two hands and kissed her lips, and she cast her arms about him and kissed him, and then sank down on the grass again, and turned from him, and laid her face amongst the grass and the bracken, and they could see that she was weeping, and her body was shaken with sobs. But the Sun-beam knelt down to her, and caressed her with her hand, and spake kind words to her softly, while Face-of-god went his ways to meet Folk-might.

Now was the dawn fading into full daylight; and between dawn and sunrise were all men stirring; for the watch had waked the hundred-leaders, and they the leaders of scores and half-scores, and they the whole folk; and they sat quietly in the wood and made no noise.

In the night the watch of the Sickle had fallen in with a thrall who had stolen up from the Dale to set gins for hares, and now in the early morning they brought him to the War-leader. He was even such a man as those with whom Face-of-god had fallen in before, neither better nor worse than most of them: he was sore afraid at first, but by then he was come to the captains he understood that he had happened upon friends; but he was dull of comprehension and slow of speech. Albeit Folk-might gathered from him that the Dusky Men had some inkling of the onslaught; for he said that they had been gathering together in the market-place of Silver-stead, and would do so again soon. Moreover, the captains deemed from his speech that those new tribes had come to hand sooner than was looked for, and were even now in the Dale. Folk-might smiled as one who is not best pleased when he heard these tidings; but Face-of-god was glad to hear thereof; for what he loathed most was that the war should drag out in hunting of scattered bands of the foe. Herewith came Dallach to them as they talked (for Face-of-god had sent for him),

325

and he fell to questioning the man further; by whose answers it seemed that many men also had come into the Dale from Rose-dale, so that they of the kindreds were like to have their hands full. Lastly Dallach drew from the thrall that it was on that very morning that the great Folk-mote of the Dusky Men should be holden in the market-place of the Stead, which was right great, and about it were the biggest of the houses wherein the men of the kindred had once dwelt.

So when they had made an end of questioning the thrall, and had given him meat and drink, they asked him if he would take weapons in his hand and lead them on the ways into the Dale, bidding him look about the wood and note how great and mighty an host they were. And the carle yeasaid this, after staring about him a while, and they gave him spear and shield, and he went with the vanward as a way-leader.

Again presently came a watch of the Shepherds, and they had found a man and a woman dead and stark naked hanging to the boughs of a great oak-tree deep in the wood. This men knew for some vengeance of the Dusky Men, for it was clear to see that these poor people had been sorely tormented before they were slain. Also the same watch had stumbled on the dead body of an old woman, clad in rags, lying amongst the rank grass about a little flow; she was exceeding lean and hunger-starved, and in her hand was a frog which she had half eaten. And Dallach, when he heard of this, said that it was the wont of the Dusky Men to slay their thralls when they were past work, or to drive them into the wilderness to die.

Lastly came a watch from the men of the Face, having with them two more thralls, lusty young men; these they had come upon in company of their master, who had brought them up into the wood to shoot him a buck, and therefore they bare bows and arrows. The watch had slain the master straightway while the thralls stood looking on. They were much afraid of the weaponed men, but answered to the questioning much readier than the first man; for they were household thralls, and better fed and clad than he, who was but a toiler in the fields. They yeasaid all his tale, and said moreover that the Folk-mote of the Dusky Men should be holden in the market-place that forenoon, and that most of the warriors should be there, both the new-comers and the Rose-dale lords, and that without doubt they should be under arms.

To these men also they gave a good sword and a helm each, and bade them be brisk with their bows, and they said yea to marching with the Host; and indeed they feared nothing so much as being left behind; for if they fell into the hands of the Dusky Men, and their master missing, they should first be questioned with torments, and then slain in the evillest manner.

Now whereas things had thus betid, and that they knew thus much of their foemen, Face-of-god called all the chieftains together, and they sat on the green grass and held counsel amongst them, and to one and all it seemed good that they should suffer the Dusky Men to gather together before they meddled with them, and then fall upon them in such order and such time as should seem good to the captains watching how things went; and this would be easy, whereas they were all lying in the wood in the same order as they would stand in battle-array if they were all drawn up together on the brow of the hill. Albeit Face-of-god deemed it good, after he had heard all that they who had been in the Stead could tell him thereof, that the Shepherd-Folk, who were more than three long hundreds, and they of the Steer, the Bridge, and the Bull, four hundreds in all, should take their places eastward of the Woodlanders who had led the vanward.

Straightway the word was borne to these men, and the shift was made: so that presently the Woodlanders were amidmost of the Host, and had with them on their right hands the Men of the Steer, the Bridge, and the Bull, and beyond them the Shepherd-Folk. But on their left hand lay the Men of the Vine, then they of the Sickle, and lastly the Men of the Face, and these three kindreds were over five hundreds of warriors: as for the Men of the Wolf, they abode at first with those companies which they had led through the wastes, though this was changed afterwards.

All this being done, Face-of-god gave out that all men should break their fast in peace and leisure; and while men were at their meat, Folk-might spake to Face-of-god and said: 'Come, brother, for I would show thee a goodly thing; and thou, Dallach, come with us.'

Then he brought them by paths in the wood till Face-of-god saw the sky shine white between the tree-boles, and in a little while they were come well-nigh out of the thicket, and then they went warily; for before them was nought but the slopes of Wood-dale, going down steeply into Silver-dale, with nought to hinder the sight of it, save here and there bushes or scattered trees; and so fair and lovely it was that Face-of-god could scarce forbear to cry out. He saw that it was only at the upper or eastern end, where the mountains of the Waste went round about it, that the Dale was narrow; it soon widened out toward the west, and for the most part was encompassed by no such straight-sided a wall as was Burgdale, but by sloping hills and bents, mostly indeed somewhat higher and steeper than the pass wherein they were, but such as men could well climb if they had a mind to, and there were any end to their journey. The Dale went due west a good way, and then winded about to the south-west, and so was hidden from them thereaway by the bents that lay on their left hand. As it was wider, so it was not so plain a ground as was Burgdale, but rose in knolls and little hills here and there. A river greater than the Weltering Water wound about amongst the said mounds; and along the side of it out in the open dale were many goodly houses and homesteads of stone. The knolls were mostly covered over with vines, and there were goodly and great trees in groves and clumps, chiefly oak and sweet chestnut and linden; many were the orchards, now in blossom, about the homesteads; the pastures of the neat and horses spread out bright green up from the water-side, and deeper

328

green showed the acres of the wheat on the lower slopes of the knolls, and in wide fields away from the river.

Just below the pitch of the hill whereon they were, lay Silverstead, the town of the Dale. Hitherto it had been an unfenced place; but Folk-might pointed to where on the western side a new white wall was rising, and on which, young as the day yet was, men were busy laying the stones and spreading the mortar. Fair seemed that town to Face-of-god: the houses were all builded of stone, and some of the biggest were roofed with lead, which also as well as silver was dug out of the mountains at the eastern end of the Dale. The market-place was clear to see from where they stood, though there were houses on all sides of it, so wide it was. From their standing-place it was but three furlongs to this heart of Silver-dale; and Face-of-god could see brightly-clad men moving about in it already. High above their heads he beheld two great clots of scarlet and yellow raised on poles and pitched in front of a great stone-built hall roofed with lead, which stood amidmost of the west end of the Place, and betwixt those poles he saw on a mound with long slopes at its sides somewhat of white stone, and amidmost of the whole Place a great stack of faggot-wood built up four-square. Those red and yellow things on the poles he deemed would be the banners of the murder-carles; and Folk-might told him that even so it was, and that they were but big bunches of strips of woollen cloth, much like to great rag-mops, save that the rags were larger and longer: no other token of war, said Folk-might, did those folk carry, save a crook-bladed sword, smeared with man's blood, and bigger than any man might wield in battle.

'Art thou far-seeing, War-leader?' quoth he. 'What canst thou see in the market-place?'

Said Face-of-god: 'Far-seeing am I above most men, and I see in the Place a man in scarlet standing by the banner, which is pitched in front of the great stone hall, near to the mound with the white stone on it; and meseemeth he beareth a great horn in his hand.'

Said Folk-might : 'Yea, and that stone hall was our Mote-house when we were lords of the Dale, and thence it was that they who are now thralls of the Dusky Men sent to them their message and token of yielding. And as for that white stone, it is the altar of their god; for they have but one, and he is that same crook-bladed sword. And now that I look, I see a great stack of wood amidmost the market-place, and well I know what that betokeneth.'

'Lo you !' said Face-of-god, 'the man with the horn is gone up on to the altar-mound, and meseemeth he is setting the little end of the horn to his mouth.'

'Hearken then !' said Folk-might. And in a moment came the hoarse tuneless sound of the horn down the wind towards them; and Folk-might said :

'I deem I should know what that blast meaneth; and now is it time that the Host drew nigher to set them in array behind these very trees. But if ye will, War-leader, we will abide here and watch the ways of the foemen, and send Dallach with the word to the Host; also I would have thee suffer me to bid hither at once two score and ten of the best of the bowmen of our folk and the Woodlanders, and Wood-wise to lead them, for he knoweth well the land hereabout, and what is good to do.'

'It is good,' said Face-of-god. 'Be speedy, Dallach !'

So Dallach departed, running lightly, and the two chiefs abode there ; and the horn in Silver-stead blew at whiles for a little, and then stayed; and Folk-might said :

'Lo you ! they come flockmeal to the Mote-stead; the Place will be filled ere long.'

Said Face-of-god : 'Will they make offerings to their god at the hallowing in of their Folk-mote ? Where then are the slaughter-beasts ?'

'They shall not long be lacking,' said Folk-might. 'See you it is getting thronged about the altar and the Mote-house.'

Now there were four ways into the Market-place of Silver-stead

330

turned toward the four airts, and the midmost of the kindreds' battle looked right down the southern one, which went up to the wood, but stopped there in a mere woodland path, and the more part of the town lay north and west of this way, albeit there was a way from the east also. But the hill-side just below the two captains lay two furlongs west of this southern way; and it went down softly till it was gotten quite near to the backs of the houses on the south side of the Market-place, and was sprinkled scantly with bushes and trees as aforesaid ; but at last were there more bushes, which well-nigh made a hedge across it, reaching from the side of the southern way ; and a foot or two beyond these bushes the ground fell by a steep and broken bent down to the level of the Market-place, and betwixt that fringe of bushes and the backs of the houses on the south side of the Place was less it maybe than a full furlong : but the southern road aforesaid went down softly into the Market-place, since it had been fashioned so by men.

Now the two chiefs heard a loud blast of horns come up from the town, and lo ! a great crowd of men wending their ways down the road from the north, and they came into the market-place with spears and other weapons tossing in the air, and amidst of these men, who seemed to be all of the warriors, they saw as they drew nigher some two score and ten of men clad in long raiment of yellow and scarlet, with tall spiring hats of strange fashion on their heads, and in their hands long staves with great blades like scythes done on to them ; and again, in the midst of these yellow and red glaive-bearers, in the very heart of the throng were some score of naked folk, they deemed both men and women, but were not sure, so close was the throng ; nor could they see if they were utterly naked.

'Lo you, brother!' quoth Folk-might, 'said I not that the beasts for the hewing should not tarry ? Yonder naked folk are even they : and ye may well deem that they are the thralls of the Dusky Men ; and meseemeth by the whiteness of their skins they be of

331

the best of them. For these felons, it is like, look to winning great plenty of thralls in Burgdale, and so set the less store on them they have, and may expend them freely.'

As he spake they heard the sound of men marching in the wood behind them, and they turned about and saw that there was come Wood-wise, and with him upwards of two score and ten of the bow-men of the Woodlanders and the Wolf—huntsmen, cragsmen, and scourers of the Waste; men who could shoot the chaffinch on the twig a hundred yards aloof; who could make a hiding-place of the bennets of the wayside grass, or the stem of the slender birch-tree. With these must needs be Bow-may, who was the closest shooter of all the kindreds.

So then Wood-wise told the War-leader that Dallach had given the word to the Host, and that all men were astir and would be there presently in their ordered companies; and Face-of-god spake to Folk-might, and said: 'Chief of the Wolf, wilt thou not give command to these bowmen, and set them to the work; for thou wottest thereof.'

'Yea, that will I,' said Folk-might, and turned to Wood-wise, and said: 'Wood-wise, get ye down the slope, and loose on these felons, who have a murder on hand, if so be ye have a chance to do it wisely. But in any case come ye all back; for all shall be needed yet to-day. So flee if they pursue, for ye shall have us to flee to. Now be ye wary, nor let the curse of the Wolf and the Face lie on your slothfulness.'

Wood-wise did but nod his head and lift his hand to his fellows, who set off after him down the slope without more tarrying. They went very warily, as if they were hunting a quarry which would flee from them; and they crept amongst the grass and stones from bush to bush like serpents, and so, unseen by the Dusky Men, who indeed were busied over their own matters, they came to the fringe of bushes above the broken ground aforesaid, and there they took their stand, and before them below those steep banks was but the space at the back of the houses. As to the houses, as aforesaid,

332

they were not so high as elsewhere about the Market-place; and at the end of a long low hall there was a gap between its gable and the next house, whereby they had a clear sight of the Place about the god's altar and the banners, and the great hall of Silverdale, with the double stair that went up to the door thereof.

There then they made them ready, and Wood-wise set men to watch that none should come sidelong on them unawares; their bows were bent and their quivers open, and they were eager for the fray.

Thus they beheld the Market-place from their cover, and saw that those folk who were to be hewn to the god were now standing facing the altar in a half-ring, and behind them in another half-ring the glaive-bearers who had brought them thither stood glaive in hand ready to hew them down when the token should be given; and these were indeed the priests of the god.

There was clear space round about these poor slaughter-thralls, so that the bowmen could see them well, and they told up a score of them, half men, half women, and they were all stark naked save for wreaths of flowers about their middles and their necks; and they had shackles of lead about their wrists; which same lead should be taken out of the fire wherein they should be burned, and from the shape it should take after it had passed through the fire would the priests foretell the luck of the deed to be done.

It was clear to be seen from thence that Folk-might was right when he said that these slaughter-thralls were of the best of the house-thralls and bed-mates of the Dusky Men, and that these felons were open-handed to their god, and would not cheat him, or withhold from him the best and most delicate of all they had.

Now spake Wood-wise to those about him: 'It is sure that Folk-might would have us give these poor thralls a chance, and that we must loose upon the felons who would hew them down; and if we are to come back again, we can go no nigher. What sayest thou, Bow-may? Is it nigh enough? Can aught be done?'

'Yea, yea,' she said, 'nigh enough it is; but let Gold-ring

333

be with me and half a score of the very best, whether they be of
our folk or the Woodlanders, men who cannot miss such a mark;
and when we have loosed, then let all loose, and stay not till our
shot be spent. Haste, now haste! time presseth; for if the Host
showeth on the brow of the hill, these felons will hew down their
slaughter-beasts before they turn on their foemen. Let the grey-
goose wing speed trouble and confusion amongst them.'

But ere she had done her words Wood-wise had got to speaking quietly with the Woodlanders; and Bears-bane, who was
amidst them, chose out eight of the best of his folk, men who
doubted nothing of hitting whatever they could see in the Market-place; and they took their stand for shooting, and with them
besides Bow-may were two women and four men of the Wolf,
and Gold-ring withal, a carle of fifty winters, long, lean, and
wiry, a fell shooter if ever anyone were.

So all these notched their shafts and laid them on the yew,
and each had between the two last fingers of the shaft-hand
another shaft ready, and a half score more stuck into the ground
before him.

Now giveth Wood-wise the word to these sixteen as to which
of the felons with the glaives they shall each one aim at; and he
saith withal in a soft voice: 'Help cometh from the Hill; soon
shall battle be joined in Silver-dale.'

Thus stand they watching Bow-may and Gold-ring till they
draw home the notches; and amidst their waiting the glaive-
bearing felons fall a-singing a harsh and ugly hymn to their
crooked-sword god, and the Market-stead is thronged endlong
and overthwart with the tribes of the Dusky Men.

There now standeth Bow-may far-sighted and keen-eyed, her
face as pale as a linen sleeve, an awful smile on her glittering
eyes and close-set lips, and she feeling the twisted string of the
red yew and the polished sides of the notch, while the yelling
song of the Dusky priests quavers now and ends with a wild shrill
cry, and she noteth the midmost of the priests beginning to handle

334

his weapon: then swift and steady she draweth home the notches, while the yew bow standeth still as the oak-bole ere the summer storm ariseth, and the twang of the sixteen strings maketh but one fell sound as the feathered bane of men goeth on its way.

There was silence for a moment of time in the Market of Silver-stead, as if the bolt of the Gods had fallen there; and then arose a huge wordless yell from those about the altar, and one of the priests who was left hove up his glaive two-handed to smite the naked slaughter-thralls; but or ever the stroke fell, Bow-may's second shaft was through his throat, and he rolled over amidst his dead fellows; and the other fifteen had loosed with her, and then even as they could Wood-wise and the others of their company; and all they notched and loosed without tarrying, and no shout, no word came from their lips, only the twanging strings spake for them; for they deemed the minutes that hurried by were worth much joy of their lives to be. And few indeed were the passing minutes ere the dead men lay in heaps about the Altar of the Crooked Sword, and the wounded men wallowed amidst them.

CHAPTER XLIV.   OF THE ONSLAUGHT OF THE MEN OF THE STEER, THE BRIDGE, AND THE BULL.

WILD was the turmoil and confusion in the Market-stead; for the more part of the men therein knew not what had befallen about the altar, though some clomb up to the top of that stack of faggots built for the burning of the thralls, and when they saw what was toward fell to yelling and cursing; and their fellows on the plain Place could not hear their story for the clamour, and they also fell to howling as if a wood full of wild dogs was there.

And still the shafts rained down on that throng from the Bent of the Bowmen, for another two score men of the Woodlanders had crept down the hill to them, and shafts failed them not. But the Dusky Men about the altar, for all their terror, or even maybe because of it, now began to turn upon the scarce-seen foemen, and to press up wildly toward the hill-side, though as it were without any order or aim. Every man of them had his weapons, and those no mere gilded toys, but their very tools of battle; and some, but no great number, had their bows with them and a few shafts; and these began to shoot at whatsoever they could see on the hill-side, but at first so wildly and hurriedly that they did no harm.

It must be said of them that at first only those about the altar fell on toward the hill; for those about the road that led southward knew not what had betided nor whither to turn. So that at this beginning of the battle, of all the thousands in the great Place it was but a few hundreds that set on the Bent of the Bowmen, and at these the bowmen of the kindreds shot so close and so wholly together that they fell one over another in the narrow ways between the houses whereby they must needs go to gather on the plain ground betwixt the backs of the houses and the break of the hill-side. But little by little the archers of the Dusky Men gathered behind the corpses of the slain, and fell to shooting at what they could see of the men of the kindreds, which at that while was not much, for as bold as they were, they fought like wary hunters of the Wood and the Waste.

But now at last throughout all that throng of Felons in the Market-place the tale began to spread of foemen come into the Dale and shooting from the Bents, and all they turned their faces to the hill, and the whole set of the throng was thitherward; though they fared but slowly, so evil was the order of them, each man hindering his neighbour as he went. And not only did the Dusky Men come flockmeal toward the Bent of the Bowmen, but also they jostled along toward the road that led southward. That beheld Wood-wise from the Bent, and he was minded to get him and his aback, now that they had made so

336

great a slaughter of the foemen; and two or three of his fellows
had been hurt by arrows, and Bow-may, she would have been
slain thrice over but for the hammer-work of the Alderman. And
no marvel was that; for now she stood on a little mound not
half covered by a thin thorn-bush, and notched and loosed at
whatever was most notable, as though she were shooting at the
mark on a summer evening in Shadowy Vale. But as Wood-
wise was at point to give the word to depart, from behind them
rang out the merry sound of the Burgdale horns, and he turned
to look at the wood-side, and lo! thereunder was the hill bright
and dark with men-at-arms, and over them floated the Banners
of the Wolf, and the Banners of the Steer, the Bridge, and the
Bull. Then gave forth the bowmen of the kindreds their first
shout, and they made no stay in their shooting; but shot the
eagerer, for they deemed that help would come without their
turning about to draw it to them: and even so it was. For
straightway down the bent came striding Face-of-god betwixt
the two Banners of the Wolf, and beside him were Red-wolf
the tall and War-grove, and therewithal Wood-wont and Wood-
wicked, and many other men of the Wolf; for now that the
men of the kindreds had been brought face to face with the
foe, and there was less need of them for way-leaders, the more
part of them were liefer to fight under their own banner along
with the Woodlanders; so that the company of those who went
under the Wolves was more than three long hundreds and a
half; and the bowmen on the edge of the bent shouted again
and merrily, when they felt that their brothers were amongst
them, and presently was the arrow-storm at its fiercest, and
the twanging of bow-strings and the whistle of the shafts was
as the wind among the clefts of the mountains; for all the new-
comers were bowmen of the best.

But the kindreds of the Steer, the Bridge, and the Bull,
they hung yet a while longer on the hills' brow, their banners
floating over them and their horns blowing; and the Dusky

The kindreds
set the battle
in array on
the wood's
edge.

A song of
onset of the
kindreds of
the Upper
Dale.

Felons in the Market-place beheld them, and fear and rage at
once filled their hearts, and a fierce and dreadful yell brake out
from them, and joyously did the Men of Burgdale answer them,
and song arose amongst them even such as this:

*The Men of the Bridge sing:*
Why stand ye together, why bear ye the shield,
Now the calf straineth tether at edge of the field?

Now the lamb bleateth stronger and waters run clear,
And the day groweth longer and glad is the year?

Now the mead-flowers jostle so thick as they stand,
And singeth the throstle all over the land?

*The Men of the Steer sing:*
No cloud the day darkened, no thunder we heard,
But the horns' speech we hearkened as men unfeared.

Yea, so merry it sounded, we turned from the Dale,
Where all wealth abounded, to wot of its tale.

*The Men of the Bridge sing:*
What white boles then bear ye, what wealth of the woods?
What chafferers hear ye bid loud for your goods?

*The Men of the Bull sing:*
O the bright beams we carry are stems of the steel;
Nor long shall we tarry across them to deal.

Hark the men of the cheaping, how loudly they cry
On the hook for the reaping of men doomed to die!

*They all sing:*
Heave spear up! fare forward, O Men of the Dale!
For the Warrior, our war-ward, shall hearken the tale.

Therewith they ceased a moment, and then gave a great and hearty shout all together, and all their horns blew, and they moved on down the hill as one man, slowly and with no jostling, the spearmen first, and then they of the axe and the sword ; and on their flanks the deft archers loosed on the stumbling jostling throng of the Dusky Men, who for their part came on drifting and surging up the road to the hill.

But when those big spearmen of the Dale had gone a little way the horns' voice died out, and their great-staved spears rose up from their shoulders into the air, and stood so a moment, and then slowly fell forward, as the oars of the longship fall into the rowlocks, and then over the shoulders of the foremost men showed the steel of the five ranks behind them, and their own spears cast long bars of shadow on the whiteness of the sunny road. No sound came from them now save the rattle of their armour and the tramp of their steady feet ; but from the Dusky Men rose up hideous confused yelling, and those that could free themselves from the tangle of the throng rushed desperately against the on-rolling hedge of steel, and the whole throng shoved on behind them. Then met steel and men ; here and there an ash-stave broke ; here and there a Dusky Felon rolled himself unhurt under the ash-staves, and hewed the knees of the Dalesmen, and a tall man came tottering down ; but what men or wood-wights could endure the push of spears of those mighty husbandmen ? The Dusky Ones shrunk back yelling, or turned their backs and rushed at their own folk with such fierce agony that they entered into the throng, till the terror of the spear reached to the midmost of it and swayed them back on the hindermost ; for neither was there outgate for the felons on the flanks of the spearmen, since there the feathered death beset them, and the bowmen (and the Bride amongst the foremost) shot wholly together, and no shaft flew idly. But the wise leaders of the Dalesmen would not that they should thrust in too far amongst the howling throng of the Dusky Men, lest they should be hemmed in by them ; for they were but a handful in regard to them : so there they

339

stayed, barring the way to the Dusky Men, and the bowmen still
loosed from the flanks of them, or aimed deftly from betwixt the
ranks of the spearmen.

And now was there a space of ten strides or more betwixt the
Dalesmen and their foes, over which the spears hung terribly, nor
durst the Dusky Men adventure there; and thereon was nought but
men dead or sorely hurt. Then suddenly a horn rang thrice shrilly
over all the noise and clamour of the throng, and the ranks of the
spearmen opened, and forth into that space strode two score of the
swordsmen and axe-wielders of the Dale, their weapons raised in
their hands, and he who led them was Iron-hand of the House of
the Bull: tall he was, wide-shouldered, exceeding strong, but
beardless and fair-faced. He bore aloft a two-edged sword, broad-
bladed, exceeding heavy, so that few men could wield it in battle,
but not right long; it was an ancient weapon, and his father before
him had called it the Barley-scythe. With him were some of the
best of the kindreds, as Wolf of Whitegarth, Long-hand of Oak-
holt, Hart of Highcliff, and War-well the captain of the Bridge.
These made no tarrying on that space of the dead, but cried aloud
their cries: 'For the Burg and the Steer! for the Dale and the
Bridge! for the Dale and the Bull!' and so fell at once on the
Felons; who fled not, nor had room to flee; and also they feared not
the edge-weapons so sorely as they feared those huge spears. So
they turned fiercely on the swordsmen, and chiefly on Iron-hand, as
he entered in amongst them the first of all, hewing to the right
hand and the left, and many a man fell before the Barley-scythe;
for they were but little before him. Yet as one fell another took his
place, and hewed at him with the steel axe and the crooked sword;
and with many strokes they clave his shield and brake his helm
and rent his byrny, while he heeded little save smiting with the
Barley-scythe, and the blood ran from his arm and his shoulder and
his thigh.

But War-well had entered in among the foe on his left hand,
and unshielded hove up a great broad-bladed axe, that clave the

340

iron helms of the Dusky Men, and rent their horn-scaled byrnies. Great strokes
He was not very tall, but his shoulders were huge and his arms stricken.
long, and nought could abide his stroke. He cleared a ring round
Iron-hand, whose eyes were growing dim as the blood flowed from
him, and hewed three strokes before him; then turned and drew the
champion out of the throng, and gave him into the arms of his fellows to stanch the blood that drained away the might of his limbs;
and then with a great wordless roar leaped back again on the
Dusky Men as the lion leapeth on the herd of swine; and they
shrank away before him; and all the swordsmen shouted, 'For the
Bridge, for the Bridge!' and pressed on the harder, smiting down
all before them. On his left hand now was Hart of Highcliff
wielding a good sword hight Chip-driver, wherewith he had slain
and hurt a many, fighting wisely with sword and shield, and
driving the point home through the joints of the armour. But
even therewith, as he drave a great stroke at a lord of the Dusky
Ones, a cast-spear came flying and smote him on the breast, so
that he staggered, and the stroke fell flatlings on the shield-boss
of his foe, and Chip-driver brake atwain nigh the hilts; but
Hart closed with him, and smote him on the face with the pom-
mel, and tore his axe from his hand and clave his skull therewith, and slew him with his own weapon, and fought on valiantly
beside War-well.

Now War-well had fought so fiercely that he had rent his own
hauberk with the might of his strokes, and as he raised his arm to
smite a huge stroke, a deft man of the Felons thrust the spike of his
war-axe up under his arm; and when War-well felt the smart of
the steel, he turned on that man, and, letting his axe fall down to
his wrist and hang there by its loop, he caught the foeman up by
the neck and the breech, and drave him against the other Dusky
Ones before him, so that their weapons pierced and rent their own
friend and fellow. Then he put forth the might of his arms and
the pith of his body, and hove up that felon and cast him on to the
heads of his fellow murder-carles, so that he rent them and was

341

rent by them. Then War-well fell on again with the axe, and
all the champions of the Dale shouted and fell on with him, and
the foe shrank away; and the Dalesmen cleared a space five fathoms'
length before them, and the spearmen drew onward and stood on the
space whereon the first onslaught had been.

Then drew those hewers of the Dale together, and forth from
the company came the man that bare the Banner of the Bridge,
and the champions gathered round him, and they ordered their
ranks and strode with the Banner before them three times to and
fro across the road athwart the front of the spearmen, and then
with a great shout drew back within the spear-hedge. Albeit five
of the champions of the Dale had been slain outright there, and
the more part of them hurt more or less.

But when all were well within the ranks, once again blew the
horn, and all the spears sank to the rest, and the kindreds drave
the spear-furrow, and a space was swept clear before them, and
the cries and yells of the Dusky Men were so fierce and wild that
the rough voices of the Dalesmen were drowned amidst them.

Forth then came every bowman of the kindred that was there
and loosed on the Dusky Men; and they forsooth had some
bowmen amongst them, but cooped up and jostled as they were,
they shot but wildly; whereas each shaft of the Dale went
home truly.

But amongst the bowmen forth came the Bride in her glittering
war-gear, and stepped lightly to the front of the spearmen. Her
own yew bow had been smitten by a shaft and broken in her hand:
so she had caught up a short horn bow and a quiver from one of
the slain of the Dusky Men; and now she knelt on one knee under
the shadow of the spears nigh to her grandsire Hall-ward, and
with a pale face and knitted brow notched and loosed, and notched
and loosed on the throng of foemen, as if she were some daintily
fashioned engine of war.

So fared the battle on the road that went from the south into
the Market-stead. Valiantly had the kindred fought there, and

no man of them had blenched, and much had they won; but the way was perilous before them, for the foe was many and many.

## CHAPTER XLV.   OF FACE-OF-GOD'S ONSLAUGHT.

NOW the banners of the Wolf flapped and rippled over the heads of the Woodlanders and the Men of the Wolf; and the men shot all they might, nor took heed now to cover themselves against the shafts of the Dusky Men. As for these, for all they were so many, their arrow-shot was no great matter, for they were in very evil order, as has been said; and moreover, their rage was so great to come to handy strokes with these foemen, that some of them flung away their bows to brandish the axe or the sword. Nevertheless were some among the kindred hurt or slain by their arrows.

Now stood Face-of-god with the foremost; and from where he stood he could see somewhat of the battle of the Dalesmen, and he wotted that it was thriving; therefore he looked before him and close around him, and noted what was toward there. The space betwixt the houses and the break of the bent was crowded with the fury of the Dusky Men tossing their weapons aloft, crying to each other and at the kindred, and here and there loosing a bow-string on them; but whatever was their rage they might not come a many together past a line within ten fathom of the bent's end; for three hundred of the best of bowmen were shooting at them so ceaselessly that no Dusky man was safe of any bare place of his body, and they fell over one another in that penfold of slaughter, and for all their madness did but little.

Yet was the heart of the War-leader troubled; for he wotted that it might not last for ever, and there seemed no end to the throng of murder-carles; and the time would come when the arrow-shot would be spent, and they must needs come to handy strokes, and that with so many.

Now a voice spake to him as he gazed with knitted brows
and careful heart on that turmoil of battle :

'What now hast thou done with the Sun-beam, and where is
her brother ? Is the Chief of the Wolf skulking when our work
is so heavy? And thou meseemeth art overlate on the field: the
mowing of this meadow is no sluggard's work.'

He turned and beheld Bow-may, and gazed on her face for a
moment, and saw her eyes how they glittered, and how the pommels of her cheeks were burning red and her lips dry and grey;
but before he answered he looked all round about to see what was
to note ; and he touched Bow-may on the shoulder and pointed
to down below where a man of the Felons had just come out of
the court of one of the houses : a man taller than most, very gaily
arrayed, with gilded scales all over him, so that, with his dark
face and blue eyes, he looked like some strange dragon. Bow-
may spake not, but stamped her foot with anger. Yet if her
heart were hot, her hand was steady; for she notched a shaft, and
just as the Dusky Chief raised his axe and brandished it aloft,
she loosed, and the shaft flew and smote the felon in the arm-
pit and the default of the armour, and he fell to earth. But even
as she loosed, Face-of-god cried out in a loud voice:

'O lads of battle ! shoot close and all together. Tarry not,
tarry not ! for we need a little time ere sword meets sword, and
the others of the kindreds are at work ! '

But Bow-may turned round to him and said : 'Wilt thou not
answer me ? Where is thy kindness gone ?'

Even as she was speaking she had notched and loosed another
shaft, speaking as folk do who turn from busy work at loom or
bench.

Then said Face-of-god : 'Shoot on, sister Bow-may! The
Sun-beam is gone with her brother, and he is with the Men of
the Face.'

He broke off here, for a man fell beside him hurt in the neck,
and Face-of-god took his bow from his hands and shot a shaft,

while one of the women who had been hurt also tended the newly-wounded man. Then Face-of-god went on speaking:

' She was unwilling to go, but Folk-might and I constrained her; for we knew that this is the most perilous place of the battle—hah! see those three felons, Bow-may! they are aiming hither.'

And again he loosed and Bow-may also, but a shaft rattled on his helm withal, and another smote a Woodlander beside him, and pierced through the calf of his leg, as he turned and stooped to take fresh arrows from a sheaf that lay there; but the carle took it by the notch and the point, and brake it and drew it out, and then stood up and went on shooting. And Face-of-god spake again:

' Folk-might skulketh not; nor the Men of the Vine, and the Sickle, and the Face, nor the Shepherd-Folk: soon shall they be making our work easy to us, if we can hold our own till then. They are on the other roads that lead into the square. Now suffer me, and shoot on!'

Therewith he looked round about him, and he saw on the left hand that all was quiet; and before him was the confused throng of the Dusky Men trampling their own dead and wounded, and not able as yet to cross that death-line of the arrow so near to them. But on his right hand he saw how they of the kindreds held them firm on the way. Then for a moment of time he considered and thought, till him-seemed he could see the whole battle yet to be foughten; and his face flushed, and he said sharply: ' Bow-may, abide here and shoot, and show the others where to shoot, while the arrows hold out; but we will go further for a while, and ye shall follow when we have made the rent great enough.'

She turned to him and said: ' Why art thou not more joyous? thou art like an host without music or banners.'

' Nay,' said he, ' heed not me, but my bidding!'

She said hastily: ' I think I shall die here; since for all we have shot we minish them nowise. Now kiss me this once amidst the battle, and say farewell.'

345                                                        Y Y

Face-of-god
falleth on to
handy strokes.

He said: 'Nay, nay; it shall not go thus. Abide a little while, and thou shalt see all this tangle open, as the sun cleaveth the clouds on the autumn morning. Yet lo thou! since thou wilt have it so.'

And he bent forward and kissed her face, and now the tears ran over it, and she said smiling somewhat : ' Now is this more than I looked for, whatso may betide.'

But while she was yet speaking he cried in a great voice : ' Ye who have spent your shot, or have nigh spent it, to axe and sword, and follow me to clear the ground 'twixt the bent and the halls. Let each help each, but throng not each other. Shoot wisely, ye bowmen, and keep our backs clear of the foe. On, on ! for the Burg and the Face, for the Burg and the Face !'

Therewith he leapt down the steep of the hill, bounding like the hart, with Dale-warden naked in his hand ; and they that followed were two score and ten ; and the arrows of their bowmen rained over their heads on the Dusky Men, as they smote down the first of the foemen, and the others shrieked and shrank from them, or turned on them smiting wildly and desperately.

But Face-of-god swept round the great sword and plunged into that sea of turmoil and noise and evil sights and savours, and even therewith he heard clearly a voice that said : ' Gold-ring, I am hurt; take my bow a while !' and knew it for Bow-may's; but it came to his ears like the song of a bird without meaning ; for it was as if his life were changed at once ; and in a minute or two he had cut thrice with the edge and thrust twice with the point, eager, but clear-eyed and deft; and he saw as in a picture the foe before him, and the grey roofs of Silver-stead, and through the gap in them the tops of the blue ridges far aloof. And now had three fallen before him, and they feared him, and turned on him, and smote so many together that their strokes crossed each other, and one warded him from the other; and he laughed aloud and shielded himself, and drave the point of Dale-warden amidst the tangle of weapons through the open.

mouth of a captain of the Felons, and slashed a cheek with a back-stroke, and swept round the edge to his right hand and smote off a blue-eyed snub-nosed head; and therewith a pole-axe smote him on the left side of his helm, so that he tottered; but he swung himself round, and stood stark and upright, and gave a short hack with the edge, keeping Dale-warden well in hand, and a gold-clad felon, a champion of them, and their tallest on the ground, fell aback, his throat gaping more than the mouth of him.

Then Face-of-god shouted and waved Dale-warden aloft to the Banner of the Wolf that floated behind and above him, and he cried out: 'As I have promised so have I done!' And he looked about, and beheld how valiantly his fellows had been doing; for before him now was a space of earth with no man standing on his feet thereon, like the swathe of the mowers of June; and beyond that was the crowd of the Dusky Men wavering like the tall grass abiding the scythe.

But a minute, and they fell to casting at Face-of-god and his fellows spears and knives and shields and whatsoever would fly; and a spear smote him on the breast, but entered not; and a bossed shield fell over his face withal, and a plummet of sling-lead smote his helm, and he fell to earth; but leapt up again straightway, and heard as he arose a great shout close to him, and a shrill cry, and lo! at his left side Bow-may, her sword in her hand, and the hand red with blood from a shaft-graze on her wrist, and a white cloth stained with blood about her neck; and on his right side Wood-wise bearing the banner and crying the Wolf-whoop; for the whole company was come down from the slope and stood around him.

Then for a little while was there such a stilling of the tumult about him there, that he heard great and glad cries from the Road of the South of 'The Burg and the Steer! The Dale and the Bridge! The Dale and the Bull!' And thereafter a ter-rible great shrieking cry, and a huge voice that cried: 'Death,

347

death, death to the Dusky Men!' And thereafter again fierce
cries and great tumult of the battle.

Then Face-of-god shook Dale-warden in the air, and strode
forward fiercely, but not speedily, and the whole company went
foot for foot along with him; and as he went, would he or
would he not, song came into his mouth, a song of the meadows
of the Dale, even such as this:

The wheat is done blooming and rust 's on the sickle,
   And green are the meadows grown after the scythe.
Come, hands for the dance! For the toil hath been mickle,
   And 'twixt haysel and harvest 'tis time to be blithe.

And what shall the tale be now dancing is over,
   And kind on the meadow sits maiden by man,
And the old man bethinks him of days of the lover,
   And the warrior remembers the field that he wan?

Shall we tell of the dear days wherein we are dwelling,
   The best days of our Mother, the cherishing Dale,
When all round about us the summer is telling,
   To ears that may hearken, the heart of the tale?

Shall we sing of these hands and these lips that caress us,
   And the limbs that sun-dappled lie light here beside,
When still in the morning they rise but to bless us,
   And oft in the midnight our footsteps abide?

O nay, but to tell of the fathers were better,
   And of how we were fashioned from out of the earth;
Of how the once lowly spurned strong at the fetter;
   Of the days of the deeds and beginning of mirth.

And then when the feast-tide is done in the morning,
   Shall we whet the grey sickle that bideth the wheat,

Till wan grow the edges, and gleam forth a warning
 Of the field and the fallow where edges shall meet.

And when cometh the harvest, and hook upon shoulder
 We enter the red wheat from out of the road,
We shall sing, as we wend, of the bold and the bolder,
 And the Burg of their building, the beauteous abode.

As smiteth the sickle amid the sun's burning
 We shall sing how the sun saw the token unfurled,
When forth fared the Folk, with no thought of returning,
 In the days when the Banner went wide in the world.

Many saw that he was singing, but heard not the words of his
mouth, for great was the noise and clamour. But he heard Bow-
may, how she laughed by his side, and cried out:
 'Gold-mane, dear-heart, now art thou merry indeed; and glad am
I, though they told me that I am hurt.—Ah! now beware, beware!'
 For indeed the Dusky Men, seeing the wall of steel rolling
down on them, and cooped up by the houses, so that they scarce
knew how to flee, turned in the face of death, the foremost of
them, and rushed furiously on the array of the Woodlanders, and
all those behind pressed on them like the big wave of the ebbing
sea when the gust of the wind driveth it landward.
 The Woodlanders met them, shouting out: 'The Greenwood
and the Wolf, the Greenwood and the Wolf!' But not a few
of them fell there, though they gave not back a foot; for so fierce
now were the Dusky Men, that hewing and thrusting at them
availed nought, unless they were slain outright or stunned; and
even if they fell they rolled themselves up against their tall foemen, heeding not death or wounds if they might but slay or
wound. There then fell War-grove and ten others of the Woodlanders, and four men of the Wolf, but none before he had slain
his foeman; and as each man fell or was hurt grievously, another
took his place.

349

Now a felon leapt up and caught Gold-ring by the neck and drew him down, while another strove to smite his head off; but the stout carle drave a wood-knife into the side of the first felon, and drew it out speedily and smote the other, the smiter, in the face with the same knife, and therewith they all three rolled together on the earth amongst the feet of men. Even so did another felon by Bow-may, and dragged her down to the ground, and smote her with a long knife as she tumbled down; and this was a feat of theirs, for they were long-armed like apes.

But as to this felon, Dale-warden's edge split his skull, and Face-of-god gathered his might together and bestrode Bow-may, till he had hewed a space round about him with great two-handed strokes; and yet the blade brake not. Then he caught up Bow-may from the earth, and the felon's knife had not pierced her hauberk, but she was astonied, and might not stand upon her feet; and Face-of-god turned aside a little with her, and half bore her, half thrust her through the throng to the rearward of his folk, and left her there with two carlines of the Wolf who followed the host for leechcraft's sake, and then turned back shouting: 'For the Face, for the Face!' and there followed him back to the battle, a band of those who were fresh as yet, and their blades unbloodied, the young men of the Woodlands.

The wearier fighters made way for them as they came on shouting, and Face-of-god was ahead of them all, and leapt at the foemen as a man unwearied and striking his first stroke, so wondrous hale he was; and they drave a wedge amidst of the Dusky Men, and then turned about and stood back to back hewing at all that drifted on them. But as Face-of-god cleared a space about him, lo! almost within reach of his sword-point up rose a grim shape from the earth, tall, grey-haired, and bloody-faced, who uttered the Wolf-whoop from amidst the terror of his visage, and turned and swung round his head an axe of the Dusky Men, and fell to smiting them with their own weapon. The Dusky Men shrieked in answer to his whoop, and all shrunk from him and Face-of-god; but a cry of joy went up from the kindred, for they knew Gold-ring, whom they deemed had been slain. So they all pressed on together, smiting down the foe before them, and the Dusky Men, some turned their backs and drave those behind them, till they too turned and were strained through the passages and courts of the houses, and some were overthrown and trodden down as they strove to hold face to the Woodlanders, and some were hewn down where they stood; but the whole throng of those that were on their feet drifted toward the Market-place, the Woodlanders following them ever with point and edge, till betwixt the bent and the houses no foeman stood up against them.

Then they stood together, and raised the whoop of victory, and blew their horns long and loud in token of their joy, and the Woodland men lifted up their voices and sang:

> Now far, far aloof
> Standeth lintel and roof,
> The dwelling of days
> Of the Woodland ways:
> Now nought wendeth there
> Save the wolf and the bear,
> And the fox of the waste
> Faring soft without haste.

No carle the axe whetteth on oak-laden hill;
No shaft the hart letteth to wend at his will;
None heedeth the thunder-clap over the glade,
And the wind-storm thereunder makes no man afraid.
Is it thus then that endeth man's days on Mid-earth,
For no man there wendeth in sorrow or mirth?

> Nay, look down on the road
> From the ancient abode!
> Betwixt acre and field
> Shineth helm, shineth shield.

351

And high over the heath
Fares the bane in his sheath;
For the wise men and bold
Go their ways o'er the wold.
Now the Warrior hath given them heart and fair day,
Unbidden, undriven, they fare to the fray.
By the rock and the river the banners they bear,
And their battle-staves quiver 'neath halbert and spear;
On the hill's brow they gather, and hang o'er the Dale
As the clouds of the Father hang, laden with bale.

Down shineth the sun
On the war-deed half done;
All the fore-doomed to die,
In the pale dust they lie.
There they leapt, there they fell,
And their tale shall we tell;
But we, e'en in the gate
Of the war-garth we wait,
Till the drift of war-weather shall whistle us on,
And we tread all together the way to be won,
To the dear land, the dwelling for whose sake we came
To do deeds for the telling of song-becrowned fame.
Settle helm on the head then! Heave sword for the Dale!
Nor be mocked of the dead men for deedless and pale.

## CHAPTER XLVI. MEN MEET IN THE MARKET OF SILVER-STEAD.

SO sang they; but Face-of-god went with Red-wolf, who was
hurt sorely, but not deadly, and led him back toward the place
just under the break of the bent; and there he found Bow-
may in the hands of the women who were tending her hurts. She

smiled on him from a pale face as he drew nigh, and he looked kindly at her, but he might not abide there, for haste was in his feet. He left Red-wolf to the tending of the women, and clomb the bent hastily, and when he deemed he was high enough, he looked about him ; and somewhat more than half an hour had worn since Bow-may had sped the first shaft against the Dusky Men.

He looked down into the Market-stead, and deemed he could see that nigh the Mote-house the Dusky Men were gathering into some better order ; but they were no longer drifting toward the southern bents, but were standing round about the altar as men abiding somewhat ; and he deemed that they had gotten more bowshot than before, and that most of them bare bows. Though so many had been slain in the battles of the southern bents, yet was the Market-stead full of them, so to say, for others had come thereto in place of those that had fallen.

But now as he looked arose mighty clamour amongst them ; and a little west of the Altar was a stir and a hurrying onward and around as in the eddies of a swift stream. Face-of-god wotted not what was betiding there, but he deemed that they were now ware of the onfall of Folk-might and Hall-face and the men of Burgdale, for their faces were all turned to where that was to be looked for.

So he turned and looked on the road to the east of him, where had been the battle of the Steer, but now it was all gone down toward the Market-place, and he could but hear the clamour of it ; but nought he saw thereof, because of the houses that hid it.

Then he cast his eyes on the road that entered the Market-stead from the north, and he saw thereon many men gathered ; and he wotted not what they were ; for though there were weapons amongst them, yet were they not all weaponed, as far as he could see.

Now as he looked this way and that, and deemed that he must tarry no longer, but must enter into the courts of the houses

before him and make his way into the Market-stead, lo! a
change in the throng of Dusky Warriors nigh the Mote-house,
and the ordered bands about the Altar fell to drifting toward
the western way with one accord, with great noise and hurry and
fierce cries of wrath. Then made Face-of-god no delay, but
ran down the bent at once, and at the break of it came upon
Bow-may standing upright and sword in hand; and as he passed,
she joined herself to him, and said: 'What new tidings now,
Gold-mane?'

'Tidings of battle!' he cried; 'tidings of victory! Folk-might
hath fallen on, and the Dusky Men run hastily to meet him.
Hark, hark!'

For as he spoke came a great noise of horns, and Bow-may
said: 'What horn is that blowing?'

He stayed not, but shouted aloud: 'For the Face, for the
Face! Now will we fall upon their backs!'

Therewith was he come to his company, and he cried out to
them: 'Heard ye the horn, heard ye the horn? Now follow me
into the Market-place; much is yet to do!'

Even therewith came the sound of other horns, and all men were
silent a moment, and then shouted all together, for the Woodlanders knew it for the horn of the Shepherds coming on by the
eastward way.

But Face-of-god waved his sword aloft and set on at once, and
they followed and gat them through the courts of the houses and
their passages into the Market-place. There they found more
room than they looked to find; for the foemen had drawn away
on the left hand toward the battle of Folk-might, and on the right
hand toward the battle of the Steer; and great was the noise and
cry that came thence.

Now stood Face-of-god under the two banners of the Wolf in
the Market-place of Silver-stead, and scarce had he time to be high-
hearted, for needs must he ponder in his mind what thing were
best to do. For on the left hand he deemed the foe was the

354

strongest and best ordered; but there also were the kindreds the Face-of-god pondereth which way he shall fall on. doughtiest, and it was little like that the felons should overcome the spear-casters of the Face and the glaive-bearers of the Sickle, and the bowmen of the Vine : there also were the wisest leaders, as the stark elder Stone-face, and the tall Hall-face, and his father of the unshaken heart, and above all Folk-might, fierce in his wrath, but his anger burning steady and clear, like the oaken butt on the hearth of the hall.

Then as his mind pictured him amongst the foe, it made therewith another picture of the slender warrior Sun-beam caught in the tangle of battle, and longing for him and calling for him amidst the hard hand-play. And thereat his face flushed, and all his body waxed hot, and he was on the very point of leading the onset against the foe on the left. But therewith he bethought him of the bold men of the Steer and the Bridge and the Bull weary with much fighting ; and he remembered also that the Bride was amongst them and fighting, it might be, amidst the foremost, and if she were slain how should he ever hold up his head again. He bethought him also that the Shepherds, who had fallen on by the eastern road, valiant as they were, were scarce so well armed or so well led as the others. Therewithal he bethought him (and again it came like a picture into his mind) of falling on the foemen by whom the southern battle was beset, and then the twain of them meeting the Shepherds, and lastly, all those three companies joined together clearing the Market-place, and meeting the men under Folk-might in the midst thereof.

Therefore, scant had he been pondering these things in his mind for a minute ere he cried out : 'Blow up horns, blow up! forward banners, and follow me, O valiant men ! to the helping of the Steer, the Bridge, and the Bull ; deep have they thrust into the Dusky Throng, and belike are hard pressed. Hark how the clamour ariseth from their besetters ! On now, on !'

Therewith hung a star of sunlight on his sword as he raised it aloft, and the Wolf-whoop rang out terribly in the Market-

They fall on
the besetters
of the south-
ern road.

place, for now had the Woodlanders also learned it, and the hearts
of the foemen sank as they heard the might and the mass thereof.
Then the battle of the Woodlanders swept round and fell upon
the flank of them who were besetting the kindreds, as an iron bar
smiteth the soft fir-wood; and they of the kindreds heard their
cry, but faintly and confusedly, so great was the turmoil of battle
about them.

Now once more was Bow-may by the side of Face-of-god;
and if she had not the might of the mightiest, yet had she the
deftness of the deftest. And now was she calm and cool, shield-
ing herself with a copper-bossed target, and driving home the
point of her sharp sword; white was her face, and her eyes
glittered amidst it, and she seemed to men like to those on whose
heads the Warrior hath laid the Holy Bread.

As to Wood-wise, he had given the Banner of the red-jawed
Wolf to Stone-wolf, a huge and dreadful warrior some forty
winters old, who had fought in the Great Overthrow, and now
hewed down the Dusky Men, wielding a heavy short-sword left-
handed. But Wood-wise himself fought with a great sword,
giving great strokes to the right hand and the left, and was no
more hasty than is the hewer in the winter wood.

Face-of-god fought wisely and coldly now, and looked more
to warding his friends than destroying his foes, and both to Bow-
may and Wood-wise his sword was a shield; for oft he took the
life from the edge of the upraised axe, and stayed the point of
the foeman in mid-air.

Even so wisely fought the whole band of the Woodlanders
and the Wolves, who got within smiting space of the foe; for
they had no will to cast away their lives when assured victory
was so nigh to them. Sooth to say, the hand-play was not so
hard to them as it had been betwixt the bent and the houses;
for the Dusky Men were intent on dealing with the men of the
kindreds from the southern road, who stood war-wearied before
them; and they were hewing and casting at them, and baying

and yelling like dogs ; and though they turned about to meet the Evil tidings.
storm of the Woodlanders, yet their hearts failed them withal,
and they strove to edge away from betwixt those two fearful
scythes of war, fighting as men fleeing, not as men in onset.
But still the Woodlanders and the Wolves came on, hewing and
thrusting, smiting down the foemen in heaps, till the Dusky
Throng grew thin, and the staves of the Dalesmen and their
bright banners in the morning sun were clear to see, and at last
their very faces, kindly and familiar, worn and strained with the
stress of battle, or laughing wildly, or pale with the fury of the
fight.    Then rose up to the heavens the blended shout of the
Woodlanders and the Dalesmen, and now there was nought of
foemen betwixt them save the dead and the wounded.

Then Face-of-god thrust his sword into its sheath all bloody
as it was, and strode over the dead men to where Hall-ward stood
under the banner of the Steer, and cast his arms about the old
carle, and kissed him for joy of the victory.    But Hall-ward thrust
him aback and looked him in the face, and his cheeks were pale
and his lips clenched, and his eyes haggard and staring, and he
said in a harsh voice:

'O young man, she is dead! I saw her fall.    The Bride is
dead, and thou hast lost thy troth-plight maiden.    O death, death
to the Dusky Men!'

Then grew Face-of-god as pale as a linen sleeve, and all the
new-comers groaned and cried out.    But a bystander said: 'Nay,
nay, it is nought so bad as that ; she is hurt, and sorely ; but she
liveth yet.'

Face-of-god heard him not.    He forgot Dale-warden lying
in his sheath, and he saw that the last speaker had a great wood-
axe broad and heavy in his hand, so he cried : ' Man, man, thine
axe!' and snatched it from him, and turned about to the foe
again, and thrust through the ranks, suffering none to stay him
till all his friends were behind and all his foes before him.    And
as he burst forth from the ranks waving his axe aloft, bare-headed

357

now, his yellow hair flying abroad, his mouth crying out, 'Death, death, death to the Dusky Men!' fear of him smote their hearts, and they howled and fled before him as they might; for they said that the Dalesmen had prayed their Gods into the battle. But not so fast could they flee but he was presently amidst them, smiting down all about him, and they so terror-stricken that scarce might they raise a hand against him. All that blended host followed him mad with wrath and victory, and as they pressed on, they heard behind them the horns and war-cries of the Shepherds falling on from the east. Nought they heeded that now, but drave on a fearful storm of war, and terrible was the slaughter of the Felons.

It was but a few minutes ere they had driven them up against that great stack of faggots that had been dight for the burnt-offering of men, and many of the felons had mounted up on to it, and now in their anguish of fear were shooting arrows and casting spears on all about them, heeding little if they were friend or foe. Now were the men of the kindreds at point to climb this twiggen burg; but by this time the fury of Face-of-god had run clear, and he knew where he was and what he was doing; so he stayed his folk, and cried out to them: 'Forbear, climb not! let the torch help the sword!' And therewith he looked about and saw the fire-pot which had been set down there for the kindling of the bale-fire, and the coals were yet red in it; so he snatched up a dry brand and lighted it thereat, and so did divers others, and they thrust them among the faggots, and the fire caught at once, and the tongues of flame began to leap from faggot to faggot till all was in a light low; for the wood had been laid for that very end, and smeared with grease and oil so that the burning to the god might be speedy.

But the fierceness of the kindreds heeded not the fire, nor over-much the men who leapt down from the stack before it, but they left all behind them, faring straight toward the western outgate from the Market-stead; and Face-of-god still led them on;

though by now he was wholly come to his right mind again, albeit the burden of sorrow yet lay heavy on his heart. He had broken his axe, and had once more drawn Dale-warden from his sheath, and many felt his point and edge.

But now, as they chased, came a rush of men upon them again, as though a new onset were at hand. That saw Face-of-god and Hall-ward and War-well, and other wise leaders of men, and they bade their folk forbear the chase, and lock their ranks to meet the onfall of this new wave of foemen. And they did so, and stood fast as a wall; but lo! the onrush that drave up against them was but a fleeing shrieking throng, and no longer an array of warriors, for many had cast away their weapons, and were rushing they knew not whither; for they were being thrust on the bitter edges of Face-of-god's companies by the terror of the fleers from the onset of the men of the Face, the Sickle, and the Vine, whom Hall-face and Stone-face were leading, along with Folk-might. Then once again the men of Face-of-god gave forth the whoop of victory, and pressed forward again, hewing their way through the throng of fleers, but turning not to chase to the right or the left; while at their backs came on the Shepherd-folk, who had swept down all that withstood them; for now indeed was the Market-stead getting thinner of living men.

So led the War-leader his ordered ranks, till at last over the tangled crowd of runaways he saw the banners of the Burg and the Face flashing against the sun, and heard the roar of the kindreds as they drave the chase towards them. Then he lifted up his sword, and stood still, and all the host behind him stayed and cast a huge shout up to the heavens, and there they abode the coming of the other Dalesmen.

But the War-leader sent a message to Hound-under-Greenbury, bidding him lead the Shepherds to the chase of the Dusky Men, who were now all fleeing toward the northern outgate of the Market. Howbeit he called to mind the throng he had seen on the northern road before they were come into the Market-

359

stead, and deemed that way also death awaited the foemen, even
if the men of the kindreds forbore them.

But presently the space betwixt the Woodlanders and the men
of the Face was clear of all but the dead, so that friend saw the
face of friend; and it could be seen that the warriors of the Face
were ruddy and smiling for joy, because the battle had been easy
to them, and but few of them had fallen; for the Dusky Men,
who had left the Market-stead to fall on them, had had room for
fleeing behind them, and had speedily turned their backs before
the spear-casting of the men of the Face and the onrush of the
swordsmen.

There then stood these victorious men facing one another, and
the banner-bearers on either side came through the throng, and
brought the banners together between the two hosts; and the
Wolf kissed the Face, and the Sickle and the Vine met the Steer
and the Bridge and the Bull: but the Shepherds were yet chasing
the fleers.

There in the forefront stood Hall-face the tall, with the joy of
battle in his eyes. And Stone-face, the wise carle in war, stood
solemn and stark beside him; and there was the goodly body
and the fair and kindly visage of the Alderman smiling on the
faces of his friends. But as for Folk-might, his face was yet
white and aweful with anger, and he looked restlessly up and
down the front of the kindreds, though he spake no word.

Then Face-of-god could no longer forbear, but he thrust Dale-
warden into his sheath, and ran forward and cast his arms about
his father's neck and kissed him; and the blood of himself and
of the foemen was on him, for he had been hurt in divers places,
but not sorely, because of the good hammer-work of the Alderman.

Then he kissed his brother and Stone-face, and he took Folk-
might by the hand, and was on the point of speaking some word
to him, when the ranks of the Face opened, and lo! the Sun-
beam in her bright war-gear, and the sword girt to her side, and
she unhurt and unsullied.

Then was it to him as when he met her first in Shadowy
Vale, and he thought of little else than her; but she stepped
lightly up to him, and unashamed before the whole host she
kissed him on the mouth, and he cast his mailed arms about her,
and joy made him forget many things and what was next to do,
though even at that moment came afresh a great clamour of
shrieks and cries from the northern outgate of the Market-stead :
and the burning pile behind them cast a great wavering flame
into the air, contending with the bright sun of that fair day, now
come hard on noontide. But ere he drew away his face from
the Sun-beam's, came memory to him, and a sharp pang shot
through his heart, as he heard Folk-might say : ' Where then is
the Shield-may of Burgstead? where is the Bride?'

And Face-of-god said under his breath : ' She is dead, she is
dead!' And then he stared out straight before him and waited
till someone else should say it aloud. But Bow-may stepped
forward and said : ' Chief of the Wolf, be of good cheer ; our
kinswoman is hurt, but not deadly.'

The Alderman's face changed, and he said : ' Hast thou seen
her, Bow-may?'

' Nay,' she said. ' How should I leave the battle? but others
have told me who have seen her.'

Folk-might stared into the ranks of men before him, but said
nothing. Said the Alderman : ' Is she well tended?'

' Yea, surely,' said Bow-may, ' since she is amongst friends,
and there are no foemen behind us.'

Then came a voice from Folk-might which said : 'Now were it
best to send good men and deft in arms, and who know Silver-dale,
from house to house, to search for foemen who may be lurking there.'

The Alderman looked kindly and sadly on him and said :
' Kinsman Stone-face, and Hall-face my son, the brunt of the
battle is now over, and I am but a simple man amongst you ;
therefore, if ye will give me leave, I will go see this poor kinswoman of ours, and comfort her.'

361                                        3 A

They bade him go: so he sheathed his sword, and went through the press with two men of the Steer toward the southern road; for the Bride had been brought into a house nigh the corner of the Market-place.

But Face-of-god looked after his father as he went, and remembrance of past days came upon him, and such a storm of grief swept over him, as he thought of the Bride lying pale and bleeding and brought anigh to her death, that he put his hands to his face and wept as a child that will not be comforted; nor had he any shame of all those bystanders, who in sooth were men good and kindly, and had no shame of his grief or marvelled at it, for indeed their own hearts were sore for their lovely kins-woman, and many of them also wept with Face-of-god. But the Sun-beam stood by and looked on her betrothed, and she thought many things of the Bride, and was sorry, albeit no tears came into her eyes; then she looked askance at Folk-might and trembled; but he said coldly, and in a loud voice:

'Needs must we search the houses for the lurking felons, or many a man will yet be murdered. Let Wood-wicked lead a band of men at once from house to house.'

Then said a man of the Wolf hight Hardgrip: 'Wood-wicked was slain betwixt the bent and the houses.'

Said Folk-might: 'Let it be Wood-wise then.'

But Bow-may said: 'Wood-wise is even now hurt in the leg by a wounded felon, and may not go afoot.'

Then said Folk-might: 'Is Crow the Shaft-speeder anigh?'

'Yea, here am I,' quoth a tall man of fifty winters, coming from out the ranks where stood the Wolves.

Said Folk-might: 'Kinsman Crow, do thou take two score and ten of doughty men who are not too hot-headed, and search every house about the Market-place; but if ye come on any house that makes a stout defence, send ye word thereof to the Mote-house, where we will presently be, and we shall send you help. Slay every felon that ye fall in with; but if ye find in the

362

houses any of the poor folk crouching and afraid, comfort their hearts all ye may, and tell them that now is life come to them.'

So Crow fell to getting his band together, and presently departed with them on his errand.

## CHAPTER XLVII. THE KINDREDS WIN THE MOTE-HOUSE.

THE din and tumult still came from the north side of the Market-place, so that all the air was full of noise; and Face-of-god deemed that the thralls had gotten weapons into their hands and were slaying their masters.

Now he lifted up his face, and put his hand on Folk-might's shoulder, and said in a loud voice:

'Kinsmen, it were well if our brother were to bid the banners into the Mote-house of the Wolf, and let all the Host set itself in array before the said house, and abide till the chasers of the foe come to us thither; for I perceive that they are now become many, and are more than those of our kindred.'

Then Folk-might looked at him with kind eyes, and said:

'Thou sayest well, brother; even so let it be!'

And he lifted up his sword, and Face-of-god cried out in a loud voice: 'Forward, banners! blow up horns! fare we forth with victory!'

So the Host drew its ranks together in good order, and they all set forward, and old Stone-face took the Sun-beam by the hand and led on behind Folk-might and the War-leader. But when they came to the Hall, then saw they how the steps that led up to the door were high and double, going up from each side without any railing or fool-guard; and crowding the stairs and the platform thereof was a band of the Dusky Men, as many as could stand thereon, who shot arrows at the host of the kindreds, howling like dogs, and chattering like apes; and arrows and

363

spears came from the windows of the Hall ; yea, and on the very roof a score of these felons were riding the ridge and mocking like the trolls of old days.

Now when they saw this they stayed a while, and men shielded them against the shafts ; but the leaders drew together in front of the Host, and Folk-might fell to speech ; and his face was very pale and stern; for now he had had time to think of the case of the Bride, and fierce wrath, and grief unholpen filled his soul.  So he said:

' Brothers, this is my business to deal with ; for I see before me the stair that leadeth to the Mote-house of my people, and now would I sit there whereas my fathers sat, when peace was on the Dale, as once more it shall be to-morrow.  Therefore up this stair will I go, and none shall hinder me ; and let no man of the host follow me till I have entered into the Hall, unless perchance I fall dead by the way ; but stand ye still and look on.'

' Nay,' said Face-of-god, ' this is partly the business of the War-leader.  There are two stairs.  Be content to take the southern one, and I will take the northern.  We shall meet on the plain stone at the top.'

But Hall-face said : ' War-leader, may I speak ? '

' Speak, brother,' said Face-of-god.

Said Hall-face : ' I have done but little to-day, War-leader.  I would stand by thee on the northern stair ; so shall Folk-might be content, if he doeth two men's work who are not little-hearted.'

Said Face-of-god: 'The doom of the War-leader is that Folk-might shall fall on by the southern stair to slake his grief and increase his glory, and Face-of-god and Hall-face by the northern. Haste to the work, O brothers !

And he and Hall-face went to their places, while all looked on.  But the Sun-beam, with her hand still in Stone-face's, she turned white to the lips, and stared with wild eyes before her, not knowing where she was ; for she had deemed that the battle was over, and Face-of-god saved from it.

But Folk-might tossed up his head and laughed, and cried out, 'At last, at last!' And his sword was in his hand, the Sleep-thorn to wit, a blade of ancient fame; so now he let it fall and hang to his wrist by the leash, while he clapped his hands together and uttered the Wolf-whoop mightily, and all the men of the Wolf that were in the host, and the Woodlanders withal, uttered it with him. Then he put his shield over his head and stood before the first of the steps, and the Dusky Men laughed to see one man come against them, though there was death in their hearts. But he laughed back at them in triumph, and set his foot on the step, and let Sleep-thorn's point go into the throat of a Dusky lord, and thrust amongst them, hewing right and left, and tumbling men over the edge of the stair, which was to them as the narrow path along the cliff-side that hangeth over the unfathomed sea. They hewed and thrust at him in turn; but so close were they packed that their weapons crossed about him, and one shielded him from the other, and they swayed staggering on that fearful verge, while the Sleep-thorn crept here and there amongst them, lulling their hot fury. For, as desperate as they were, and fighting for death and not for life, they had a horror of him and of the sea of hatred below them, and feared where to set their feet, and he feared nought at all, but from feet to sword-point was but an engine of slaughter, while the heart within him throbbed with fury long held back as he thought upon the Bride and her wounding, and all the wrongs of his people since their Great Undoing.

So he smote and thrust, till him-seemed the throng of foes thinned before him: with his sword-pommel he smote a lord of the Dusky Ones in the face, so that he fell over the edge amongst the spears of the kindred; then he thrust the point of Sleep-thorn towards the Hall-door through the breast of another, and then it seemed to him that he had but one before him; so he hove up the edges to cleave him down, but ere the stroke fell, close to his ears exceeding loud rang out the cry, 'For the Burg and the Face! for the Face, for the Face!' and he drew aback a little, and his eyes

365

cleared, and lo! it was Hall-face the tall, his long sword all reddened with battle; and beside him stood Face-of-god, silent and
panting, his face pale with the fierce anger of the fight, and the
weariness which was now at last gaining upon him. There stood
those three with no other living man upon the plain of the stairs.

Then Face-of-god turned shouting to the Folk, and cried:

'Forth now with the banners! For now is the Wolf come
home. On into the Hall, O Kindred of the Gods!'

Then poured the Folk up over the stairs and into the Hall of
the Wolf, the banners flapping over their heads; and first went
the War-leader and Folk-might and Hall-face, and then the
three delivered thralls, Wolf-stone, God-swain, and Spear-fist,
and Dallach with them, though both he and Wolf-stone had been hurt
in the battle; and then came blended together the Men of the Face
along with them of the Wolf who had entered the Market-stead
with them, and with these were Stone-face and Wood-wont and
Bow-may, leading the Sun-beam betwixt them; and now was
she come to herself again, though her face was yet pale, and her
eyes gleamed as she stepped across the threshold of the Hall.

But when a many were gotten in, and the first-comers had had
time to handle their weapons and look about them, a cry of the
utmost wrath broke from Folk-might and those others who remembered the Hall from of old. For wretched and befouled was
that well-builded house: the hangings rent away; the goodly
painted walls daubed and smeared with wicked tokens of the Alien
murderers: the floor, once bright with polished stones of the
mountain, and strewn with sweet-smelling flowers, was now as
foul as the den of the man-devouring troll of the heaths. From
the fair-carven roof of oak and chestnut-beams hung ugly
knots of rags and shapeless images of the sorcery of the Dusky
Men. And furthermore, and above all, from the last tie-beam of
the roof over the daïs dangled four shapes of men-at-arms, whom
the older men of the Wolf knew at once for the embalmed bodies
of their four great chieftains, who had been slain on the day of the

366

Great Undoing; and they cried out with horror and rage as they saw them hanging there in their weapons as they had lived.
There was the Hostage of the Earth, his shield painted with the green world circled with the worm of the sea. There was the older Folk-might, the uncle of the living man, bearing a shield with an oak and a lion done thereon. There was Wealth-eker, on whose shield was done a golden sheaf of wheat. There was he who bore a name great from of old, Folk-wolf to wit, bearing on his shield the axe of the hewer. There they hung, dusty, befouled, with sightless eyes and grinning mouths, in the dimmed sunlight of the Hall, before the eyes of that victorious Host, stricken silent at the sight of them.

Underneath them on the daïs stood the last remnant of the battle of the Dusky Men; and they, as men mad with coming death, shook their weapons, and with shrieking laughter mocked at the overcomers, and pointed to the long-dead chiefs, and called on them in the tongue of the kindreds to come down and lead their dear kinsmen to the high-seat; and then they cried out to the living warriors of the Wolf, and bade them better their deed of slaying, and set to work to make alive again, and cause their kinsmen to live merry on the earth.

With that last mock they handled their weapons and rushed howling on the warriors to meet their death; nor was it long denied them; for the sword of the Wolf, the axe of the Woodland, and the spear of the Dale soon made an end of the dreadful lives of these destroyers of the Folks.


CHAPTER XLVIII. MEN SING IN THE MOTE-HOUSE.

THEN strode the Warriors of the Wolf over the bodies of the slain on to the daïs of their own Hall; and Folk-might led the Sun-beam by the hand, and now was his sword in its sheath, and his face was grown calm, though it was stern and sad. But even as he trod the daïs comes a slim swain of the Wolves twisting himself through the throng, and so maketh way to Folk-might, and saith to him:

'Chieftain, the Alderman of Burgdale sendeth me hither to say a word to thee; even this, which I am to tell to thee and the War-leader both: It is most true that our kinswoman the Bride will not die, but live. So help me, the Warrior and the Face! This is the word of the Alderman.'

When Folk-might heard this, his face changed and he hung his head; and Face-of-god, who was standing close by, beheld him and deemed that tears were falling from his eyes on to the hall-floor. As for him, he grew exceeding glad, and he turned to the Sun-beam and met her eyes, and saw that she could scarce refrain her longing for him; and he was abashed for the sweetness of his love. But she drew close up to him, and spake to him softly and said:

'This is the day that maketh amends; and yet I long for another day. When I saw thee coming to me that first day in Shadowy Vale, I thought thee so goodly a warrior that my heart was in my mouth. But now how goodly thou art! For the battle is over, and we shall live.'

'Yea,' said Face-of-god, 'and none shall begrudge us our love. Behold thy brother, the hard-heart, the warrior; he weepeth because he hath heard that the Bride shall live. Be sure then that she shall not gainsay him. O fair shall the world be to-morrow!'

But she said: 'O Gold-mane, I have no words. Is there no minstrelsy amongst us?'

Now by this time were many of the men of the Wolf and the Woodlanders gathered on the daïs of the Hall; and the Dalesmen noting this, and wotting that these men were now in their own Mote-house, withdrew them as they might for the press toward the nether end thereof. That the Sun-beam noted, and that all those about her save the War-leader were of the kin-

368

dreds of the Wolf and the Woodland, and, still speaking softly, she said to Face-of-god :

'Gold-mane, meseemeth I am now in my wrong place; for now the Wolf raiseth up his head, but I am departing from him. Surely I should now be standing amongst my people of the Face, whereto I am going ere long.'

He said: 'Beloved, I am now become thy kindred and thine home, and it is meet for thee to stand beside me.'

She cast her eyes adown and answered not; and she fell a-pondering of how sorely she had desired that fair dale, and now she would leave it, and be content and more than content.

But now the kindreds had sundered, they upon the daïs ranked themselves together there in the House which their fathers had builded; and when they saw themselves so meetly ordered, their hearts being full with the sweetness of hope accomplished and the joy of deliverance from death, song arose amongst them, and they fell to singing together; and this is somewhat of their singing :

> Now raise we the lay
> Of the long-coming day!
> Bright, white was the sun
> When we saw it begun :
> O'er its noon now we live;
> It hath ceased not to give ;
> It shall give, and give more
> From the wealth of its store.

O fair was the yesterday ! Kindly and good
Was the wasteland our guester, and kind was the wood;
Though below us for reaping lay under our hand
The harvest of weeping, the grief of the land ;
Dumb cowered the sorrow, nought daring to cry
On the help of to-morrow, the deed drawing nigh.

All increase throve
In the Dale of our love;
There the ox and the steed
Fed down the mead;
The grapes hung high
'Twixt earth and sky,
And the apples fell
Round the orchard well.
Yet drear was the land there, and all was for nought;
None put forth a hand there for what the year wrought,
And raised it o'erflowing with gifts of the earth.
For man's grief was growing beside of the mirth
Of the springs and the summers that wasted their wealth;
And the birds, the new-comers, made merry by stealth.

Yet here of old
Abode the bold;
Nor had they wailed
Though the wheat had failed,
And the vine no more
Gave forth her store.
Yea, they found the waste good
For the fearless of mood.
Then to these, that were dwelling aloof from the Dale,
Fared the wild-wind a-telling the worst of the tale;
As men bathed in the morning they saw in the pool
The image of scorning, the throne of the fool.
The picture was gleaming in helm and in sword,
And shone forth its seeming from cups of the board.

Forth then they came
With the battle-flame;
From the Wood and the Waste
And the Dale did they haste:

370

They saw the storm rise,
And with untroubled eyes
The war-storm they met ;
And the rain ruddy-wet.
O'er the Dale then was litten the Candle of Day,
Night-sorrow was smitten, and gloom fled away.
How the grief-shackles sunder ! How many to morn
Shall awaken and wonder how gladness was born !
O wont unto sorrow, how sweet unto you
Shall be pondering to-morrow what deed is to do !

They sing of
their slain.

Fell many a man
'Neath the edges wan,
In the heat of the play
That fashioned the day.
Praise all ye then
The death of men,
And the gift of the aid
Of the unafraid !
O strong are the living men mighty to save,
And good is their giving, and gifts that we have !
But the dead, they that gave us once, never again ;
Long and long shall they save us sore trouble and pain.
O Banner above us, O God of the strong,
Love them as ye love us that bore down our wrong !

So they sang in the Hall; and there was many a man wept,
as the song ended, for those that should never see the good days
of the Dale, and all the joy that was to be ; and men swore, by
all that they loved, that they would never forget those that had
fallen in the Winning of Silver-dale ; and that when each year the
Cups of Memory went round, they should be no mere names to
them, but the very men whom they had known and loved.

371

## CHAPTER XLIX. DALLACH FARETH TO ROSE-DALE: CROW TELLETH OF HIS ERRAND: THE KINDREDS EAT THEIR MEAT IN SILVER-DALE.

Dallach would follow hard on the fleers.

NOW Dallach, who had gone away for a while, came back again into the Hall; and at his back were a half score of men who bore ladders with them: they were stout men, clad in scanty and ragged raiment, but girt with swords and bearing axes, those of them who were not handling the ladders. Men looked on them curiously, because they saw them to be of the roughest of the thralls. They were sullen and fierce-eyed to behold, and their hands and bare arms were flecked with blood; and it was easy to see that they had been chasing the fleers, and making them pay for their many torments of past days.

But when Face-of-god beheld this he cried out: ' Ho, Dallach! is it so that thou hast bethought thee to bring in hither men to fall to the cleansing of the Hall, and to do away the defiling of the Dusky Men?'

' Even so, War-leader,' said Dallach; ' also ye shall know that all battle is over in Silver-stead; for the thralls fell in numbers not to be endured on the Dusky Men who had turned their backs to us, and hindered them from fleeing north. But though they have slain many, they have not slain all, and the remnant have fled by divers ways westaway, that they may gain the wood and the ways to Rose-dale; and the stoutest of the thralls are at their heels, and ever as they go fresh men from the fields join in the chase with great joy. I have gathered together of the best of them two hundreds and a half well-armed; and if thou wilt give me leave, I will get to me yet more, and follow hard on the fleers, and so get me home to Rose-dale; for thither will these runaways to meet whatso of their kind may be left there. Also I would fain be there to set some order amongst the poor folk of mine own people, whom this day's work hath delivered from torment.    And if thou wilt suffer a few men of the Folk-might would go an errand. Dalesmen to come along with me, then shall all things be better done there.'

'Luck go with thine hands!' said Face-of-god. 'Take whomso thou wilt of the Burgdalers that have a mind to fare with thee to the number of five score; and send word of thy thriving to Folk-might, the chieftain of the Dale; as for us, meseemeth that we shall abide here no long while.    How sayest thou, Folk-might, shall Dallach go?'

Then Folk-might, who stood close beside him, looked up and reddened somewhat, as a man caught heedless when he should be heedful; but he looked kindly on Face-of-god, and said:

'War-leader, so long as thou art in the Dale which ye kindreds have won back for us, thou art the chieftain, and no other, and I bid thee do as thou wilt in this matter, and in all things; and I hereby give command to all my kindred to do according to thy will everywhere and always, as they love me; and indeed I deem that thy will shall be theirs; since it is only fools who know not their well-wishers.    How say ye, kinsmen?'

Then those about cried out: 'Hail to Face-of-god! Hail to the Dalesmen! Hail to our friends!'

But Folk-might went up to Face-of-god, and threw his arms about him and kissed him, and he said therewithal, so that most men heard him:

'Herewith I kiss not only thee, thou goodly and glorious warrior! but this kiss and embrace is for all the men of the kindreds of the Dale and the Shepherds; since I deem that never have men more valiant dwelt upon the earth.'

Therewith all men shouted for joy of him, and were exceeding glad; but Folk-might spake apart to Face-of-god and said: 'Brother, I suppose that thou wilt deem it good to abide in this Hall or anigh it; for hereabouts now is the heart of the Host. But as for me, I would have leave to depart for a little; since I have an errand, whereof thou mayest wot.'

373

Crow telleth
of the clearing
of the houses.

Then Face-of-god smiled on him, and said : ' Go, and all good go with thee; and tell my father that I would have tidings, since I may not be there.' So he spake; yet in his heart was he glad that he might not go to behold the Bride lying sick and sorry. But Folk-might departed without more words; and in the door of the Hall he met Crow the Shaft-speeder, who would have spoken to him, and given him the tidings; but Folk-might said to him : ' Do thine errand to the War-leader, who is within the Hall.' And so went on his way.

Then came Crow up the Hall, and stood before Face-of-god and said : ' War-leader, we have done that which was to be done, and have cleared all the houses about the Market-stead. Moreover, by the rede of Dallach we have set certain men of the poor folk of the Dale, who are well looked to by the others, to the burying of the slain felons ; and they be digging trenches in the fields on the north side of the Market-stead, and carry the carcasses thither as they may. But the slain whom they find of the kindreds do they array out yonder before this Hall. In all wise are these men tame and biddable, save that they rage against the Dusky Men, though they fear them yet. As for us, they deem us Gods come down from heaven to help them. So much for what is good: now have I an ill word to say; to wit, that in the houses whereas we have found many thralls alive, yet also have we found many dead; for amongst these murder-carles were some of an evil sort, who, when they saw that the battle would go against them, rushed into the houses hewing down all before them—man, woman, and child ; so that many of the halls and chambers we saw running blood like to shambles. To be short: of them whom they were going to hew to the Gods, we have found thirteen living and three dead, of which latter is one woman ; and of the living, seven women; and allt hese, living and dead, with the leaden shackles yet on them wherein they should be burned. To all these and others whom we have found, we have done what of service we could in the way of victual and clothes, so that they scarce believe that they are on this lower earth. Moreover, I have with me two score of them, who are men of some wits, and who know of the stores of victual and other wares which the felons had, and these will fetch and carry for you as much as ye will. Is all done rightly, War-leader?'

'Right well,' said Face-of-god, 'and we give thee our thanks therefor. And now it were well if these thy folk were to dight our dinner for us in some green field the nighest that may be, and thither shall all the Host be bidden by sound of horn. Meantime, let us void this Hall till it be cleansed of the filth of the Dusky Ones; but hereafter shall we come again to it, and light a fire on the Holy Hearth, and bid the Gods and the Fathers come back and behold their children sitting glad in the ancient Hall.'

Then men shouted and were exceeding joyous; but Face-of-god said once more: 'Bear ye a bench out into the Market-place over against the door of this Hall: thereon will I sit with other chieftains of the kindreds, that whoso will may have recourse to us.'

So therewith all the men of the kindreds made their ways out of the Hall and into the Market-stead, which was by this time much cleared of the slaughtered felons; and the bale for the burnt-offering was now but smouldering, and a thin column of blue smoke was going up wavering amidst the light airs of the afternoon. Men were somewhat silent now; for they were stiff and weary with the morning's battle; and a many had been hurt withal; and on many there yet rested the after-grief of battle, and sorrow for the loss of friends and well-wishers.

For in the battle had fallen one long hundred and two of the men of the Host; and of these were two score and five of the kindreds of the Steer, the Bull, and the Bridge, who had made such valiant onslaught by the southern road. Of the Shepherds died one score save three; for though they scattered the foe at once, yet they fell on with such headlong valour, rather than wisely, that many were trapped in the throng of the Dusky Men.

375

Of the Woodlanders were slain one score and nine; for hard had been the fight about them, and no man of them spared himself one whit. Of the men of the Wolf, who were but a few, fell sixteen men, and all save two of these in Face-of-god's battle. Of the Burgdale men whom Folk-might led, to wit, them of the Face, the Vine, and the Sickle, were but seven men slain outright. In this tale are told all those who died of their hurts after the day of battle. Therewithal many others were sorely hurt who mended, and went about afterwards hale and hearty.

So as the folk abode in the Market-place, somewhat faint and weary, they heard horns blow up merrily, and Crow the Shaft-speeder came forth and stood on the mound of the altar, and bade men fare to dinner, and therewith he led the way, bearing in his hand the banner of the Golden Bushel, of which House he was; and they followed him into a fair and great mead on the south-west of Silver-stead, besprinkled about with ancient trees of sweet chestnut. There they found the boards spread for them with the best of victual which the poor down-trodden folk knew how to dight for them; and especially was there great plenty of good wine of the sun-smitten bents.

So they fell to their meat, and the poor folk, both men and women, served them gladly, though they were somewhat afeard of these fierce sword-wielders, the Gods who had delivered them. The said thralls were mostly not of those who had fallen so bitterly on their fleeing masters, but were men and women of the households, not so roughly treated as the others, that is to say, those who had been wont to toil under the lash in the fields and the silver-mines, and were as wild as they durst be.

As for these waiting-thralls, the men of the kindreds were gentle and blithe with them, and often as they served them would they stay their hands (and especially if they were women), and would draw down their heads to put a morsel in their mouths, or set the wine-cup to their lips; and they would stroke them and caress them, and treat them in all wise as their dear friends. Moreover,

376

when any man was full, he would arise and take hold of one of They make the poor folk feast. the thralls, and set him in his place, and serve him with meat and drink, and talk with him kindly, so that the poor folk were much bewildered with joy. And the first that arose from table were the Sun-beam and Bow-may and Hall-face, with many of the swains and the women of the Woodlanders; and they went from table to table serving the others.

The Sun-beam had done off her armour, and went about exceeding fair and lovely in her kirtle ; but Bow-may yet bore her hauberk, for she loved it, and indeed it was so fine and well-wrought that it was no great burden. Albeit she had gone down with the Sun-beam and other women to a fair stream thereby, and there had they bathed and washed themselves ; and Bow-may's hurts, which were not great, had been looked to and bound up afresh, and she had come to table unhelmed, with a wreath of wind-flowers round her head.

There then they feasted ; and their hearts were strengthened by the meat and drink ; and if sorrow were blended with their joy, yet were they high-hearted through both joy and sorrow, looking forward to the good days to be in the Dales at the Roots of the Mountains, and the love and fellowship of Folks and of Houses.

But as for Face-of-god, he went not to the meadow, but abode sitting on the bench in the Market-place, where were none else now of the kindreds save the appointed warders. They had brought him a morsel and a cup of wine, and he had eaten and drunk ; and now he sat there with Dale-warden lying sheathed across his knees, and seeming to gaze on the thralls of Silver-dale busied in carrying away the bodies of the slain felons, after they had stripped them of their raiment and weapons. Yet indeed all this was before his eyes as a picture which he noted not. Rather he sat pondering many things ; wondering at his being there in Silver-dale in the hour of victory; longing for the peace of Burgdale and the bride-chamber of the Sun-beam. Then went his thought out toward his old playmate lying hurt in Silver-

dale ; and his heart was grieved because of her, yet not for long,
though his thought still dwelt on her; since he deemed that she
would live and presently be happy—and happy thenceforward
for many years. So pondered Face-of-god in the Market-place
of Silver-dale.


CHAPTER L.   FOLK-MIGHT SEETH THE BRIDE AND
SPEAKETH WITH HER.

NOW tells the tale of Folk-might, that he went his ways
from the Hall to the house where the Bride lay ; and the
swain who had brought the message went along with him,
and he was proud of walking beside so mighty a warrior, and he
talked to Folk-might as they went ; and the sound of his voice
was irksome to the chieftain, but he made as though he hearkened. Yet when they came to the door of the house, which was
just out of the Place on the Southern road (for thereby had the
Bride fallen to earth), he could withhold his grief no longer, but
turned on the threshold and laid his head on the door-jamb, and
sobbed and wept till the tears fell down like rain. And the boy
stood by wondering, and wishing that Folk-might would forbear
weeping, but durst not speak to him.

In a while Folk-might left weeping and went in, and found a
fair hall sore befouled by the felons, and in the corner on a bed
covered with furs the wounded woman ; and at first sight he
deemed her not so pale as he looked to see her, as she lay with
her long dark-red hair strewed over the pillow, her head moving
about wearily. A linen cloth was thrown over her body, but
her arms lay out of it before her. Beside her sat the Alderman,
his face sober enough, but not as one in heavy sorrow ; and anigh
him was another chair as if someone had but just got up from it.
There was no one else in the hall save two women of the Woodlanders, one of whom was cooking some potion on the hearth, and

378

another was sweeping the floor anigh of bran or some such stuff,
which had been thrown down to sop up the blood.

So Folk-might went up to the Bride, sorely dreading the image
of death which she had grown to be, and sorely loving the woman
she was and would be.

He knelt down by the bedside, heeding Iron-face little, though
he nodded friendly to him, and he held his face close to hers;
but she had her eyes shut and did not open them till he had been
there a little while; and then they opened and fixed themselves
on his without surprise or change. Then she lifted her right hand
(for it was in her left shoulder and side that she had been hurt)
and slowly laid it on his head, and drew his face to hers and
kissed it fondly, as she both smiled and let the tears run over
from her eyes. Then she spake in a weak voice :

' Thou seest, chieftain and dear friend, that I may not stand
by thy victorious side to-day. And now, though I were fain if
thou wouldst never leave me, yet needs must thou go about thy
work, since thou art become the Alderman of the Folk of Silver-
dale. Yea, and even if thou wert not to go from me, yet in a
manner should I go from thee. For I am grievously hurt, and I
know by myself, and also the leeches have told me, that the fever
is a-coming on me ; so that presently I shall not know thee, but
may deem thee to be a woman, or a hound, or the very Wolf that
is the image of the Father of thy kindred; or even, it may be,
someone else—that I have played with time agone.'

Her voice faltered and faded out here, and she was silent a
while ; then she said :

' So depart, kind friend and dear love, bearing this word with
thee, that should I die, I call on Iron-face my kinsman to bear
witness that I bid thee carry me to bale in Silver-dale, and lay
mine ashes with the ashes of thy Fathers, with whom thine own
shall mingle at the last, since I have been of the warriors who
have helped to bring thee aback to the land of thy folk.'

Then she smiled and shut her eyes and said : ' And if I live,

379

as indeed I hope, and how glad and glad I shall be to live, then shalt thou bring me to thy house and thy bed, that I may not depart from thee while both our lives last.'

And she opened her eyes and looked at him ; and he might not speak for a while, so ravished as he was betwixt joy and sorrow.  But the Alderman arose and took a gold ring from off his arm, and spake :

' This is the gold ring of the God of the Face, and I bear it on mine arm betwixt the Folk and the God in all man-motes, and I bore it through the battle to-day ; and it is as holy a ring as may be ; and since ye are plighting troth, and I am the witness thereof, it were good that ye held this ring together and called the God to witness, who is akin to the God of the Earth, as we all be.  Take the ring, Folk-might, for I trust thee ; and of all women now alive would I have this woman happy.'

So Folk-might took the ring and thrust his hand through it, and took her hand, and said :

' Ye Fathers, thou God of the Face, thou Earth-god, thou Warrior, bear witness that my life and my body are plighted to this woman, the Bride of the House of the Steer ! '

His face was flushed and bright as he spoke, but as his words ceased he noted how feebly her hand lay in his, and his face fell, and he gazed on her timidly.  But she lay quiet, and said softly and slowly :

' O Fathers of my kindred ! O Warrior and God of the Earth ! bear witness that I plight my troth to this man, to lie in his grave if I die, and in his bed if I live.'

And she smiled on him again, and then closed her eyes ; but opened them presently once more, and said :

' Dear friend, how fared it with Gold-mane to-day ? '

Said Folk-might : 'So well he did, that none might have done better.  He fared in the fight as if he had been our Father the Warrior : he is a great chieftain.'

She said : ' Wilt thou give him this message from me, that in

380

no wise he forget the oath which he swore upon the finger-ring as it lay on the sundial of the Garden of the Face? And say, moreover, that I am sorry that we shall part, and have between us such breadth of wild-wood and mountain-neck.'

'Yea, surely will I give thy message,' said Folk-might; and in his heart he rejoiced, because he heard her speak as if she were sure of life. Then she said faintly:

'It is now thy work to depart from me, and to do as it behoveth a chieftain of the people and the Alderman of Silver-dale. Depart, lest the leeches chide me: farewell, my dear!'

So he laid his face to hers and kissed her, and rose up and embraced Iron-face, and went his ways without looking back.

But just over the threshold he met old Hall-ward of the House of the Steer, who was at point to enter, and he greeted him kindly. The old man looked on him steadily, and said: 'To-morrow or the day after I will utter a word to thee, O Chief of the Wolf.'

'In a good hour,' said Folk-might, 'for all thy words are true.'

Therewith he gat him away from the house, and came to Face-of-god, where he sat before the altar of the Crooked Sword; and now were the chiefs come back from their meat, and were sitting with him; there also were Wood-father and Wood-wont; but Bow-may was with the Sun-beam, who was resting softly in the fair meadow after all the turmoil.

So men made place for Folk-might beside the War-leader, who looked upon his face, and saw that it was sober and unsmiling, but not heavy or moody with grief. So he deemed that all was as well as it might be with the Bride, and with a good heart fell to taking counsel with the others; and kindly and friendly were the redes which they held there, with no gainsaying of man by man, for the whole folk was glad at heart.

So there they ordered all matters duly for that present time, and by then they had made an end, it was past sunset, and men were lodged in the chief houses about the Market-stead.

Albeit, though they ate their meat with all joy of heart, and

381

were merry in converse one with the other, the men of the Wolf
would by no means feast in their Hall again till it had been cleansed
and hallowed anew.

### CHAPTER LI. THE DEAD BORNE TO BALE: THE MOTE-HOUSE RE-HALLOWED.

ON the morrow they bore to bale their slain men, and therewithal what was left of the bodies of the four chieftains of
the Great Undoing. They brought them into a most fair
meadow to the west of Silver-stead, where they had piled up a
very great bale for the burning. In that meadow was the Doom-
ring and Thing-stead of the Folk of the Wolf, and they had hallowed it when they had first conquered Silver-dale, and it was
deemed far holier than the Mote-house aforesaid, wherein the
men of the kindred might hold no due court; but rather it was
a Feast-hall, and a house where men had converse together,
and wherein precious things and tokens of the Fathers were
stored up.

The Thing-stead in the meadow was flowery and well-grassed,
and a little stream winding about thereby nearly cast a ring around
it; and beyond the stream was a full fair grove of oak-trees,
very tall and ancient. There then they burned the dead of the
Host, wrapped about in exceeding fair raiment. And when the
ashes were gathered, the men of Burgdale and the Shepherds left
those of their folk for the kindred to bury there in Silver-dale;
for they said that they had a right to claim such guesting for them
that had helped to win back the Dale.

But when the Burning was done and the bale quenched, and the
ashes gathered and buried (and that was on the morrow), then
men bore forth the Banners of the Jaws of the Wolf, and the Red
Hand, and the Silver Arm, and the Golden Bushel, and the Ragged
Sword, and the Wolf of the Woodland; and with great joy and

triumph they brought them into the Mote-house and hung them up over the daïs; and they kindled fire on the Holy Hearth by holding up a disk of bright glass to the sun; and then they sang before the banners. And this is somewhat of the song that they sang before them:

Why are ye wending? O whence and whither?
  What shineth over the fallow swords?
What is the joy that ye bear in hither?
  What is the tale of your blended words?

No whither we wend, but here have we stayed us,
  Here by the ancient Holy Hearth;
Long have the moons and the years delayed us,
  But here are we come from the heart of the dearth.

We are the men of joy belated;
  We are the wanderers over the waste;
We are but they that sat and waited,
  Watching the empty winds make haste.

Long, long we sat and knew no others,
  Save alien folk and the foes of the road;
Till late and at last we met our brothers,
  And needs must we to the old abode.

For once on a day they prayed for guesting;
  And how were we then their bede to do?
Wild was the waste for the people's resting,
  And deep the wealth of the Dale we knew.

Here were the boards that we must spread them
  Down in the fruitful Dale and dear;
Here were the halls where we would bed them:
  And how should we tarry otherwhere?

383

Over the waste we came together:
　　There was the tangle athwart the way;
There was the wind-storm and the weather;
　　The red rain darkened down the day.

But that day of the days what grief should let us,
　　When we saw through the clouds the dale-glad sun?
We tore at the tangle that beset us,
　　And stood at peace when the day was done.

Hall of the Happy, take our greeting!
　　Bid thou the Fathers come and see
The Folk-signs on thy walls a-meeting,
　　And deem to-day what men we be.

Look on the Holy Hearth new-litten,
　　How the sparks fly twinkling up aloof!
How the wavering smoke by the sunlight smitten,
　　Curls up around the beam-rich roof!

For here once more is the Wolf abiding,
　　Nor ever more from the Dale shall wend,
And never again his head be hiding,
　　Till all days be dark and the world have end.


CHAPTER LII. OF THE NEW BEGINNING OF GOOD
DAYS IN SILVER-DALE.

ON the third day there was high-tide and great joy amongst
all men from end to end of the Dale; and the delivered
thralls were feasted and made much of by the kindreds,
so that they scarce knew how to believe their own five senses that
told them the good tidings.

For none strove to grieve them and torment them; what they

would, that did they, and they had all things plenteously; since for all was there enough and to spare of goods stored up for the Dusky Men, as corn and wine and oil and spices, and raiment and silver. Horses were there also, and neat and sheep and swine in abundance. Withal there was the good and dear land ; the waxing corn on the acres ; the blossoming vines on the hill-side ; and about the orchards and alongside the ways, the plum-trees and cherry-trees and pear-trees that had cast their blossom and were overhung with little young fruit; and the fair apple-trees a-blossoming, and the chestnuts spreading their boughs from their twisted trunks over the green grass. And there was the goodly pasture for the horses and the neat, and the thymy hill-grass for the sheep ; and beyond it all, the thicket of the great wood, with its unfailing store of goodly timber of ash and oak and holly and yoke-elm. There need no man lack unless man compelled him, and all was rich enough and wide enough for the waxing of a very great folk.

Now, therefore, men betook them to what was their own before the coming of the Dusky Men ; and though at first many of the delivered thrall-folk feasted somewhat above measure, and though there were some of them who were not very brisk at working on the earth for their livelihood; yet were the most part of them quick of wit and deft of hand, and they mostly fell to presently at their cunning, both of husbandry and handicraft. Moreover, they had great love of the kindreds, and especially of the Woodlanders, and strove to do all things that might plea-sure them. And as for those who were dull and listless because of their many torments of the last ten years, they would at least fetch and carry willingly for them of the kindreds ; and these last grudged them not meat and raiment and house-room, even if they wrought but little for it, because they called to mind the evil days of their thralldom, and bethought them how few are men's days upon the earth.

Thus all things throve in Silver-dale, and the days wore on
3 D

toward the summer, and the Yule-tide rest beyond it, and the
years beyond and far beyond the winning of Silver-dale.

### CHAPTER LIII. OF THE WORD WHICH HALL-WARD OF THE STEER HAD FOR FOLK-MIGHT.

BUT of the time then passing, it is to be said that the whole
host abode in Silver-dale in great mirth and good liking,
till they should hear tidings of Dallach and his company,
who had followed hot-foot on the fleers of the Dusky Men. And
on the tenth day after the battle, Iron-face and his two sons and
Stone-face were sitting about sunset under a great oak-tree by
that stream-side which ran through the Mote-stead; there also
was Folk-might, somewhat distraught because of his love for
the Bride, who was now mending of her hurts. As they sat
there in all content they saw folk coming toward them, three in
number, and as they drew nigher they saw that it was old Hall-
ward of the Steer, and the Sun-beam and Bow-may following
him hand in hand.

When they came to the brook Bow-may ran up to the elder
to help him over the stepping-stones; which she did as one who
loved him, as the old man was stark enough to have waded the
water waist-deep. She was no longer in her war-gear, but was
clad after her wont of Shadowy Vale, in nought but a white
woollen kirtle. So she stood in the stream beside the stones,
and let the swift water ripple up over her ankles, while the elder
leaned on her shoulder and looked down upon her kindly. The
Sun-beam followed after them, stepping daintily from stone to
stone, so that she was a fair sight to see; her face was smiling
and happy, and as she stepped forth on to the green grass the
colour flushed up in it, but she cast her eyes adown as one somewhat shamefaced.

So the chieftains rose up before the leader of the Steer, and

Folk-might went up to him, and greeted him, and took his hand
and kissed him on the cheek.   And Hall-ward said:
' Hail to the chiefs of the kindred, and my earthly friends!'
Then Folk-might bade him sit down by him, and all the men
sat down again; but the Sun-beam leaned her back against a
sapling ash hard by, her feet set close together; and Bow-may
went to and fro in short turns, keeping well within ear-shot.
Then said Hall-ward: 'Folk-might, I have prayed thy kinswoman Bow-may to lead me to thee, that I might speak with
thee; and it is good that I find my kinsmen of the Face in thy
company; for I would say a word to thee that concerns them
somewhat.'
Said Folk-might: 'Guest, and warrior of the Steer, thy
words are ever good; and if this time thou comest to ask aught
of me, then shall they be better than good.'
Said Hall-ward: 'Tell me, Folk-might, hast thou seen my
daughter the Bride to-day?'
' Yea,' said Folk-might, reddening.
' What didst thou deem of her state?' said Hall-ward.
Said Folk-might: 'Thou knowest thyself that the fever hath
left her, and that she is mending.'
Hall-ward said: 'In a few days belike we shall be wending
home to Burgdale: when deemest thou that the Bride may travel,
if it were but on a litter?'
Folk-might was silent, and Hall-ward smiled on him and said:
' Wouldst thou have her tarry, O chief of the Wolf?'
' So it is,' said Folk-might, 'that it might be labour lost for
her to journey to Burgdale at present.'
' Thinkest thou?' said Hall-ward; 'hast thou a mind then that
if she goeth she shall speedily come back hither?'
' It has been in my mind,' said Folk-might, 'that I should wed
her.  Wilt thou gainsay it?  I pray thee, Iron-face my friend, and
ye Stone-face and Hall-face, and thou, Face-of-god, my brother,
to lay thy words to mine in this matter.'

387

Hall-ward
asketh a price
for the Bride.
Then said Hall-ward stroking his beard : 'There will be a seat missing in the Hall of the Steer, and a sore lack in the heart of many a man in Burgdale if the Bride come back to us no more. We looked not to lose the maiden by her wedding ; for it is no long way betwixt the House of the Steer and the House of the Face. But now, when I arise in the morning and miss her, I shall take my staff and walk down the street of Burgstead ; for I shall say, The Maiden hath gone to see Iron-face my friend ; she is well in the House of the Face. And then shall I remember how that the wood and the wastes lie between us. How sayest thou, Alderman ?'

'A sore lack it will be,' said Iron-face ; 'but all good go with her ! Though whiles shall I go hatless down Burgstead street, and say, Now will I go fetch my daughter the Bride from the House of the Steer ; while many a day's journey shall lie betwixt us.'

Said Hall-ward : 'I will not beat about the bush, Folk-might ; what gift wilt thou give us for the maiden ?'

Said Folk-might : 'Whatever is mine shall be thine ; and whatsoever of the Dale the kindred and the poor folk begrudge thee not, that shalt thou have ; and deemest thou that they will begrudge thee aught ? Is it enough ?'

Hall-ward said : 'I wot not, chieftain ; see thou to it ! Bowmay, my friend, bring hither that which I would have from Silver-dale for the House of the Steer in payment for our maiden.'

Then Bow-may came forward speedily, and went up to the Sun-beam, and led her by the hand in front of Folk-might and Hall-ward and the other chieftains. Then Folk-might started, and leapt up from the ground ; for, sooth to say, he had been thinking so wholly of the Bride, that his sister was not in his mind, and he had had no deeming of whither Hall-ward was coming, though the others guessed well enough, and now smiled on him merrily, when they saw how wild Folk-might stared.

As for the Sun-beam, she stood there blushing like a rose in June, but looking her brother straight in the face, as Hall- The price of the Bride.

'Folk-might, chief of the Wolf, since thou wouldst take our maiden the Bride away from us, I ask thee to make good her place with this maiden ; so that the House of the Steer may not lack, when they who are wont to wed therein come to us and pray us for a bedfellow for the best of their kindred.'

Then became Folk-might smiling and merry like unto the others, and he said : 'Chief of the Steer, this gift is thine, together with aught else which thou mayst desire of us.'

Then he kissed the Sun-beam, and said : 'Sister, we looked for this to befall in some fashion. Yet we deemed that he that should lead thee away might abide with us for a moon or two. But now let all this be, since if thou art not to bear children to the kindreds of Silver-dale, yet shalt thou bear them to their friends and fellows. And now choose what gift thou wilt have of us to keep us in thy memory.'

She said : 'The memory of my people shall not fade from me ; yet indeed I ask thee for a gift, to wit, Bow-may, and the two sons of Wood-father that are left since Wood-wicked was slain ; and belike the elder and his wife will be fain to go with their sons, and ye will not hinder them.'

'Even so shall it be done,' said Folk-might, and he was silent a while, pondering ; and then he said :

'Lo you, friends! doth it not seem strange to you that peace sundereth as well as war ? Indeed I deem it grievous that ye shall have to miss your well-beloved kinswoman. And for me, I am now grown so used to this woman my sister, though at whiles she hath been masterful with me, that I shall often turn about and think to speak to her, when there lie long days of wood and waste betwixt her voice and mine.'

The Sun-beam laughed in his face, though the tears stood in her eyes, as she said : 'Keep up thine heart, brother; for at least

389

the way is shorter betwixt Burgdale and Silver-dale than betwixt life and death ; and the road we shall learn belike.'

Said Hall-face : 'So it is that my brother is no ill woodman, as ye learned last autumn.'

Iron-face smiled, but somewhat sadly ; for he beheld Face-of-god, who had no eyes for anyone save the Sun-beam ; and no marvel was that, for never had she looked fairer. And forsooth the War-leader was not utterly well-pleased ; for he was deeming that there would be delaying of his wedding, now that the Sun-beam was to become a maid of the Steer ; and in his mind he half deemed that it would be better if he were to take her by the hand and lead her home through the wild-wood, he and she alone ; and she looked on him shyly, as though she had a deeming of his thought. Albeit he knew it might not be, that he, the chosen War-leader, should trouble the peace of the kindred ; for he wotted that all this was done for peace' sake.

So Hall-ward stood forth and took the Sun-beam's right hand in his, and said :

'Now do I take this maiden, Sun-beam of the kindred of the Wolf, and lead her into the House of the Steer, to be in all ways one of the maidens of our House, and to wed in the blood wherein we have been wont to wed. Neither from henceforth let anyone say that this woman is not of the blood of the Steer ; for we have given her our blood, and she is of us duly and truly.'

Thereafter they talked together merrily for a little, and then turned toward the houses, for the sun was now down ; and as they went Iron-face spake to his son, and said :

'Gold-mane, wilt thou verily keep thine oath to wed the fairest woman in the world ? By how much is this one fairer than my dear daughter who shall no more dwell in mine house ?'

Said Face-of-god : 'Yea, father, I shall keep mine oath ; for the Gods, who know much, know that when I swore last Yule I was thinking of the fair woman going yonder beside Hall-ward, and of none other.'

'Ah, son!' said Iron-face, 'why didst thou beguile us? Hadst
thou but told us the truth then!'

'Yea, Alderman,' said Face-of-god smiling, 'and how thou
wouldest have raged against me then, when thou hast scarce
forgiven me now! In sooth, father, I feared to tell you all: I
was young; I was one against the world. Yea, yea; and even
that was sweet to me, so sorely as I loved her—Hast thou forgotten, father?'

Iron-face smiled, and answered not; and so came they to the
house wherein they were guested.


## CHAPTER LIV. TIDINGS OF DALLACH: A FOLK-MOTE IN SILVER-DALE.

THREE days thereafter came two swift runners from Rose-
dale with tidings of Dallach. In all wise had he thriven,
and had slain many of the runaways, and had come happily to Rose-dale: therein by the mere shaking of their swords
had they all their will; for there were but a few of the Dusky
Warriors in the Dale, since the more part had fared to the
slaughter in Silver-stead. Now therefore had Dallach been
made Alderman of Rose-dale; and the Burgdalers who had gone
with him should abide the coming thither of the rest of the Burgdale Host, and meantime of their coming should uphold the new
Alderman in Rose-dale. Howbeit Dallach sent word that it was
not to be doubted but that many of the Dusky Men had escaped
to the woods, and should yet be the death of many a mother's
son, unless it were well looked to.

And now the more part of the Burgdale men and the Shepherds began to look toward home, albeit some amongst them
had not been ill-pleased to abide there yet a while; for life was
exceeding soft to them there, though they helped the poor folk
gladly in their husbandry. For especially the women of the Dale,

391

of whom many were very goodly, hankered after the fair-faced
tall Burgdalers, and were as kind to them as might be. Forsooth not a few, both carles and queens, of the old thrall-folk
prayed them of Burgdale to take them home thither, that they
might see new things and forget their old torments once for all,
yea, even in dreams. The Burgdalers would not gainsay them,
and there was no one else to hinder ; so that there went with the
Burgdale men at their departure hard on five score of the Silver-
dale folk who were not of the kindreds.

And now was a great Folk-mote holden in Silver-dale, whereto
the Burgdale men and the Shepherds were bidden ; and thereat
the War-leader gave out the morrow of the morrow for the day
of the departure of the Host. There also were the matters of
Silver-dale duly ordered : the Men of the Wolf would have had
the Woodlanders dwell with them in the fair-builded stead, and
take to them of the goodly stone houses there what they would ;
but this they naysaid, choosing rather to dwell in scattered
houses, which they built for themselves at the utmost limit of
the tillage.

Indeed, the most abode not even there a long while ; for they
loved the wood and its deeds. So they went forth into the wood,
and cleared them space to dwell in, and builded them halls such
as they loved, and fell to their old woodland crafts of charcoal-
burning and hunting, wherein they throve well. And good for
Silver-dale was their abiding there, since they became a sure defence and stout outpost against all foemen. For the rest, wheresoever they dwelt, they were guest-cherishing and blithe, and
were well beloved by all people ; and they wedded with the other
Houses of the Children of the Wolf.

As to the other matters whereof they took rede at this Folk-
mote, they had mostly to do with the warding of the Dale, and the
learning of the delivered thralls to handle weapons duly. For men
deemed it most like that they would have to meet other men of the
kindred of the Felons ; which indeed fell out as the years wore.

Moreover, Folk-might (by the rede of Stone-face) sent messengers to the Plain and the Cities, unto men whom he knew there, doing them to wit of the tidings of Silver-dale, and how that a peaceful and guest-loving people, having good store of wares, now dwelt therein, so that chapmen might have recourse thither. Folk-might will give the Burgdalers gifts.

Lastly spake Folk-might and said :

' Guests and brothers-in-arms, we have been looking about our new house, which was our old one, and therein we find great store of wares which we need not, and which we can but use if ye use them. Of your kindness therefore we pray you to take of those things what ye can easily carry. And if ye say the way is long, as indeed it is, since ye are bent on going through the wood to Rose-dale, and so on to Burgdale, yet shall we furnish you with beasts to bear your goods, and with such wains as may pass through the woodland ways.'

Then rose up Fox of Upton and said : ' O Folk-might, and ye men of the Wolf, be it known unto you, that if we have done anything for your help in the winning of Silver-dale, we have thus done that we might help ourselves also, so that we might live in peace henceforward, and that we might have your friendship and fellowship therewithal, so that here in Silver-dale might wax a mighty folk who joined unto us should be strong enough to face the whole world. Such are the redes of wise men when they go a-warring. But we have no will to go back home again made rich with your wealth ; this hath been far from our thought in this matter.'

And there went up a murmur from all the Burgdalers yea-saying his word.

But Folk-might took up the word again and spake :

' Men of Burgdale and the Sheepcotes, what ye say is both manly and friendly ; yet, since we look to see a road made plain through the woodland betwixt Burgdale and Silver-dale, and that often ye shall face us in the feast-hall, and whiles stand beside us in the fray, we must needs pray you not to shame us

393                    3 E

by departing empty-handed; for how then may we look upon your faces again? Stone-face, my friend, thou art old and wise; therefore I bid thee to help us herein, and speak for us to thy kindred, that they naysay us not in this matter.'

Then stood up Stone-face and said: ' Forsooth, friends, Folkmight is in the right herein; for he may look for anger from the wights that come and go betwixt his kindred and the Gods, if they see us faring back giftless through the woods. Moreover, now that ye have seen Silver-dale, ye may wot how rich a land it is of all good things, and able to bring forth enough and to spare. And now meseemeth the Gods love this Folk that shall dwell here; and they shall become a mighty Folk, and a part of our very selves. Therefore let us take the gifts of our friends, and thank them blithely. For surely, as saith Folk-might, henceforth the wood shall become a road betwixt us, and the thicket a halting-place for friends bearing goodwill in their hands.'

When he had spoken, men yeasaid his words and forbore the gifts no longer; and the Folk-mote sundered in all lovingkindness.

### CHAPTER LV.  DEPARTURE FROM SILVER-DALE.

ON the morrow of the morrow were the Burgdale men and they of the Shepherds gathered together in the Marketstead early in the morning, and they were all ready for departure; and the men of the Wolf and the Woodlanders, and of the delivered thralls a great many, stood round about them grieving that they must go. There was much talk between the folk of the Dale and the Guests, and many promises were given and taken to come and go betwixt the two Dales. There also were the men of the thrall-folk who were to wend home with the Burgdalers; and they had been stuffed with good things by the men of the kindreds, and were as fain as might be.

As for the Sun-beam, she was somewhat out of herself at first, being eager and restless beyond her wont, and yet at whiles weeping-ripe when she called to mind that she was now leaving all those things, the gain whereof had been a dream to her both waking and sleeping for these years past. But at last, as she stood in the door of the Mote-house, and beheld all the throng of folk happy and friendly, it came over her that she herself had done her full share to bring all this about, and that all those pleasant places of Silver-dale now full of the goodly life of man would be there even as she had striven for them, and that they would be a part of her left behind, though she were dwelling otherwhere.

Therewithal she said to herself that it was now her part to wield the life of men in Burgdale, and begin once more her days of a chieftain and a swayer of the Folk, and the life of a stirring woman, which the edge of the sword and the need of the hard hand-play had taken out of her hands for a while, making her as a child in the hands of the strong wielders of the blades.

So now she became calm once more, and her face was clad again with the full measure of that majesty of beauty which had once overawed Face-of-god amidst his love of her ; and folk beheld her and marvelled at her fairness, and said : ' She hath an inward sorrow at leaving the fair Dale wherein her Fathers dwelt, and where her mother's ashes lie in earth.' Albeit now was her sorrow but little, and much was her hope, and her foresight of days to be ; though all the Dale, yea, every leaf and twig of it whereby her feet had ever passed, and each stone of the fair houses, was to her as a picture that she could look on from henceforth for ever.

Of the Bride it is to be said that she was now much mended, and she caused men bear her on a litter out into the Market-place, that she might look on the departure of her folk. She had seen Face-of-god once and again since the Day of Battle, and each time had been kind and blithe with him ; and for Iron-face,

395

she loved him so well that she was ever loth to let him depart from her, save when Folk-might was with her.

And now was the Alderman standing beside her, and she said to him : ' Friend and kinsman, this is the day of departure, and though I must needs abide behind, and am content to abide, yet doth mine heart ache with the sundering ; for to-morrow when I wake in the morning there will be no more sending of a messenger to fetch thee to me. Indeed, great hath been the love between me and my people, and nought hath come between us to mar it. Now, kinsman, I would see Gold-mane, my cousin, that I may bid him farewell ; for who knoweth if I shall see him again hereafter ? '

Then went Iron-face and found Face-of-god where he was speaking with Folk-might and the chieftains, and said to him : ' Come quickly, for thy cousin the Bride would speak with thee.'

Face-of-god reddened, and paled afterwards, but he went along with his father silently ; and his heart beat as he came and stood before the litter whereas the Bride lay, clad all in white and propped up on fair cushions of red silk. She was frail to look on, and worn and pale yet ; but he deemed that she was very happy.

She smiled on him, and reached out her hand and said :

' Welcome once more, cousin ! ' And he held her hand and kissed it, and was nigh weeping, so sore was he beset by a throng of memories concerning her and him in the days when they were little ; and he bethought him of her loving-kindness of past days, beyond that of most children, beyond that of most maidens ; and how there was nothing in his life but she had a share in it, till the day when he found the Hall on the Mountain.

So he said to her : ' Kinswoman, is it well with thee ?'

' Yea,' she said, ' I am now nigh whole of my hurts.'

He was silent a while ; then he said :

' And otherwise art thou merry at heart ?'

' Yea, indeed,' said she ; ' yet thou wilt not find it hard to deem that I am sorry of the sundering betwixt me and Burgdale.'

Again was he silent, and said in a while : 'Dost thou deem that I wrought that sundering?'

She smiled kindly on him and said : 'Gold-mane, my playmate, thou art become a mighty warrior and a great chief; but thou art not so mighty as that. Many things lay behind the sundering which were neither thou nor I.'

'Yet,' said he, 'it was but such a little time agone that all things seemed so sure ; and we—to both of us was the outlook happy.'

'Let it be happy still,' she said, 'now begrudging is gone. Belike the sundering came because we were so sure, and had no defence against the wearing of the days ; even as it fareth with a folk that hath no foes.'

He smiled and said : 'Even as it hath befallen *thy* folk, O Bride, a while ago.'

She reddened, and reached her hand to him, and he took it and held it, and said : 'Shall I see thee again as the days wear?'

Said she : 'O chieftain of the Folk, thou shalt have much to do in Burgdale, and the way is long. Yet would I have thee see my children. Forget not the token on my hand which thou holdest. But now get thee to thy folk with no more words ; for after all, playmate, the sundering is grievous to me, and I would not spin out the time thereof. Farewell!'

He said no more, but stooped down and kissed her lips, and then turned from her, and took his ways to the head of the Host, and fell to asking and answering, and bidding and arraying; and in a little time was his heart dancing with joy to think of the days that lay before him, wherein now all seemed happy.

So was all arrayed for departure when it lacked three hours of noon. As Folk-might had promised, there were certain light wains drawn by bullocks abiding the departure of the Host, and of sumpter bullocks and horses no few; and all these were laden with fair gifts of the Dale, as silver, and raiment, and weapons. There were many things fair-wrought in the time of the Sorrow,

397

that henceforth should see but little sorrow. Moreover, there was plenty of provision for the way, both meal and wine, and sheep and neat; and all things as fair as might be, and well-arrayed.

It was the Shepherds who were to lead the way; and after them were arrayed the men of the Vine and the Sickle; then they of the Steer, the Bridge, and the Bull; and lastly the House of the Face, with old Stone-face leading them. The Sun-beam was to journey along with the House of the Steer, which had taken her in as a maiden of their blood; and though she had so much liefer have fared with the House of the Face, yet she went meekly as she was bidden, as one who has gotten a great thing, and will make no stir about a small one.

Along with her were Wood-father and Wood-mother, and Wood-wise, now whole of his hurt, and Wood-wont, and Bow-may. Save Bow-may, they were not very joyous; for they were fain of Silver-dale, and it irked them to leave it; moreover, they also had liefer have gone along with the House of the War-leader.

Last of all went those people of the once thralls of the Dusky Men who had cast in their lot with the Burgdalers, and they were exceeding merry; and especially the women of them, they were chattering like the stares in the autumn evening, when they gather from the fields in the tall elm-trees before they go to roost.

Now all the men of the Dale, both of the kindreds and of the thrall-folk, made way for the Host and its havings, that they might go their ways down the Dale; albeit the Woodlanders clung close to the line of their ancient friends, and with them, as men who were sorry for the sundering, were Wolf-stone and God-swain and Spear-fist. But the chiefs, they drew around Folk-might a little beside the way.

Now Red-coat of Waterless, who had been hurt, and was now whole again, cast his arms about Folk-might and kissed him, and said:

' All the way hence to Burgdale will I sow with good wishes

for thee and thine, and especially for my dear friend God-swain of the Silver Arm ; and I would wish and long that they might turn into spells to draw thy feet to usward; for we love thee well.'

In like wise spake other of the Burgdalers ; and Folk-might was kind and blithe with them, and he said :

'Friends, forget ye not that the way is no longer from you to us than it is from us to you. One half of this matter it is for you to deal with.'

'True is that,' said Red-beard of the Knolls, 'but look you, Folk-might, we be but simple husbandmen, and may not often stir from our meadows and acres ; even now I bethink me that May is amidst us, and I am beginning to be drawn by the thought of the haysel. Whereas thou—' (and therewith he reddened) 'I doubt that thou hast little to do save the work of chieftains, and we know that such work is but little missed if it be undone.'

Thereat Folk-might laughed ; and when the others saw that he laughed, they laughed also, else had they foreborne for courtesy's sake.

But Folk-might answered: 'Nay, chief of the Sickle, I am not altogether a chieftain, now we have gotten us peace; and somewhat of a husbandman shall I be. Moreover, doubt ye not that I shall do my utmost to behold the fair Dale again; for it is but mountains that meet not.'

Now spake Face-of-god to Folk-might, smiling and somewhat softly, and said : 'Is all forgiven now, since the day when we first felt each other's arms ? '

'Yea, all,' said Folk-might; 'now hath befallen what I foretold thee in Shadowy Vale, that thou mightest pay for all that had come and gone, if thou wouldest but look to it. Indeed thou wert angry with me for that saying on that eve of Shadowy Vale ; but see thou, in those days I was an older man than thou, and might admonish thee somewhat ; but now, though but few days have gone over thine head, yet many deeds have abided in thine hand, and thou art much aged. Anger hath left thee, and wisdom hath

399

waxed in thee. As for me, I may now say this word : May the
Folk of Burgdale love the Folk of Silver-dale as well as I love
thee ; then shall all be well.'

Then Face-of-god cast his arms about him and kissed him, and
turned away toward Stone-face and Hall-face his brother, where
they stood at the head of the array of the Face ; and even therewith came up the Alderman somewhat sad and sober of countenance, and he pushed by the War-leader roughly and would not
speak with him.

And now blew up the horns of the Shepherds, and they began
to move on amidst the shouting of the men of Silver-dale ; yet
were there amongst the Woodlanders those who wept when they
saw their friends verily departing from them.

But when they of the foremost of the Host were gotten so far
forward that the men of the Face could begin to move, lo! there
was Redesman with his fiddle amongst the leaders; and he had
done a man's work in the day of battle, and all looked kindly on
him. About him on this morn were some who had learned the
craft of singing well together, and knew his minstrelsy, and he
turned to these and nodded as their array moved on, and he drew
his bow across the strings, and straightway they fell a-singing,
even as it might be thus :

Back again to the dear Dale where born was the kindred,
   Here wend we all living, and liveth our mirth.
Here afoot fares our joyance, whatever men hindred,
   Through all wrath of the heavens, all storms of the earth.

O true, we have left here a part of our treasure,
   The ashes of stout ones, the stems of the shield ;
But the bold lives they spended have sown us new pleasure,
   Fair tales for the telling in fold and on field.

For as oft as we sing of their edges' upheaving,
   When the yellowing windows shine forth o'er the night,

Their names unforgotten with song interweaving
　　Shall draw forth dear drops from the depths of delight.

Or when down by our feet the grey sickles are lying,
　　And behind us is curling the supper-tide smoke,
No whit shall they grudge us the joyance undying,
　　Remembrance of men that put from us the yoke.

When the huddle of ewes from the fells we have driven,
　　And we see down the Dale the grey reach of the roof,
We shall tell of the gift in the battle-joy given,
　　All the fierceness of friends that drave sorrow aloof.

Once then we lamented, and mourned them departed ;
　　Once only, no oftener.　Henceforth shall we fling
Their names up aloft, when the merriest hearted
　　To the Fathers unseen of our life-days we sing.

Then was there silence in the ranks of men ; and many mur-
mured the names of the fallen as they fared on their way from
out the Market-place of Silver-stead.　Then once more Redesman and his mates took up the song :

Come tell me, O friends, for whom bideth the maiden
　　Wet-foot from the river-ford down in the Dale ?
For whom hath the goodwife the ox-waggon laden
　　With the babble of children, brown-handed and hale ?

Come tell me for what are the women abiding,
　　Till each on the other aweary they lean ?
Is it loitering of evil that thus they are chiding,
　　The slow-footed bearers of sorrow unseen ?

Nay, yet were they toiling if sorrow had worn them,
　　Or hushed had they bided with lips parched and wan.
The birds of the air other tidings have borne them—
　　How glad through the wood goeth man beside man.

Then fare forth, O valiant, and loiter no longer
  Than the cry of the cuckoo when May is at hand ;
Late waxeth the spring-tide, and daylight grows longer,
  And nightly the star-street hangs high o'er the land.

Many lives, many days for the Dale do ye carry ;
  When the Host breaketh out from the thicket unshorn,
It shall be as the sun that refuseth to tarry
  On the crown of all mornings, the Midsummer morn.

Again the song fell down till they were well on the western
way down Silver-dale ; and then Redesman handled his fiddle once
more, and again the song rose up, and such-like were the words
which were borne back into the Market-place of Silver-stead :

And yet what is this, and why fare ye so slowly,
  While our echoing halls of our voices are dumb,
And abideth unlitten the hearth-brand the holy,
  And the feet of the kind fare afield till we come?

For not yet through the wood and its tangle ye wander ;
  Now skirt we no thicket, no path by the mere ;
Far aloof for our feet leads the Dale-road out yonder ;
  Full fair is the morning, its doings all clear.

There is nought now our feet on the highway delaying
  Save the friend's loving-kindness, the sundering of speech ;
The well-willer's word that ends words with the saying,
  The loth to depart while each looketh on each.

Fare on then, for nought are ye laden with sorrow ;
  The love of this land do ye bear with you still.
In two Dales of the earth for to-day and to-morrow
  Is waxing the oak-tree of peace and good-will.

Thus then they departed from Silver-dale, even as men who
were a portion thereof, and had not utterly left it behind.   And

that night they lay in the wild-wood not very far from the Dale's end ; for they went softly, faring amongst so many friends.

## CHAPTER LVI.   TALK UPON THE WILD-WOOD WAY.

ON the morrow morning when they were on their way again Face-of-god left his own folk to go with the House of the Steer a while; and amongst them he fell in with the Sun-beam going along with Bow-may.  So they greeted him kindly, and Face-of-god fell into talk with the Sun-beam as they went side by side through a great oak-wood, where for a space was plain green-sward bare of all underwood.

So in their talk he said to her : ' What deemest thou, my speech-friend, concerning our coming back to guest in Silver-dale one day ? '

' The way is long,' she said.

' That may hinder us  but not stay us,' said Face-of-god.

' That is sooth,' said the Sun-beam.

Said Face-of-god : ' What things shall stay us?  Or deemest thou that we shall never see Silver-dale again ? '

She smiled : ' Even so I think thou deemest, Gold-mane.  But many things shall hinder us besides the long road ? '

Said he : ' Yea, and what things ? '

' Thinkest thou,' said the Sun-beam, ' that the winning of Silver-stead is the last battle which thou shalt see ? '

' Nay,' said he, ' nay.'

' Shall thy Dale—our Dale—be free from all trouble within itself henceforward?   Is there a wall built round it to keep out for ever storm, pestilence, and famine, and the waywardness of its own folk ? '

' So it is as thou sayest,' quoth Face-of-god, ' and to meet such troubles and overcome them, or to die in strife with them, this is a great part of a man's life.'

403

'Yea,' she said, 'and hast thou forgotten that thou art now a great chieftain, and that the folk shall look to thee to use thee many days in the year?'

He laughed and said: 'So it is. How many days have gone by since I wandered in the wood last autumn, that the world should have changed so much!'

'Many deeds shall now be in thy days,' she said, 'and each deed as the corn of wheat from which cometh many corns; and a man's days on the earth are not over many.'

'Then farewell, Silver-dale!' said he, waving his hand toward the north. 'War and trouble may bring me back to thee, but it maybe nought else shall. Farewell!'

She looked on him fondly but unsmiling, as he went beside her strong and warrior-like. Three paces from him went Bowmay, barefoot, in her white kirtle, but bearing her bow in her hand; a leash of arrows was in her girdle, her quiver hung at her back, and she was girt with a sword. On the other side went Wood-wont and Wood-wise, lightly clad but weaponed. Woodmother was riding in an ox-wain just behind them, and Woodfather went beside her bearing an axe. Scattered all about them were the men of the Steer, gaily clad, bearing weapons, so that the oak-wood was bright with them, and the glades merry with their talk and singing and laughter, and before them down the glades went the banner of the Steer, and the White Beast led them the nearest way to Burgdale.

CHAPTER LVII. HOW THE HOST CAME HOME AGAIN.

IT was fourteen days before they came to Rose-dale; for they had much baggage with them, and they had no mind to weary themselves, and the wood was nothing loathsome to them, whereas the weather was fair and bright for the more part. They fell in with no mishap by the way. But a score and three of runaways joined themselves to the Host, having watched their goings and wotting that they were not foemen. Of these, some had heard of the overthrow of the Dusky Men in Silverdale, and others not. The Burgdalers received them all, for it seemed to them no great matter for a score or so of new-comers to the Dale.

But when the Host was come to Rose-dale, they found it fair and lovely; and there they met with those of their folk who had gone with Dallach. But Dallach welcomed the kindreds with great joy, and bade them abide; for he said that they had the less need to hasten, since he had sent messengers into Burgdale to tell men there of the tidings. Albeit they were mostly loth to tarry; yet when he lay hard on them not to depart as men on the morrow of a gild-feast, they abode there three days, and were as well guested as might be, and on their departure they were laden with gifts from the wealth of Rose-dale by Dallach and his folk.

Before they went their ways Dallach spake with Face-of-god and the chiefs of the Dalesmen, and said:

'Ye have given me much from the time when ye found me in the wood a naked wastrel; yet now I would ask you a gift to lay on the top of all that ye have given me.'

Said Face-of-god: 'Name the gift, and thou shalt have it; for we deem thee our friend.'

'I am no less,' said Dallach, 'as in time to come I may perchance be able to show you. But now I am asking you to suffer a score or two of your men to abide here with me this summer, till I see how this folk new-born again is like to deal with me. For pleasure and a fair life have become so strange to them, that they scarce know what to do with them, or how to live; and unless all is to go awry, I must needs command and forbid; and though belike they love me, yet they fear me not; so that when my commandment pleaseth them, they do as I bid, and when it pleaseth them not, they do contrary to my

405

bidding; for it hath got into their minds that I shall in no case
lift a hand against them, which indeed is the very sooth. But
your folk they fear as warriors of the world, who have slain the
Dusky Men in the Market-place of Silver-stead; and they are
of alien blood to them, men who will do as their friend biddeth
(think our folk) against them who are neither friends or foes.
With such help I shall be well holpen.'

In such wise spake Dallach; and Face-of-god and the chiefs
said that so it should be, if men could be found willing to abide
in Rose-dale for a while. And when the matter was put abroad,
there was no lack of such men amongst the younger warriors,
who had noted that the dale was fair amongst dales and its
women fairer yet amongst women.

So two score and ten of the Burgdale men abode in Rose-
dale, no one of whom was of more than twenty and five winters.
Forsooth divers of them set up house in Rose-dale, and never
came back to Burgdale, save as guests. For a half score were
wedded in Rose-dale before the year's ending; and seven more,
who had also taken to them wives of the goodliest of the Rose-
dale women, betook them the next spring to the Burg of the
Runaways, and there built them a stead, and drew a garth about
it, and dug and sowed the banks of the river, which they called
Inglebourne. And as years passed, this same stead throve exceedingly, and men resorted thither both from Rose-dale and
Burgdale; for it was a pleasant place; and the land, when it
was cured, was sweet and good, and the wood thereabout was full
of deer of all kinds. So their stead was called Inglebourne after
the stream; and in latter days it became a very goodly habita-
tion of men.

Moreover, some of the once-enthralled folk of Rose-dale, when
they knew that men of their kindred from Silver-dale were going
home with the men of Burgdale to dwell in the Dale, prayed
hard to go along with them; for they looked on the Burgdalers
as if they were new Gods of the Earth. The Burgdale chiefs

would not gainsay these men either, but took with them three score and ten from Rose-dale, men and women, and promised them dwelling and livelihood in Burgdale.

So now with good hearts the Host of Burgdale turned their faces toward their well-beloved Dale; and they made good diligence, so that in three days' time they were come anigh the edge of the woodland wilderness. Thither in the even-tide, as they were making ready for their last supper and bed in the wood, came three men and two women of their folk, who had been abiding their coming ever since they had had the tidings of Silver-dale and the battles from Dallach. Great was the joy of these messengers as they went from company to company of the warriors, and saw the familiar faces of their friends, and heard their wonted voices telling all the story of battle and slaughter. And for their part the men of the Host feasted these stay-at-homes, and made much of them. But one of them, a man of the House of the Face, left the Host a little after nightfall, and bore back to Burgstead at once the tidings of the coming home of the Host. Albeit since Dallach's tidings of victory had come to the Dale, the dwellers in the steads of the country-side had left Burgstead and gone home to their own houses; so that there was no great multitude abiding in the Thorp.

So early on the morrow was the Host astir; but ere they came to Wildlake's Way, the Shepherd-folk turned aside westward to go home, after they had bidden farewell to their friends and fellows of the Dale; for their souls longed for the sheep-cotes in the winding valleys under the long grey downs; and the garths where the last year's ricks shouldered up against the old stone gables, and where the daws were busy in the tall unfrequent ash-trees; and the green flowery meadows adown along the bright streams, where the crowfoot and the paigles were blooming now, and the harebells were in flower about the thorn-bushes at the down's foot, whence went the savour of their blossom over sheep-walk and water-meadow.

So these went their ways with many kind words ; and two
hours afterwards all the rest of the Host stood on the level
ground of the Portway ; but presently were the ranks of war
disordered and broken up by the joy of the women and children,
as they fell to drawing goodman or brother or lover out of the
throng to the way that led speediest to their homesteads and
halls. For the War-leader would not hold the Host together
any longer, but suffered each man to go to his home, deeming
that the men of Burgstead, and chiefly they of the Face and the
Steer, would suffice for a company if any need were, and they
would be easily gathered to meet any hap.

So now the men of the Middle and Lower Dale made for their
houses by the road and the lanes and the meadows, and the
men of the Upper Dale and Burgstead went their ways along
the Portway toward their halls, with the throng of women
and children that had come out to meet them. And now men
came home when it was yet early, and the long day lay before
them ; and it was, as it were, made giddy and cumbered with
the exceeding joy of return, and the thought of the day when
the fear of death and sundering had been ever in their hearts.
For these new hours were full of the kissing and embracing of
lovers, and the sweetness of renewed delight in beholding the fair
bodies so sorely desired, and hearkening the soft wheedling of
longed-for voices. There were the cups of friends beneath the
chestnut trees, and the talk of the deeds of the fighting-men, and
of the heavy days of the home-abiders; many a tale told oft and
o'er again. There was the singing of old songs and of new,
and the beholding the well-loved nook of the pleasant places,
which death might well have made nought for them ; and they
were sweet with the fear of that which was past, and in their
pleasantness was fresh promise for the days to come.

So amid their joyance came evening and nightfall ; and though
folk were weary with the fulness of delight, yet now for many
their weariness led them to the chamber of love before the rest of

408

deep night came to them to make them strong for the happy life to be begun again on the morrow.

House by house they feasted, and few were the lovers that sat not together that even. But Face-of-god and the Sun-beam parted at the door of the House of the Face ; for needs must she go with her new folk to the House of the Steer, and needs must Face-of-god be amongst his own folk in that hour of high-tide, and sit beside his father beneath the image of the God with the ray-begirt head.

## CHAPTER LVIII. HOW THE MAIDEN WARD WAS HELD IN BURGDALE.

NOW May was well worn when the Host came home to Burgdale; and on the very morrow of men's home-coming they began to talk eagerly of the Midsummer Weddings, and how the Maiden Ward would be the greatest and fairest of all yet seen, whereas battle and the deliverance from battle stir up the longing and love both of men and maidens ; much also men spake of the wedding of Face-of-god and the Sun-beam ; and needs must their wedding abide to the time of the Maiden Ward at Midsummer, and needs also must the Sun-beam go on the Ward with the other Brides of the Folk. So then must Face-of-god keep his soul in patience till those few days were over, doing what work came to hand ; and he held his head high among the people, and was well looked to of every man.

In all matters the Sun-beam helped him, both in doing and in forbearing ; and now so wonderful and rare was her beauty, that folk looked on her with somewhat of fear, as though she came from the very folk of the Gods.

Indeed she seemed somewhat changed from what she had been of late ; she was sober of demeanour during these last days of her maidenhood, and sat amongst the kindred as one communing with herself : of few words she was and little laughter ; but her face clear, not overcast by any gloom or shaken by passion : soft and kind was she in converse with others, and sweet were the smiles that came into her face if others' faces seemed to crave for them. For it must be said that as some folk eat out their hearts with fear of the coming evils, even so was she feeding her soul with the joy of the days to be, whatever trouble might fall upon them, whereof belike she foreboded some.

So wore the days toward Midsummer, when the wheat was getting past the blossoming, and the grass in the mown fields was growing deep green again after the shearing of the scythe ; when the leaves were most and biggest ; when the roses were beginning to fall ; when the apples were reddening, and the skins of the grape-berries gathering bloom. High aloft floated the light clouds over the Dale ; deep blue showed the distant fells below the ice-mountains ; the waters dwindled ; all things sought the shadow by daytime, and the twilight of even and the twilight of dawn were but sundered by three hours of half-dark night.

So in the bright forenoon were seventeen brides assembled in the Gate of Burgstead (but of the rest of the Dale were twenty and three looked for), and with these was the Sun-beam, her face as calm as the mountain lake under a summer sunset, while the others many were restless, and babbling like April throstles ; and not a few talked to her eagerly, and in their restless love of her dragged her about hither and thither.

No men were to be seen that morning ; for such was the custom, that the carles either departed to the fields and the acres, or abode within doors on the morn of the day of the Maiden Ward ; but there was a throng of women about the Gate and down the street of Burgstead, and it may well be deemed that they kept not silence that hour.

So fared the Brides of Burgstead to the place of the Maiden Ward on the causeway, whereto were come already the other brides from steads up and down the Dale, or were even then close at hand on the way; and among them were Long-coat and her two fellows, with whom Face-of-god had held converse on that morning whereon he had followed his fate to the Mountain.

There then were they gathered under the cliff-wall of the Portway; and by the road-side had their grooms built them up bowers of green boughs to shelter them from the sun's burning, which were thatched with bulrushes, and decked with garlands of the fairest flowers of the meadows and the gardens.

Forsooth they were a lovely sight to look on, for no fairer women might be seen in the world; and the eldest of them was scant of five and twenty winters. Every maiden was clad in as goodly raiment as she might compass; their sleeves and gown-hems and girdles, yea, their very shoes and sandals were embroidered so fairly and closely, that as they shifted in the sun they changed colour like the king-fisher shooting from shadow to sunshine. According to due custom every maiden bore some weapon. A few had bows in their hands and quivers at their backs; some had nought but a sword girt to their sides; some bore slender-shafted spears, so as not to overburden their shapely hands; but to some it seemed a merry game to carry long and heavy thrust-spears, or to bear great war-axes over their shoulders. Most had their flowing hair coifed with bright helms; some had burdened their arms with shields; some bore steel hauberks over their linen smocks: almost all had some piece of war-gear on their bodies; and one, to wit, Steed-linden of the Sickle, a tall and fair damsel, was so arrayed that no garment could be seen on her but bright steel war-gear.

As for the Sun-beam, she was clad in a white kirtle embroidered from throat to hem with work of green boughs and flowers of the goodliest fashion, and a garland of roses on her head. Dale-warden himself was girt to her side by a girdle fair-wrought of golden wire, and she bore no other weapon or war-gear; and she let him lie quiet in his scabbard, nor touched the hilts once; whereas some of the other damsels would be ever drawing their swords out and thrusting them back. But all noted that goodly weapon, the yoke-fellow of so many great deeds.

There then on the Portway, between the water and the rock-wall, rose up plenteous and gleeful talk of clear voices shrill and soft ; and whiles the maidens sang, and whiles they told tales of old days, and whiles they joined hands and danced together on the sweet summer dust of the highway. Then they mostly grew aweary, and sat down on the banks of the road or under their leafy bowers.

Noon came, and therewithal goodwives of the neighbouring Dale, who brought them meat and drink, and fruit and fresh flowers from the teeming gardens ; and thereafter for a while they nursed their joy in their bosoms, and spake but little and softly while the day was at its hottest in the early afternoon.

Then came out of Burgstead men making semblance of chap-men with a wain bearing wares, and they made as though they were wending down the Portway westward to go out of the Dale. Then arose the weaponed maidens and barred the way to them, and turned them back amidst fresh-springing merriment.

Again in a while, when the sun was westering and the shadows growing long, came herdsmen from down the Dale driving neat, and making as though they would pass by into Burgstead, but to them also did the maidens gainsay the road, so that needs must they turn back amidst laughter and mockery, they them-selves also laughing and mocking.

And so at last, when the maidens had been all alone a while, and it was now hard on sunset, they drew together and stood in a ring, and fell to singing ; and one Gold-may of the House of the Bridge, a most sweet singer, stood amidst their ring and led them. And this is somewhat of the meaning of their words :

The sun will not tarry ; now changeth the light,
Fail the colours that marry the Day to the Night.

412

Amid the sun's burning bright weapons we bore,
For this eve of our earning comes once and no more.

For to-day hath no brother in yesterday's tide,
And to-morrow no other alike it doth hide.

This day is the token of oath and behest
That ne'er shall be broken through ill days and best.

Here the troth hath been given, the oath hath been done,
To the Folk that hath thriven well under the sun.

And the gifts of its giving our troth-day shall win
Are the Dale for our living and dear days therein.

O Sun, now thou wanest! yet come back and see
Amidst all that thou gainest how gainful are we.

O witness of sorrow wide over the earth,
Rise up on the morrow to look on our mirth!

Thy blooms art thou bringing back ever for men,
And thy birds are a-singing each summer again.,

But to men little-hearted what winter is worse
Than thy summers departed that bore them the curse?

And e'en such art thou knowing where thriveth the year,
And good is all growing save thralldom and fear.

Nought such be our lovers' hearts drawing anigh,
While yet thy light hovers aloft in the sky.

Lo the seeker, the finder of Death in the Blade!
What lips shall be kinder on lips of mine laid?

Lo he that hath driven back tribes of the South!
Sweet-breathed is thine even, but sweeter his mouth.

413

Come back from the sea then, O sun! come aback,
Look adown, look on me then, and ask what I lack!

Come many a morrow to gaze on the Dale,
And if e'er thou seest sorrow remember its tale!

For 'twill be of a story to tell how men died
In the garnering of glory that no man may hide.

O sun sinking under! O fragrance of earth!
O heart! O the wonder whence longing has birth!

So they sang, and the sun sank indeed; and amidst their
singing the eve was still about them, though there came a happy
murmur from the face of the meadows and the houses of the
Thorp aloof. But as their song fell they heard the sound of
footsteps a many on the road; so they turned and stood with
beating hearts in such order as when a band of the valiant draw
together to meet many foes coming on them from all sides, and
they stand back to back to face all comers. And even therewith, their raiment gleaming amidst the gathering dusk, came
on them the young men of the Dale newly delivered from the
grief of war.

Then in very deed the fierce mouths of the raisers of the war-
shout were kind on the faces of tender maidens. Then went
spear and axe and helm and shield clattering to the earth, as
the arms of the new-comers went round about the bodies of the
Brides, weary with the long day of sunshine, and glee and loving
speech, and the maidens suffered the young men to lead them
whither they would, and twilight began to draw round about
them as the Maiden Band was sundered.

Some, they were led away westward down the Portway to
the homesteads thereabout; and for divers of these the way was
long to their halls, and they would have to wend over long
stretches of dewy meadows, and hear the night-wind whisper in

many a tree, and see the east begin to lighten with the dawn before they came to the lighted feast that awaited them. But some turned up the Portway straight towards Burgstead; and short was their road to the halls where even now the lights were being kindled for their greeting.

As for the Sun-beam, she had been very quiet the day long, speaking as little as she might do, laughing not at all, and smiling for kindness' sake rather than for merriment; and when the grooms came seeking their maidens, she withdrew herself from the band, and stood alone amidst the road nigher to Burgstead than they; and her heart beat hard, and her breath came short and quick, as though fear had caught her in its grip; and indeed for one moment of time she feared that he was not coming to her. For he had gone with the other grooms to that gathered band, and had passed from one to the other, not finding her, till he had got him through the whole company, and beheld her awaiting him. Then indeed he bounded toward her, and caught her by the hands, and then by the shoulders, and drew her to him, and she nothing loth; and in that while he said to her:

'Come then, my friend; lo thou! they go each their own way toward the halls of their houses; and for thee have I chosen a way—a way over the foot-bridge yonder, and over the dewy meadows on this best even of the year.'

'Nay, nay,' she said, 'it may not be. Surely the Burgstead grooms look to thee to lead them to the gate; and surely in the House of the Face they look to see thee before any other. Nay, Gold-mane, my dear, we must needs go by the Portway.'

He said: 'We shall be home but a very little while after the first, for the way I tell of is as short as the Portway. But hearken, my sweet! When we are in the meadows we shall sit down for a minute on a bank under the chestnut trees, and thence watch the moon coming up over the southern cliffs. And I shall behold thee in the summer night, and deem that I see

415

He telleth of
the Path of
the Wedding.
all thy beauty; which yet shall make me dumb with wonder
when I see it indeed in the house amongst the candles.'

'O nay,' she said, 'by the Portway shall we go; the torch-
bearers shall be abiding thee at the gate.'

Spake Face-of-god: 'Then shall we rise up and wend first
through a wide treeless meadow, wherein amidst the night we
shall behold the kine moving about like odorous shadows; and
through the greyness of the moonlight thou shalt deem that
thou seest the pink colour of the eglantine blossoms, so fragrant
they are.'

'O nay,' she said, 'but it is meet that we go by the Portway.'

But he said: 'Then from the wide meadow come we into
a close of corn, and then into an orchard-close beyond it. There
in the ancient walnut-tree the owl sitteth breathing hard in the
night-time; but thou shalt not hear him for the joy of the
nightingales singing from the apple-trees of the close. Then
from out of the shadowed orchard shall we come into the open
town-meadow, and over its daisies shall the moonlight be lying
in a grey flood of brightness.

'Short is the way across it to the brim of the Weltering Water,
and across the water lieth the fair garden of the Face; and I have
dight for thee there a little boat to waft us across the night-dark
waters, that shall be like wavering flames of white fire where
the moon smites them, and like the void of all things where the
shadows hang over them. There then shall we be in the garden,
beholding how the hall-windows are yellow, and hearkening
the sound of the hall-glee borne across the flowers and blending
with the voice of the nightingales in the trees. There then shall
we go along the grass paths whereby the pinks and the cloves
and the lavender are sending forth their fragrance, to cheer us,
who faint at the scent of the over-worn roses, and the honey-
sweetness of the lilies.

'All this is for thee, and for nought but for thee this even;
and many a blossom whereof thou knowest nought shall grieve if

416

thy foot tread not thereby to-night; if the path of thy wedding which I have made, be void of thee, on the even of the Chamber of Love.

'But lo! at last at the garden's end is the yew-walk arched over for thee, and thou canst not see whereby to enter it; but I, I know it, and I lead thee into and along the dark tunnel through the moonlight, and thine hand is not weary of mine as we go. But at the end shall we come to a wicket, which shall bring us out by the gable-end of the Hall of the Face. Turn we about its corner then, and there are we blinking on the torches of the torch-bearers, and the candles through the open door, and the hall ablaze with light and full of joyous clamour, like the bale-fire in the dark night kindled on a ness above the sea by fisher-folk remembering the Gods.'

'O nay,' she said, 'but by the Portway must we go; the straightest way to the Gate of Burgstead.'

In vain she spake, and knew not what she said; for even as he was speaking he led her away, and her feet went as her will went, rather than her words; and even as she said that last word she set her foot on the first board of the foot-bridge; and she turned aback one moment, and saw the long line of the rock-wall yet glowing with the last of the sunset of midsummer, while as she turned again, lo! before her the moon just beginning to lift himself above the edge of the southern cliffs, and betwixt her and him all Burgdale, and Face-of-god moreover.

Thus then they crossed the bridge into the green meadows, and through the closes and into the garden of the Face and unto the Hall-door; and other brides and grooms were there before them (for six grooms had brought home brides to the House of the Face); but none deemed it amiss in the War-leader of the folk and the love that had led him. And old Stone-face said: 'Too many are the rows of bee-skeps in the gardens of the Dale that we should begrudge wayward lovers an hour's waste of candle-light.'

3 H

So at last those twain went up the sun-bright Hall hand in
hand in all their loveliness, and up on to the daïs, and stood
together by the middle seat ; and the tumult of the joy of the
kindred was hushed for a while as they saw that there was
speech in the mouth of the War-leader.

Then he spread his hands abroad before them all and cried
out : ' How then have I kept mine oath, whereas I swore on the
Holy Boar to wed the fairest woman of the world ? '

A mighty shout went rattling about the timbers of the roof in
answer to his word ; and they that looked up to the gable of the
Hall said that they saw the ray-ringed image of the God smile
with joy over the gathered folk.

But spake Iron-face unheard amidst the clamour of the Hall :
' How fares it now with my darling and my daughter, who
dwelleth amongst strangers in the land beyond the wild-wood ? '

CHAPTER LIX. THE BEHEST OF FACE-OF-GOD TO
THE BRIDE ACCOMPLISHED : A MOTE-STEAD AP-
POINTED FOR THE THREE FOLKS, TO WIT, THE
MEN OF BURGDALE, THE SHEPHERDS, AND THE
CHILDREN OF THE WOLF.

THREE years and two months thereafter, three hours after
noon in the days of early autumn, came a wain tilted over
with precious webs of cloth, and drawn by eight white
oxen, into the Market-place of Silver-stead : two score and ten
of spearmen of the tallest, clad in goodly war-gear, went beside it,
and much people of Silver-dale thronged about them. The wain
stayed at the foot of the stair that led up to the door of the Mote-
house, and there lighted down therefrom a woman goodly of
fashion, with wide grey eyes, and face and hands brown with the
sun's burning. She had a helm on her head and a sword girt to
her side, and in her arms she bore a yearling child.

And there was come Bow-may with the second man-child born to Face-of-god.

She stayed not amidst the wondering folk, but hastened up the stair, which she had once seen running with the blood of men : the door was open, and she went in and walked straightway, with the babe in her arms, up the great Hall to the daïs.

There were men on the daïs : amidmost sat Folk-might, little changed since the last day she had seen him, yet fairer, she deemed, than of old time ; and her heart went forth to meet the Chieftain of her Folk, and the glad tears started in her eyes and ran down her cheeks as she drew near to him.

By his side sat the Bride, and her also Bow-may deemed to have waxed goodlier. Both she and Folk-might knew Bow-may ere she had gone half the length of the hall ; and the Bride rose up in her place and cried out Bow-may's name joyously.

With these were sitting the elders of the Wolf and the Woodlanders, the more part of whom Bow-may knew well.

On the daïs also stood aside a score of men weaponed, and looking as if they were awaiting the word which should send them forth on some errand.

Now stood up Folk-might and said : 'Fair greeting and love to my friend and the daughter of my Folk ! How farest thou, Bow-may, best of all friendly women ? How fareth my sister, and Face-of-god my brother ? and how is it with our friends and helpers in the goodly Dale ?'

Said Bow-may : 'It is well both with all those and with me ; and my heart laughs to see thee, Folk-might, and to look on the elders of the valiant, and our lovely sister the Bride. But I have a message for thee from Face-of-god : wilt thou that I deliver it here ?'

'Yea surely,' said Folk-might, and came forth and took her hand, and kissed her cheeks and her mouth. The Bride also came forth and cast her arms about her, and kissed her ; and they led her between them to a seat on the daïs beside Folk-might.

But all men looked on the child in her arms and wondered

The Bride
taketh Gold-
mane's babe.
A message to
Folk-might.

what it was. But Bow-may took the babe, which was both fair
and great, and set it on the knees of the Bride, and said :
'Thus saith Face-of-god : "Friend and kinswoman, well-
beloved playmate, the gift which thou badest of me in sorrow do
thou now take in joy, and do all the good thou wouldest to the
son of thy friend. The ring which I gave thee once in the garden
of the Face, give thou to Bow-may, my trusty and well-beloved,
in token of the fulfilment of my behest." '

Then the Bride kissed Bow-may again, and fell to fondling of
the child, which was loth to leave Bow-may.

But she spake again : 'To thee also, Folk-might, I have a
message from Face-of-god, who saith : " Mighty warrior, friend
and fellow, all things thrive with us, and we are happy. Yet is
there a hollow place in our hearts which grieveth us, and only
thou and thine may amend it. Though whiles we hear tell of
thee, yet we see thee not, and fain were we, might we see thee,
and wot if the said tales be true. Wilt thou help us somewhat
herein, or wilt thou leave us all the labour ? For sure we be that
thou wilt not say that thou rememberest us no more, and that thy
love for us is departed." This is his message, Folk-might, and
he would have an answer from thee.'

Then laughed Folk-might and said : 'Sister Bow-may, seest
thou these weaponed men hereby ?'

'Yea,' she said.

Said he : 'These men bear a message with them to Face-of-
god my brother. Crow the Shaft-speeder, stand forth and tell
thy friend Bow-may the message I have set in thy mouth, every
word of it.'

Then Crow stood forth and greeted Bow-may friendly, and
said : 'Friend Bow-may, this is the message of our Alderman :
"Friend and helper, in the Dale which thou hast given to us do
all things thrive ; neither are we grown old in three years' wearing, nor are our memories worsened. We long sore to see you
and give you guesting in Silver-dale, and one day that shall

befall. Meanwhile, know this : that we of the Wolf and the Woodland, mindful of the earth that bore us, and the pit whence we were digged, have a mind to go see Shadowy Vale once in every three years, and there to hold high-tide in the ancient Hall of the Wolf, and sit in the Doom-ring of our Fathers. But since ye have joined yourselves to us in battle, and have given us this Dale, our health and wealth, without price and without reward, we deem you our very brethren, and small shall be our hall-glee, and barren shall our Doom-ring seem to us, unless ye sit there beside us. Come then, that we may rejoice each other by the sight of face and sound of voice ; that we may speak together of matters that concern our welfare ; so that we three Kindreds may become one Folk. And if this seem good to you, know that we shall be in Shadowy Vale in a half-month's wearing. Grieve us not by forbearing to come." Lo, Bow-may, this is the message, and I have learned it well, for well it pleaseth me to bear it.'

Then said Folk-might : ' What say'st thou to the message, Bow-may ? '

' It is good in all ways,' said she, ' but is it timely ? May our folk have the message and get to Shadowy Vale, so as to meet you there ? '

' Yea surely,' said Folk-might, ' for our kinsmen here shall take the road through Shadowy Vale, and in four days' time they shall be in Burgdale, and as thou wottest, it is scant a two days' journey thence to Shadowy Vale.'

Therewith he turned to those men again, and said : ' Kinsman Crow, depart now, and use all diligence with thy message.'

So the messengers began to stir ; but Bow-may cried out : ' Ho ! Folk-might, my friend, I perceive thou art little changed from the man I knew in Shadowy Vale, who would have his dinner before the fowl were plucked. For shall I not go back with these thy messengers, so that I also may get all ready to wend to the Mote-house of Shadowy Vale ? '

But the Bride looked kindly on her, and laughed and said:
'Sister Bow-may, his meaning is that thou shouldest abide here
in Silver-dale till we depart for the Folk-thing, and then go
thither with us; and this I also pray thee to do, that thou mayst
rejoice the hearts of thine old friends; and also that thou mayst
teach me all that I should know concerning this fair child of my
brother and my sister.'

And she looked on her so kindly as she caressed the babe,
that Bow-may's heart melted, and she cried out:

'Would that I might never depart from the house wherein
thou dwellest, O Bride of my Kinsman! And this that thou biddest me is easy and pleasant for me to do. But afterwards I
must get me back to Burgdale; for I seem to have left much
there that calleth for me.'

'Yea,' said Folk-might, 'and art thou wedded, Bow-may?
Shalt thou never bend the yew in battle again?'

Said Bow-may soberly: 'Who knoweth, chieftain? Yea,
I am wedded now these two years; and nought I looked for
less when I followed those twain through the wild-wood to
Burgdale.'

She sighed therewith, and said: 'In all the Dale there is no
better man of his hands than my man, nor any goodlier to look
on, and he is even that Hart of Highcliff whom thou knowest
well, O Bride!'

Said the Bride: 'Thou sayest sooth, there is no better man in
the Dale.'

Said Bow-may: 'Sun-beam bade me wed him when he pressed
hard upon me.' She stayed awhile, and then said: 'Face-of-god
also deemed I should not naysay the man; and now my son by
him is of like age to this little one.'

'Good is thy story,' said Folk-might; 'or deemest thou, Bow-
may, that such strong and goodly women as thou, and women so
kind and friendly, should forbear the wedding and the bringing
forth of children? Yea, and we who may even yet have to gather

422

to another field before we die, and fight for life and the goods of life.'

'Thou sayest well,' she said; 'all that hath befallen me is good since the day whereon I loosed shaft from the break of the bent over yonder.'

Therewith she fell a-musing, and made as though she were hearkening to the soft voice of the Bride caressing the new-come baby; but in sooth neither heard nor saw what was going on about her, for her thoughts were in bygone days. Howbeit presently she came to herself again, and fell to asking many questions concerning Silver-dale and the kindred, and those who had once been thralls of the Dusky Men; and they answered all duly, and told her the whole story of the Dale since the Day of the Victory.

So Bow-may and the carles who had come with her abode for that half-month in Silver-dale, guested in all love by the folk thereof, both the kindreds and the poor folk. And Bow-may deemed that the Bride loved Face-of-god's child little less than her own, whereof she had two, a man and a woman; and thereat was she full of joy, since she knew that Face-of-god and the Sun-beam would be fain thereof.

Thereafter, when the time was come, fared Folk-might and the Bride, and many of the elders and warriors of the Wolf and the Woodland, to Shadowy Vale; and Dallach and the best of Rose-dale went with them, being so bidden; and Bow-may and her following, according to the word of the Bride. And in Shadowy Vale they met Face-of-god and Alderman Iron-face, and the chiefs of Burgdale and the Shepherds, and many others; and great joy there was at the meeting. And the Sun-beam remembered the word which she spoke to Face-of-god when first he came to Shadowy Vale, that she would be wishful to see again the dwelling wherein she had passed through so much joy and sorrow of her younger days. But if anyone were fain of this meeting, the Alderman was glad above all, when he took the

They meet in
Shadowy
Vale.

Those kindreds grow into one Folk.

Bride once more in his arms, and caressed her whom he had deemed should be a very daughter of his House.

Now telleth the tale of all these kindreds, to wit, the Men of Burgdale and the Sheepcotes; and the Children of the Wolf, and the Woodlanders, and the Men of Rose-dale, that they were friends henceforth, and became as one Folk, for better or worse, in peace and in war, in waning and waxing; and that whatsoever befell them, they ever held Shadowy Vale a holy place, and for long and long after they met there in mid-autumn, and held converse and counsel together.

NO MORE AS NOW TELLETH THE TALE OF THESE KINDREDS AND FOLKS, BUT MAKETH AN ENDING.